CHANCE MEDLEY

He slammed the oven door shut and set to work on the second batch of loaves. A tiny corner of Povin's brain queried why the boy didn't go outside to smoke as he usually did, but the question went unanswered and unheeded.

Don't go so fast, he chided himself. It didn't have to be Chance Medley. Bryant was familiar with the code but he hadn't used it for years; why resurrect it without any prior warning for the last, most important time of all?

Because the woman was interested in music, that's why.

Somewhere, locked away in the interstices of his mind, Povin knew he had a piece of information – but he didn't know what it was. He didn't have the key.

As Povin turned away from the table to carry the last batch of bread to the oven he registered that triple-oh-eight's chair was empty, but he still didn't pay any heed. It was only when he set himself to scrub down the tabletops that his eyes missed the knife and, much too late, his brain hurled all its combined resources into defending the yawning breach, now so obvious; he had time to scream, very loudly but only once, before the hand silenced him and he was falling backwards towards the blade . . .

Also by John Trenhaile in Sphere Books:

KYRIL
A VIEW FROM THE SQUARE

Nocturne for the General

JOHN TRENHAILE

SPHERE BOOKS LIMITED
London and Sydney

First published in Great Britain by
The Bodley Head Ltd 1985
Copyright © John Trenhaile 1985
Published by Sphere Books Ltd 1986
30–32 Gray's Inn Road, London WC1X 8JL

Quotations on pages 113, 143, and 223 from *The Bratsk Station and Other New Poems* by Yevgeny Yevtushenko. Reproduced with permission from Granada Publishing Ltd.

Printed and bound in Great Britain by
Collins, Glasgow

For Julian Friedmann and Carole Blake
Joint Chiefs of *the* Main Directorate
With love and gratitude

The man that hath no music in himself,
Nor is not moved with concord of sweet sounds,
Is fit for treasons, stratagems and spoils;
The motions of his spirit are dull as night,
And his affections dark as Erebus:
Let no such man be trusted. Mark the music.

The Merchant of Venice, Act V, Scene I

Peace! Would you not rather die
Reeling, — with all the cannons at your ear?
    So, at least, would I,
And I may not be here
Tonight, tomorrow morning or next year.
Still I will let you keep your life a little
while,
        See dear?
    I have made you smile.

Charlotte Mew, from 'On the Road to the Sea'

1

'*Dedushka* was a railway man also,' said Belikov. 'Until they shot him, that is.'

He eyed his companion anxiously, uncertain whether he had perhaps gone too far. But the journalist's face disclosed only polite interest.

'Why did they shoot him?'

Belikov hesitated. He still wasn't quite sure where he was with this Englishman, foisted on him at the last moment by an uncompromising official of the Ministry in Moscow. To speak or to remain silent? Belikov never knew.

'Anti-Soviet activity,' he said at last. 'He joined the wrong union. *Vikzhel*, that was what they called it. The Reds were all for *Vikzhedor*. Big rivals, they were. Granddad ended up arguing with the wrong people.' Belikov shrugged, cocked his head on one side and raised an eyebrow. 'See?'

'More or less. Trade unions are a bit like that where I come from, only they don't shoot each other.'

While Belikov poured more coffee into their cracked mugs Anthony Lowe stood up and wandered over to the window to see if it had stopped snowing.

The scene before him was bleak. A couple of days previously he and a select delegation of other foreign correspondents had accompanied Yakov Belikov from Sverdlovsk up to the small township of Mendelejewa, the end of the branchline from Tobolsk. Railways were hardly his field. Lowe, the Moscow-based correspondent of the London *Times*, normally concerned himself with matters weightier than the five-year plan of the Sverdlovsk Regional Division. At first he wanted to refuse the assignment, but now he was glad he'd decided to come after all. As a foreign journalist he was not permitted to travel more than twenty-five miles from the Kremlin without official permission, and almost any chance to escape from the capital for a few days was to be welcomed. Then again, it was difficult to refuse an express invitation from the Ministry, although god knew what the TASS mandarins thought they'd find of interest in the glum marches of Siberia. February — hardly the best of months for travel within the Soviet Union. Outside, the narrow street was still thick with snow from last night's fall; in the sticks, in out-of-the-way places like Mendelejewa, street-clearing took time to organize.

He returned to the table and sat down, pushing aside the huge map of the Sverdlovsk region which Belikov had earlier spread out in order to illustrate his points on the proposed development of the branchline north of Mendelejewa to Uwat. Lowe liked his Russian host. At the age of fifty-five Yakov Belikov had made it to chief of the planning sector in his division and he was realistic enough to accept that he wasn't going any farther. By now he had hardly any hair left, his Joe Stalin moustache was a uniform battleship grey and he had finally stopped arguing the toss with the bathroom scales. ('The scales I can fix,' said the black-market repairman down the block. 'The scales I *have* fixed. You I can't fix. Go away.') Lowe too was stouter than a man in his early fifties ought to be, and like Belikov he devoted more and more time to scheming for early retirement on a full pension that wasn't yet due. Before their train reached Mendelejewa both men had discovered a mutual ambition: to blow their accumulated life savings on the best stereo equipment money could buy and spend their declining years, semi-drunk, listening to the entire Beethoven canon, over and over again. So while the French, the Dutch, the Italian and the Swiss trooped out into the snow to hear the chief divisional engineer earnestly declaim the merits of electric traction over diesel oil, Lowe and Belikov made an unspoken agreement to treat these few days as a little holiday, a brief, companionable respite from Life.

'Tell me about your grandfather.'

Belikov drained his mug as a way of covering his hesitation. He had never been in close contact with a foreigner before.

10

The man from the Ministry had been very specific in his instructions for handling Lowe — 'Make friends with him, Yakov, you'll find him a lot more fun than the rest' — but everybody knew you had to be a bit careful with outsiders, especially newspapermen.

'I never knew him,' he said at last. 'He died before I was born. It's time we went to lunch, come on.'

The two men shouldered their way into heavy overcoats and donned their fur hats. As Belikov slipped the catch on the outer door he began to whistle. Lowe recognized it as Chopin and told him so.

'You're right.'

'I can't quite place it. A nocturne . . .?'

'Yes.'

'I'll get it, I'll get it, don't tell me.'

As they began to saunter down the nearly deserted street Belikov whistled the melody again, more slowly this time.

'Once more,' said Lowe.

But before Belikov could comply there was an interruption. Somewhere behind them and to one side another voice took up the tune.

'Dar! Dar! Dan-dum-dum-dum-*tum*!'

'Come on,' said Belikov quickly. 'It's bloody freezing out here.'

But Lowe had already stopped. He turned his head and there, slumped in the scant shelter afforded by a doorway, was the owner of the cracked and discordant voice which had intruded on their private game: a man, quite an old man by the look of him, whose clothes gave only slight protection against the extreme winter's day. Long, unkempt hair, thin arms and legs, torn trousers, a cotton shirt under some shapeless woollen garment now full of holes, shoes that might have been made of cardboard, mittens . . .

Lowe frowned. There was something familiar about this pitiful wreck of a human being but Lowe couldn't place it, couldn't absolutely lay his hand on his heart and swear, yet there was something, *something* . . .

'Hello,' he said quietly.

The beggar looked up at him, grinning stupidly. At the side

11

of his mouth a bubble of saliva grew and shrank, grew and shrank. The eyes were empty of understanding. Most of his teeth had gone, Lowe noticed, and those that were left were almost black. The antiseptic cold isolated him from the beggar's smell, but Lowe knew he stank, his breath, his body, everything about him stank.

Nevertheless, he moved closer. The beggar raised his arms across his face and squeezed himself even farther into the doorway, as if willing his emaciated body to pass through the wood and stone, away from the piercing interest displayed by the threatening stranger who loomed over him; and Lowe understood that this man had been beaten. Very slowly so as not to frighten the beggar, he knelt down. He had been right about the smell, but that didn't matter. Recognition. He had been on the point of identifying the Chopin nocturne and now he was within an ace of putting a name, yes a *name*, to this heap, this shrunken apology for a man — dammit, it was there, next second he'd have it . . .

Nocturne no. 18. Of course.

Lowe began to whistle the tune softly. For a moment the beggar's face did not change; then, or so it seemed to Lowe, a glimmer of light showed at the back of the soulless eyes, the ghost of a smile gathered at the corners of the slack mouth.

'Dan-dum-dum-dum-tum.'

Lowe smiled and nodded. 'Listen,' he heard Belikov say behind him, 'you want to leave him, OK? Your colleagues'll be coming back soon, won't they wonder . . . ?'

Lowe continued to smile at the beggar, suddenly desperate to preserve the gossamer-thin line of communication between them.

'Listen, it's a crime to beg.' Belikov's voice was becoming urgent, less friendly. 'You want to get us both into trouble?'

'Shut up.'

Chopin. The eighteenth nocturne. Moscow Conservatoire. December 1981. Lead artist.

Dar-*dum*-te-tum . . .

Lead artist, lead artist. . .

The beggar was not so old, Lowe now realized. And at one time he must have been very good-looking. Moscow Con-

12

servatoire. December 1981. Lead artist, lead artist, *lead artist*.

Suddenly his eyes flickered downwards and narrowed with surprise. The hands. My god, he thought, the fingers, ruined, what a mess. An industrial accident? The ghostly miasma of recognition was dissipating quickly; silly of him, strange how the human brain plays such tricks, nothing so treacherous as the human brain . . .

'Here,' he said softly. 'Take this.'

He fumbled in his overcoat pocket, searching blindly for his wallet. Belikov's jealous, frightened eyes bulged at the sight of this latest outrage.

'Six roubles!' he exploded. 'It's too much!'

The beggar took the money and stared, as if unaware of its significance. Lowe folded his own hands around the notes, around the beggar's mittens, averting his eyes from the mauled hands.

'Militia! *Shit!*'

At the end of the street a blue and white car was slowly turning towards them. Lowe uneasily realized that he had placed Belikov in danger while at the same time making an idiot of himself, all for this beggar, this — he 'tcha'd' in anger, cursing his own folly. Now there would be awkward questions, papers, hostility, suspicion . . .

The car cruised up to them and stopped. Four militiamen got out. Two of them approached the beggar and took him by the arms. At that the beggar cried out in fear, but now his distress touched no answering chord in Lowe's busily working mind.

'Your identification.'

As Lowe placed his *propiska* into the militiaman's black-gloved hand he felt a second of premature relief. This was low-key stuff.

The militiaman scarcely bothered to read the documents which Lowe and Belikov handed over. For a moment his face remained expressionless. Then he said, 'This person has been bothering you, Comrades. We will deal with him. I am sorry that it should have happened.'

Lowe stared at the man with growing professional interest. Three years' residence in the Soviet Union had led him to

13

anticipate a good deal of unpleasantness from any encounter with the police, however trifling. This was unexpected. This was, to a newspaperman, interesting.

The beggar was being searched next to the car. One of the militiamen approached with the two *treshkas* which Lowe had handed over earlier.

'This money belongs to you.'

It was not a question but Lowe and Belikov both shook their heads, the latter with some show of reluctance.

'This money belongs to you,' the militiaman repeated, his eyes fixed on Lowe. When the Englishman did not reply the militiaman forced the notes into his hands, much as Lowe had made the beggar take the money a few minutes previously. Then, just as suddenly as they had arrived and with as little fuss, the militiamen withdrew. They slung the beggar into the back seat of their car, closed the doors and drove off. Lowe stood in the middle of the street and watched them go, Belikov by his side. The car reached an intersection and turned right, vanishing almost immediately. Belikov plucked Lowe's arm.

'Lunch,' he said aggressively. 'Come. *Please!*'

But Lowe did not move. His gaze was still fixed on the spot where he'd had his last sight of the beggar sitting between the two militiamen on the back seat. Belikov looked greedily at the three-rouble notes in his companion's hands and damned himself for an idiot in not claiming the money when he'd had the chance. Lowe muttered something.

'What?'

'I said . . .' Lowe seemed to collect himself. He pocketed the notes, replaced his gloves, and turned to face Belikov. 'I said I've remembered the nocturne. Number 18 . . .'

'Yes. Good.'

'. . . And where I last heard it.'

'Ah.'

Lowe put an arm round Belikov's shoulders and the two men began to walk down the street together, as if linked by a common resolve to pretend that the whole recent incident had never occurred.

'. . . And who was playing it.'

In the traction sector of the Sverdlovsk Railway's divisional headquarters there is a fully comprehensive electronic display indicator. In Belikov's eyes this machine was capable of wonderful things. A flick of a switch would cause the entire freight network of the division to light up, with green lines joining all the far-flung railheads. Another switch, and there was the passenger network, the various towns conjoined by white lines along which moved red cursors, indicating trains travelling between stations. Yet another switch, and those lines disappeared, leaving only the principal towns illuminated, with no obvious means of communication between them. Sometimes Belikov would leave his office and stroll down to the first floor to watch this marvel of modern electronics for an hour or more, while the planning sector got on as best it could without him.

It so happens that the KGB have a similar facility at their headquarters overlooking Moscow's Dzerzhinsky Square, although neither Belikov nor Lowe was aware of this. The KGB's display is not electronic, nor in a sense is it even a display, because it exists only in the mind of the Chairman himself. Still, it exists. Inside the Chairman's brain a switch is pulled and lines appear, connections are made, links forged, until at last a railwayman's nightmare is born, a veritable cat's cradle of criss-cross lines and points and junctions and U-turns and conflicting signals, through which the blood-red cursor of the Chairman's thought must move, now fast, now slow, but always with a purpose, a sense of mission.

Anthony Lowe returned to Moscow with the rest of the press delegation. A few days later he strolled down to Maurice Thorez Embankment to call at the British Embassy where he remained (according to the KGB's logbook) for twenty-seven minutes. And suddenly, in the mind of the Chairman, the display became alive.

The duty officer's instructions were very strict and he obeyed them punctiliously. As soon as he saw the words 'Sight C 24 hours' appear at the top of the printout he reached for his red phone and dialled Sir Richard Bryant's home number. The fact that it was two o'clock in the morning made no difference; anything designated 'Sight C 24 hours' had to be laid before the Head of the Service at once. The telex was waiting on C's desk when, forty-five minutes later, he entered his office on the very top floor. Seeing the coded groups he tut-tutted with annoyance; then he looked again, saw that it was a cipher reserved for Head of Service and departmental chiefs and mentally squared his shoulders.

An hour later he sat back and stared into space while he allowed his thoughts time in which to settle. Then he stood up and walked round the desk to activate his IBM console.

'What?' asked the green screen.

'Select: Hunt List,' he instructed it. The machine whirred and hummed, lights flickered, a cursor raced across the top of the screen.

HUNT LIST.

'Scroll,' ordered Bryant, and the machine began to review the spies, the terrorists, the saboteurs. The list was a long one; several minutes passed before the machine arrived at 'S'.

Bryant tapped a key marked 'Stop'; the machine complied. Bryant flexed his fingers and began laboriously to pick out an instruction.

'Item . . . 790 . . . query.'

The screen dissolved, reassembled itself. Now the print was smaller and Bryant found it harder to read. He reached for his glasses and leaned a little closer to the screen. After he had digested what it had to say he reverted to the keyboard.

'Edit * ?'

'OK,' agreed the machine.

Bryant tapped again, watching intently while the little green cursor danced across the screen like a nervy will-o'-the-wisp.

'Yes?' asked the machine.

'Endit,' tapped Bryant. 'Review . . . . whole.'

The screen dissolved, rescrambled, became still. Bryant felt mildly pleased with his efforts; he was old enough to take perverse pleasure in mastering the modern technology.

His eyes scanned the self-contained message several times before they turned opaque and he found himself transported through the screen to another dimension. Geneva. Two years ago. A KGB general, making his first move in an attempt to stave off Armageddon, showed himself on the streets for just long enough to catch the eye of an eager young British agent . . . Now, stumbling across the path of a journalist, there came a beggar who wore scarcely any clothes but nevertheless seemed immune to cold. And it occurred to Bryant that the message on the screen was not self-contained after all, but was a code superimposed on the events of Geneva two years ago; 'Look at me,' the screen seemed to be saying, 'Note the similarities, observe the pattern . . .'

It was fortunate that they had used Lowe; he was trustworthy as well as sharp-eyed. A less observant man might not even have noticed the beggar, let alone remembered him. Bryant shrugged. Luck. If not this time then next. Kazin was patient, always ready to try again.

He picked up the telex, searching for 'Place of Origin'. BE Moscow. British Embassy. That was wrong. Say rather . . . DS Moscow. Dzerzhinsky Square.

Then his face clouded and he was abruptly drawn back to immediate realities. Something was wrong. For reasons best known to itself the machine had begun to flash the entry on and off, on and off . . . He sat down, mute with helpless frustration, while the green light came and went, alternately illuminating his face in a garish glare and plunging the office into darkness — light, dark, green, black, light, dark . . .

PYOTR STOLYINOVICH flashed the screen: on-off, on-off, green-black, light-dark. And underneath that, the words which Bryant had typed in himself; on-off, green-black, light-dark . . .

FOUND ALIVE . . . FOUND ALIVE . . . FOUND ALIVE . . .

After a few minutes the machine, bored with waiting for fresh instructions, did what it was programmed to do and blacked out the screen, leaving visible only the will-o'-the-wisp shimmer of the cursor, constant and tireless, unsleeping as its blood-red counterpart in the KGB Chairman's brain.

2

Inna Karsovina faced up to the fact that there was going to be a quarrel and struggled to repress a surge of irritation. She knew perfectly well that this was the time to put into practice what the keep-fit class instructor had told her so often and take half a dozen deep breaths, but she didn't. Instead she waited until her whole body was so tense that a musician could have plucked a high C from it, and bawled, 'Volodiya! Turn off that television *at once*!'

Her six-year-old son was lying in front of the set on his stomach with his head propped up on his hands. From the spasm which ran the length of his skinny little body Inna deduced that he had heard, but he made no move to obey.

'Volodiya! Did you hear what I said just then?'

'I heard.'

His tone was one of jaunty insouciance. Inna's body unscrewed itself a couple of turns; she wanted to giggle. You stop that, she told herself sharply. The child has to learn. She swept up to the TV, plunged her finger on to the button with a theatrical gesture and swung round to stand with hands on hips, defying the boy to make a fuss.

For a moment he remained in the same position, one bare leg swinging and the expression on his face unchanged. Then, very slowly, he rolled over on to his back and smiled. To Inna, looking down at him, the smile was inverted. Wrong-way-round smiles always seemed so funny. Her body gave another wrench and this time her lips twitched.

Volodiya saw that. He saw everything.

'Is supper ready yet?'

'Never you mind about supper.' For a grisly second of self-awareness Inna had a mental picture of herself actually wagging a sharp-looking finger at her son. 'When I tell you to do a thing, you do it. Understood?'

The little boy sighed, a purely distilled exhalation of all the world-weariness in an utterly weary world. The sigh of a very old man who has seen everything and yet somehow managed to survive it all. A thoroughly adult sigh. Inna felt irrationally crushed by it.

'Oh-*kay*.'

'What?'

'Oh . . . Yes, Mum.'

'*What*?'

'Yes, Mother. Shall I wash now?'

Damn, thought Inna. How does he always succeed in making me lose the thread? Why is it never possible to win an argument with a son, with any child? Was it like this when I was a girl? Surely not. And yet . . .

'Inna — help!'

Her mother's cry was immediately followed by the sound of a heavy object landing on the floor. Inna forgot about Volodiya and raced across to the sliding partition which separated their living room from the tiny kitchen. To her relief she saw that her mother was still upright.

'What happened?' Inna's voice was unnecessarily harsh. Her words often came out that way, without her meaning them to.

'The cake tin. It fell.'

'The cake tin! Is that all?'

'That's all.'

'Then why shout for help, as if the whole house is falling down on your head?'

Inna squeezed herself into the minute space between the cooker and the fridge and bent down to retrieve the tin. Her mother, not at all perturbed, smiled sweetly. She was a short, plump woman whose grey hair lent refinement to an otherwise somewhat moony face, with happy, twinkling eyes and a

19

straight back which many another sixty-two-year-old might have envied. Inna herself frequently envied Anfisa for a number of reasons, not least the ability to take whatever life threw at her and make the best of it. When distributing the genes they had unfortunately managed to miss that one out of Inna's allocation.

She reached up to put the tin on its shelf. She wanted to ask her mother how it had come to fall in the first place but she acknowledged to herself that there was no point. Explanations only led to arguments in this house, and you cannot win arguments with the old any more than you can with the young. Inna-in-the-middle, she thought impatiently. That's me. Why is it that Volodiya and Mother never seem to argue with each other? So it *is* my fault . . .

'Shut up,' she said aloud.

'Mm?'

Inna smiled tautly at her mother. 'Nothing. Is there anything I can do to help?'

'You can lay the table,' said Anfisa. 'It'll be another five minutes. Those tomatoes were a mistake after all, we can't eat them cold. I'm having to simmer them.'

Inna bit her lip. She hated queuing with the great mass of the population, the *narod*, and her position as an executive officer of the Committee for State Security ensured that she didn't have to very often. But last Saturday, to please her mother, she had waited for an hour to buy fresh vegetables, standing patiently in the cold March wind because she felt the family deserved a treat. And now it wasn't a treat after all.

Inna sent Volodiya to wash his hands while she laid the table. A bigger place, that's what we need, she muttered as she dealt mats, knives, forks, spoons, three rooms, one for you, one for me, one for Mother, glass for you, glass for me, glass for Mother, plate for you . . .

Dreams never did anyone any harm, but in her heart Inna knew that they were stuck with this apartment for years. No use complaining, then; and indeed they had been lucky to get it. The accommodation — two rooms, bathroom-with-lavatory and minuscule kitchen — was in good repair and excellently located. In order to reach the old apartment house

20

you had to duck through a little archway on Arbat Street, just opposite the Vakhtangov Theatre, follow a damp, narrow passage which led to an open courtyard with a fountain in the centre, and then take another passage leading off the far side. The KGB approved of the building because it could be approached only from the street; there was no back door. The neighbourhood, buried deep in Moscow's old quarter, suited Inna and her mother very well; Volodiya pleaded for a high-rise with a lift and a view of the ring road, but in vain.

Notwithstanding KGB approval, Inna had had to fight for this apartment. The family suffered a shortage of housing points. Her mother was a widow (bad) of a university lecturer (not too good) who lived with her grown-up daughter, another widow (getting better) with a young son (ah!) of junior-school age (good!), the daughter being employed by the Committee for State Security (excellent!!), in a relatively senior grade for her age (well done!). But even so, the neighbourhood was really out of their league. By Soviet standards it was a high-class district, fairly reeking of *blat*, that mysterious mixture of money, access and influence which characterized the *nomenklatura*, the capital's power elite. Inna had sized up the situation and decided to talk to her superior — not the head of her section, not the Chief of Division, but the major general who commanded the Fifth Main Directorate, where she was working then. The general was charmed, not to say infatuated. As well he might be; for Inna had drawn out her savings, which by then consisted of a whole month's salary, and squandered the lot on a tight dress and some Western perfume to wear at the interview, so that in the course of a ten-minute discussion she secured both the apartment and a prickly perception of what it must be like to whore for a living.

To Inna's relief Volodiya ate a good supper and went to bed without complaining. She never could depend on that. Sometimes he would eat nothing all day, then stay awake until past ten, clinging and whiny. Inna wanted him to grow up strong and self-reliant; sometimes it looked as though he might turn out that way, and sometimes not. Often she

21

thought to herself that she didn't much care how he turned out as long as he inherited nothing from his father.

After they had eaten she helped her mother clear away the dishes. Inna wanted a quiet time in which to reflect but her mother, standing at the sink with her hands deep in sudsy water, was immune to atmosphere.

'You're worried, aren't you? It was obvious at dinner, I can always tell. It's starting this week, the job's starting, isn't it?'

'I'm not worried.'

'Well you should be! You think I'm old and stupid but I know enough to realize that when a KGB officer's put on probation . . .'

'Probation! What rubbish you do talk.' Inna calmly folded up her dishcloth and draped it over the radiator. 'They're reviewing my role, that's all. It's quite normal when you reach a certain level.'

'And what does that mean? "Adequate level of ideological commitment", wasn't that the phrase?'

'Yes, Mother. *Adequate!* Sufficient, in other words. Acceptable.'

'Exactly! Just enough to get by! We both know it's a reprimand, and you should be doing something about it, my girl.'

Inna folded her arms and rested her back against the refrigerator. 'I am doing something about it. For once they gave me a choice. They offered me the Murmansk job and I took it. I've *told* you all this.'

Her mother pulled out the plug, swished water round the sink and dried her hands. 'Murmansk! That's the last we'll see of you, then.'

'I'll be home for the weekends. Sometimes.'

'And the idea of you as an interrogator. *You're* no interrogator! Persecuting Catholics, that's more your line.'

'Don't be silly! I wasn't always an interrogator, but there's such a thing as training, you know,' said Inna, bravely stifling her own doubts. 'And what's all this nonsense about persecution . . .?'

'Training, hooey.' Her mother folded up her tea towel and slapped it down on to the dresser. 'Well, you'd better make a success of it, hadn't you.'

Yes, thought Inna, suddenly furious at her mother's interference — yes, I bloody well had! And a fat lot of help I'll get here. Persecution, indeed! Hadn't her mother yet woken up to the fact that Russia wasn't still a tsarist tyranny? But she kept her thoughts to herself because it was easier that way. She waited while the old lady settled herself in front of the television with the sound turned down low, so as not to disturb Volodiya next door. That disposed of Mother for the night; when she was tired she would switch off the set and make up the folding sofa-divan, thus transforming the living area into her bedroom.

Inna took a shower, put on her night things and climbed into the big double bed next to her sleeping son, gently so as not to wake him. She wanted to think and she always thought best when tucked up in bed. She put on the shaded light, quietly arranging herself on her side so that she could see the photograph.

It was a black and white print of good quality, about twenty centimetres by fifteen, set in a plain wooden frame. The frame had been a whim, born of a desire to nettle her mother rather than any deep-felt aesthetic sense. When she had first put the photograph out on the table next to the bed Volodiya asked her, Is that Daddy? No. A sweetheart, then? Mind your own business. It's just a photograph of someone Mummy knows well, that's all. Then she bought the frame, and: Well, *is* it a sweetheart?, her mother asked nervously. He looks rather old for you . . .

In the meagre light he didn't look very old, she decided, although no doubt he would have aged a good deal since the photograph was taken. He was in his early fifties then; the department couldn't be more precise than that. Well-brushed grey hair, a good suit, Western-style tie . . . a girl of twenty-eight, on her way to the top, could surely do worse for a sugar daddy?

Inna propped herself up on one elbow and pulled the frame a shade nearer the bed. It was an interesting, experienced face; the face of a man who had seen the world and succeeded in manipulating it to his own ends. She considered it dispassionately. The skin was taut and healthy-looking, the eyes

23

good-humoured. She couldn't quite make up her mind if she thought him handsome. He wasn't bad as older men go, but the ears spoiled the overall effect: they were long and pointed, and they stuck out from his head at too sharp an angle. He might have been handsome in the flesh. Not now, of course, but then.

How would he be now? Would he be strong? Stronger than her? Well, she'd know soon enough.

Inna picked up the frame and lay back on the pillow, holding the photograph at the best angle for catching the light. We've altered his face for him, the Project Committee had told her, smiling; don't expect miracles. The camps aren't exactly a health spa, you know.

Inna, worldly-wise, had laughed when they said that, but — she wasn't sure. She might be an experienced statistician, but she was still very much a 'new girl' when it came to interrogation. She found it hard to conceive of Gulag. We've altered his face for him . . .

Traitors deserved the worst there was. They ought to have shot him long ago, obviously, so if they kept him alive it was because he was meant to suffer. If he'd been right about all that doctrinal God nonsense then the KGB could simply have shoved him off to hell to burn for ever. (For the past five years Inna had been working on sect analysis in the KGB's Religious Affairs Department and regarded herself as something of an expert on spiritual matters of this kind.) But since he was wrong they had to keep him here just a little longer, so that he could pay — and be seen by others to pay.

Whatever the Personnel Directorate might imply in their mealy-mouthed reports, she had no doubts concerning her own commitment to the Party, to the Soviet Union and all it stood for. But now, as she held the photograph against the dim light, it occurred to her that this face, those eyes, had belonged to a man who once was rather special. If someone like that had strode into the midst of the silly boys at Lomonosov University with their childish games, perhaps she would have sat up and taken notice. Perhaps she would even have wanted to hear what he had to say.

In the room next door the phone rang.

Before it could ring a second time Inna was out of bed and through the door. Her mother hadn't moved from in front of the television set. She disliked the phone and never answered it if Inna was at home.

'Yes?'

Inna fought to quell her temper, remembering, too late, her breathing exercises. She realized that she was jamming the receiver against her ear so hard that it hurt.

'Central Registry. Identify yourself.'

Inna hesitated only a second, but during that second every muscle in her body was still. 'Karsovina, Inna Marietta, HN double-oh-nine-six-three-eight-four, Second Main Directorate, Fourth Direction.'

'You will report to the office of the Chairman of the Committee for State Security of the Council of Ministers of the USSR in Dzerzhinsky Square at nine o'clock tomorrow morning. Enter by the door marked F.'

Inna drew breath to speak but before she could do so the connection was broken. She held the receiver away from her ear and stared at it. The prospect of Kazin was always alarming, but to be summoned in such a strange way was positively ominous. Why didn't Kazin go through Lieutenant Colonel Borodin, her Chief of Direction? What would Borodin have said when he heard? Or . . . Inna swallowed. Suppose he *hadn't* heard . . .

After an initial moment of near-panic her brain began to reassert control. It was necessary to be practical. In the bathroom cupboard she kept some *oblepikh* bush oil, a natural tranquillizer. She found the bottle and took a carefully measured dose. Then she returned to the bedroom, lay down and extinguished the light. Inna closed her eyes and strove to meditate, only half succeeding.

There had to be a rational explanation. First and foremost, she knew she had done nothing wrong. She was 'clean'. But, of course, being clean didn't rule out some terrible misunderstanding, she'd heard such dreadful stories of innocent people — shut up, shut *up*, don't be ridiculous. If she had done nothing wrong, perhaps her mother . . . little Volodiya . . . Should she ask Anfisa? Ask her son? Better not. Better say nothing until after she'd heard what Kazin had to say. Only, what if then it was too late . . .?

Kazin. Oleg Kazin. In spite of her carefully controlled effort to relax, the name drummed over and over in her brain. A myth . . . That's all it was, of course, a tale, a legend, very useful when it came to dealing with subordinates — that story about killing his own daughter, for example, now that really *was* a lot of rubbish, no father ever murdered his own daughter, and it was equally preposterous to suggest that he and Stalin . . .

Inna fluffed up the pillows and lay down again, sighing with impatience at her fears. But rumour said that Kazin never bothered with junior personnel. He was a recluse, dealing only with heads of directorates and keeping even them at a distance. For someone of her lowly rank to be summoned to his presence was unheard of. *How had she attracted his attention? What had she done?*

In her heart she knew what the summons meant. It was, it had to be, the Murmansk assignment.

Her mother shrieked when she saw her next morning. 'You look like a ghost! Didn't you sleep?'

'Not much.'

Inna couldn't face the thought of another confrontation with her mother, so she whisked Volodiya off to school, not giving him time to complain, and caught the bus by the skin of her teeth. She saw her wasted reflection in the window and grunted with displeasure. Was it a mistake to have chosen the plain blue suit with the white neck-bow? Should she perhaps have dolled herself up, as she had for the major general when she so desperately wanted the apartment?

The apartment. Inna's breath hissed through her teeth and she raised both hands to her face, damning her own idiocy in not thinking of that before. Had Kazin discovered her dealings with the major general? There was a word for that kind of thing, not a new word, but one which was being increasingly spoken of late. Corruption. She was guilty of corruption. And if the Chairman had found out . . .

Inna lowered her hands and swallowed hard. It was essential to keep her fears in proportion and not panic. What would be best: bring it up herself, come straight to the point, confess everything? Or wait? Suppose it was only Murmansk, after all, and not the business over the apartment; wouldn't she be asking for trouble if she raised it first?

Questions. No answers, only questions, questions without number.

She had never before set foot inside the KGB's Dzerzhinsky Square headquarters, although she had been an executive officer for more than five full years. The long-planned process of decentralization was virtually complete, and now only the cream were located at 'The Square'. Didn't people say that Kazin was slowly making it into his personal fortress by fencing it off from the rest of the organization? Inna began to wish she had been in the habit of paying more attention to office rumours.

Progress through the building was frustratingly slow but at last she found herself alone in the centre of a huge oak-pannelled, high-ceilinged room, almost the size of her entire apartment. Standing by the window with his hands behind his back was a man wearing the uniform of a full colonel. Inna's tongue was gummed to the roof of her mouth. It felt as if two huge ball bearings had been inserted at the base of her throat. For a long time the colonel stared at her, and Inna knew that this man not only understood to the last refined millimetre how she felt, he had also arranged it that way. He wanted her to experience genuine terror . . . but the effort was counterproductive, because instead Inna began to feel angry.

The colonel, seeing that also, at last was satisfied. Scarcely taking his eyes off Inna's face he raised his forearm very deliberately and glanced at his watch.

'You can go in now.'

Inna looked around her. Several doors led off from this huge office. Her lips parted, as if to speak, but her tongue still clove to the roof of her mouth.

'Through there.' With a slight inclination of his elegantly tonsured grey head the colonel indicated the double doors on Inna's left. 'Don't bother to knock. He doesn't like people to knock.'

Inna turned and cautiously approached the doors. Now her

heart was beating uncomfortably fast. Was this a trap? Surely she ought to knock, everybody knocked when calling on the *nachalstvo*, those-in-power.

'Go on,' murmured the colonel. 'He's expecting you. He won't bite you.'

Inna straightened her shoulders, reached out and pushed on one of the doors. The prospect before her was not encouraging. Kazin's office felt enormous but she couldn't be sure because it was also in virtually total darkness.

At the far end of the room, perhaps a quarter of a mile away (or so it seemed to her), a man was sitting behind a vast desk, writing with the aid of a single lamp. Between her and the desk stretched out only the dark. The man did not look up from his work, but by straining her ears she was able to hear him mutter, 'Come here.' She began to traverse the huge expanse of space which separated her from the desk. The parquet floor was bare and her heels clicked ominously in the gloom.

'Sit.'

Opposite the desk was a chair. As Inna lowered herself into it a light came on, shining directly down at her. Inna nervously clutched the arms of the chair and then she looked, for the first time really looked, at Oleg Kazin.

He was very old, that was her first impression; old and inexplicably powerful, as if the legends understated rather than exaggerated the truth. He was wearing a crumpled white suit. Thick pebble spectacles had the effect of magnifying his pale blue eyes into great round hypnotic orbs. The shabby suit and the blue eyes contrasted eerily with his blooming, pink skin: pallor set against blood. She watched in fascination as he lit a cigarette from the butt of an old one and inhaled, snatching the smoke deep inside his lungs as if it were a substitute for oxygen.

'Smoke?'

The voice was bloodless, to match the eyes and the suit, but Inna was momentarily reassured.

'No thank you, Comrade Chairman.'

'No, you don't smoke. Why not?'

'Because I always understood it is bad for the health, Comrade Chairman.'

There was silence. Inna was pleased to hear how cool she sounded.

'Oh? Do I look unhealthy?'

As he spoke these words Kazin let his glance slide, as if by accident, to one side. Without moving her head Inna felt her eyes follow his and light on a thick metal door, just visible in the far wall. Her lips parted. The Door. It existed. *It existed!*

As if from a great distance, way outside herself, she heard a far from cool voice whisper, 'No, Comrade Chairman. You look . . . very well.'

There was another long silence. Then Kazin chuckled and Inna's eyes darted back to his face. He was smiling.

'Shall I tell you something, Inna Marietta? Until I was appointed Chairman of the KGB I had never set foot inside this room. Not once. And I used to say to myself, That hoary old tale about the door. A rumour. A legend. But, you know, Inna Marietta . . . it's real. There. In that wall.'

Inna felt a stab of pain in her chest and realized that all through Kazin's speech she had been holding her breath.

'You see the chair I'm sitting in?' The way he said it put invisible but unmistakable quotation marks round 'the chair'. 'Another myth. Another rumour. Yet . . . the truth.'

For the first time she saw that Kazin's body was enveloped, overshadowed even, by a carved oak throne. From where she was sitting it was little more than a black shape blending into the darkness.

'But, Inna Marietta, not all the rumours are true.'

Kazin seemed content for her to sit silently and think about that proposition for a while. When next he spoke his cracked, catarrhal voice seemed somehow softer, less menacing.

'Do you know what this is?'

He used the cigarette to point out four thick cardboard folders perched on the right-hand side of his desk. Inna shook her head.

'This is you.' Kazin chuckled again. 'Isn't there a lot of you?'

Her dossier. Actions, thoughts, views, feelings, failures, assessments: all were there. Inna swallowed hard.

'It's very good.'

Inna's eyebrows shot up.

'Most of it. It's not easy for a woman to make headway in the KGB, but you've managed well enough. There are a few things which puzzle me, however. Why did you stop playing the piano, for instance?'

Inna took a few moments to adjust. First her imagination had her passing through The Door, now the Chairman was asking her about her hobbies.

'It took too long to practise, Comrade Chairman. You have to devote so many hours to it a day, or it's no good.'

To her relief her voice sounded strong and confident again. She knew a moment of pride. Not everyone could stand up to Kazin like this . . .

The Chairman nodded slowly. 'I see. And you weren't prepared to put in the necessary time.'

'It was incompatible with the demands of my career.'

Kazin nodded again, as if he found the explanation predictable. 'And the child,' he said after a pause. 'Is Volodiya "compatible", as you put it, with a career?'

'I think so, yes.'

'Although a husband wasn't.'

'That was different. He was guilty of anti-Soviet tendencies. Bad both for my career and my child.'

'Not "our" child, I notice.'

Inna flushed. 'I felt it was necessary to remove Volodiya from his influence. There was danger of moral corruption. The judge thought so, and the Personnel Directorate here on the Square agreed with him.'

'I would express that differently. The Personnel Directorate thought so. And the judge did what he is paid to do: he complied.'

Inna said nothing. No one could speak of such things without courting endless trouble. No one but Kazin.

'So you see, Inna Marietta, you owe us a great debt. Here. On the square.'

Inna looked deep inside herself and realized with a mental shrug that Kazin had merely made explicit what she herself had long suspected.

'You agree with me, I see. Good. I have chosen to deal

plainly with you, because it is simpler than the other ways I have at my disposal. I know all about your next assignment, up in Murmansk. I developed it. I directed it. From now on, I intend to oversee it personally. I selected you because where you are going your weaknesses are as useful to me as your strengths. Oh yes, don't look so surprised. From now on you are working for me, as a personal assistant. Others will know it and will treat you accordingly. For you, Inna Marietta —' Kazin's lips curled in a sarcastic smile — 'socialism has finally arrived.'

Until the night before Inna had never imagined in her wildest dreams that the Chairman even knew of her existence. Then came the phone call and now he was telling her . . . What exactly *was* he telling her?

'Take this notepad, look at the number I have written and memorize it.'

Inna stretched out a hand which trembled slightly. At the last moment Kazin flicked the pad, so that it landed in her palm with a slap. The digits danced before her eyes and steadied. When she could recall the numbers exactly she placed the pad on Kazin's desk.

'It is a telephone number. It belongs to an instrument in the next room. Somebody will always be there to receive your calls. Make sure you keep the number to yourself.'

'Yes, Comrade Chairman.'

'A moment ago I mentioned your weaknesses. The task ahead requires a woman: someone of resource, strength and guile who nevertheless combines with those qualities the warmth, tenderness even, of femininity. All this has been explained to you, I know. Now it is necessary to underline some things. What I will call the masculine side of you has always to be in control, understood?'

Inna nodded. This at least was old ground: the interrogators had imparted their craft well.

'Your child will have to learn to do without you for long periods at a stretch. That should come as no hardship to you when you consider the importance to us of the task ahead.'

Inna was dimly coming to realize that somehow, amongst all the disruption, her career had advanced farther in the last few minutes than most KGB workers achieved in a lifetime. Volodiya would reap the benefit; so too he must help her pay the price.

'I understand perfectly, Comrade Chairman.'

'Good. Don't think of us as unsympathetic. We will keep an eye on the boy's welfare, your mother's too. You have no compunction about leaving her, I take it?'

'None whatsoever.'

It came out a little pat. Kazin and Inna noticed that simultaneously; the conspiratorial smile on his face mirrored her own rather less confident one.

'Good. Then let us move on. They tell me you are ready, Inna Marietta. They may be right. I propose to find out for myself. Forget about strategy for one moment, forget about tactics. Tell me, in your own words, what is the object of my sending you to interrogate General Stepan Ilyich Povin?'

'To break the Chance Medley code, Comrade Chairman.'

Kazin's eyes widened in mock appreciation. 'Yes. And now tell me this — what is the . . . Chance Medley code? How does it work?'

'It is a variation on the two-key system. The recipient is sent the coded message in two parts on consecutive days. What he receives on day one is incomprehensible, to him or to anyone else. What he receives on day two is equally indecipherable when read by itself, but if he then puts the two parts of the message together and applies the key he can decode the complete text.'

Kazin regarded her with benign approval. 'Where does the Chance Medley element come in?'

'May I use an example?'

'If it is pertinent.'

'A variation on the typical two-key system might involve the recipient not actually knowing that what he receives on the first day is part of a message at all. The day two material not only completes the message, it also identifies the other part of it. In my chosen example, the recipient is a local Party secretary who gets five administrative circulars through the post on the first day. He has been forewarned that one of the documents contains his message, but only when the post

32

arrives on day two does he know which of the previous day's circulars contains the first part of the text. That is known as the Chance Medley variation.'

'Excellent. Clear and concise. Now for the next step. How does this affect Povin?'

Inna's mind seized up. She knew the answer, but before she could respond Kazin became impatient and prompted her.

'Povin planned to defect to the West and was getting help from outside, yes? They wanted to send him a message telling him who would meet him and escort him over the border, a courier from the Travel Agency. To use the language of your earlier exposition, on day one Stolyinovich brought into the country a number of objects which together or singly comprised the first part of the message. What about the day two material?'

Now the words spilled out of Inna as if from a high-speed printer. 'Stolyinovich himself carried the day two material in the form of lines from a Shakespearean sonnet, Comrade Chairman. He never communicated those lines to Povin, who was accordingly arrested while still in a state of total ignorance about the message. The interrogators have already extracted those lines from Stolyinovich, but he is unaware of the nature of the day one material.'

She paused for breath and Kazin murmured, 'Yes. We don't know what they . . . the day one objects were. Or at least, we're not sure. And your job, Inna Marietta . . . is to find out.' His voice tailed away, as if his mind were elsewhere.

'So.' He returned to the present with a jolt. 'Why have I chosen you, Inna Marietta? Why you, when the real interrogators have been working on him for these past two years, mm?'

This time Inna's pause was quite genuine. She raised her head but found no reassurance in Kazin's gaze. 'Because you are reluctant to ask him directly,' she ventured. 'In this one, isolated area you can never be sure whether he is lying. There is no crosscheck. So direct methods are to be avoided. Instead . . .'

'Yes. Be quick!'

'Instead you have chosen someone to take by guile what

33

cannot be taken by storm. Someone whose personal characteristics are thought, are . . . believed, to overlap with those of Povin's only close friend, of Stolyinovich. For that task you have chosen . . . me.'

Kazin nodded. He was pleased with the woman sitting in front of him. His instincts had not lied.

'Although I must confess . . . I do not understand why you have not chosen . . .'

'A man.' Kazin spoke testily, as if the woman had let him down. 'In the case of Povin it never does to be too obvious. Let me ask you this. What are your feelings towards Povin?'

'I detest him.' The words came out in a long hiss.

'Why?'

'Because . . . he is a traitor. A fascist. A spy and a counter-revolutionary . . .' She spread her hands in an uneasy gesture of frustration. 'I am sorry, Chairman, I do not . . .'

'I understand. But do *you* understand, Inna Marietta? Do you understand what I said earlier, about needing your weaknesses?'

Inna looked at the floor and mutely shook her head, but this time Kazin was neither angry nor disappointed. 'Until your recent transfer, all your work had been done for the Fifth Direction: the Fifth Directorate's Department of Religious Affairs. You are by training a statistician; that is why we recruited you — we had need of statisticians. Now, we have also made an interrogator out of you — of a sort. There are limits, of course, but yes, you are an interrogator. Do you follow me?'

Again the mute shake of the head. Kazin leaned forward.

'If you worked with radioactive material, we'd be concerned for you. For your health, your wellbeing. It's the same with Christianity. Are you *sure* you don't feel the attraction, the emotional draw? Povin did.'

'No!'

'Don't be so quick to answer next time. Not so — what is it you musicians say — not so staccato.'

Inna took the hint and deliberately paused; then wished she hadn't. It was as if Kazin's question struck an invisible tuning fork to send out vibrations of a kind which she found distinctly unsettling. But, of course, there was only one possible answer. 'No, Comrade Chairman. My researches for the department have convinced me that all religions have one thing in common: superstition based on fear. So no attraction, except that which a conscientious worker always tries to cultivate towards the subject matter of his duties. What worries me is my other weakness. The other reason why you chose me. The reason why I was put on probation in the first place.'

'And what is that?'

Inna subjected him to a long stare before she answered. 'My weakness is that I . . . I think for myself.' She faltered. 'Too much.'

Kazin slapped the desktop with his palm and laughed out loud. Inna, hearing that laugh, felt her skin turn cold.

'Don't think you can buy yourself out of trouble by being bold with me, Karsovina. That may work at some levels, when you're wheedling an apartment for yourself, for example, but with me . . .' He raised his palm from the desk and waved it to and fro before once more bringing it down with a slap. 'You'll be watching him. But *we* . . . will be watching you. Always. Do you understand, Karsovina?'

Inna stiffened. The apartment. He knew about that. 'Yes.'

'Good.' Kazin allowed her a few more moments in which to digest the message. When next he spoke it was in an altogether softer tone of voice. 'Then it remains only to repeat that you go with my personal good wishes — which in their turn carry my personal guarantee of rewards for the successful.'

'Thank you. Comrade Chairman . . .?'

Kazin's lips wrinkled in distaste. 'You have a question?'

'I am sorry, but . . . the telephone number you mentioned earlier. I am to use it — when?'

Kazin remained perfectly still. She knew his rages were supposed to begin with a moment of calm before the storm broke and could have bitten out her tongue as the price of her own stupidity. Then the Chairman shook his head, very slowly, half a dozen times, like an old professor whose prize student has for once blundered.

'He — ' the merest emphasis on the word, the slightest pause — 'will leave you in no doubt.'

The interview was over, but Inna knew that no one ever left his presence without permission. And now Kazin gave it. He resumed writing, one hand supporting his head.

'Out.'

Inna stood up, turned and walked towards the place where she imagined the door to be. But once beyond the pool of light shed by the overhead lamp she rapidly became disorientated, missing the exit by several feet. She had to grope her way along the wall; and as she did so it came over her with complete conviction and a prickly sense of unease that Kazin had risen silently from his desk and was walking across the room towards her. Her fingers scrabbled for the handle, the pain burned in her chest, somewhere deep in her throat she heard the beginnings of a whimper ... then her hand made contact with brass, she wrenched downwards and, to her unutterable relief, a narrow streak of white light opened up. As the door closed behind her she caught a last glimpse of Kazin, still sitting in The Chair, one hand supporting his chin, iron-grey shafts of smoke rising up to be lost in the black cavern around him.

Inna leaned back against the door, eyes shut, while her heart hammered itself into silence. She awoke from the daze to find herself in the presence of a blazing row.

The colonel who had received her earlier was still standing by the window, but his hands were no longer clasped behind his back. He was using them to grapple with a short, thick-set general whose own hands were firmly fixed on the colonel's lapels. Inna had emerged so quietly that neither man was conscious of her presence. They were speaking simultaneously, the words tumbling out so fast that it was several moments before she managed to distinguish them.

'I tell you, Krubykov —'

Suddenly the colonel's head swivelled and Inna knew he had seen her. In the same instant the general, becoming aware that all was not well, broke off in mid-sentence. He released the colonel's lapels and for an embarrassed moment the two men self-consciously straightened their uniforms, as if they had been engaged in nothing more unusual than moving a dusty piece of furniture. Inna continued to stare at them through eyes filled with trepidation. After the three of them had held this silent tableau for a moment longer the colonel redirected his gaze to the confused general and forced a chilly smile.

'I can assure you, my dear Frolov, in a week, ten days at the most. That's the absolute best I can do for you at present.'

Inna's eyes widened. So *that* was Frolov. She had been reading about him in the Murmansk papers a day or two previously. He didn't at all accord with her mental picture of him. She'd expected someone authoritative, charismatic . . .

The general backed away. He was still breathing heavily and he never once removed his gaze from the colonel's face. For him Inna simply did not exist. A big purple vein throbbed in his forehead, like an obscene worm. By his shoulder-boards he represented the very epitome of the unspeakable power housed within these walls, yet the impression he conveyed was one of frustrated impotence.

Without a word more the general turned on his heel and walked out, slamming the door behind him. The other man turned to face Inna and she saw that he was angry enough to be physically dangerous.

'You were given a number,' the colonel said suddenly, and Inna jumped. 'Repeat it.'

Was this a trap? Suppose Kazin had asked the colonel to seek the number from her and given orders that if she complied she was to be shot . . .

'Re-*peat* . . . *it!*'

'Eight-nine-six-four-four-four.'

The words seemed to ricochet around the room, echoing themselves with contemptuous derision. How could she? *How could she be such a fool?*

'Nine-eight, six-four, double-four,' she muttered.

The colonel said nothing and Inna began the long walk to the door through which the indignant general had earlier made his exit. As she reached it the colonel said, 'If ever you do have to use it — the number I mean — you will get it right?'

Inna, seething, halted in the doorway. For the first time she recognized at the back of his grey eyes something that she had seen before, in the stares of other men, and in that second he ceased to hold any but conventional terrors for her.

'After all,' he went on softly, 'you never know who you might end up talking to. Do you?'

3

Daybreak. Every morning it was the same. The old man woke to see the first light of an Arctic dawn insinuate itself like a thief through the grimy pane of glass let high in the wall opposite his bunk; then, after a moment of numbness, pain renewed its grip on his life. Daybreak was the worst time for him. He hated it. In the camp, even the light was soiled, as if the sun knew it had no right to be there.

The temperature in the blockhouse hovered a few degrees above freezing. The stove in the middle of the floor was almost out. It paid the contractors to supply only the poorest-quality chips which had lain in the snow all winter and now could not be disposed of except to the Gulag administration's procurement officer. There was a precise art to drying out these chips of wood. The occupant of each little cell in the blockhouse spread them by the stove last thing at night, after the guard had completed his final round, and hoped that the chips would dry out enough for them to be used as fuel the following morning. But sometimes the wood was too wet, or the guard too late, and then the embers died. So, occasionally, did the inhabitants of the cells. It all depended on the weather.

He lay motionless, listening to the bitter sough of the wind outside. Far away, on the other side of the compound, a dog howled, signalling the start of a furious bout of barking. Meat. They could smell meat.

His stomach contracted in a painful spasm. Change the subject.

His leg was smarting again. Change *that* subject also. What about the bladder? Not too bad, thank God. He drew a deep breath and struggled to move his arms. It was a universal Gulag rule that all prisoners must sleep with their arms outside the blanket. (Blanket! What a joke!) Now the pins and needles began to torment him as he strove to bring his frozen body back to life. A grunt forced its way through the old man's clenched teeth. Tremors of pain shot up and down his arms. It took the best part of five minutes to ease the muscles into play, but eventually it was done and he heaved a sigh of contentment at the first small success of the morning.

Each day was a self-contained triumph, a victory simply because he was there to see it. Now, as he lay watching the grey square of window turn off-white, the old man prayed. It sounded more like a statement than a prayer, but he knew he was talking to God, and God knew.

'There is bread to eat. Water to drink. And air to breathe.'

He repeated it several times, like a mantra, his lips scarcely moving. The bread was tasteless and sometimes mouldy, the water was cloudy often as not, and the air so cold that it scraped the sinuses like a knife. That didn't matter. None of it mattered. God had seen him through, buoyed up by faith like a castaway on a fragile raft. He was alive. There was bread to eat. There was water to drink. There was air to breathe.

There was revenge to think about, too. Someone had put him in this camp. A jealous deputy, hungry for a promotion that he didn't deserve. Frolov . . . he usually had an early-morning thought to spare for Frolov.

The old man dragged himself painfully over on to his stomach and reached behind the headboard of the bunk, one hand scrabbling blindly for the hole in the wainscot. After a moment his eyes closed in relief. It was still there. Very cautiously, so as not to make the slightest noise, he withdrew the long, pointed sliver of wood. His eyes had lighted on it several weeks before as he was helping sort chips for the stove and he'd pounced at once, pretending to slip on the wet floor, covering the precious sliver with his frail body. The wood was hard and sound. Even such a weapon as that was beyond price, here in the camp. None of the other prisoners knew his identity, to them he was merely a number, but if ever they found out what he had been in the outside world, they would destroy him. The camp authorities, knowing this, guarded the old man day and night; but two years of deprivation had not blunted his mind. He understood how 'accidents' happened. He would have killed in order to preserve the sliver of wood.

With slow, careful movements he transferred his stiletto from the hole in the wainscot to the inside of his jacket sleeve, where he had sewn a thread to hold it. A risk, but one worth taking. If the guards found it in the course of a casual search they might give him ten days' solitary, but nothing more, and he had lived through worse than that. Two years in this and other camps on the archipelago had taught him everything he needed to know about 'living through'.

He could use the stiletto. Victor, his old friend and helper in the outside world, had shown him how to fight with a blade. Victor. Whatever happened to him . . . ?

The barking of the dogs was louder now. That meant they were coming. He gripped the frayed edge of the thin blanket, his breath wheezing faster. Another day . . .

Torch beams suddenly flickered through the window, crisscrossing the ceiling of the old man's cell. Then came the cry which heralded the start of every working day.

'To the corridor! Now!'

In a second he was up, pulling on his boots. He stumbled into the narrow passage and turned to face the door at the far end of the blockhouse, while the nine other inmates did the same with varying degrees of haste and enthusiasm. Then the outer door was hurled open to admit a blast of icy wind and a flurry of snow from the roof; the lights went on; 'All out! Outside! Get a move on, out, out, *out*!'

In the doorway stood a cluster of grey-coated, fur-hatted, faceless guards with rifles slung over their shoulders, and a Doberman on a taut leash, its jaws snapping wildly. For a moment they merely watched, allowing the rush of cold air, frozen ice vapour, to do their work for them. The old man,

40

who had been awake for a long time by now, was one of the first to jump down the steps.

Not a bad day, he reflected as he jogged up and down, warming his hands under his armpits. The snow was turning to slush, the cloud was high and light, spring was coming. Even on the northernmost tip of Russia, above the Arctic Circle, there was a spring. It would not warm up properly until about June but then the temperature might reach fifteen or sixteen degrees Celsius, or so they told him; he hadn't been in this camp long enough to experience it for himself. The old man couldn't imagine such a temperature. Why, they'd all be tearing their clothes off and running about naked! Personally, he'd believe it when it happened. For now, it was enough to see that the snow was melting and the sky was a little lighter than it had been at the same time last week. One day at a time. One *hour* at a time.

'Form up. Hurry it along there! You want us to let the dogs loose? They can always manage a little more *breakfast*.'

The guards' coarse laughter was stilled by the approach of an officer. The old man kept his head buried in his chest but his eyes flickered this way and that, seeing everything. The officer's name was Zuyev. He interested the old man greatly. It so happened that in his former life, outside Gulag, the old man had come to learn a lot about Captain Zuyev, and now as a result he had plans for him. Plans which had Captain Zuyev known about them, would have caused him to be even more short-tempered than usual.

The zeks from blockhouse C formed up in a line. In front of them the inhabitants of blocks A and B were likewise falling in; behind them the rest of the two hundred odd prisoners did the same. Oh-six-thirty hours. Roll call.

As far as officialdom was concerned there were no names in this compound, only numbers. Not that it bothered the old man; he recognized a lot of people who passed through Ristikent MU/12, peering at them through the mask of anonymity which the Gulag administration had — so far — allowed him, and matching up their faces with the files inside his head. Only Colonel Trofimov, the camp commander, knew the old man's true identity, no one else.

First names were another matter. Everybody knew everybody else's patronymic. No matter what the guards said, you couldn't call a fellow-prisoner by his number. You just couldn't.

Talking by the zeks was strictly prohibited, but in practice roll call meant the big news exchange of the day. Prisoners soon learned to communicate in a low murmur, broken up into jerky phrases which could, if challenged, be passed off as a suppressed cough. This compound was like any other prison in one respect: its internal grapevine was excellent.

'God be with you, Stepan Ilyich,' murmured a low voice on the old man's right. Without raising his eyes from the ground in front of him he replied, 'And with you. Sergei Petrovich.' A pause. The old man murmured again. 'God be with you. Aleksei . . . Anatolovich.' And a moment later the soft acknowledgment came from his left. The guards noticed nothing suspicious. Another few moments of precious human contact were notched up for the record. Another triumph.

'No dead,' he heard a man say, and promptly passed it on. Good news was welcome. Fewer night-time deaths meant that spring *was* coming.

The roll call drew to a close.

'*Ruki nazad*! Hands behind your backs! Forward!'

The three rows of zeks turned to face the bitter wind. The old man was careful never to stand at the end of the line. That way he ensured he didn't have to take the polar blast full in his face; there was always at least one other body to shield him from it. This morning he could feel his feet. Good. The weather was improving. *Good*.

The mess hall was on the other side of the compound, behind the big house. Smoke was rising from the chimney stacks of the sturdy, brick-built dacha and the old man thought longingly of the stoves within. He'd heard camp officers curse their luck at being exiled to the Ristikent Special Camp, but Christ! They didn't know they were born.

Although he kept his eyes down, nothing escaped him. He knew exactly where he was at every step. The cell block-houses were at the very back of the compound, fifty metres from the electrified wire fence with its watchtowers, mined strips and dog patrols. A makeshift road led through a birch grove up to the big house, with its corrugated-iron mess hall and officers' quarters tacked on like an ugly wart growing from a handsome face. Beyond that, a slope thinly planted with birch trees rolled down to the white lake in which an escaping zek might live for half a minute before he turned to stone and sank like one. For this was an *ozerlag*, a lakeshore camp, yet it was no ordinary offshoot of Gulag. Nothing about Ristikent MU/12 was ordinary.

The old man's eyes flickered up to the façade of the dacha, very close now. All the windows were sealed, the blinds drawn . . . what happened behind those windows, those unseeing, inward turning eyes? He should know, he *did* know — with his background how could he not? But now he was seeing things from a different viewpoint, whence the familiar attributes of his former existence took on all the terrors of the unknown. He had never yet penetrated the house, although it was the centre of camp operations and the scene of much activity. Throughout the day a steady stream of cars came and went, carrying braided generals and beribboned admirals, Party secretaries in their Savile Row suits, and god knew who else. For Ristikent MU/12 was special, very special. Its location in the Arctic north, deliberately far away from Moscow, was a secret known only to a carefully chosen few; because according to Party ideology the State had no need for an institution such as this and therefore it could not, did not exist.

In Ristikent MU/12, as well as rank-and-file prisoners they housed some of the idols of the Soviet Union who had toppled the farthest: the traitors who came from the top.

Not only the traitors. A month ago the news had rippled through the morning line-up: 'Sakharov is here!' Maybe he was; the old man never saw him. All he knew was that three days later the rumour was different: 'Sakharov has gone, in the middle of the night, no one knows where . . .' No one ever knew. Turnover was high. People came and went in an endless succession of new faces, a pathetic tide which ebbed and flowed through the lakeshore camp, beaching its human wreckage for a brief moment before finally flushing it out to be lost at sea.

All but the old man. He stayed, dreading the inevitable day when he would look down the line at roll call to see a man from the past who recognized him.

The zeks shuffled to a halt outside the corrugated-iron mess hall and waited to be called. At a sign from one of the guards the old man broke ranks and, with a couple of other prisoners, stumbled across to the compound bakery. He had been inside the mess hall only once, on the night of his arrival, the previous October. He could still remember the stench: a rank mixture of sweat, damp, mould and rotting cabbage which rammed itself down his nostrils into his stomach, into his brain, almost — but not quite — preventing him from eating. Not to eat was a crime, the worst in the old man's calendar. But he was grateful when, next day, they assigned him to the bakery. The cooks ate there, instead of in the mess hall with the others.

That was a piece of luck so stupendous that at first it had troubled him deeply. For the past two years, in other camps, they had been beating the hell out of him. Then, suddenly, and without any warning — this. A warm, dry job. An *inside* job, the dream of every zek. A fifteen-hour day, yes, insanitary conditions, certainly, only one short break in the afternoon, of course — but none of that mattered. It all paled into insignificance when set against the single great guarantee which the job represented: he would survive. At the end of his first day in the bakery the old man had lain down on his bunk and wept. God was with him. *He would survive!*

He turned on the lights and blinked owlishly round his domain. Over the five months which had elapsed since his transfer to this camp he had established a regular routine. The first hour was easy. All the cooks had to do was draw off hot water from the storage tanks and make weak tea for the prisoners who comprised the bulk of the work force. That, together with porridge and three hundred grammes of bread apiece, was their breakfast. Then each man was given another three hundred grammes of bread, some dried fish or meat, and two lumps of sugar to keep him going through the day. In the evening there was a proper meal, of variable quality it was true, but a meal none the less, served with yet more bread.

That all added up to a lot of bread. It was the old man's job to bake it. And he had to do everything by hand.

He had four helpers, each responsible for a different part of the process. Mix the heavily adulterated flour with the mouldy yeast and cloudy water. Knead. Leave to rise while you started another batch. Knead the first batch again, leave it to rise, bake it. Start early, no slacking, that was important. Always remember: if the bread wasn't baked, the zeks would kill you unless the guards did it first — that helped concentrate the mind.

A young zek, assigned to bakery work because in his previous camp they had all but blinded him, heaved a sack of flour on to the old man's table: the only part of the process he couldn't manage for himself. He looked at the youngster, who returned his gaze through half-closed eyes. One of the corneas was milky white. At first the old man had sensed that the zek recognized him from the past, but after a while he came to think it was his imagination playing tricks. This zek was only a number, triple-oh-eight, and a first name: Lev. The boy's face was one of the very few that the old man couldn't recall, and the zek never said anything to show that he knew the old man. He just stared at the world from behind the ghastly milk-white screen and did what he was told.

The old man shrugged. Alexander the Chechen would look after triple-oh-eight, he was almost as good as Victor. Alexander, or the wooden stiletto. One threat he could cope with. As long as there was only one . . .

He took off his jacket and hung it on a hook behind the door, then went to fill a plastic bucket from the tap. Hot water was better, but in the morning it was all being used for tea so he had to make do with cold. He looked around for salt. Sometimes there was salt and sometimes there wasn't. Today there wasn't. He dearly loved a bit of salt, but he knew you could get by without it. Additional salt wasn't essential to support human life as long as you had a reasonable diet otherwise. He smiled grimly to himself. A healthy diet, yes, that was the secret.

Kneading the first batch soon got him into a sweat. He was ravenously hungry but experience had taught him to get ahead of the day's work before eating. At last it was done. He left the grey, sodden mass to rise and went to pour himself a tin of tea. He sipped it slowly. By dragging out the hot drink he could often take the edge off his hunger, thus making it easier to eat his bread a nibble at a time.

None of the cooks ever took one bite more than their allotted ration. That would be cheating the rest of the zeks, and most of these men were still civilized enough to see the evil involved. But with the guards it was another matter.

In a side room off the main bakery, half a dozen 'trusties' were responsible for cooking the guards' food under the supervision of an NCO. (No one supervised the old man and his cronies in the main bakery; it was assumed that they wouldn't poison their own kind.) The guards fared little better than the prisoners, but their bread was of superior quality and they were sure of getting meat twice a week. It somehow happened that on most days a little bit of food trickled through into the main bakery from the guards' kitchen, though quality and quantity both varied a lot. The old man didn't always eat his bit of mutton or fish head; sometimes he traded it for *makhorka*, the coarse tobacco of the camps, which in turn he used to barter for a sliver of soap, or for information. Nearly all the guards could be bought with tobacco, as long as you didn't ask too much of them. If you wanted to learn something important it was necessary to lay your hands on vodka, which was possible but extremely difficult. There the guards' usefulness ended. They would sell knowledge but they wouldn't take messages out. Not that this troubled the old man. He had a plan for getting round it. The old man had lots of plans.

He nibbled on a bit of bread, sucking the crust. He sucked all his food before he swallowed it; that way it gave up whatever goodness it had and wasn't just lost in his guts. He weighed the last morsel in his fingers, debating whether to finish it or save it for later. Better save it. That was the advice you always gave to new prisoners: if in doubt, save it for later.

He tapped Lev triple-oh-eight on the shoulder, resisting the urge to wince when the zek turned his malevolent stare towards him. 'Come on,' he muttered. 'Let's get started.'

It was a day like any other. The routine went on undisturbed. The old man liked to think while he worked. He was trying to find the answer to a particular and very unusual problem.

Life was too easy.

It was as simple as that. They were treating him too well. It wasn't like the previous camps. There he'd been ground into the dirt. They'd given him a dose of hard labour, the dreaded *katorga*, and when that didn't finish him off they followed it up with 'general assignment work', their euphemism for legalized murder. He'd survived beatings by guards, beatings by prisoners, interrogations by the Special Investigation Department of the KGB (and by god, those interrogators were 'special' all right), starvation, squalor. He could not walk properly; thanks to the endless cold and damp he'd contracted rheumatoid arthritis. Twice he'd crawled his way back over the narrow line which separated life in the camps from death. And now, all of a sudden, it was easy.

Why?

The old man wiped the sweat off his forehead and rested his arms on the table. Perhaps they were just softening him up in readiness for the next real battering: stick-and-carrot, the old story. Maybe Chairman Kazin was preparing for one last interrogation, doing it the way the old man himself would have chosen. And that meant there would be a change of cast, too, Povin was sure of it; soon Kazin would send his chosen interrogator, lance in hand, like a medieval champion come to joust. Someone different. Someone — the old man raised his head and smiled — *special*.

What would that special someone's instructions be? The old man's smile faded. He didn't know, or at least — he couldn't be sure. But he had ideas, and one of them was starting to exert a peculiar hold over his imagination. Kazin wanted to find out whatever it was that the old man knew . . . but didn't know he knew. He had cooperated, he had told them what he could, and still they wanted something else . . . Suppose he was right? Who would the Chairman send? Who would he himself have sent . . .?

Hearing the door behind him open he instinctively resumed his work, not wanting to be caught unoccupied. A harsh voice called out his number.

'Here.'

He turned to see that Alexander the Chechen had silently come to stand a few feet away from him, and at once he smiled ingratiatingly. The stocky zek did not return the smile. His yellowish, rounded features contracted into a frown. He had been in the compound almost as long as the old man; each recognized the other as different. The old man needed him. But in an odd kind of way the Chechen seemed to need the old man also. There was a tacit interdependence which neither would ever acknowledge openly.

'To the house. Now!'

The old man vainly tried to wipe the wet dough from his hands on the backs of his denim trousers and shambled over to collect his jacket. Never ask why, he reminded himself bitterly. You'll find out soon enough. He had to push past the burly Chechen, who made no move to let him through. As he shuffled away the old man was conscious of Alexander's calculating eyes on his back.

An armed guard was waiting for him by the side door which led into the house. 'Come on, you. Hurry up!'

Even the tiny conservatory in which he found himself was warmer than the bakery. The old man darted cunning glances here and there, garnering information. Solid doors, barred windows, a curious smell of decay. The guard motioned him to follow. When nothing happened the guard turned, his face creased with irritation, and jerked the old man's arm. 'This way, you!'

A short, bare passage led from the conservatory into a large entrance hall; he was aware of dusty pictures, a table on which stood a long-faded arrangement of ferns, a nondescript square of carpet. And that smell . . . furniture polish, decay, mustiness. Then the guard was leading him through a heavy oak door, down a flight of steps to the cellars. His heart began to pound. Ahead of him was another door, steel this time, with a large keyhole and rivets round the edge. The guard thrust him through it, using the old man's weight to swing the heavy door open. When the guard shoved him across the threshold his legs refused to cooperate and he fell, bruising his forehead on the hard edge of a wooden chair which lay just inside the cellar. Pain flooded through his body.

The door closed behind him.

'Get up.'

The camp commander's voice snapped across him like a knout, but he couldn't comply. Only when Colonel Trofimov repeated the order did he manage to haul himself blindly upright. He was panting with exhaustion and fear.

'Identify yourself.'

The old man took a deep breath, tottered and heaved. Somehow he managed to say his number out loud. In the long silence that followed he tried to summon up some courage, but it was difficult. The room seemed to be full of another incredibly heavy, pungent smell, one which bore back memories long ago forgotten.

He was in a large underground room poorly lit by a single overhead bulb. At one end was a thick wooden stake embedded in the concrete floor. At the other . . .

At the other end of the room, perhaps fifteen metres from the stake, were six soldiers drawn up in a line, their rifles at the ready. A firing squad. And behind them, a little to one side, stood an impossible illusion, the product of hunger and exhaustion. A vision.

A woman.

The guard dragged him over to the stake where another man was waiting with ropes, but he could not take his eyes from the woman's face. She was white and tense, making no effort to conceal her revulsion. Her gaze did not meet his.

'Present!'

The squad raised their rifles; the old man heard the bolts click. The ropes bound him fast to the stake. His breath came and went in short panting groans. Please God, no, not now, it was too soon, too soon . . .

'Aim!'

The colonel stood with his legs apart, arms folded across his chest. The old man's eyes jerked from the woman to

Trofimov's cold, sneering face and he read there no possibility of mercy, no hope. Without unfolding his arms the colonel turned to one side and began to walk slowly towards the wall, out of range of the guns; the old man knew that when Trofimov passed beyond the last man in the line he would give the order to fire and he cried aloud, 'No! For God's sake . . . *Please*!'

As the colonel reached the wall the woman said, without looking at him but in a voice which easily carried to the stake, 'Weak. Weak and useless. You old queers, all the same. They should have shot you years ago, Povin.'

The old man remembered, just in time, to open his bladder. As the urine trickled down his legs Trofimov raised his head and cried aloud to the wall, 'Fire!'

Povin was aware of the woman beginning to stalk towards him with an enigmatic look on her face, one hand stretched out as if in succour; then darkness descended.

4

Far away to the south it was breakfast-time in another world.

'*Babushka*, I love my new trousers you bought for me.'

Volodiya ran up to his grandmother and impulsively threw his arms round her waist, burying his head in her apron. Anfisa Kostrytsina picked up the boy and carried him through into the living room.

'They suit you,' she said. 'Hungarian. I was lucky to find some still in stock. Thanks to Mrs Yuryn . . .'

She stood the boy on his chair and gauged him with a dressmaker's eye. 'I like to see little boys in long. Short pants went out of fashion years ago.'

Volodiya's eyes were almost on a level with her own.

'Mummy likes me in shorts,' he said impishly, tossing back his head the better to see how she took it.

'And when Mummy comes home you can wear your shorts again.' Anfisa's manner was brisk and businesslike. She had no time for Volodiya's playing-off-one-against-the-other games. The boy, seeing her mood, sat down and turned his attention to the egg.

'Where's Hungary?' he asked suddenly.

'Oh, a long way away. South. And West. Is that egg done?'

'West? Is Hungary near Paris, then?'

'It looks a bit runny . . . No, nowhere near Paris. Paris is in France.'

'I know. Miss Chekmasov said so. We had to paint the French flag yesterday. Red and white and blue. Miss Chekmasov says France is very decadent. Grandma, what does decadent mean?'

'It's what happens to little boys who don't eat up all their breakfast. They grow weak and skinny. Then they're decadent.'

Rot those teachers, thought Anfisa Kostrytsina. Filling little heads with big ideas . . .

'I'd rather be decadent. So I won't have my egg.'

He threw down his spoon and made as if to wriggle off the chair. Quick as a flash his grandmother reached out to grab his ear.

'Ow! You *hurt* me.'

For a second the scowl he turned on her reminded the old lady of his father: those terrible clefts in the middle of the forehead, the hooded eyes . . . She twisted his ear without meaning to and tears spurted from the little boy's eyes.

'*I* didn't hear you say, "May I please get down, Grandmother?" Or wasn't I listening properly?'

Volodiya was silent for the length of time it took him to work out that he wasn't going to be able to free himself from his grandmother's grip. Then he tried another tack. Instead of wrestling with the old lady he lowered his head and glanced up at her with well-feigned timidity, fluttering his eyelashes. She always fell for that . . .

Only this time she didn't. Volodiya fluttered some more.

51

'You didn't hear properly,' he ventured.

Anfisa turned her head away, very deliberately, so that she was looking at him out of the corner of her right eye, and allowed her face to assume a dreadful frown. Her grip on Volodiya's ear did not slacken. The boy saw that all was lost and ran up the white flag.

'May I get down, Grandmother? Please?'

'Not until you've finished your egg.'

'But . . .'

'But me no buts, young master. That's what the boyars used to say in the old days, "But me no buts, young master," when their sons were naughty — have you read that with Miss Chekmasov yet?'

'No! You're teasing. What else did the bad boyars say. The *bad . . . bold . . . boy*-ars . . .'

Anfisa Kostrytsina kept up a steady flow of patter while he finished his egg and ate his bread and butter, washed his hands and face, brushed his hair and collected his lunch bag. She never ceased to be amazed at how easy it was to deal with a child that wasn't your own. Don't give them time to think, be firm, let them see you love them all the same . . . Why had she never realized the simplicity of it when Inna was Volodiya's age?

As he reached the front door she hauled him back.

'Call that brushing your hair? Come here —'

He reached for the latch, laughing, but again she was too quick for him: she held his wrists together and flicked the comb through his fine blond hair a dozen times, until he looked presentable, while Volodiya struggled and panted and protested between giggles.

'There,' gasped Anfisa Kostrytsina, almost out of breath herself. 'You'd be one too many for a wagonful of wolves, you would! Where do you get your energy from? I wish you'd give me some.'

'I *would* give you some, *babushka*, if only I knew how. I promise I would!'

'Mind those stairs, now . . .'

She walked with him to the school gate, where she held him at arm's length for final inspection and said goodbye.

'Now, don't forget. This evening I have to go to a fitting, but I'll try and be back as soon as I can. You've got your key?'

'Yes.'

'Show me.'

He delved into one of the pockets of his brand new trousers and fished out the key. She knew he was perfectly capable of using it; all the same she felt troubled and somehow guilty. It wasn't right that he should have to come home alone. But her part-time dressmaking brought in a very useful supplement to the family's income, and they really could use the money from that fitting, it was an evening gown . . .

'Put it back, then. Have a lovely day, won't you.'

'You too, Grandma. Bye-ee!'

She stayed to watch him fly across the playground, his sparkling red and white legs marking him out from the other boys, and shook her head knowingly. Hungarian or not, those trousers wouldn't last. Well, at six years old, pushing seven, what to expect?

'Volodiya,' she shouted, suddenly remembering something. The boy stopped just short of the door and turned back towards her.

'Come straight home,' Anfisa yelled, hoping her voice would carry the distance. 'Don't talk to anyone on the way!'

He raised a hand to show that he had heard, and quickly disappeared inside the school building. Anfisa pursed her lips doubtfully before letting them dissolve into a smile. On the way home, she decided, she would see if she could buy some wool for a matching scarf and mitts — he'd need another pair soon, and by knitting them herself she could help Inna make the money stretch farther. Inna wouldn't mind, of course; she'd be grateful. Although — Anfisa shook her head — you never could tell with Inna, these days.

5

They allowed her to choose the best room in the house, what had once been a large salon right in the centre overlooking the lake. The high ceiling and whitewashed walls reflected the cold northern light, drawing it in, diffusing it, ready to expose whatever the room's occupants might want to hide. She elected to sit with her back to the tall double windows, her face in shadow, so that she could observe all that happened without disclosing her own reactions to whoever sat in the chair opposite.

Inna Karsovina placed a pencil diagonally across the block of white paper on the desk, folded her hands in her lap and waited.

The guard dumped Povin in the chair and retreated to the door. For a long time there was silence in the room while youth and age surveyed each other.

'They told me they'd reworked your face,' the woman said slowly. 'The rest of you they left to my imagination. What a mess. What a . . . *shitty* mess.'

Povin said nothing. It was a long time since Kazin had mounted a direct attack on his mind. For the moment he was content to wait and see how things developed.

'Mock executions,' Inna Karsovina drawled. 'What a joke! Have you any idea how pathetic you looked, Povin . . . lying there with piss all down your pants, shivering, mumbling?' She grunted. 'Treat it as a rehearsal for the real thing. This interrogation begins and ends with a firing squad, you know that, don't you?'

Povin remained silent. He was a connoisseur of details. The woman's handbag lay on the sideboard by the window, behind her left shoulder. Next to it was a copy of *Izvestia*, which seemed entirely appropriate, and the latest edition of *Komsomolskaya Pravda*, which did not. A Party hack who read liberal youth magazines . . .

The woman leaned forward to rest her hands on the edge of the desk, spreading them wide. To Povin her appearance represented all that was beautiful and wholesome in a world he had left behind for ever. Blonde hair, recently washed, framed her face in thick, layered tresses. Two large blue, perfectly balanced eyes stared down at him from under a high, intelligent forehead. When she opened her lips to speak he caught a glimpse of white, even teeth. And that scent, that glorious heady aroma which flowed from every pore . . .

His mind flashed back to the moment when he had first inhaled that delicious perfume, in the cellar. The fragrance of death.

This woman reminded him of someone long since dead. A friend, his only real friend, used to hold his head erect in just that way. The hair, the eyes, exactly the same. Stolyinovich.

Someone special. Someone different. Someone *appealing*.

'It is necessary to establish a few points before we start,' the woman said. Her voice was harsh and unmusical, but Povin knew it did not always sound like that. 'In the past I have never found it necessary to employ physical compulsion. I am, however, quite prepared to find that you are the exception.' Her eyes flickered away from his face and briefly focused on the guard behind him. 'Blood doesn't upset me. Violence doesn't worry me. The guard remains here.'

'I have always cooperated. The records will show that.'

'The records show, Povin, that once you open your mouth it's difficult for the interrogators to shut it again. If you call that cooperating then, yes, I agree with you. Here things will be different. When I tell you to be quiet you'll *be* quiet. Understand?'

Someone who might be amenable to . . . *pressure*.

'I have been beaten enough. Two years. After that a man has only one concern: to avoid the next blow. Ask your questions, Comrade Interrogator. But — what should I call you?' He sighed inwardly and tensed his body for what was about to happen. 'May I please know the Comrade Interrogator's name?'

The woman hesitated for a moment. Then she raised one hand from the desk and snapped her fingers. The guard took a couple of paces forward and swung his fist against Povin's ear. The old man, lifted out of his chair by the force of the blow, collapsed on the floor.

'Get up.'

He staggered to his feet and groped his way back into the chair. His ear throbbed painfully, but he was learning, learning all the time.

'That's what'll happen if you ask a question again.'

Povin nodded. His instincts were right. He must pile on the pressure and to hell with the agony.

'Do you know what this is?' The woman was tapping a large cardboard box with the end of her pencil. 'This is you. All of you.' Her lips parted briefly in a sarcastic smile. 'Isn't there a lot of you?'

Povin was an expert on voices. Who had taught her that gambit with the box and the pencil? He knew that she had picked it up somewhere, that it wasn't natural. He made himself ignore the pain in his head and strove to concentrate.

'These files are the result of the two years' intensive interrogation which you have already undergone in other camps,' the woman went on. 'To a certain degree you are correct to speak of cooperation. What you have told us proved almost entirely accurate. Note, I stress "almost". My task is different.' She paused. 'My task is to elicit your motives.'

Povin raised his head very slowly, as if the action was in defiance of his will. The woman read his expression and nodded dismissively. She stood up and walked round the desk to within a few inches of Povin's side, lowering her face close to his.

'Yes, you're right. It's a waste of time. But somebody's got to do it. Personally, I don't give a fig for your motives. All I know from those files over there on the desk is that on eight separate occasions, eight historical watersheds, you went out and betrayed the Motherland to the best of your quite exceptional ability. And the question I've been sent to ask you — as if it mattered — is: why?'

She backed away from Povin and walked round the desk to resume her seat. He noticed how she kicked her feet forward with every step; the walk of a defiant woman. But who was there to defy here?

'If it weren't for General Frolov we might never have caught you.' She saw how murder flared in his eyes and smiled. 'Thank goodness for Frolov. It just shows you should never underestimate your deputy, Povin. Unfortunately, it's too late for you to draw any useful conclusions from the experience. But we don't want to have to rely on Frolovs. Prevention rather than cure, that's the watchword now.'

The old man resumed his intent study of the floorboards.

'So.' The woman sat back in her seat and folded her arms. 'The purpose and scope of this interrogation. We wish to build up the profile of a traitor, Povin. This will involve detailed study of your personal life and early background, in particular your deviant religious tendencies.'

Press. *Attack*. 'Oh surely not?'

'Be careful, Povin. I did not tell you to speak.'

'I'm sorry, but . . . you see, I don't want to waste your time. I suppose I should, really, because that way I prolong my life — do you know the story of the Arabian Nights? — but there's hardly much point in that, is there? No, the thing is that I don't think you know what you're looking for.'

He tensed his body in anticipation of a blow, but the woman merely leaned forward to rest her elbows on the table. There was a look of amusement on her face. 'No?'

'No.' His courage increased and he pushed harder. 'Oh, I'm sure Chairman Kazin has given you something, a peg to hang the interrogation on — any old thing would do for *that*. But I don't believe he's chosen to confide in *you*.'

Inna Karsovina smiled. The Project Committee were right after all. They had promised her it wouldn't be boring. 'I should stick to that, if I were you,' she said. 'It'll comfort you during the nights, help you sleep, like a baby with its thumb.' Again the taut smile, this time a deliberate provocation. 'Frolov sleeps well at night, Povin. Kazin tells him everything now. Why not? As head of the First Main Directorate with overall responsibility . . .'

'Thank you so much for the reminder.'

'I shall be reminding you of much in the weeks to come, Povin.'

'I'm sure you will. If I may say so, your ability is already conspicuous. The Chairman chose you for this job and I can see why. So — may I please say it? — so young.'

A tiny spot of colour appeared in the woman's cheeks and her lips twisted in a pout of displeasure. 'Let's get down to specifics, shall we?' Although her voice was bored, the old man's stock of learning increased by the minute. There were limits to what she would tolerate from him, but in her heart she recoiled from the idea of violence, so it became a question of constantly drawing and redrawing the boundaries. Provoke, move, *press* . . .

'Almost anything will do. For instance . . . the Mexican fiasco. Nineteen seventy-one. You betrayed Nechiporenko, had him expelled. Come on, let's see how good you are at following my line of thought. Why did you do that, Povin? What was in it for you?'

He made his voice sound apologetic. 'There was the money . . .'

'Which was paid into a UNICEF bank account. Every kopeck, every rouble.'

'Yes indeed.'

There was silence, each protagonist apparently of the view that he or she had successfully refuted the other's point.

'So!' The woman broke first. 'There was nothing in it *for* you, was there?'

'No, no, I am sorry. Please forgive me, Comrade Interrogator, but I have failed to make myself clear. I was so happy to be able to help the children. I love the little ones. By taking money from the West I was able to assist them much more than on the salary of a colonel general in the KGB. The people in the West are callous when dealing with children. It seemed so . . . just.'

The old man could not resist glancing up to see what effect his words had had. The woman was sitting in her original position, arms spread wide to grasp the lip of her desk, her head a little to one side. He saw at once that she wasn't taken in and grudgingly conceded her half a point. Only half, because by now he knew she wasn't stupid, she was cunning, and if she couldn't see through what he'd just said she had no business being here.

'Povin,' she said quietly.

'Yes?'

The woman shook her head from side to side, as if ticking off a precocious child. 'Don't call me Comrade Interrogator.'

Povin gave her the other half point. She had the beginnings of style, as well as enough brains to preserve her from the trap of subjecting him to ceaseless brutality. He lifted his hands from his lap and spread them in a gesture of mute apology.

'Let's pursue this for a moment. You liked the thought of all that money going to UNICEF?'

'Oh yes.'

'It gave you pleasure . . . a kick?'

'Oh yes, very good. Exactly.'

'Then why confine yourself to eight betrayals? Why not make a career of it, do the thing properly?'

'I had . . . other motives. Each time there was a different motive. You'll laugh when I say this, but it caused me great pain to betray the Motherland. If you think I enjoyed it, you're mistaken.'

The woman appeared not to have heard. 'And yet,' she said thoughtfully, 'there's something in what you say. About the money. It suited the image you had of yourself. No, no I'm wrong . . .' She held the pencil up to her forehead. 'It suited . . . the image you *wanted* to have of yourself.'

Povin stared down at his hands. That rattled him. Kazin had sent someone appealing, yes, but there was more to it than that. This champion was able.

'You're wrong.' Her voice assumed a matter-of-fact tone. 'I never doubted it hurts to be a traitor. A form of masochism, isn't that it? No wonder you and Stolyinovich were friends.'

Povin directed a look of such venomous hatred at Inna that for a moment the woman drew back, her head involuntarily

59

turning to the guard by the door. Then she abruptly changed her mind and the subject together.

'Mexico. What was Nechiporenko to you?'

Povin was growing tired; the unexpected reference to Stol-yinovich had unnerved him. He badly needed time to think, to regroup. He must somehow get rid of her, if not for ever then at least for now. No, it would not be for ever. With a sudden chill of apprehension the old man realized that this woman was merely dusting off her weapons.

'Listen,' he said, leaning forward. 'There was the money. There was the Christianity — you know all about that. And there was something called the balance of power? Do you understand? Peace ultimately depends on it.' His voice grew stronger, more rapid. 'Neither side must be allowed to gain an overweening advantage over the other. I worked hard, damned hard, to see the Americans didn't get the edge over us. Sometimes it was necessary to redress the balance. You know what those murderous bastards in the Kremlin can be like. If they saw their way clear to taking over the world, they'd do it tomorrow. I wanted to prevent that. Study the AWACS file. Then maybe you'll understand.'

He had hoped to provoke her into that vital snap of the fingers which would bring the guard running, but the woman merely picked up her pencil and began to toy with it, sliding her fingers up and down its length; and to Povin's surprise she blushed. For a second of remarkable empathy the old man knew that her face was burning, actually painful with the strain of coping with all that hot blood.

'You mustn't think I'm stupid,' she said slowly. 'You really mustn't, you know.'

Povin's lips parted. He was so astonished he couldn't move, couldn't even think. The floor behind him creaked as the guard uneasily shifted his weight from one foot to the other. Time was arrested.

No, she was not stupid. She was clever enough to make herself seem vulnerable. And that made her dangerous be-yond all calculation.

'Take him away.' Inna Karsovina threw down her pencil and stood up. 'We'll continue later, Povin.' She turned her back on him and walked across to the tall windows for a view of the wintry scene outside. As he reached the threshold she spoke condescendingly to the moist glass. 'Inna Marietta Karsovina. My name.'

Then he was in the ice-cold corridor, the guard's grip tight on his shoulder, and the first session was over.

Inna continued to stare out over the strip of snow-covered grass which separated the house from the lake. How had she done? Not too badly . . . What would Kazin think when he heard the tape? She had the beginnings of a headache. The violence played an important role at the start, of course, but she hoped it wouldn't be necessary to resort to it again. The mock execution had made her feel physically sick, and she knew that Povin had noted the second of hesitation before she could bring herself to set the guard on him. She shrugged her shoulders and tried to push away the memory; lack of experience, that's all it was, she'd learn . . .

But it was going to be a long haul. Somehow she had to win his confidence, make him talk to her like a friend, trust her to the point where she could question him about those last hours of freedom wherein the first part of the Chance Medley code lay concealed. It was difficult to think of going through all that with such a repellent man, the worst traitor she'd ever encountered or was ever likely to. Yet she could do it. She could do anything they asked. If only . . .

Her headache was growing worse. If only they hadn't insisted that she tell Povin her real name. But when she suggested to the Project Committee that an invented one would do they merely laughed. 'Don't you trust us?' they'd said mockingly. 'Does the first-year student know better than the professors?'

Suddenly she wished she hadn't given Povin her real name, and to hell with the 'professors'. They hadn't read Genesis. They couldn't know the power that was in a name.

Back in the main bakery Povin rested all his weight on his arms and stared down at the table. Lev triple-oh-eight, his young zek helper, was watching him. The old man had been taken away by 'them'. Now he was back, but in quarantine. Had he talked? Did he tell them how they fiddled food from the guards? Had he become a *seksot*, a secret collaborator?

Povin knew what Lev was thinking, but he ignored him. For the present there were other, more pressing things to occupy his mind.

Kazin had made his move at last. It was vital for him to divine the Chairman's plan without delay, but that wasn't easy. It all came back to the one big question: why had they kept him alive these past two years?

Because he was useful, that's why.

No, he wasn't useful, not any more. At the beginning, perhaps. By confessing nearly everything he had helped his camp interrogators advance the KGB's stock of intelligence by leaps and bounds. Mistakes had been exposed and corrected. Counter-intelligence techniques had been changed for the better. The conduct of covert operations abroad had been revolutionized. Povin simply told them the truth, and truth was addictive; 'they' wanted more and more of it. So he kept right on talking.

But the supply wasn't inexhaustible. He had spun it out for as long as he could, thereby prolonging his life, until last autumn when he'd finally dried up. They should have shot him then, yet they didn't; which was illogical.

Unless they knew he was holding back on them. But he wasn't! Not consciously.

Povin banged the table with his fists. Not *consciously*! Was that it — a secret he didn't even realize he possessed and nobody else knew? He had been guessing when he'd taunted the woman with her own lack of knowledge, but suppose it was right? How would he himself have gone about unveiling such a secret?

By sending someone special, different, appealing . . .

Povin closed his eyes and spoke briefly to God. God alone had kept him going through the past few years. Without religion, without faith, he would have died or gone mad. That, and a desire for revenge on his treacherous deputy, that Judas, Boris Frolov . . .

It was time to make a move.

*

Through the bakery window he could see a group of officers outside, chatting and smoking. They had little with which to occupy themselves during the day; the occupants of Ristikent MU/12 tended to be model prisoners. As Povin watched, the group broke up. One man remained behind, apparently undecided what to do next. He looked at the sky, which was clear; then he considered the half-smoked cigarette in his hand. Povin read his mind as clearly as if the officer had written his thoughts on a blackboard.

The old man chewed his lip. He had plans for Zuyev, yes, but he didn't want to implement them, not yet. It was still too early, the danger appalled him . . . What choice did he have?

Povin made up his mind and moved across to the bakery door. He could sense triple-oh-eight growing ever more restless, but still he ignored him. He let himself out and eased the door shut, hesitating for a moment longer while his courage gathered.

'Captain Zuyev.'

The officer turned quickly. He was in his mid-thirties, tall and broad and good-looking, not the kind of man to take any shit from a zek.

'Get back to work,' he said; and then, without any change in his even tone, 'or I'll feed you to the dogs myself.'

Povin drew a deep breath. His heart was pounding but he could not retreat now.

'I want to talk to you about Major General Ognev and certain financial arrangements which you and others came to while Ognev was in command of the Number Five Suvorov Military Academy; also certain irregularities concerning conduct of the Komsomol summer camps.' Povin paused and drew another deep breath. 'Or should I say . . . abnormalities?'

During Povin's speech Zuyev's hand dropped slowly to his side. Now the burning tip fell from his cheap cigarette and was extinguished in the snow, but he did not notice. His eyes were fixed on Povin's face. For several minutes he could not speak.

'Who are you?' he said at last. He spoke very softly, as though afraid someone might overhear. 'You're the man without a name . . . what are you?'

While Zuyev waited for an answer it seemed to him that the old man was not a zek addressing an officer, but rather a representative of some secret, all-powerful organization, perhaps even . . .

'You are from the Organs,' he whispered. 'A plant from the KGB . . .'

'Don't trouble yourself about the past. Think of the here and now. And before you touch that pistol — ' Zuyev's hand froze on his belt — 'all I have on you is written down and in safe keeping. I have friends here, Captain. Lots of friends.'

The officer's eyes seemed to shrink back inside his skull. Povin, seeing it, rammed home his advantage. Zuyev hadn't shot him. It was going to work.

'All you need to know is that I once had a friend who was a musician.' Povin paused. 'A very well-known musician. Who liked to talk when he was drunk.'

'You knew Stoly?'

'Stoly? Is that what you called him?' For a brief instant his gaze left the frightened officer's face and he grunted. 'I told you not to think about the past, Captain. I had a friend. Who was a musician. Who used to recount marvellous stories about where a man could buy discreet "chickens", isn't that what you call them, Captain Zuyev, boys of fifteen or sixteen who do it at summer camp out of sheer terror, and older boys too, in the military academies, for money, for advancement, for men like *you*, Captain. And how many of them, I wonder, go on like that through life, all because someone in a brave captain's epaulettes knew a major general who knew a musician. A pianist. Stoly.'

Povin had not raised his voice. His tone throughout was one of quiet, conversational reasonableness, yet the effect on Captain Zuyev was paralytic. He stood rooted to the spot, his eyes scarcely visible through the surrounding folds of clammy flesh.

It was necessary to keep up the momentum. The old man talked inexorably on, denying Zuyev an opportunity to think, to remember where the real power lay.

'In the past, in history, it was one of my duties to transmit those stories, Captain Zuyev. But — I did not. Instead, I wrote them up for my amusement. I used an exercise book, of a kind which the cadets in Ognev's military academy used, because that tickled my sense of humour. Do you remember the notebooks, Zuyev? The last ten pages . . . the edges are cut and marked with letters of the alphabet, so as to provide the means of making an index. And in my index I kept an orderly list of names. A list which grew. And grew. From A —'

Povin raised his forefinger and slowly drew a line in the air between him and the officer — 'to Z.'

Povin allowed his voice to tail away, losing the last syllable on the Arctic wind. When Zuyev swallowed Povin heard his throat creak.

'Then there was the album. For photographs. You remember the parties? On the houseboat. My friend kept the albums — there were several, by the end. He didn't know I'd seen them. But in the past, in history, I saw . . . everything. Which is how I came to know you, Zuyev. I never forgot a face, not once. Or a scar.'

Zuyev's breath whistled through his teeth, as if the word 'scar' laid bare the original wound. Seeing that, Povin raised his forefinger again and, scarcely touching the cloth of the officer's greatcoat, drew another line.

'From here . . . to here.'

For what seemed like a very long time the wind moaned between the two men, providing the only sound on the deserted sward. Then Zuyev spoke.

'What do you want?'

Povin let him hang a moment longer.

'I want you to ensure safe delivery of a letter to Moscow, then bring me the reply.'

He stood back a pace and watched Zuyev's face for a reaction. The officer said nothing and after a while Povin went smoothly on.

'It can go in your own mail. The censors will notice nothing amiss, I can assure you of that. And even if they did, Zuyev . . . which is worse? Eh? A slap on the wrist for accepting a bribe from a zek? Or a companionable evening with the photographs. In Dzerzhinsky Square . . .'

Zuyev breathed heavily. Povin, scenting victory, spoke faster now.

'Something else from history, Captain. A dinner party, very select. A pink-faced man who wears thick spectacles was telling us his plans for the future of the Motherland. To promulgate a law whereby all perverts who corrupted minors would automatically be put to death.'

The old man was seized with sudden animation. His eyes blazed, his voice rose. 'To be shot!' he cried. 'All of them, every one! *To be shot*!'

Zuyev tottered backwards, drawing in a great gulp of air with an audible groan. For a fleeting second he seemed to see the pink-faced man, his thick glasses glinting . . . then there was only a skinny old zek, his hands tucked tightly under his armpits, one leg seemingly shorter than the other and his eyes fixed obediently to the ground.

Zuyev pivoted on his heel and began to walk away. Immediately in front of him, leaning against the wall of the bakery, was Alexander the Chechen. Alexander did not look at Zuyev. He was cleaning his nails with a splinter of wood and every so often he raised his eyes in Povin's direction with a questioning stare. It was as if the two of them had made an unspoken pact to keep the captain a prisoner. He was no longer free to do as he wanted. He could not leave.

Zuyev wheeled round. Povin still occupied his old position, motionless as a statue, a figure of stone without compromise or pity. Then very slowly the old man raised his eyes, nodded once at Alexander and turned away, leaving Zuyev to shiver in the wind like a rabbit who sees the snake depart and cannot believe his luck.

6

Another phase of the long-planned decentralization process involved winkling the First Main Directorate out of its stronghold in Dzerzhinsky Square and installing it in a long, modern, concave-fronted building just off Moscow's outer ring road. On the top floor, bang in the middle of the façade, was the palatial suite of offices assigned to the Head of the Directorate, Colonel General Boris Andreyavich Frolov. Major Valyalin, Frolov's principal assistant, occupied a rather less sumptuous room next door.

After trotting happily along behind Frolov for many humdrum years, quite content to be a senior lieutenant for the rest of his life, Valyalin had recently discovered that leap-frogging promotion brought its own set of problems. None of his old friends would speak to him now, he had risen so high; while people he scarcely knew, important people, occupied his time with their cajolery, threats, even occasionally their physical allurements. The common object was always the same: to gain access to the chief. What none of them realized was that the chief himself now spent a quite disproportionate amount of his own time vainly trying to achieve precisely the same objective.

The door to the major's office flew open and Frolov poked his head round it.

'Valyalin! Come in here.'

Valyalin rose from his desk with a sigh and walked through into Frolov's spacious suite. He pulled up a chair without being invited and gloomily lowered himself into it. He missed their former cluttered quarters in the Square. There everything was in a mess, but somehow he always knew where to find that missing file or the last half-litre of vodka. Here everything was chromium and glass, or beige upholstery. Valyalin hated beige.

He also increasingly dreaded having to deal with Boris Frolov, who was showing all the signs of incipient paranoia.

On the surface, Frolov was one of the select company to have benefited from Kazin's dramatic rise and Povin's equally spectacular departure. The climacteric left him in charge of Russia's foreign spy system, with the coveted rank of colonel general, a new apartment, a dacha by the Black Sea and the very latest Chaika. But he wasn't happy. The quickest road to the top could also be the hardest.

'Listen, how about this . . .' Frolov was leaning across his desk, drumming on the plate glass with a pencil. 'I think they may've got themselves a new girl in Kazin's main office. Not at all his usual style . . . long blonde hair and this cute little blue dress with a bow at the top. You should have seen her. D'you think the old madman's got sex on the brain?'

Valyalin thought. 'No,' he said finally.

Frolov leaned back, discouragement written all over his face. He looked his age. The rheumy eyes, sunk deep in hollows of dark flesh, had recently started to give off an alarming signal to his subordinates. Frolov was frightened. It wasn't just the deteriorating situation with Kazin. There was something else, something more sinister, but Valyalin didn't know what.

'I suppose it is a bit late in the day,' Frolov said. 'But you do hear things.'

'Not,' said Valyalin, 'about Chairman Kazin.'
Frolov sank back into his chair and allowed his shoulders to sag. 'Perhaps it's Krubykov,' he muttered.

'Far too discreet. They say he's got any number of women, but he keeps them tucked away. Why flaunt a mistress in the office? Anyway, how do you know this girl works there? She might have been visiting.'

'Visiting! Visiting *Kazin*! That's just the point, idiot, no one ever gets to visit the old wizard. Why d'you think we spend half our time trying to beat down that fucking door? Which, I may say, she breezed through as though she owned it. She was actually in Kazin's private room when I arrived, I saw her come out! That's why I think she must work there — what other explanation could there be?'

68

Valyalin shrugged, unimpressed. 'How many times have you seen her down there?'

'Only once.'

'Once! That's not much to go on, is it?' Valyalin made no attempt to hide his scepticism.

'Well, it's all we've got. I can't get anywhere, so now you're going in to play. That's the new idea, understand?'

Valyalin shook his head and Frolov leaned forward impatiently. 'Go down there and get to know her. She's younger than you, you'll like her. Take her out, buy her a bottle of champagne, anything!'

'Do I have to?' Valyalin asked lugubriously.

'Yes!' snarled Frolov. 'Yes, you fucking well do have to. I haven't been given an appointment to see Kazin for over two months now. It's got to the point where I can't even find out who that woman is, do you realize that? So now I'm giving you a free hand. A long shot, but it might work. You, handsome . . . well, never mind, personable say . . . youngest major in the KGB, all charm and charisma . . . eh? Get the idea? Chairman's new secretary or whatever she is, overcome with confusion, doesn't know which way to look . . .'

'But if *you* can't find out who she is, how the hell . . .?'

'Because you're not me!' Frolov thumped the desk. 'That's the point.'

'Couldn't you do it?' bleated Valyalin.

Frolov was about to give Valyalin a tongue-lashing he wouldn't forget, when he had a sudden mental picture of the pretty young girl in the blue dress. That hair, he'd never seen anything like it. Those eyes. That figure, those legs. As scrumptious a little morsel as ever made a man want to open his mouth wide. Not even Ilinichna, his wife . . .

Ilinichna.

'No!' snapped Frolov, jumping up from his desk. 'No, I fucking well couldn't, moron!'

He marched across to the door of his office and flung it open, indicating to Valyalin with a sideways toss of the head that he was to pass through it.

'You've got a week. *One week!*'

7

Povin entered the large, white room for the second session feeling better prepared, but the woman had another surprise for him. She was standing by the desk, arranging flowers in a vase. Nine, ten, eleven . . . one dozen big red roses. His eyes widened. He calculated for a second; it was worth the risk. 'I haven't seen any flowers for two years,' he blurted out.

The sentry roughly pushed him down into the chair and Inna Karsovina directed a stony stare towards him in reproof for having spoken first. After a moment, however, she seemed fractionally to thaw.

'From Georgia. I had them in my room, but I don't spend much time there. Whereas I have to spend a lot of time with you, Povin.'

She continued to arrange the flowers. Povin rubbed his eyes. Despite his fatigue he noticed that her fingers were long and slim and artistic; they seemed to caress the stems, carefully avoiding contact with the thorns.

'Flown up from Baku in somebody's suitcase,' Inna said. 'Some little black-market racketeer with a bundle of roubles in an elastic band and the good wishes of the local Party chief ringing in his ears.' She laughed sarcastically. 'Well, we don't care, do we, Povin?'

When she had finished arranging the flowers she carried the vase across to the window-ledge behind the desk, before sitting down. A nice touch, Povin thought. His eyes strayed to the copy of *Izvestia* beside the vase. 'Imperialist Walk-Out at Geneva,' the bold headline proclaimed, and there was something in smaller type about grain-production figures. The world went on as ever, it seemed.

'You never see a newspaper here, I suppose?'

'Never.'

'They can be so stupid sometimes. Stupid and predictable, that's what I think about some of my colleagues, you know? I'll see if I can persuade the commander to let you read a paper now and then.'

Povin wanted to laugh. To denigrate one's colleagues, such a transparent ploy. 'Thank you.'

'There must be lots of things you miss. And people . . . D'you ever think about Victor?'

'Sometimes.'

'Did you know he'd bought himself a hotel by the side of a lovely lake?'

Povin glared at her. 'How should I know?'

'Don't pretend, Povin. Camps aren't hermetically sealed. What exactly *was* Victor, by the way?'

'How do you mean, what was . . .?'

'What role did he play in your life, I wonder?' She was almost teasing him, but there must be a point; always there had to be a point.

'Role?'

'He carried your bags, paid your bills . . . it wouldn't surprise me at all to learn that he washed out your socks at night. And, of course, he killed for you. Killed to order. What else?'

It was a neat summary. Povin shook his head. 'Nothing.'

'Perhaps. Victor reminds me of the little Georgian who brought up those flowers: moonlighting perfected. So we're back to Georgia again. Your grandfather was Georgian.'

'Yes,' said Povin. 'From Tbilisi. A dear old boy. He used to take me fishing. He had a great woolly moustache, like . . .'

'Povin.'

The old man at once fell silent.

'Povin, when it's time to bring out the family snapshots, I'll ask for them. When I want to give you time to think, I'll give you time to think. Understood?'

'Certainly, Comrade Karsovina.'

Inna banged the desk with her clenched fist and spat out her next words in a spray of neat acid. 'I've told you. I've told you before. Don't . . . call . . . me . . . that.'

Povin's voice oozed humility. 'So sorry. I thought it was "Comrade Interrogator" you objected to.'

'It is "Comrade" that I resent. Coming from you, it is an insult. Remember, I have only to say the word, one word, and your fellow-prisoners will know that they have a former KGB general in their midst. We've been more than generous so far: Gulag take very good care to see that no one who knew you on the outside is assigned to Ristikent. That can change overnight. Would you like that, Povin?'

The old man was silent and Inna went on, 'Frolov would like that. He is taking a close personal interest in your interrogation, Povin. It would give the General much pleasure to see you thrown to the wolves.'

'What a pity that we shall be disappointing him then.'

'Who says he's going to be disappointed?'

'I do.' Inna suddenly found it inexplicably difficult to meet his eyes.

'You are taking such very great care to keep me alive, even to the extent of providing me with a personal bodyguard, for which, incidentally, I am grateful.'

Her face remained impassive but the ensuing silence gave the old man all the confirmation he needed. He rubbed his temples, wishing he did not feel so tired. 'Would you not agree that there is no sense in sending me to an ordinary camp? Putting it bluntly — ' Povin stretched his stiff legs out in front of him and looked at the ceiling — 'you do not dare.' He jerked his head downwards so that Inna, without meaning to, once more found herself staring into his eyes. 'I wish I knew what to call you,' he added.

'There is no need for you to call me anything,' she said testily. 'You will never need to attract my attention, Povin. You have it. Always. Now. Today I'm going to start with your background. Let's examine your maternal grandfather, from Tbilisi. He was a Chekist, one of the first. A great man in the eyes of the Party.'

'For a while.'

'He started late, you mean. Yes, but so did many others. You remember the parable of the labourers in the vineyard, of course?' Povin's eyes widened a fraction. What was that . . .?

'The advantages of socialism were not always immediately apparent. He became a great man none the less — yet your first memory is of fishing!'

'Oh yes.' (Parable? Had she really said that?) 'He was my grandfather first and always. We never once talked about politics.'

'Forget the fishing and tell me this. What is your very earliest memory of anything?'

Povin frowned. 'This is not interrogation,' he said with quiet good humour. 'This is psychoanalysis.' He allowed his voice to rise in apparent anxiety. 'You think I am mentally ill, is that it?'

'Your question betrays abysmal ignorance. The mentally ill do not qualify for psychoanalysis. They derive no benefit from it. They require other treatment, Povin, as you well know. Were you yourself not in the Fifth Direction of the Fifth Directorate when they first conceived the idea of locking up religious dissidents in mental hospitals?'

The old man said nothing.

'And injecting them with lethal dosages of prescribed drugs? And wrapping them in straitjackets, dropping them in ice-filled baths, then leaving them to dry out in the sun, until the water evaporated and the jackets tightened . . .'

Povin's lips writhed in what might have been a smile.

'I, too, began my career in the Fifth Direction of the Fifth Main Directorate. Yes, Povin, we actually have something in common: a shared experience which taught both of us the difference between the two concepts. For psychoanalysis *is* different. Only the *nomenklatura* qualify for that. This — is interrogation. The subject: your background and childhood. Now. Your earliest memory?'

Povin thought. 'There was a quince tree,' he said slowly. 'Birds were nesting in it . . . we'd gone to Baku on holiday. I was very young then . . . four years old, perhaps. I remember opening the window, and all the birds in the tree flew away . . . but the funny thing was, for a moment, although they were up in the air, they kept their formation, their respective places . . . so that it was like another tree peeling itself off from the first one, a shadow, if you like . . .

then the shadow broke up and the birds flew away.'

The memory had a curious effect on them both. He looked up wonderingly to find the woman's eyes boring into his own. She seemed to be sharing the picture he had created. She could see it. Povin was sure she could see it.

'My first memory,' she said softly, 'is of a bird in a cage . . .' Suddenly her expression hardened and she was back to business.

'Interesting. I expected your first memory to be of your mother. Tanya — that was her name, I think?'

'Tanya, yes.'

'You have memories of that time?'

'Not then. I didn't spend much time at home then. Father was often away on Praesidium business, and Mother . . .'

'. . . Had a drink problem and other assorted personality defects, quite so. Don't get angry, Povin — save yourself a beating and speed things up at the same time. So father absent, mother a drunk with religious tendencies. Not quite the classic homosexual childhood, but close, I would have said. So you spent a lot of time with your grandparents at Baku in the early days. You like the Georgians?'

Povin made no reply.

'Everyone likes the Georgians,' said the woman. 'I like them. They keep the black economy going. Where would I get my roses in March if it weren't for some leather-coated Georgian with his strapped-up suitcases and a bought travel permit in his pocket? Come on, admit it. You find the Georgians attractive.'

'Put like that, yes.'

'How would you put it?'

The old man shrugged. 'Of course, we all need the black economy to keep going in style, but the men who run it give the Organs one big headache. It got out of hand a long time ago.'

'But there's Georgian blood in you. It shows, Povin. It shows in your face, and in your record. You ran a black market in information which gave the Organs more than a headache. It's hardly surprising. Your very first memory is of the south, the warm, lazy south where no one does any work.'

Povin felt a long-dormant chord of memory plucked by her words.

' "O for a beaker full of the warm south . . .",' he murmured in English.

'With beaded bubbles winking at the brim?' The woman's voice was ironical. 'Who do you think I am, Povin, a cog from the bureaucratic machine? Can you see the nuts and bolts? I've always been fond of poetry. Do you remember how it goes on? "Now more than ever seems it rich to die, To cease upon the midnight with no pain . . ." ' She reverted to Russian. 'Appropriate, don't you think?'

'Please, I hope not.' Inside his skull he could feel the first stirrings of a migraine. He hadn't quite found the way of dealing with this girl, not yet. She made demands on his intellectual defences which his weakened body could not always meet. 'I would congratulate you on your English, incidentally.'

'Keep your congratulations to yourself. All I want from you is your complete attention. And in future, don't think to distract me by drifting off into verse.'

'Sorry. You're quite right, of course.'

Inna, exasperated, banged the desk with her fist. 'What do you mean, I'm quite right?'

'We mustn't allow ourselves to be distracted, must we? Kazin wouldn't like that.' For a second his eyes shone with amusement. 'Or would he?'

She failed to react, but Povin didn't care; what mattered was that the two of them had known a moment's sweetness which neither of them would easily be able to forget. He made an effort to shake off his exhaustion and sought to focus all his attention on her next words. There was a battle to fight, and the opening skirmishes had only just begun.

8

The door of the Gasthof zum Röten Löwen opened just as Bryant reached it, to reveal the figure of a tall man standing between him and the light.

'The season has not begun. We are closed . . .' There was a long pause. 'Come in.'

Bryant stepped across the threshold and looked about him. The inside of the small hotel was clean, neat — and cluttered. Seemingly hundreds of small pictures and photographs occupied the whitewashed walls, fighting the myriad china ornaments and assorted copper vases for his attention. Thick, faded druggets lay on a highly polished wooden floor, each plank of which boasted the well-trodden dip of long usage. It was very comfortable, very homely, very nice. *Gemütlich* was the word which came to Bryant's mind: a place families would return to year after year.

'In here. Sit down, why don't you. You must have had a job finding this place. I'll fix you a drink.'

Bryant sank down wearily into the nearest chair. The man was right: it had taken him a long time to locate the inn. He'd driven down from Vienna, turning off the E5 at Parndorf before following the Breitenbrunn road along the shore of Lake Neusiedler. It was late evening by the time he reached his destination, and he felt exhausted.

'What will you take?'

'Some local wine, if you have it.'

'Weiner Nussberger?'

'Very good. Thank you.'

The innkeeper returned to the table carrying a tray with a bottle, a corkscrew and two goblets.

'I will join you.'

While he poured the wine Bryant fingered the thick, ringed green stem of his glass and mused uneasily on the next step.

'Health.'

The two men drank. A Dalmatian dog lay toasting its stomach in front of the log fire. Bryant snapped his fingers gently, but the dog did not stir. Too comfortable to move, his back seemed to say; even for a dog-loving Englishman like you.

Bryant discreetly tried to study the innkeeper, who looked to be in his late forties or early fifties; the lines in his face cut deep. The harsh, Slavonic accent, the unsmiling expression coupled with the shadow in his cold, narrow eyes: these were things that suggested resolution and the attainment of goals long marked out. Somehow he did not look the part of honest Austrian innkeeper. His expression was too grim for that. The tall, broad-shouldered frame, in keeping with the face, suggested an altogether tougher existence, won from a hostile environment at some cost . . . And that scar, the ugly old wound which ran the length of his throat, that surely never came from the careless extraction of a cork . . .

Bryant compared the man opposite him with his private mental picture of Victor and was satisfied.

'I was wondering,' he said diffidently, 'if you could help me. I am looking for a man called . . . Victor. Someone suggested that he might live in this area. Perhaps in this very hotel.'

His host banged the cork back in the bottle with a chop of his fist. 'Who wants him?'

'My name is Richard Bryant. I have business with Victor.'

'Does Richard Bryant style himself Mister, or something more grand?'

Bryant coughed. 'Sir Richard Bryant.'

'Kindly call me God,' the innkeeper said solemnly, before breaking into a delighted laugh at the other man's startled expression. 'Isn't that how it goes? "Call Me God, Kindly Call Me God, God Calls Me God." The General liked that one very much. Remember the message he sent you when you got your, your . . . how do I say it? Your "K"? "Now I shall call you God." '

'I remember.'

'You are very welcome, Sir Richard Bryant KCMG. Have another glass.'

Watching him pour, Bryant said cautiously, 'You are Victor?'

'Oh yes. I do not have to ask who you are. I saw your photograph at the Square often enough.'

'Does it surprise you to see me here?'

'It does. How did you find me? I made the Americans promise never to disclose my whereabouts to DI6.'

'Binderhaven. He owed me too many favours to refuse.' Bryant's lips wrinkled in a tired smile. 'He told me how you all got out, you and he and the girl. Manchuria . . .'

Victor laughed. 'Mongolia. Helicopter to Mongolia, then a month's trek to China.' His face hardened. 'Where they flung us in jail. But we got out eventually.' He took a long drink and topped up his glass. 'What happened to them?'

'Oh, they went back to the States. They lived together for a while, I believe. Then they drifted apart. She's living in San Diego now. Kirk's busy trying to raise a mission to El Salvador — he doesn't change.'

'And you? What are *you* doing, eh?'

Bryant twirled the stem of his glass and grunted. 'I dither between mission, crusade and pilgrimage as apposite terms. Which of them do you find least pretentious?'

'Ah! You're coming to the point, I see.' Now there was a look of sly calculation on Victor's face. 'Perhaps I lied. Perhaps I wasn't so surprised to see you. I had a hunch you might turn up one day soon.'

'May I ask why?'

Victor chuckled, a hoarse guttural sound which Bryant found unnerving. 'When they found the pianist alive. That's when I told myself, Victor, better watch out for God . . .'

Victor turned out to be an excellent cook. As Bryant ate his dinner he silently wondered whether to ask Victor who had told him about Stolyinovich. Better not, he decided. If the source was in Moscow, Victor wouldn't divulge it; if in London, Bryant preferred not to know. For Bryant's money, the news had filtered back to Lake Neusiedler via Anthony Lowe, but he would never be sure.

'Do you do everything yourself?' he asked, wiping his mouth with a napkin.

'I have help in season. Not too much — I like my profits to be my own. My affairs also. You want a brandy? *I* want a brandy.'

Bryant waited until he was busy at the bar, then called, 'Do you know where the General is now?'

'No. I heard he was alive, that's all.'

'He's in a special maximum security compound just south of Murmansk. By the side of Lake Not.'

Victor did not reply at once and when he turned round with the tray Bryant saw that he was frowning.

'Yes . . . odd, isn't it? They're sending me a message. Kazin's inviting me inside. By putting Povin on the very border with Norway he's saying: "Come, all of you, come and get your friend — see how easy it is!" Only it isn't easy. It's hard as hell.'

'I'm glad you realize that, God.'

'Oh, I know. Kazin knows it too. He intends to compromise me, then bargain. "If I keep quiet about your old man's foolishness and you give me the Travel Agency on a plate, I'll give you Povin." '

Victor returned to the table and sat down. The Dalmatian yawned, raised his head briefly from the fire rug, and settled back to sleep.

'And just what foolishness is this old man thinking of doing, eh?'

'Ever watch any old World War Two films?'

'Sure. What's that got to do . . .?'

'You remember the scenes in Bomber Command during the Blitz? There are the pretty girls pushing wooden models around the table while officers sit above them, directing, and above the officers sits the great Air Marshal himself. That's me. Where I sit it's always been very quiet and remote. There's a lot going on below me but I can't even see the real activity, just as the Air Marshal in the old film couldn't see the planes represented by those models on the table in front of him.'

'Well, so what?'

79

Bryant sighed. 'I'm due to retire soon. But before I do I'm going out into the field and I'm going to bring General Povin back with me. Alive. Whole. The West owes him that and I intend to discharge the debt.'

'Why do *you* have to do all this? Are DI6 on strike?'

'No. But I've been turned down. Too sensitive. Too expensive.' The bitterness in Bryant's voice took Victor by surprise. 'I've given them a bloody lifetime. But they won't give me Povin.' Bryant slowly unclenched his fists. 'Forgive me,' he muttered, 'but . . . you also miss him very much, don't you.'

For an instant Victor's face darkened, as if he suspected a trap; then he relaxed and a slow smile strayed across his face.

'You want an answer?' he said. 'Hey, God — I'm talking to you! You want an answer, eh?' There was silence. 'Well then . . .' Victor settled back in his chair. Suddenly he jutted out his chin and bared his teeth. 'Frolov,' he hissed, drawing his right forefinger across his throat in a swift retributive gesture. For a moment it looked as though he had more to say, but he seemed to think better of it and snapped his fingers dismissively.

'I've been drawing a map,' said Bryant after a pause. 'I need your help to double-check it.'

'Why not? If it will help the General. Just as long as you remember I'm a respectable hotelier now.'

Bryant picked up the brandy bottle and poured each of them a generous tot while he ordered his thoughts.

'They arrested the General at the airport. Another few hours and he'd have been on the Turkish border. But in order to do that, he'd have needed a courier. We'd provided one. From the Travel Agency.'

Victor took a swig of brandy. 'We always assumed you would. Several times General Stepan worked hard to cover up for them. They owed him a passage.'

'Agreed. Besides, they were — are — the best. They've been smuggling people out of the Soviet Bloc since the war and never lost a man. We relied on them, and when it came to the General we wanted nothing but the best.'

'I'm glad to hear that, God.'

'The question arose: how to give the General the name of his contact in the Agency? We decided on a variation of a code we knew the General was familiar with: the two-key code. We used Stolyinovich to send him part one of the message, disguised as a batch of gramophone records. You know how the two-key code works?'

'Certainly. I helped him decipher your stuff. You transmit in two parts. General Stepan wouldn't realize what the first half of the message meant until you fed him the second part. Then he'd put the two halves together and have whatever it was you wanted to tell him.'

'Precisely. In this case, we did what seemed obvious at the time. We sent the second part of the message via Stolyinovich himself.'

Bryant paused. Victor swilled brandy around in his glass and said contemptuously, 'So Kazin has part two of the message.'

Bryant smiled. 'We think so.'

'He must do. Stolyinovich would have told everything he knew on that first night. Kazin leered at him and he pissed himself. Of course Kazin broke him. Why else would they throw him out on the street for all to see? It was a signal — a signal to you.'

'Ah, of course. You heard about that.'

'I hear lots of things.'

'Typical Kazin,' mused Bryant. 'No finesse. Stolyinovich was wearing scarcely any clothes, but he wasn't even shivering. So they'd obviously let him out a few moments before Lowe walked down that street. Very hit and miss, too — there must have been a good chance that Lowe wouldn't see him.'

He flashed a look at his companion to see if the name Lowe caused a reaction. Victor's face remained impassive. 'Naturally,' he said. 'But Kazin's a patient man. He could always have tried again. He would have gone on trying until someday someone noticed. Maybe this was the second or third time he'd tried, only no one'd seen Stolyinovich on the earlier occasions. You know what I think?'

'What?'

'It was a good gamble on Kazin's part. Floating the pianist out like that — almost an exact duplicate of the General's trick in Geneva two years ago; you could hardly fail to see it.'

'I agree. Whatever the answer, the Travel Agency is intact. They've had to pay a high price: no Soviet operations for the last couple of years, no contact with the Moscow courier, nothing moving at all. But it's paid off. Kazin still needs to get his hands on part one, which the pianist never knew.'

'You're sure of that?'

'Oh yes. So far I'm sure. This isn't the difficult part of the map. Stolyinovich was given the job of carrying the records into Russia, but he didn't realize they had any significance. He never knew anything about the two-key code.'

'So where is the difficult part, as you call it? The thing is so obvious. All Kazin has to do now is crack the General, and he'll have the name of the Travel Agency's courier. And then we can kiss goodnight to the Agency. Simple.'

'No. Not simple at all. That's where it starts to get tiresome.'

Victor rubbed the base of his glass on the table. 'I don't follow you.'

Bryant leaned forward anxiously, willing Victor to concentrate. 'I want to make you try and see my line of thought. Check it for flaws. You know the two-key system. Did General Stepan ever talk to you about the musical Chance Medley code?'

'No.'

'It was quite simple. We used it a lot in the early days, when the General first began to help us. Probably before your time. It was based on opus numbers and keys. Suppose I wrote the General a letter containing a reference to Grieg's Piano Concerto in A Minor, Opus 16. That would give him A 16. You follow?'

Victor nodded. 'Yes. You never used it while I was working for him.'

'We hadn't used it for a long time. But we intended to resurrect it for the final message, the one with the name of the courier. Hence the records we sent in with Stolyinovich.'

'I never knew that. My job was in Irkutsk, at the airbase. As far as the General's escape was concerned, he was working on his own.'

'The General didn't know it either. He wouldn't have realized it until Stolyinovich handed over the second part of the message — which was to the effect that he was to use the Chance Medley code on the records which he'd received a few days previously.'

'Let me get this straight.' To Bryant's enormous relief Victor was beginning to show signs of interest. 'You're telling me that to this very day the General still doesn't know that the records had any significance at all? To him, they've never been anything more than a present from his friend . . .'

Bryant smiled encouragingly. 'Go on.'

'But . . . Kazin knows, because he's broken the pianist, that . . . What does Kazin know?'

'I told you it became complicated. Suppose this. Suppose Kazin knows it's the musical Chance Medley code, that his computer analysts have got that far. It's not impossible. We ran the model through our own computer in London; the machine broke it in eighty hours. Anything that Stolyinovich told them should have proved sufficient for Dzerzhinsky Square to identify Chance Medley.'

He broke off, his eyes staring into space, as if trying to penetrate Kazin's mind.

'So — why doesn't Kazin just work General Stepan over until he coughs the names of the records?'

'That's it! Why not, indeed? Well, tell me. What's the answer?'

Bryant rose and moved thoughtfully across to the fireplace where the Dalmatian, sensing his approach, lifted its head and sang softly deep in its throat. Bryant knelt down to pat the dog, which went limp, indicating with a roll of its eyeballs that this was permitted.

'The answer,' Victor said from his chair, 'is that Povin never got the records. Or he never bothered to unpack them — Stolyinovich used to bring him such junk.' He came across to join Bryant by the fire, lowering himself into an armchair with a disdainful 'tchah!'.

'Think again.'

Bryant left off fondling the sleepy dog and retreated to another armchair opposite Victor's. The fire was dying now; the logs were enveloped in a dull red glare which seemed to throb in time with the Dalmatian's soft, regular breathing.

'Try this, then,' said Bryant after a long pause. 'What if Kazin hasn't asked the General about the records at all?'

Victor raised his eyes and faced Bryant inquisitively. 'You mean the old tyrant's gone insane?'

'Not at all. Think about it. Concentrate your thoughts on the answers the General might give.'

There was a moment of silence, broken by Victor's soft 'Ah . . .'

'You see? The General is interrogated about records. Now why on earth, why in the name of all that's holy, should Kazin be interested in records? What *possible* justification could there be for such a question — unless . . .'

'Unless those records had a significance which he hadn't appreciated until that point . . .'

'But which he appreciated now. Precisely. Povin's not a fool. It wouldn't take him long to calculate the odds of us using the Chance Medley code to send him a message through the gramophone records. He applies the code, invents a list of records, and fingers — who? Krubykov? Kazin himself?' Bryant grunted. 'Chernenko?'

'It's too risky. Suppose he named records which weren't in the collection?'

'With approaching eight thousand records to choose from, unlikely.' Bryant hauled himself up to the edge of his chair. 'Suppose the records had been absorbed into the collection before Kazin's men ransacked the apartment. Suppose there was nothing to identify the new records, nothing to distinguish them from the rest . . .'

Victor shook his head. 'You're asking me to swallow a big heap of "ifs".'

Bryant slapped his knee. 'Yes! But there's one "if" I *don't* ask you to swallow. The Travel Agency is still intact! That's a *fact*.'

He sank back into his former position, his eyes fixed on Victor's face, insisting that he believe.

'We all know there's only so much torture a man can take. We have to assume that by now, after two whole years, he's told them everything. What other explanation can there be?

Povin doesn't know he knows! They haven't shot him. We know he's alive. *You* know he's alive — God knows how, but you do. There's still one link in the chain they haven't broken — and they're too scared to ask him outright!'

'Then why Murmansk? Why the move?'

Bryant hesitated. 'I told you it would become difficult,' he said. 'But — try this. Suppose they've decided to leave his body alone. Suppose they've gone to work on his mind.'

'I don't understand what you're saying.'

'They're going to try and burgle the house while the owner's got his back turned. Trick out of him what he knows-but-doesn't-know. You get the idea?'

'The subtle approach.'

'Precisely! Now tell me — what, in your view, are their chances of succeeding?'

Victor did not answer immediately. Instead he rose from his seat by the fireplace and went across to the table where they had eaten supper earlier, to collect the bottle of brandy. Keeping his back turned to Bryant he said thoughtfully, 'General Stepan, too, is subtle. I think . . .'

He returned to the fire and made as if to pour spirit into his companion's glass, but Bryant put his hand over it.

'. . . I think it would depend on who they sent in to play the game with him. Someone unexpected. Someone . . . aach!' He struggled to find the right word. 'Someone who would throw him off balance, someone . . . demoralizing. You know who I think they would use? Stolyinovich.'

The same thought had occurred to Bryant earlier, but it was intriguing to hear it confirmed from the lips of Povin's closest confidant. Then Victor slowly shook his head.

'No. It would put General Stepan too much on his guard. But if they could find someone *like* the pianist, somebody to fill the same role . . .'

'Which was?' Bryant asked, too quickly; and Victor shrugged.

'Your guess is as good as mine. I knew when not to pry. But one thing I do know: Stolyinovich was the only man General Stepan ever relaxed, completely relaxed with. When they were alone together, just the two of them. Sometimes they'd go up to the dacha in Zhukovka for a week at a stretch, and the difference when they came down again was amazing. You could see it in his eyes. He was happy. Peaceful. They were two of a kind, all right. Whatever *that* was!' He rounded on Bryant with a snarl — 'What do you want from me?'

There was a long silence. Then Bryant said, 'Do you know if General Stepan is still in contact with anyone . . . outside?'

'Not me, if that's what you're thinking.'

'Not you, but . . . someone, perhaps?'

Victor hesitated, and Bryant saw that he wasn't sure whether to trust him, wasn't sure where the General's true interests lay.

'I would guess . . . maybe,' he said at last. 'When you get so high in an organization like the KGB, you never quite . . . there's cronies, jackals, all kinds. If he can get a message out then, yes, there are probably people in Moscow to receive it. But I don't know who.' He looked up aggressively. 'That's the truth!'

'I'm sure it is.'

'So — why do you ask?'

'Kazin's tired of waiting. He is about to move against the General. And I need to be sure that he won't talk.' His measured, level tone did not falter. 'I want him brought out. Made safe. And there's another aspect to the problem. As a former KGB general Povin is in mortal danger from his fellow-prisoners. So far Kazin has chosen to protect him. But he could change his mind whenever it suited him; and besides, you know and I know that however carefully the Gulag authorities guard him, he's at risk. Every moment of the day, he's at risk.

Victor threw back his head and laughed. 'So you come to me!'

'Who else could I go to? There's no help for me in London. I've asked and been given the thumbs down. Even the preservation of something as important as the Travel Agency is considered to be above current budget, and as for Povin . . . an elderly KGB general whose information is at least two years out of date . . .'

'But I come cheap and willing. I get it — so easy to sell if

86

anything went *wrong*. An old associate and friend, gone crazy in retirement, acting out of misguided loyalty. A snatch that failed. How they'd love that in the embassies, in the newsrooms, at the Foreign Ministry in Moscow. Jesus, *God*, but you have a sense of humour.'

'Do I?' Bryant smiled, as if the idea tickled his fancy. 'Well yes, perhaps I do.'

'You really think that I would be tempted by such a . . . such a mad scheme? You really believe that, eh?'

'Everything I was ever told about you led me to believe that you might be tempted, yes.'

'Oh! Ooh-hoo! And what were you . . . *told*, Sir Richard Bryant?'

'That you were a brave and resourceful man of action whose single greatest quality was loyalty to his master.' Bryant spoke with cold, level emphasis. 'Shall I go on?'

Victor remained silent, staring into the fire.

'That as long as it did not hurt the General, you would sell your own mother at a cut-price rate. That you were utterly ruthless, totally efficient, dedicated above all to the preservation of General Stepan, right or wrong . . .'

Victor banged his glass down on the mantelpiece and wheeled round.

'Yes!' he shouted. 'Yes to all of it, yes, yes, *yes*! Yet you come to me with a proposal that I should walk in there and have my head shot off! *He's* at risk — maybe you think it would be a joyride for *me*? Are you crazy? Are you?'

Bryant waited for him to subside.

'I expressed a wish, a personal wish, to have the General brought out alive,' he said quietly. 'The official view is not so generous. A hit-and-run snatch is considered too dangerous, too likely to fail. Particular emphasis is laid on the Soviet decision to transfer the General to Murmansk, near the border with Finland. The official view is that this is a trap. Therefore, the most that can be considered is an assassination run. There is no alternative; furthermore, it is proposed that the executioner should be sent *soon*. I have noted the official view and placed it on file for no immediate future action. When I go back tomorrow, I shall have to do something about it. What I do depends on you. And for you, my dear Victor . . . there is an alternative.'

The last of the logs collapsed into the hearth with a shower of sparks. The startled Dalmatian raised its head, licked its chops and then, reassured, settled comfortably down once more to sleep.

When Bryant came downstairs next morning his host was still sitting by the fireside, a Europa road map in his hands but there was no sign of the dog. Hearing Bryant's footsteps he raised his head and said, 'I'll get you some breakfast.'

'Coffee only, please. And only if it's no trouble.'

'For God, it's no trouble.'

As Victor stood up and closed the map Bryant thought he saw a glimpse of the Kola Peninsula, but he wouldn't have staked money on it.

'Sleep well?'

'Very well, thank you. A nice place you have here. I imagine it becomes very crowded in the summer.'

'Oh yes. It's a good business. But hellish boring out of season.' Victor sighed, his lined face suddenly rueful. 'In season, too, if you want the truth.'

Bryant poured himself a cup of black coffee and added sugar. 'It's an isolated spot, this. Do you ever find it perhaps a touch lonely?'

Victor brought another cup and sat down opposite him before answering.

'Yes, it's lonely here. I thought of getting married a while back. Everything was arranged, in fact.'

Bryant raised an eyebrow. 'What happened?'

'She was offered a job in Vienna, just before the big day. I don't blame her for taking it. This place is hardly a lifetime's dream for a girl.'

'I am so sorry.' Bryant looked nervously at his watch, aware that his response was inadequate. 'I must go. How much do I owe you?'

'Nothing. It's on the house. There's other ways you can pay me back.'

'Such as?'

'Suppose I wanted a quick guided tour of Norway. Could you arrange that?'

'Without any trouble. But might I ask —'

'No. No questions, not at this stage. I want time to think, and I think best on the ground. The timing: well, it's important. Spring is nearly here. In the north it will be later, but still not long. If we go, we must go soon. You are right about the risk. The General is already a dead man, in there with the zeks.'

Bryant nodded.

'But you must understand: at this stage I am only asking for time in which to think. You are seeking the impossible. The chances of success are almost non-existent. I need to consider this.'

Bryant could think of nothing else to say. He shook hands with Victor, stowed his case in the boot of his car and walked round to the driver's door. Victor waited until he had disappeared round a bend in the track before going back inside the hotel and resuming his study of the map.

As he spread out the section which showed the Kola Peninsula and the tip of Norway it occurred to him that he had scarcely exaggerated: the difficulties involved were astronomical. After two years of dull, mostly honest trading he still had all his wits about him; he realized that to rescue Povin would require the utmost care, both in the planning and the execution. At the moment he frankly didn't see how it could be accomplished with the resources available to him.

He raised his head and stared into the middle distance. He knew that he was missing something, something obvious. There was another dimension; and as the wider implications began to expand to fill his horizon Victor slowly laid down his pencil.

Suppose by some remote chance he succeeded — what then? Months of debriefing in an English country house followed by a dreary existence lived out under a false name, constantly afraid of discovery — what kind of future for the general was that?

Suppose, Bryant had said. Suppose this, suppose that. Why not start by supposing that there was an alternative, fashioned by someone who owed General Stepan an incalculable debt of gratitude going back years and years and years? Someone who owed no favours to East or West . . .

Victor picked up his pencil and quickly began to make notes on the blue of the Gulf of Finland.

9

Krubykov very carefully put his head round the door of the Chairman's office and as it were 'took the air'. The room was in its usual state of near-total darkness, with only Kazin's reading lamp to illuminate a small area in the immediate vicinity of the huge desk. At nine o'clock at night, however, this created a somewhat less sinister impression, and things were obviously quiet since the Chairman was playing patience.

Krubykov approached as if walking on eggs and saw that it was his master's favourite game. The player took a pack of fifty-two cards and dealt them out in four piles from left to right. If two cards were the same, two sevens say, or two aces, he took the left-hand one and laid it on the right-hand match. It was the same with threes of a kind: the cards on the left were transferred to the match on the farthest right. When all the cards had been dealt the player picked up the piles from right to left and began again. If four of a kind came up in a row he put them aside; the game was over when all the fours had been discarded thus.

The curious thing about this patience was that it always seemed to come out for Kazin but Krubykov could never make it work. It was called The Insomniac and in Krubykov's case at least it amply lived up to its name.

As the colonel arrived by the side of Kazin's desk the Chairman finished a deal and swept up the cards, aligning them with a violent bang on the blotter before starting all over again. 'This game, it's like people,' Kazin said abruptly. 'You meet them for the first time, you learn a few things about them, you part . . . Then you start to think over what you learned at that meeting . . .' Slap, slap, slap went the cards. Two tens appeared and he promptly transferred the left-hand card to the right-hand pile. 'People are like cards, their characters, their habits . . . you deal them out, one, two, three . . . rearrange them . . . until at last . . . you've got it . . . straight.'

Krubykov smiled. 'I wish it was so easy.'

'Oh, it is.' Kazin reached the end of another deal and deftly shot the four piles into the palm of his left hand. 'When you've had sufficient practice. What have you got there, Krubykov?'

The colonel looked down at the folders he was carrying and hesitated. You could never rely on there being a 'right time' to beard Kazin with anything, but it was too late to back out now. Of all the innumerable matters which required the Chairman's attention Krubykov unhesitatingly chose the one which was uppermost in his own mind.

'About Frolov, Comrade Chairman. I'm having trouble with him. He wants to see you.'

Kazin's stony glare was not reassuring to Krubykov. 'He can't.'

'I've told him that, Chairman, but he's very persistent. He is, after all, head of a main directorate. It would be customary . . .'

'No.'

Krubykov spread his hands appealingly. 'Then what am I to tell him?'

Kazin did not answer at once. The last four cards of the deal were knaves. He knocked them aside without any obvious expression of satisfaction and resumed the game. Only when he had dealt another dozen cards did he say, 'There is no need to explain anything to General Frolov. We made a mistake there, Krubyov.'

The colonel said nothing. Kazin continued to ruminate aloud.

'But then, what options did we have? He was close behind

91

us, could have ruined everything if he'd a mind to. He helped us all get here and so we owed him something. Unfortunately, we chose the wrong something.'

'Water under the bridge, Chairman. Frolov has some powerful friends in the Kremlin now.'

'You should never say too late, Krubykov. Not to me.' Kazin's smile was glacial. 'There are always ways. Sit down. I want to talk to you.' The colonel pulled up a chair. 'I am in the course of taking care of General Frolov.'

Krubykov concealed his astonishment with difficulty. He had been trying to plan a long-term strategy for dealing with Frolov, something that would see them both through to the ends of their careers. It had not occurred to him that the commander of the First Main Directorate might have weaknesses worthy of exploitation. 'I'm sorry, Chairman, I was not aware of that.'

'There is no reason why you should be. His removal can be arranged, but not directly. As you say, he has powerful allies now. They are going to have to be convinced by solid evidence which at present we lack. As a by-product of something else, however, all is possible. You understand?'

Krubykov shook his head. With Kazin you should never pretend. The Chairman subjected him to a look of scathing contempt and went on, 'It doesn't matter. The less you know about it the better, at least for the present. I shall need you later, not now. Now I want to talk about something else. The woman, Karsovina. What news?'

The colonel's voice was strained. 'Nothing, Chairman. The Project Committee doesn't meet until the end of next week.'

Kazin removed four aces and pursed his lips. 'You don't approve, do you?'

'I am . . . just a little sceptical.'

'Why?'

'She is so new to the game, Chairman. And her character . . . well, you've read the profiles as often as I have. Hardly a model of ideological perfection, is she? If you hadn't assigned her to the present job she'd be for the axe.'

'Probably. But the weaknesses to which you draw my attention are, in my hands, strengths.' Kazin gathered up the cards and commenced yet another deal. 'Povin will latch on to her character defects before long. At that point she is going to become extremely useful to us.'

'But useful enough to crack the Chance Medley code? Is she really subtle enough for that? And when I consider the importance of the product ... the Travel Agency! Going strong for thirty-nine years with never a break. Is it likely, I appeal to you, Comrade Chairman, is it really likely that a fundamentally unstable, inexperienced girl ...'

Kazin chuckled to himself and the colonel saw that four queens had appeared in sequence. 'Appropriate,' he heard the Chairman mutter. There were very few cards left in his hand now. 'The Travel Agency is important.' He raised his head and stared across the desk at Krubykov. 'It would be satisfying to solve a problem which defeated Andropov as well as Stanov. But even if we do not get the Travel Agency out of Povin, we shall still get something of use. And don't underestimate the woman. She's not as unstable as you seem to think.'

He removed four kings from the piles in front of him and picked up the cards slowly, as if anxious not to disturb his luck.

'I want you to go to Murmansk yourself and talk to the committee. There's something still troubling me at the moment.' His voice was moody, dissatisfied. 'Something amiss.'

'Amiss?' Krubykov uneasily shifted his weight in the chair.

'We have to pile the pressure on to Povin. He has to be made to attempt a breakout.'

Krubykov found it pleasant to have his suspicions confirmed, but he knew it would be as well to pretend surprise. Considering that he was Kazin's principal aide, the Chairman told him very little. 'To *escape*?'

'That's right. How would you arrange that?'

Krubykov considered the proposition. He found it distinctly unattractive. 'I think I might threaten him with exposure, Chairman. Tell the other zeks who he was, something of the kind.'

'We will make that threat. The girl's instructions are quite explicit. But *that* won't work by itself. No, there's more. Something else. Guess again.'

Krubykov disliked the word 'guess' in this context. It implied a lack of professionalism on his part. 'Drop the defences? Make it look easy?'

Kazin shook his head impatiently. The cards flickered through his hands with dazzling speed. 'Guess again.'

Krubykov thought for a moment longer before shaking his head, and Kazin compressed his lips. 'I've already arranged what I have in mind,' he said. 'I just hope I haven't overdone it, that's all. Liaise with the committee. They'll brief you fully. Go tomorrow.'

The last four cards were swept away. 'If you want a man to get out of bed, try putting a cobra under the sheet.' Kazin did not smile. He picked up the pack, shuffled it once and laid it aside.

'Game over,' he said.

10

'No guards today,' Inna Karsovina said briskly. 'They put me off my stroke. And besides —' she shot a contemptuous glance at the pathetic looking human huddle opposite — 'you're hardly up to any tricks, are you, old man?'

Povin was very watchful. The girl seemed comparatively new to the techniques of interrogation, and as such she might be expected to follow the book. The book dictated regular alternation of stick with carrot and since the last session had been reasonably soft the old man was expecting violence. But the atmosphere was wrong. She had put aside the book in favour of improvisation. He decided to delay his first move for as long as possible. Besides, he was tired, so tired . . .

There was a lengthy silence, followed by the woman saying, 'Povin.'

He slowly raised his head to find that she had placed one clenched fist on top of the other and was resting her chin in the hollow formed by the upper thumb and forefinger. Their faces were almost level. After a moment the woman, without moving her chin, shook her head from side to side, like a mother who unwillingly realizes that her child must be indulged this once.

'You can have a cup of coffee. If you want.'

She sat up and reached for a flask which stood on the side of the desk. Povin watched her movements, his face devoid of expression; then his glance fell on the vase of roses in the window and he noticed (for he noticed everything) that the water was no longer cloudy, she had changed it before the session began. And something else was new. Next to the vase of flowers stood a tape recorder.

The room was suddenly rich with the aroma of fresh coffee. Before Povin could stop himself he had taken a deep breath and was all but overwhelmed by the unaccustomed savour. The effect on him was extraordinary: he retched, suddenly desperate that she should bottle up the delicious smell, that evil genie escaped from its lamp; he longed to cry out, 'No! I don't want any. I don't want it!'

But she had poured him a cupful of dark, bitter liquid and was holding it out to him, hot blackness, and a serpent watching from behind a tree . . .

He took the cup. He always tried hard to make himself appear even more feeble than he really was, but on this occasion the acting came easily. His hands were shaking — he needed both of them to hold the beaker steady; then it rattled against his teeth, scalding steam seared his nostrils, and he sipped . . .

Inna watched him curiously, years of fascinated study yielding up their memories of rapt communicants with round eyes full of light . . . 'Religion,' she said slowly. 'Why *Roman* Catholicism? This is an Orthodox country, by and large.'

Very slowly, so as not to spill one drop from the precious

cup, Povin replaced it on the desk and held it down on the flat surface until he was sure it was stable.

'Was the Krinsky Square sect Roman?'

'Krinsky Square?'

'You know. The Oblensky diaries.'

Povin's eyes at last made contact with hers, but after a pause he mutely shook his head.

'Major Oblensky, your first commanding officer. He kept a diary. You were in it; he thought , correctly as it turned out, that you were in the process of becoming a Christian. Oblensky himself was purged, but his diary survived. General Frolov found it right at the start of his investigation — a brilliant piece of field-work. Inspired.'

Povin made a mental note of that and filed it away for leisurely dissection in the future. 'No,' he said. 'Krinsky Square was Orthodox, as I recall.'

'What about your mother then?'

'Ah, Mother. She had a confessor . . .'

'Father Michael.'

He scanned Inna's face apprehensively. 'You warned me not to ask questions. I implore you, let me now ask just one.'

The woman appeared to consider it, her lower lip thrust out in the way of a salesman who says, 'A question! What a pity, now if it had been an answer you were trying to part-exchange . . .'

'As long as you don't get any fancy ideas into your head about a dialogue, Povin. Anyway, I can guess what your question is — you want to know what we did with the priest.'

Povin nodded humbly.

'Nothing. He's too useful to us. There are quite a few interesting ones in among that flock.'

The old man nodded again, apparently satisfied with this answer. 'The priest lent me books. He was sympathetic to Rome. A lot of my reading was Roman-biased, you see.'

'Was that your only reason for choosing Roman Catholicism?'

'No. It attracted less surveillance in those days, and I knew that the Fifth Direction had infiltrated the Orthodox leadership.'

'And yet . . . Tanya, your mother, was Orthodox. I find it strange that you should not have followed in her footsteps.'

'Would you understand what I meant if I said that that was another reason for choosing Rome?'

'I might.' Inna consulted her own stock of childhood and adolescent memories. 'Yes.'

She pulled a folder towards her and opened it to reveal a number of newspaper clippings. She studied them for a moment while her hands continued to grapple with the Thermos flask. She poured herself a cup of coffee; then, as she was about to replace the cap, she remembered Povin and held out the flask for him to take. When he failed to react immediately she looked up from the clippings and saw the indecision on his face.

'Come on,' she said. 'It's like sex: only the first time hurts. Like treachery also,' she added absently, once again diverting her attention to the folder's contents.

Povin dithered a moment longer; then he shrugged and picked up the flask.

'I want to show you something,' said Inna. 'I cut these out of the papers, all within the last six months. In Central America, some troops burned a village to the ground, having first killed all the inhabitants. Their way of dealing with the children is interesting. They roped them together, and pulled them one by one into a bonfire which they'd built in the village square. Alive, Povin.'

She paused, awaiting a reaction. The face which he raised to her was perfectly innocent.

'I'm sorry, Afghanistan you said?'

Inna smiled, yes *smiled*, and in her usual conversational tone said, 'If you do that again I'll call the guard in and tell him to break your arm. Then I'll have your true identity posted up on the wall of every blockhouse in this camp. Do you believe me, Povin?'

'No. I regret, but . . . no. You need me alive. I do not think the Chairman would be very pleased if he found out that you had publicized my whereabouts without his permission, do you?'

Inna bit her lip. Her enthusiasm had led her astray; she was

97

in danger of losing control. For an unsettling moment it almost seemed to her that Povin had greater insight into Kazin's mind than she did. But then, as she swiftly reminded herself, that was hardly surprising; the two men had worked together for long enough.

Povin gauged her reactions and smiled gently. She was not immune to flattery, he had noticed that before, but she was also afraid. Afraid of Kazin. Of fluffing her chances.

Inna hurriedly lowered her eyes to the folder. 'A gunman broke into a school, killed a teacher and a policeman who tried to grapple with him, shot three children dead, then shot himself.'

'You place great emphasis on children.'

'So?'

'I am sorry, you did not ask me to speak.'

The woman, irritated by the break in the flow, took a few seconds to regain her bearings. 'The point I am making is this. According to you, God is omnipotent. What kind of God permits such things to happen? Come on, you tell me!'

If she expected him to be taken aback she was disappointed; the expression on his face was quizzical. 'You're interested in all this, aren't you?' he said quietly.

'Answer the question!'

'I must tell you that I am no theologian. I never have been. My understanding of these matters is no greater than a peasant's.'

'And yet you must have some answers, must you not? You have faced these things in your time.'

'Of course.'

'Well, then! Explain. Convince me.'

She spread her hands wide and Povin saw with sudden certainty that she spoke the literal truth. She wanted to be convinced more than anything in the world, more even than that the children whom she had described should be brought back to life.

'Well, then,' he faltered, 'I should say the kind of God who permitted those things to happen was first and foremost . . . mysterious.'

'Is that intended as a joke?' The timbre of letdown in her

voice was as unmistakable as it was sad.

'It is not a joke. You have asked me a perfectly serious question, a question which no one has ever put to me before, and I welcome it, and I regard it as important. I am trying to give you the best answer I can. I say again, this God, my God, He is mysterious. Because He is infinitely, unimaginably superior to me in every respect there is no need for Him to let me know all His designs. What He does, He does. It is not my business to understand. My business is to stand in awe.'

There was a long pause during which Inna found she couldn't take her eyes off Povin's face. 'A fairly feeble response, wouldn't you say?' But it was her own response that failed the test.

Povin's eyes smouldered. For a moment he almost felt strong again. 'No, I would not. In Russia the State has declared itself to be God. Here it is the State that is omnipotent. Do you set yourself up against it? Challenge its judgements? Argue the toss?'

'I've warned you about the questions, Povin. Don't provoke me any more today.'

A hard, rebellious knot had formed in her guts and she couldn't make it go away. The State as God, indeed . . .

'The God of the Old Testament,' Povin said suddenly, making Inna shift uneasily in her chair, 'He exists. You've just been reading to me about Him. The bandit tribes of the eastern deserts invented Him because that was the only way they could think of to justify their land-grabbing. But there is a God of the New Testament also. A God changed by the sacrifice of His only son. Or so I believe.'

'Changed!' Inna scoffed. 'How can God change?'

Povin held up his hands as if to ward her off. 'This is where the trouble begins. I am not a theological scholar. All I know is what I feel — here.' The old man turned his upraised hands towards his breast. 'You must please understand that I am an unwilling Christian. I did not seek to be what I am. I couldn't help it. If I could have helped it, I would.'

'Then why . . .?'

'Because I had no choice, I tell you! Listen.' Povin leaned forward to clasp his hands on the edge of the desk. 'Once I watched them torture a poor boy to death. His only offence was that whenever they hit him he prayed a bit louder. They couldn't bear the reproach. So they cracked his skull for him, against a brick wall. And then, click! Bang! Povin became a Christian. Don't ask me why. Everything just came together in one great almighty explosion . . .'

'I find that interesting.' Inna sat back in her chair, lips puckered, the unwilling victim of assertive memories. 'When I was in the Fifth Direction — strange how we both started in the same place — I was continually being struck by the parallels between Christianity and sexual perversion. Of course, there's a good deal of overlap, as you know. Who better? But the pattern's there, all right. In both cases you find a minority, quite happy to be as they are. And the majority: agonized, struggling, always seeking for an "out" — or if not an out, at least a good excuse for getting on with life as *they* want it to be, irrespective of the rules. "The disciple whom Jesus loved." ' Inna laughed scornfully. 'Personally I never saw the difficulty about interpreting that little piece of Scripture.'

For a moment or so Povin just stared at her. Then he laughed, a coarse, cracked, grating sound which put another loop in the knot beneath Inna's waist.

'Such a comfort for an old man like me.' He shook his head and laughed again. 'To know that the KGB is in good hands. To know that the younger generation is in the saddle. That the whole glorious show can be kept on the road for a few seasons longer.' He opened his arms in a gesture of welcome. 'But why stop there, Interrogator Karsovina? You see, I have remembered not to denigrate you with the term "Comrade". Surely we can do better than that, if we try. Let's pool our knowledge. Do you know St Augustine, the *Confessions*?'

'Yes.'

'What — all of him?'

'Yes.'

'Well that's a hell of a lot more than I do. Remember the friend who dies of a fever, in Thagaste? Book Five . . .'

'Four, actually,' Inna corrected him. 'But go on.'

'Four, five . . . "Yet ours was not the friendship which

should be between true friends . . ." Think what the Fifth Direction could do with *that*, Madame Interrogator Karsovina. And what's more, the friend died! Of a *fever*. An early case of syphilis, no doubt. Why stop with the New Testament? Why limit ourselves? Think! Expand! The possibilities are, quite literally — ' He threw back his head, as if seeking the perfect word in the cracked plaster of the ceiling above him — 'unspeakable.'

In the silence which followed Inna put her hands together and began, very slowly, to clap. 'You're wasting your fancy speeches on me,' she said, her confidence returning as the old man's appeared to wane. 'The KGB are hardly the first to come up with these ideas. Personally, I've never seen the harm in a little organized religion.' She saw the rejection in the old man's eyes. 'No, I'm serious! That's one reason why I was glad to leave the Fifth Direction. I was convinced that we were wasting our time. Marx himself called religion the opium of the people. We ought to be putting it to good use, instead of pretending a few old priests and widows in headscarves were going to set the Soviet Union alight from Moscow to Vladivostock. It's unreal. It's also extremely wasteful. I've no time for it.'

'If I may say so, you have a remarkable insight into the Russian character. At risk of offending you, I might even say — the Russian soul.'

Inna chose to ignore the irony in his voice and shrugged. 'Much good it did me. Look where I am now.'

'Doing the rounds of the camps,' Povin said helpfully, sympathetically even. 'Softening up the difficult cases with a whiff of perfume and some philosophical chitchat.'

He saw the cruel light blaze in her eyes and felt her anger roll across the desk towards him like a wave. Then, to his astonishment, she began to laugh; and it was as if the sun had come out to brighten Povin's dismal world.

'I keep forgetting,' she said, once she had recovered herself a little. 'It's you who's the expert here. Not perfume, by the way. Soap, herb soap.' She pushed the file of clippings away from her and folded her hands on the desktop. 'That's enough about religion for today,' she said. 'We'll come back to it another time. There was something else I wanted to ask you about. What part did music play in your life?'

'Music?' Povin's surprise seemed genuine.

'Yes. In your early life. Was yours a musical family?'

'Not really.'

'Yet you yourself are fond of it.'

'Certainly.'

'What do you think of this?'

She walked across to the window ledge where the tape recorder stood and switched it on. Povin listened for a few seconds, then he said, 'Oh dear.'

She turned away from the machine. 'What?'

'Not very subtle.' He raised an eyebrow but she could see that he was distressed.

'You don't like Albéniz?'

'Well enough.'

'*Fête-dieu à Séville*. Very nice.'

'I know it.' He tried to smile, playing the game for her benefit. 'The execution's a bit rough, isn't it?'

'Stolyinovich,' said Inna. 'The Deutsche-Gramophon recording. Too much rubato here and there perhaps, but magical none the less.'

'Certainly. Why don't you turn if off?'

'You don't like it? A moment ago you said you did.'

'Well you've made your point, haven't you? A shrewd stroke, I award you the marks. Below the belt, but all's fair, isn't that what they say?'

'About love and war, yes.'

'Yes. Which is this, by the way?'

'War. As between you and me. But as between you and Stolyinovich, I really don't know. Why not talk about it, Povin? Make yourself feel better.'

'Because I don't think it would.' By now the signs of distress were becoming more pronounced. Povin was on the verge of exhaustion. Inna adjusted the volume a little and resumed her seat behind the desk.

'Try it.'

'Listen.' Povin drew on his reserves of strength and leaned forward to rest his own hands on the desktop. 'Why don't we

102

make a deal. You want to be rid of me, I want to be rid of you. I'm a dead man, I've known that these past two years. That's why your bosses tried out a mock execution on me; you don't need to be clever to understand that. But you keep reminding me of what it's like to be alive. You give me coffee. You play me music. You smile at me. And you're beautiful — you know how beautiful you are. You're a nuisance, you know that? The others, they merely hurt my body — but you go deeper. And at the same time you're an irrelevance, because you're merely Kazin's mouthpiece-cum-notebook. In fact, you're like that tape-recorder over there, a useful piece of equipment, nothing more.' Seeing her redden with anger he twisted his lips into a coaxing smile. 'Come on, out with it. Tell me what it is you want to know.'

She made a great effort to quell her irritation and appeared to consider it as a serious question before finally shaking her head. 'No,' she said, smiling faintly. 'Not yet, Povin. It's too early. Well, I don't know ... Yes, all right. Tell me what everybody's scratching their heads over. Did you ever sleep with Pyotr Stolyinovich?'

He was not quite sure if he had heard correctly. 'I don't understand.'

'Of course you do. Everyone knows he was queer. But he was your bosom friend. So tell me ... did you sleep with him?'

'You're on the wrong track,' Povin said roughly. 'Pyotr had nothing to do with anything. He's as irrelevant as you are. Forget about him. Look, why don't I tell you about the money ...?'

But he had lost her. She shook her head gently, as if too polite to put a stop to the seemingly unquenchable flow, and held up a hand.

'It doesn't matter. Save it.'

'But the money, it's important ...'

'No, not really. We understand about the money. You don't seem to see what we want to achieve here. We're out to construct the profile of a traitor, so that in future we can identify the signs early and deal with the culprit. Prevention is better than cure. In that light, surely you must see that what happened between you and Stolyinovich up at the dacha matters far more than the details of your bank account?'

Povin leaned forward to rest his forearms on the desk, spreading his hands and addressing himself to the expanse of wood between them.

'You don't know what you're doing,' he said quietly. 'You don't know what you're opening up. What you're saying is that you don't care about information, but you care about me, the real me. Don't you see how dangerous that is?'

Inna's smile faded. Suddenly she could find no words with which to answer the old man.

'Because in order to find *me* . . . they have to expose *you*.'

Inna's lips manged to curl, but her eyes were suddenly watchful. 'You know nothing of me, old man. Nothing at all.'

'Don't I?' There was a heavy silence. 'One thing I know, Inna Karsovina —' he nodded heavily, as if repeating the words to himself — 'you have a child. You should think about that . . . Comrade.'

The seconds marched on into infinity while the woman fought to control the surge of blood which swept through her body to the roots of her hair and then was gone, leaving her limp. Her arm lanced out, her finger stabbed at the bell, the door burst open . . .

But when it came to it she could not speak. She could not outface Povin's steady eyes, could find no way to repel their challenge. Instead she waved her hand, wordlessly indicating to the guard that he was to remove the old man from her sight, from her life . . .

In the doorway Povin stopped and turned back to her. 'Next time,' he said quietly, 'I will tell you the child's name. No, don't say it now. I'm very good at guessing.'

After the door had closed behind him Inna Karsovina held the same position for a long time. Terror, stark terror, had her paralysed. The room was like an oven but she was shivering. And she could not quite rid herself of the ghastly illusion that somewhere close by in the background there hovered a pink face with pebble-lensed spectacles and a thin smile, a smile which said, '*He* . . . will leave you in no doubt . . .'

11

Major Lambe took Victor for dinner at the Parrilla Española in Helsinki's Eerikinkatu. The moment they sat down he ordered two large whiskies. Lambe felt he needed a drink. Seventy-two hours spent in the company of this enigmatic Russian had sufficed to give him the creeps.

'Show him around,' Bryant's letter said. 'Show him anything he wants to see.' And Lambe, who prided himself on the excellent relationship which his section of military intelligence enjoyed with London HQ, had complied. Now he almost wished he hadn't. There was an interesting if unpleasant smell about Victor. Lambe regarded him as highly dangerous.

The Russian swallowed a tot of neat spirit and rolled his eyeballs heavenwards. 'Is it always so cold up there?'

'Not always. Usually it's colder. You didn't have to get through a *jernnatt*. It means "iron night", and that's just how it feels.'

Victor shrugged and drank more whisky. 'You can keep it.'

'Thanks, but I was under the impression that it's your problem, not mine.'

Victor rubbed his glass round and round in a circle on the tablecloth, scrutinizing Lambe from under his thick eyebrows. He didn't know much about this man but what he did know he liked. The major was euphemistically described in the embassy register as 'Military Liaison Officer (A2)', which didn't fool anybody. He was forty-five and, to judge from his careful comb-work, losing hair faster than he wanted. Victor approved of his tall, spare figure: fat men tire more easily and, contrary to popular belief, aren't well suited to work in the cold.

105

Victor knew that Bryant reposed complete trust in this man, which was as well, because the Russian was going to need a lot of help.

'You've been very kind to me. Maps. Aerial photographs. Sketch plans. Everything I asked for, in fact.'

Lambe blinked. He had a very slow blink, appearing to close his eyes deliberately, hold them shut for an instant and then open them, always with a smile. It somehow made him look trustworthy. Victor liked that blink.

'I've merely been obeying my orders. The man said to give you the works, so I did. Any complaints?'

'None.'

'Good, another satisfied customer.'

'But maybe I'll need some more help. Later.'

'I see. My instructions don't go that far, I'm afraid.'

Victor resumed circling the tablecloth with his glass. He knew that Bryant had told Lambe very little. The immediate problem was how to confide the bare minimum in the major without at the same time appearing to doubt his integrity.

'Suppose I had a friend,' he said, 'who wanted to go travelling. An old man, in need of special travel arrangements, on account of his age and the state of his health. And the weather. And the difficult terrain . . .'

The circles made by the glass were shaped with meticulous precision. Lambe watched, his face expressionless.

'. . . An old man who would need a special courier to go in and fetch him out.'

At that Lambe cleared his throat. 'I'm sorry,' he said, 'but you've lost me. Surely any reputable firm of travel agents could supply a courier?'

At that Victor tossed back his head and laughed out loud.

'There are no . . . *reputable* . . . travel agents where my old friend lives.'

'Ah. I see, then. An outlying area.'

Victor nodded, took a swig from his glass and resumed his careful circling of the tablecloth. 'As you say. And one where it is very difficult to move, unaided. In the East.'

A waiter brought their first courses. Lambe ate his in thoughtful silence. Victor pushed his chair back from the table, leaving his food untouched, and continued to toy with his glass while keeping his shrewd eyes on the Englishman's face. Lambe did not speak again until he had finished his salad and placed his knife and fork neatly in the centre of his empty plate.

'There's a way in,' Lambe said slowly. 'I can see that. The border's virtually unguarded in places, the snow leaves gaps in the defences . . . a man might make it to wherever he wanted to go. But coming back . . .'

Victor began to attack his cold food, wolfing it down as if he hadn't eaten for a week.

'What about the midnight sun?'

Victor pushed away his unfinished plate and poured himself a glass of wine without offering one to Lambe. 'Of course I have taken the midnight sun into account. My courier will want to commence his journey well before the first week in May.'

Victor lit a cigarette and began to smoke it moodily, one leg jiggling up and down against the table. Lambe wanted to ask him to stop, took a look at his face and decided not to.

'My courier . . . he travels fast, that one.'

'I dare say he does. What about your old friend — does he travel equally fast?'

The change that came over Victor's face was remarkable. It was as though he donned a smiling mask normally reserved for polite social conversations, chance encounters. 'That's the return journey.'

'So?'

Victor shrugged again. His smile was starting to annoy Lambe, who mistook it for a sign of stupidity. NATO liked things to be very well organized in Scandinavia; he was one of the people who made sure that they were. There was no room for a crazy Russian with some half-baked, harebrained scheme which had a beginning and a middle but no end.

'I see. You're going to improvise as you go along, are you?'

Victor heard the tautness in his voice and the smile faded.

'Nothing will be left to chance. Nothing at all. Please . . . I would welcome any ideas you may have for the . . . return journey.'

The second course arrived and Lambe used the pause to organize his thoughts. There were ways and means, of course, he realized that. Every so often he had to accommodate 'visitors': nameless men who disappeared 'over the wire' for a few hours or days and then had to be ferried back in a hurry. Not often, thank god, but sometimes. Those men were professionals; they played by the rules. They told you where they would be at a certain time; you sent in a two-seater Harrier to pick them up. The pilot flew at thirty feet above the steppe and staged the turnaround so quickly that the blast from the plane's Pegasus 103 engines scarcely had time to melt the snow. But it was not the kind of operation you talked about to anonymous Russians, no matter how highly recommended they came.

'I'm afraid I really haven't got any ideas,' he said; and Victor knew at once that he was lying.

'You will,' he said cheerfully.

But Lambe wasn't so sure. He spent the rest of the meal making small talk to the Russian and turning over in his mind what he had just been told. It seemed that there was need for haste. But why? Who was behind this, and what was the real objective? A clandestine operation of some kind, no doubt . . . Well, that happened — but not here in the so-called Red Zone which fringed Russia's Kola Peninsula, not if Lambe had anything to do with it.

While he drank his wine and smoked a cigarette the major sent his mind roaming back over the events of the past few days, retracing their movements through Finnmark as if on an invisible map. He concluded that Victor was by now remarkably well equipped to enter the Soviet Union unobserved and make his way towards the target — whoever that was. But afterwards came the mysterious hiatus, an almost cavalier indifference as to what happened next.

Victor could get in. Lambe wasn't at all sure that the Russian was in a position to get out again. But perhaps — the thought caused his hand to freeze while he was stirring his coffee — perhaps Victor didn't want to get out.

After dinner they parted amicably enough. Two businessmen parting after an assignment or a deal, that was how it must have looked, how it was meant to look. A casual observer would have been hard-pressed to detect the under-current of distrust which had begun to flow between them, as pervasive as it was invisible, as potentially corrosive as it was well concealed.

Victor was in no particular hurry. He lit a cigarette, drew down a lungful of smoke and began to saunter through the back streets of Helsinki towards his hotel.

It was now necessary to make a careful assessment of the major's limitations, as well as his undoubted qualities. Lambe reminded Victor of Bruno, his Dalmatian. He seemed obedient and eager to please. Orders would arrive from London and he would obey them, without deviation or ques-tion. Later, if things didn't turn out so well, at least he would have the consolation of knowing that he had done what he was told. A pat and a kindly word might keep the English major going in the right direction for a long time. Victor wondered if that was why Bryant had chosen Lambe. His frown deepened. He needed to be absolutely sure about Bryant's motives. He must check, double-check *everything*.

April. It was possible, but he must go soon. Two days to target, a week to dig in, and then . . .

Victor thought of the Kola Peninsula and in spite of himself he shivered. Limitless and unimaginable power concentrated in a few square miles of slush and snow . . . How confident they must feel, those masters of the Gulag; how secure in the knowledge that Povin was safe. Well, he *was* safe, wasn't he? Safe from the likes of Lambe . . .

Lambe was going to have to be watched every step of the way. Victor knew he hadn't fooled the major, not completely. Therefore, he had to make doubly sure of Bryant. A plane, that was essential. Once it landed in Russia Victor knew he would be able to take control. But getting it there in the first place was going to be a problem. It all came back to Bryant . . .

Victor, still frowning, strolled slowly back to the warmth of his hotel, and bed. The Russians were a hardy race, he mused; hardy and also strong. But they suffered from a

dangerous vice. They were overconfident . . . and he too was
a Russian.

A quarter of a mile away Lambe paused at the junction with
Hietalandenkatu, undecided. No, he had to return to the
office before going home. As he crossed the street his pace
quickened, while inwardly he began to draft a telex for London. 'For C, personal . . . must talk personal scrambler . . .'
  By now the major was almost trotting. As he began to rub
his gloved hands together, fighting the bitterness of the night
frost, he watched with his mind's eye how the pencil crossed
through the words 'must talk' and substituted 'must see
physically one to one,' and in that instant Lambe began to
run.

12

For the whole of the long bus journey to Moscow's Vagankovskoye Cemetery Inna fulminated against her mother in
silent rage, while Volodiya sat in the next seat staring out of
the window. How dare she, Inna kept saying to herself, over
and over again, how could she! To tell the boy his father was
dead, just like that and without consulting her was bad
enough, but to mention the name of the cemetery and then
ask him whether he wanted to see the grave . . . Every time
she managed to snatch a weekend at home there was *something*. She had to spend all her free time merely trying to undo
the damage done, with Volodiya always ready to appeal to
babushka for permissions which ran counter to some of
Inna's most cherished principles. The boy needed either a
father or a mother who was there permanently. Too bad.
Inna wasn't about to marry any of the men she knew at
present, so it seemed that until she reached the end of the

road at Murmansk, Volodiya was going to be relegated to the role of hobby.

How strange that Povin should have had problems with his mother . . .

She cast a quick, hostile glance to where Anfisa was sitting on the other side of the aisle. The old lady looked up, smiled and resumed her knitting.

Inna drew in a hard, deep breath and tried to prevent her anger from overflowing against her son. It wasn't his fault. Of course he was curious, that was only natural, what child wouldn't be? Especially when they talked about anything and everything at school these days. And, of course, at some time he would have had to know, but now? At six, pushing seven? That was her mother all over, with her traditional, muddled ideas about death and what was 'proper'. In Mother's day, children had to come face to face with death all the time, thanks to the 'Great Father', or what ever nonsensical name it was that people of her generation gave Stalin, but that was in the past — and good riddance! If it had been sex, now! Ah, that would have been different, of course — 'The boy's far too young, Inna!'

'Where do we go when we die?' Volodiya asked her, his solemn voice vibrant with awkward, unaccustomed emotion.

Inna resisted the irrational urge to appeal to her mother for help. 'Nowhere, darling. When we die, we die. It's like going to sleep for ever.'

'Yes, but where do we *go*?' He wasn't angry with her, or reproachful, but it was all too clear that in his eyes she was deliberately choosing to misunderstand.

'What keeps us alive . . . the spirit, if you like, it just goes away and leaves us for ever.'

'The spirit,' he said thoughtfully. And then, 'Do I have a spirit, Mother?'

The bus stopped opposite the peasant market. Most of the passengers were alighting here; Sunday was always popular for trips to the cemetery. 'We've arrived,' Inna said, more roughly than she'd meant to. 'Do you want to get off?'

She'd been half hoping that he would have changed his mind, but he stood up at once and said, 'Of course.' As Inna helped her mother down the steps of the bus her glance fell on a rack of newspapers outside a nearby kiosk. 'Grenada!' roared the indignant headline, and she quickly averted her gaze. Grenada, Afghanistan, what was the difference? The old man had nearly bowled her over with Afghanistan; in spite of herself she couldn't help smiling at the memory. Povin was right, of course. Few things in recent years had demonstrated more thoroughly to Inna Karsovina what a pack of fools those apes in the Kremlin could sometimes be than the invasion of Afghanistan.

'Come on,' she said, giving Volodiya's hand a vigorous jerk. 'Are we going to stand here all day?' She looked round to meet Anfisa's eyes brimming with disapproval. 'And you, Mother.'

The night before, Volodiya had carefully explained to them how he wanted the visit to go. First, he said, they would buy flowers from the market. Then they would visit the grave. Then they would talk. Inna tried to dissuade him, hearing the desperation echo in her voice, but her mother maintained a purposeful silence and without her support it was no use. Now, as they walked under the brick arch which led into Vagankovskoye, she found herself dreading that looming 'talk' most of all. The precocious way in which he spoke the word struck an ominous note in her mind. The last thing Inna wanted to do was discuss the past, or her dead ex-husband's role in it.

The grave was situated in a distant, overgrown corner of the cemetery, where few mourners ever came. The railings which surrounded each tomb were rusty, the paths unkempt. Inna felt uneasy. The only other person in sight was a little old man, bent almost double, who was shearing grass from a nearby grave. He raised his eyes to Inna's face and almost at once lowered them again without smiling. For a fleeting second the woman imagined that he had recently emerged from the earth to tend his own last resting place, and she shivered.

'Inna,' her mother hissed. 'I saw that old one on the bus. Are you being followed? Has it come to that now, eh?'

'Please do try not to be silly, Mother.' It annoyed Inna to

112

find that she herself wasn't quite certain. She knew she was on probation; Kazin was perfectly capable of having her watched. On the whole she was pleased with her recent progress but that didn't mean the high-ups had to share her view. Fairly pleased, she corrected herself.

'Look, Mother,' said Volodiya. 'There's a seat over there, underneath that tree.'

Inna eyed her son uncertainly. She found it hard to cope with this newfound sophisticated manliness. It was obvious that he wanted the women to go and sit on the seat, away from him.

She walked over to it without a word, leaving Anfisa to follow her more slowly. It was a warm spring afternoon and Inna realized with a sudden, unexpected spark of pleasure that many months had elapsed since she last sat outside in the sun. Volodiya was all right, she decided. He was standing by his father's grave in a posture of respect, head bowed, hands clasped behind his back. Who had taught him that, she wondered? Or was it natural to him, just as the complementary vice of arrogance had been natural to his father . . .

She deliberately ignored Anfisa's arrival on the seat next to her, flipped open the book she had brought and began to read at random.

> *I am past thirty. I fear the nights.*
> *I hunch the sheet with my knees.*

'Fuck!' Inna slammed the book shut again and thrust it into her bag. What a fool she'd been to bring Yevtushenko on an expedition like this. Especially *The Bratsk Station*, Leonid's first gift to her when they were still both students. She ought to have thrown it out long ago. And yet . . . Inna knew she wouldn't throw it out. A life is composed of only so many memories; one had to separate the good from the bad. He had loved her once, and while he did he gave her Yevtushenko. It wasn't the poet's fault that her husband had turned into a drunken womanizer with a propensity for violence.

Before they left to catch the bus she had picked up the book almost (but not quite) without thinking; now her mother peered down at the cover. 'Yevtushenko, eh? No wonder they're worried about you down at the Square. No wonder they're having you followed! Didn't Fedor give you that?'

'No,' Inna snapped. 'It was Leonid.'

She sighed. Soon she too would be like Yevtushenko's narrator: past thirty and fearing the nights. There had been affairs, of course. She brought herself up sharply. 'Affairs' — don't try that super-sophisticated rubbish with me! She had slept with two men since the death of her husband; her mother had just mentioned one of them. 'Fedor was all right,' she said grumpily, and her mother snorted.

Fedor had been typical Party line drink-of-water stuff, although there was nothing ordinary about the man himself: handsome, charming, sexually charismatic. He worked on the floor below her and they met in the lift; she knew from their very first encounter that she would sleep with him. She had a pretty good idea of what it would be like too, and she wasn't wrong. After a perfunctory kiss and a fondle of her breasts he produced a packet of Bakovka condoms, which somehow contrived to be fragile as well as thick (Inna shuddered at the memory) and suggested they *trakhnut*. It was all over in less than five minutes, during which time he assailed Inna's ears with more sexual swearwords, more *mat*, than she had previously known existed. When Fedor had finished he leaned over her and murmured, 'It was good for you, wasn't it? I can always tell . . .'

Inna stretched her legs out in front of her and began to massage her knees. It really was very pleasant out here under the big oak tree. Volodiya had begun a perambulation of the grave, hands still clasped behind his back like a visiting dignitary inspecting the Tomb of the Unknown Warrior. What on earth was going on inside that tousled head? Inna looked at her watch. Well, there was no hurry. And perhaps this visit would exorcise the spectre of his dead father once and for all.

'At least he was better than that other one,' her mother interrupted.

'Oh give it a rest, Mother, for goodness' sake! Haven't you got your knitting or something?'

'All I'm saying is that Fedor was a man. Not like that whatsisname!'

Fedor had taught her one thing, and that was always henceforth to take her own precautions. Because she was in the KGB she was able to lay her hands on the elusive Hungarian Infekundin pills without too much trouble. Thus accoutred, she had resolved to select her next 'glass-of-water' more carefully. A shaft of sunlight fell through the leaves of the oak tree on to her hands, dappling them white and grey, and Inna smiled at the other person she was then.

Nikolai. To her mother he had never been anything but 'whatsisname'. So straightforward and yet so complicated. She knew at once that she would never, never sleep with him — yet she did. With him it was obvious, right from the start, that they could, should, never be more than friends. But instead they became awkward, protesting lovers. It was as if neither of them wanted what had to be. Only after a month of their reluctant, uneasy affair did it occur to Inna to ask him point blank if he were married . . .

Volodiya was approaching the seat beneath the tree's spreading branches. Inna held out her hands but he walked past them and hitched himself on to the seat beside Anfisa. Inna expected him to speak, but he was silent.

'Happy now?' She tried to make it sound light and jolly, as if she had merely indulged a request for an ice cream or a visit to the zoo. Volodiya did not reply at once. Inna looked down on the top of his head, knowing that this was very nearly all the family she had left in the world and infinitely the most precious member of it; the perception left her feeling wild and breathless like an animal under threat.

'Why did the people kill Daddy?' The boy's voice was small and sad. Inna wasn't sure she had heard him correctly; only when he repeated the question and her mother stirred restlessly did the full enormity of it overwhelm her.

'Where did you get such a silly idea from? Has *babushka* . . .?'

'No. I just feel it, that's all. He was very young when he died, wasn't he? The other boys at school say young people don't die. Did the soldiers kill him?' His face knotted into momentary rage. 'I hate them!'

An iron shutter seemed to descend before Inna's vision,

obliterating sense. Her mother, normally so talkative, was strangely silent. Even as Inna made a valiant effort to recover she knew it was hopeless.

'Listen to me, Volodiya. Daddy died in an accident. It was sad, very sad.'

'Tell me about it, then.' Volodiya turned his face up to hers and she saw that he was on the verge of tears. Inna swallowed hard. She really must not cry, she told herself, not here, not yet. It was on the tip of her tongue to say, 'I'll tell you when you're grown up,' when suddenly she realized that if he was old enough, mature enough, to suffer grief for a father he had never known and want to stand by his grave, then the answer she had framed was in reality no answer at all.

Inna sighed. 'If you genuinely want to know about it, ask me again and I'll tell you. But think first.'

Anfisa jerked her head in an emphatic and totally unexpected gesture of approval but still she remained silent, and Inna realized with a sick feeling in her stomach that she was on trial for the truth.

His mother's reply had been so unexpectedly adult that Volodiya, taken aback, did think, and Inna was pleased. But when he raised his eyes again he said, 'Yes. I want to know.'

Inna was distracted by the sight of the bent old man, still at work on the nearby grave, by the sunlight rippling across her hands, by birdsong, by anything and everything. Yet she knew she must tell the boy at least an approximation of the truth.

'When . . . when Daddy and I were married, we were both very young.'

'Was that at the University? At Lomonosov?'

'Yes.'

'Was Daddy a math-ma-tish-an too?'

A moment ago Inna would have been glad of the interruption. Now she felt irrationally cheated, and hurried on.

'Yes. In those days Daddy was very clever. But then he fell sick.' Inna hesitated. That seemed like a promising line. 'Soon after you were born he started to do strange things.'

'What?'

'Oh . . . he'd break things. Without meaning to,' she added

hastily. 'And sometimes he'd . . . well, he'd hurt Mummy. Because he was so clumsy. And then one day . . .'

Volodiya looked up innocently. 'Yes?'

'One day, he was arrested. By the militia. They thought he'd done something very, very bad.' Inna chewed her lips. This was the worst part. She decided to rush it, before improvisation finally deserted her. 'And they locked him up, and during the night . . .'

'Is that when they killed him?' Volodiya asked sombrely. 'During the night?'

An evil goblin nearly tricked her into saying 'How do you know?' but fortunately she checked herself in time. There was something fey about her son this afternoon, something new and hitherto unsuspected. He frightened her. Inna's body shook in a sudden spasm — how could she even think such a wicked thing? And yet . . . it might be true.

'Nobody killed Daddy,' she whispered. 'He wasn't well. In his mind, he . . . He couldn't manage like the rest of us. He . . .' Suddenly the sight of Volodiya's pale, unnaturally mature little face was too much for her. 'He killed himself!' she all but shouted; and the bent old man actually straightened up to his full height for long enough to subject her to a shocked stare, a stare which said, 'What possesses you, woman? In front of the child!'

Anfisa sighed. Volodiya looked at his mother for a long moment, then shook his head. Inna tried to fathom what that sign of negation was meant to convey. That he rejected the story? That he found it horrifying? Inna couldn't tell. She realized sadly that her son was now a person and, like other people, he had secret places, prohibited zones.

'Come and look,' said the child, reaching out for her hand; and Inna obediently rose, leaving Anfisa to do as she pleased. When they approached Leonid's grave Volodiya's grip tightened until he was pinching the flesh of her hand so that it hurt. With a feeling akin to relief she realized that he hadn't really understood anything, that a lot of his supposed re-actions existed only in her own overheated imagination. For a moment the two of them stood looking down at the untidy mound, upon which the boy had earlier laid his posy of spring

117

flowers. Then Volodiya led his mother away. He paused just long enough to collect *babushka* before marching towards the exit, stiff and tense as a soldier on May Day Parade, and Inna, by now limp and unprotesting, went with him.

'Well, and was it true?' said Anfisa, very quietly so that the boy wouldn't hear. 'Did they kill him, eh?' But Inna had no reply to offer.

In the bus on the way home she stared out of the window, blind to the busy streets, her vivid memories running out of control. The divorce — no point in complicating matters by telling Volodiya about that — had been all but settled when Leonid suddenly demanded custody of the child. It threatened to turn into a long, drawn-out wrangle in which Inna and the boy could only be losers. She had become ill with fatigue and stress. This was immediately before a promotion board, when she needed to be at her best, and instead she was crawling in to work five, ten, fifteen minutes late and getting later, a pale ghost of her former self. Then the telephone call in the middle of the night, 'Your husband has been arrested.' 'On what charge?' 'Arson. Setting fire to a warehouse while drunk.' She had wanted to see him but they wouldn't let her; next thing she knew, he was dead. Hanged in his cell, overwhelmed by grief and remorse, his life in ruins . . . The prison doctor was very kind, Inna could still remember how his voice flowed mellifluously on over the rocky river bed of her wretched life, endlessly comforting . . .

She didn't believe a word of it.

Didn't she? Perhaps she believed it as desperately as if her own survival depended on it. And perhaps the boy must be made to believe it too. Like his mother, Volodiya must come to understand that the remains of people who committed suicide in prison were often handed over to relatives for burial, there was nothing in the slightest suspicious about that, even though the regulations stated that no corpse must ever be delivered from a state detention centre into private hands. And the fact that her work had been suffering at the time was neither here nor there; it was a coincidence, nothing more than a coincidence. Of course, she had to admit that the effect of her former husband's arrest was to resolve the custody issue in her favour even before his suicide — hadn't Kazin implied as much?

Kazin. Inna's hands tightened on the strap of her bag. At what point, she asked herself, did Kazin first come to know of her existence? Was it, by any chance, by mere coincidence, just about the time that Leonid first laid claim to custody of her child?

Was Kazin telling her the whole truth? No, rephrase that — could she believe *anything* he told her? Inna gasped out loud. Had she *really* said that, even though it was only inside her own head? What would Povin have thought?

She clenched her teeth. Povin. That old man was starting to exact a price. He dazzled her. Somehow the vision had become distorted, and it hurt. Inna had never before encountered anyone who managed to combine so much evil with such a tenacious sense of his own essential righteousness.

She became aware that Volodiya was muttering something and came back to the present with a jolt.

'What did you say?'

'I *hate* them, those people . . .'

Volodiya felt his mother grab his wrist and he looked up, startled. There was a look in her eyes he had never seen before, an expression which made him shrink back into the seat away from this suddenly strange woman with her baleful intensity and painful grip.

'Don't let me ever hear you say again that you hate anyone,' Inna said. Her voice was steely and cold. 'You understand? Not . . . *ever*!'

13

The spring mornings began early these days; the air was steadily growing milder. Now that it was worth going outside for a smoke Povin found himself looking forward to his break with real eagerness. He knew that Interrogator Karsovina would send for him soon, but he still had precious moments in which to relax, to think.

It was nearly time to stop work when the incident happened.

He had been shunting loaf tins from the table into the ovens, using a baker's long-handled spatula. Every so often he would pick up a sharp knife and pare off some dough which had grown above itself in the proving process, tossing the knife back down on the tabletop and scooping the tins on to the wooden paddle in an easy rhythm. There were a hundred tins to be dealt with in this way but the work was mechanical and not too heavy, so that his mind was free to dwell on other things, which explained why his guard was down.

The old man had crammed a lot of thinking into the last few days, until his brain cells were as stuffed with calculations as the tins which rattled so carelessly through his fingers were filled with dough. Over the years Povin had come to know a lot about Kazin's thought processes. Now the old man was reasonably satisfied that he had it all straight.

Kazin wanted to know something; but he didn't dare ask for it outright. Something, in other words, which couldn't be independently checked. Nothing verifiable, nothing tangible. An impression, perhaps, or a vague recollection. Or — the old man kept coming back to this — something he didn't even realize he knew.

Chance Medley.

He slammed the oven door shut and set to work on the second batch of loaves. Lev triple-oh-eight sat quietly watching him from the back of the bakery, his own work over for the moment. A tiny corner of Povin's brain queried why the boy didn't go outside to smoke as he usually did, but the question went unanswered and unheeded.

Don't go so fast, he chided himself. It didn't have to be Chance Medley. Bryant was familiar with the code but he hadn't used it for years; why resurrect it without any prior warning for the last, most important time of all?

Because the woman was interested in music, that's why.

Don't be ridiculous. That didn't mean a thing. You're going too far too fast. Test everything, assume nothing.

Somewhere, locked away in the interstices of his mind, Povin knew he had a piece of information – but he didn't know what it was. He didn't have the key. Bryant would have assigned him a courier, someone to see him safely across the border. Someone very senior, very good. Someone with a name. Perhaps that was what Kazin wanted. A name.

Too far too fast, he wearily reminded himself. Test, don't assume.

As Povin turned away from the table to carry the last batch of bread to the oven he registered that triple-oh-eight's chair was empty, but still he didn't pay any heed. His mind was too intent on the pursuit of Kazin's thoughts. It was only when he set himself to scrub down the tabletops that his eyes missed the knife and, much too late, his brain hurled all its combined resources into defending the yawning breach, now so obvious; he had time to scream, very loudly but only once, before the hand silenced him and he was falling backwards towards the blade . . .

Inna stood by the window of the interrogation room, staring vacantly out over the grassy expanse which sloped down to the shore of the lake. It was mid-morning and the zeks were all at work, but as usual the camp officers seemed unoccupied. A group of them strolled between the sparse trees, talking and smoking as if they had nothing else in the world

121

to think about. Inna didn't recognize any of them. Yes she did, though. She had a vague recollection of this one officer from her first day in the compound; the security man had pointed him out to her as somebody with a question mark hanging over his head. Inna tried to remember the officer's name; it began with a Z. Zorov, Zanev . . .

Zuyev. That was it. The *oper* had been very down on Zuyev; Inna wondered why.

She consulted her watch. It was nearly time to begin the session. She was about to take her seat behind the desk when the phone rang, and on picking it up she found herself in direct communication with Chairman Kazin.

'Karsovina . . . Karsovina, are you there?'

She swallowed back the bile which suddenly rose into her throat and tried to make her voice sound confident. 'Here Comrade Chairman. The phone cable, it became tangled . . .'

'I hope you're not becoming clumsy. I don't like clumsy operatives, Karsovina. You should know that by now.'

Inna swayed on her feet and said nothing.

'The reason I'm phoning you is to ascertain what progress you've been making.'

'I think it can best be described as slow but steady, Chairman.' She noted with pleasure that as the impact of the surprise faded her voice lost its hesitancy. 'It is a lengthy process, as you predicted. He's wily as a fox.' She paused. 'To be blunt, Chairman, I don't scare him any more.'

Kazin's metallic chuckle reverberated down the line and Inna trembled. Strange how this awe-inspiring old man could still magic up terror at a distance . . .

'Good. It's not your function to scare him, not now. You should have moved on from that, Karsovina. Does *he* scare *you*?'

'No.'

'Don't be too cocky. He still has a long arm, remember that.' Again the iron chuckle. 'He's begun to hurt, hasn't he?'

Inna chewed her lips. The resulting pause seemed to go on for a long time. Was it worth a lie, over the phone? Better not. 'He is . . . different, Comrade Chairman. Impressive, in a funny sort of way.'

'So. You are learning, after all. I'm glad to hear that because the hard part is yet to come. It is time we applied a little pressure to the General, Karsovina. I'm making arrangements for him to receive a visitor, a highly unofficial visitor. Tell the *oper* to step up surveillance. And take a good look at yourself, while you're at it.'

'Chairman?'

'He's confusing you.'

'I don't think —'

'Don't interrupt. He's becoming interesting, by far the most interesting man you know. You've begun to feel sorry for him. That's as it should be. It's necessary. Just don't start getting any fancy ideas, that's all. About rehabilitating him . . .'

Inna could not contain a gasp. How did Kazin know that? On the night of the visit to the cemetery she had lain awake for a long time, staring at Povin's photograph. To her surprise she realized that she had started to view him in a different light. At first she thought that the old man — she nearly said 'her' old man — was too pathetic for words; that it was simply no longer possible to derive any satisfaction from humiliating someone so sick and broken. But as time passed she came to see that his mind was intact; and on the flight up to Murmansk Inna had finally acknowledged to herself that she would go farther. Kazin was right — Povin was by far and away the most interesting man she knew. She looked forward to their sessions together. She might despise him, she certainly didn't agree with much of what he said, but he was real! And, yes again, deep inside her there had actually begun to take root the perverse idea that if there was anything at all in the theory of rehabilitation, she might succeed in redeeming Povin yet.

'Please don't trouble yourself about that, Chairman.' She tried to make herself sound bored, just a touch insulted. 'We can all forget the fairytales, I think. It seems to me —'

Although the room was double-glazed the sound of a shot penetrated with unnerving clarity.

'Yes? You were saying?'

But Inna had rushed to the window, the telephone receiver

in her hand quite forgotten. The group of officers had scattered. Zuyev was running towards the camp bakery, pistol held high in the air and even at a hundred metres' distance Inna could hear his hoarse shouts for help. A patrol came at the double from down by the lake, fanning out through the trees as if in readiness for an assault. Inna jammed her forehead against the glass, striving to see the source of all the excitement. Everything happened with frustrating slowness, as if a projectionist was deliberately holding the film in check: the soldiers took an age to clear the ridge in front of the house, Zuyev and the other officers seemed to be struggling through treacle, the old man . . .

'Karsovina?' The receiver hummed and crackled in her hand. '*Karsovina!*'

'Chairman, I . . . There's been an incident of some kind. I can't see . . . Povin's hurt.' Inna raised her hand to her mouth. 'Blood. I can see blood.'

Povin fell out of the bakery and sank down on the grass. Then the huge figure of Alexander the Chechen appeared in the doorway, his head turning back to someone or something behind him. He raised a hand just as Zuyev came panting up; in the same instant Alexander stepped aside and another zek flew through the narrow gap to land flat on his back at the officer's feet. For a moment he lay there without moving; then his back arched in a spasm and he appeared to faint.

Inna raised the receiver to white lips. She was shaking. 'He . . . he is alive, Comrade Chairman. This happened . . . outside.' She proceeded to relate what she had seen, her voice quavering.

When she had finished Kazin grunted. 'If he's conscious, take the session as usual.' His voice was brisk. 'Things are moving, Karsovina. Just make sure you're awake and moving with them, that's all.' To Inna's astonishment he seemed not at all put out by what she had told him; quite the reverse. 'Now have this call transferred to the camp commander's office.'

After she had complied with his last instruction she replaced the receiver on its rest. She needed both hands to do it. When the door opened to admit Povin she had no idea of how much time had passed. As he lowered himself into his chair she stared at him woodenly, trying to think of something to say.

'You are hurt?' Her voice came out much too high. The expression on his pale, clammy face was answer enough.

'Not really. A knife wound. Superficial.' He managed to bare his teeth in a grin. 'My buttock.'

'Knife! I heard a shot.'

'That was when the Chechen raised the alarm. As soon as one of the officers heard it he fired his pistol to attract attention.' Seeing the look of incomprehension on her face he explained, 'They are trained to do that. Nothing alerts a patrol like the sound of a shot.'

'You need . . . assistance?' Inna hated herself. She hated him for teaching her the ways of a camp.

Povin shook his head and grimaced. 'They swabbed the wound. Nothing serious. I managed to wrench myself to one side, then the Chechen stepped in. Lucky he was there.'

It was on the tip of Inna's tongue to postpone the session; only the memory of her recent conversation with Kazin held her back. The old man was speaking rationally enough but he looked awful.

'Who did it?' There was no mistaking the venom in her voice. 'I said . . . who did it?'

Povin mutely shook his head. Inna was poised to make an issue of it; then she shrugged. 'Zuyev can tell me later.'

'Zuyev. Ah yes.' He sighed and disconnected his own gaze from her piercing stare, allowing his eyes to stray to the vase of flowers. Inna, suddenly eager to relieve the tension, permitted herself a tense smile.

'Daffodils. The roses died, I'm afraid. And all the little Georgians have gone to Baku, for the sunshine.' Her voice was still pitched unnaturally high. 'Daffodils only, now.'

'But still lovely. You cannot imagine what the sight of a freshly cut flower means to someone like me.'

'You are commenting on the beauty of the flower, or the fact that it has been cut?'

'Oh, I am sorry — the beauty. I don't believe God minds us uprooting one or two of his flowers.'

'He has plenty more?'

'Always more.'

Inna knew she ought to check herself, that she was teetering on the lip of a slippery downwards slope, but instead she shrugged again and poured two cups of coffee from the big flask. This time the old man did not hesitate to accept. She noticed that he was leaning heavily to one side, obviously trying to keep his weight off the wound. The buttock. Inna suppressed another smile. Why did life often turn out to be so absurd?

'Would you like some more music today?' she said suddenly, and at once wished the words unspoken.

Povin looked up from his cup to see her wide eyes full upon him. In his dazed state they were mildly hypnotic and somehow softer than he remembered them. She too had been shocked by what had happened and in a perplexed kind of way she was offering help. So the assault had not been official policy then . . .

'No thank you.'

Inna felt repulsed. 'I suppose that after two years of deprivation music must have come as something of a surprise.'

'It was too much for me last time. Another day, perhaps.'

Inna threw herself back in her chair and began to massage the nape of her neck. Her muscles refused to relax. A dull ache was building up behind her eyes. 'I don't really feel like work today. What a weekend!' Now she treated Povin to a proper smile, still inexplicably wanting to be indulgent. 'My child — you were right about that, by the way, a good guess — gave me hell.'

'Ah, I'm sorry. And how is Volodiya?'

Povin considered her through eyes which seemed to betray nothing more than polite interest, but the horror of his innocent-sounding question overwhelmed Inna. Her lips moved soundlessly.

'I beg your pardon, Citizen Karsovina. I could not hear.'

'How did you do that?' Her voice was no more than a husky whisper.

'Do what?'

'You know very well what!'

If Povin was enjoying his triumph he gave no sign of it. As

always he seemed eager to please, anxious to assist the good citizen interrogator in any way he could. In the moment of silence which followed Inna became aware of a new emotion: anger. The façade of astonishment which the old man presented to her was perfect but she knew it was false. It had to be false. What should she do? Should she summon the guard, make him beat it out of Povin; have the swine thrown into solitary for a month?

Yes, that was it — pay him out. All her nascent feelings of pity for the old man were dashed aside. His arm is still long, that's what Kazin had said and he was right, but now she would see that arm cut off at the elbow. The thought of him knowing Volodiya's name terrified her. If he could discover the name, what else could he do? What could he *not* do? He must be neutralized. He must die. He . . .

He's beginning to hurt, that's what Kazin had said. Inna banged the desktop with her clenched fist.

'A lucky guess,' Povin murmured. His eyes were hooded slits. He was scrutinizing her more intently than ever before, as if the whole future of the interrogation depended on what happened next, and Inna steeled herself to the knowledge that she had reached the first of many watersheds.

But her heart was steadying now and at last her brain was coming to the rescue. She knew that the old man had shot his bolt; there were no more weapons in his armoury. Volodiya was safe and a thousand miles away where Povin could not touch him. The balance of power was slowly being restored to its customary slant in her favour.

It was vital to complete the recovery. Inna returned him stare for stare. Her head was still throbbing but even in such a crisis as this she did not lack resourcefulness. 'Strike!' she commanded herself. 'Strike *now*!'

'You remind me of my husband.' Her voice oozed contempt. 'In the old days. He was master of that kind of cheap conjuring trick. Are you listening to me, Povin?'

There was no need to ask: his face was rapt. Inna could have cried aloud in relief. She had done the unexpected, made a stand.

'He used to tease me, you know.' Now her voice was soft

and flat. 'Men. So strange.' Inna shook her head in a slow schoolmarmish gesture of disapproval. 'All that dominating male force. Like a wave which picks you off the sand. And the man always thinks he's shifted the woman's whole foundation in life, him and his tidal wave, but he hasn't.' She leaned slowly forward to rest her hands on the desk, not needing to raise her soft voice, knowing that now she had his attention, all of it. 'It's just a wave, Povin. It rolls over you and it's lost.' She shook her head again, this time in rejection. 'A man always wants the wave to flow *through* you. It doesn't. It doesn't, Povin.'

His face remained expressionless, as if he couldn't quite make up his mind about her words. Then he spoke, rather humbly Inna thought, almost as if he sensed he'd made a wrong move. 'I won't do it again. On my honour as a Young Pioneer.'

'Why did you do that, Povin? Why bother?'

He hesitated, trying to assess what he could make her believe. Inna tapped the desk impatiently.

'A flexing of the muscles, perhaps. To show you that you have a real fight on your hands, not just token dignity.' Another pause. 'To see if I could.'

It sounded honest.

'Oh, you could. But no one ever doubted that, Povin. No one needed to see it proved.' Her voice maintained its same, even tone. The old man fidgeted uncomfortably. The pain in his buttock was worse, he was weary, he longed to be away, anywhere but here, listening to that honied voice of hers . . . A drop of sweat trickled down his forehead into his eye and he brushed it away with a nervous flick.

'Ploys like that don't slow us down. There will be no inquiry, no investigation. You have succeeded in nettling me a little, that's all, but I'm a mother and if you couldn't find my one soft spot you'd be marked down as stupid, and you're not stupid, Povin.'

He realized that she was aware of his physical pain. She was savouring it to the full. The knowledge brought him obscure comfort. It meant there would be no formal punishment. This was the end of it. He had made her blaze with a moment's anger and fear — all for what?

'And because you are *not* stupid, Povin, you realize that now we shall go back to what we were discussing last week, and I will ask you questions about Stolyinovich, and you will answer them, precisely, accurately, quickly. So, the truth. Did . . . you . . . sleep . . . with him?'

Since she began the speech her voice had dropped a full octave and her eyes had become orbs of liquid light which seemed to move closer, now farther away. Before he could help himself Povin began to speak as if in response to a command.

'No. It was never that kind of relationship. He had plenty of lovers, and I . . . I wasn't interested in the sexual side of things. The occasional woman, yes, oh yes . . . but hardly ever on a regular basis.' He looked down at his hands, suddenly awkward. 'Does that deal with the question?'

'Admirably. Do you regret not wanting to sleep with him, by the way?'

'How did you know that?'

'Not difficult. Now. Pyotr Stolyinovich was the best friend you ever had in the world, is that not right?'

'Certainly.'

'Yet you constantly risked his life by running him as your courier.'

'He wanted to do it.' A sour blend of pain and anxiety spurred Povin into the semblance of animation. His voice, hesitant at first, began to acquire something of its former authority. 'He was perfect for the job: easy ingress and egress, international contacts all over the world, a fop, a pansy, by definition about as dangerous as a white mouse. Also, it would have been very hard to lose Stolyinovich — the West would've asked too many questions. Or so I thought,' he added bitterly.

'You never felt the slightest twinge of guilt at what you asked him to do?'

'Aach! You remind me of Bryant.'

Inna, realizing how quickly he was retrieving lost ground, went on in a rush, 'And why is that?'

'He used to think I couldn't be a real Roman Catholic

129

because I slept with women when I felt like it.' Povin shook his head in genuine bewilderment, the pain momentarily forgotten. 'I never could make him see that things are relative. Even the Pope is only quite a good man, as the Pope would usually be the first to admit. Yes, Pyotr was my friend. He was also an adult. He approved of what I was doing, which in essence was to betray only when world security called for it, and he offered to help. I let him. What's wrong with that for an analysis?'

Inna nodded. They were both holding their ground now. It struck her that the relationship was developing an equilibrium all of its own, and she made a mental note to consider the implications of that when she was by herself.

'I'll tell you what's wrong with it, if you like,' said Povin.

Inna had been about to pass on to something else, but now she checked herself. 'Well?'

The old man hesitated. Inna looked up impatiently and saw that the expression on his face was troubled. 'I shouldn't have let him. What I just told you, it's not the end of the subject, not by a long way. People don't always know what's good for them. Sometimes you have to protect them from themselves.'

Like the boys, he was thinking. Like the military cadets seduced by Zuyev and 'Stoly'.

'You knew him for many years.'

'Oh yes.'

'He, too, was a Christian.'

'Yes. One of his boyfriends had religion bad. Something else that Bryant wouldn't have understood.'

'Is that why he wanted to help you — because he was a Christian?'

'Part of it.'

'It would have required enormous motivation to run such phenomenal risks.'

'Oh, he never knew exactly what he was carrying. Not the details. And I left him right out of the two biggest trades I ever made.'

'Which were?'

'*You* know. Lyalin. And Kyril'

'You regard them as the two biggest?'

130

'Of course! One hundred and five of our diplomats expelled from London in 1971; that was my fault. Pavlov in Montreal — gone! General Vladimirov in Helsinki — gone! That was down to me too. Then take Kyril: all the Kremlin Kommandant's ciphers betrayed to Sir Richard Bryant, Head of the English Secret Intelligence Service; who did it? Me. *Not* Stolyinovich, you understand? Povin.'

He was angry and proud and at the same time ashamed. Inna decided to risk a foray into one of the old man's more fascinating grey areas.

'Music. Were you fond of music before you met him?'

Povin's preternaturally acute antennae suddenly picked up a subtle change in the atmosphere. The woman was doodling on her notepad, as if the answer to her question was of but marginal interest. He looked down again and debated within himself. It might be nothing, it might be trivial, but . . .

Kazin wants to know something. *Something you don't know you know*!

'Oh, music. What a question.'

After a while Inna realized that this was meant to stand as the old man's reply. For an indecisive moment she continued to fiddle with her pencil; then she must have reached some conclusion for she said sharply, 'It doesn't matter. Time's up, Povin. But I'll be coming back to Stolyinovich, don't doubt it. And Povin . . .'

He had already reached the doorway, where the guard was waiting to collect him. He turned back with marked reluctance.

'. . . Remember your Pioneer's oath. You'd better.'

Her own face remained expressionless but the old man could not help smiling. Then he turned to see Alexander the Chechen looming over the guard's shoulder, and he smiled no longer.

14

'The doctor wants to examine you again,' said the guard. 'You're to go to the hospital.' Povin nodded, unable to take his eyes off the Chechen's rounded face, and began to walk down the passage. When he reached the staircase Alexander drew level with him; Povin shied away and discovered that the guard had disappeared.

'I'm to take you.' The Chechen's voice was unusually soft. Povin nodded a reluctant assent, but his mind didn't go with the action. Alexander had never gone to such lengths to be alone with him before. He was starting to feel apprehensive.

The hospital consisted of three rooms on the ground floor of the dacha's west wing, the side farthest from the interrogation unit. The old man used the walk to try and dredge up all he could remember about the Chechens. It wasn't encouraging.

As a people they were ungovernable, even the KGB acknowledged that. They were a law unto themselves. If you didn't like that you could face their vendetta — and good luck to you! A Chechen respected only two things: his council of elders and the law of the knife. Once the council had given the command to kill the death of the victim was assured.

Povin found himself sidling ever closer to the wall of the passage. Until today, Alexander had always appeared to be some kind of bizarre ally. Now the atmosphere had subtly changed and Povin was no longer sure.

Kengir. When the special camp erupted into mutiny, the Chechens alone among all the inhabitants of the exile settlement at nearby Dzhezkazgan supported the rebels; yet the MVD hadn't dared move against them. 'None of our

132

business,' they declared, burying their heads in the monthly statistics. It was their business — but they knew that if they moved against the Chechens they might wake up in the morning to find their own children's throats slit, and that was even more their business. So the rebellion at Dzhezkazgan went unquelled; and when the tanks finally rolled into Kengir Special Camp to crush the mutiny the Chechens' participation in it was somehow conveniently overlooked.

Povin wiped the sweat from his forehead with the sleeve of his jacket. They were nearly at the hospital, thank god. Soon he would be free of the silent spectre by his side and then he could breathe again. The devil rot all those who were responsible for colonizing the Chechen people . . .

'In here.'

Alexander stepped aside to let Povin enter the day ward. An orderly, himself a zek, was busy counting sheets piled up on the floor, but one glance at the Chechen's face was enough to tell him that the tally could wait. He slipped out past Povin, hugging the wall and averting his eyes. If this was the prelude to a murder — not the first in Ristikent MU/12 — he didn't want to be a witness.

The old man reached out to grab him. 'Hey listen. I need to see the doctor —' But the orderly wrenched his arm away and scuttled along the passage until he was out of sight and earshot of whatever was going to happen next.

Alexander closed the door and leaned his back against it. Povin stared at him in silence for a moment; then, 'Doctor!' he cried. But there was no answer.

The white-tiled ward was an ominously bare storeroom which doubled up as a dispensary where the doctor saw his daily intake of patients for routine complaints, before giving them the stark option of getting back to work or taking ten days' solitary. Three of the walls were stacked to the ceiling with shelves containing sheets, bedding, miscellaneous articles of paramedical utility such as overalls and rubber gloves. But there were no syringes or scalpels, not even a single bottle of medicine which could be thrown or smashed into razor-sharp shivs.

No window either. And no escape.

Alexander extended one arm. Povin followed the line and saw that the Chechen was pointing at the bare examination couch. He hesitated only a second before moving across to it.

'Lie down on your stomach. You'll be more comfortable that way.'

Povin was slightly reassured. This didn't sound like the beginning of a death sentence. A trap? No. The Chechen could break his neck with a flick of his fingers, he didn't need to put the old man at a disadvantage first.

Povin gingerly hoisted himself on to the couch and lay down with a groan. For a long time nothing happened. Alexander maintained his position by the door, leaning his back against it in such a way that no one would be able to get in. But nobody tried to get in, and nobody would. The orderly had had plenty of time to spread the word. The hospital seemed to be cut off from the rest of the house. No sound penetrated the closed, stuffy room.

'You want doctor? Here. Better than doctor.'

Povin screwed his head round to see that the Chechen had moved silently away from the door and was standing level with the old man's waist. Vodka. He had taken a bottle of vodka from the capacious pocket of his padded jacket and was holding it out. For a moment Povin couldn't grasp what he was being offered; then he snatched it with a croak of gratitude and swigged three tots in quick succession.

It wasn't rubbish, either, but the real thing: Stolichnaya, or just as good, although the bottle didn't have a label. Where in hell had that come from? Never mind, it felt wonderful.

The Chechen, seeing him hesitate, laughed aloud. 'Go on. Take. Take more. Nothing to be afraid of here. The others, they think I'm going to slit your throat. Let them . . . then maybe they'll stay away, eh? Drink!'

Povin obeyed, then checked himself. The last thing he wanted to do was lose consciousness. He wasn't used to vodka, not nowadays.

'Smoke?'

He shook his head. Alexander leisurely drew out a packet of cigarettes — proper smokes, not what passed for tobacco in the compound — and lit up. He smoked for a while in silence, leaving Povin to enjoy the savour of fine Latakia. The old man felt his treacherous body relax a fraction.

'You saved my life back there.' Alexander sucked down some smoke and said nothing. 'Thank you.'

The Chechen shrugged. 'Maybe I had a reason. Normally I don't like KGB, Povin.'

The old man's heart stopped beating for the space of a second before doubling its former rate. The room was going round and round. 'How do you know my name?' he asked very quietly.

'Everyone here has a name. Only the bosses use numbers.'

'You know what I mean.' The old man's voice wavered. 'My surname.'

'I have got reasons.'

So. He had been right, then. Kazin had given him his own personal minder, together with a full set of instructions. *Why?*

'You up to talking?'

When Povin failed to reply the Chechen leaned down to see if he was still conscious. 'Eh? You awake, KGB man?'

'I'm listening. You talk.'

Alexander laughed. Not a happy sound — an audible form of sneer. 'Why not?' he said. 'It's you with the problems. What keeps you going, Povin? Your god, eh? Must be. Has to be something to keep you going with the problems you got. You, not me.'

'You're right.' The old man was slowly recovering his composure. He had courage enough and here was an opportunity to learn something which he dare not pass up. 'You don't belong in this camp. You're not one of us.'

'No. Not *important* enough. I've got my orders and a job to do. Same as triple-oh-eight.'

Povin's neck stiffened. 'Who *is* he?'

Alexander smoked quietly for a while. 'Does name Kulikov mean anything to you?'

Povin sent his mind racing back over his past life, searching for a face. His memory had never failed him yet. After a while he was forced to abandon the exercise and shake his head.

135

The name Kulikov had no connotations for him.

'Father first deputy editor of *Pravda*, or some such mush. So they tell me. Got it now?'

Povin frowned. At the mention of Kulikov's job the name did ring a soft bell, but there was nothing sinister about the connection. Kulikov . . .

'No.'

'Well try another name, then. Michaelov. General Michaelov.' Alexander dropped the butt of his cigarette on to the floor and ground it out. 'Nice work you did there, Povin. Throw all the blame on to your boss, take his job. Nice. Like Frolov do to you later, eh? Not so nice for Michaelov, though.'

Povin could think of nothing to say. Alexander leaned down close to his face, his eyes filled with curiosity. Something about the old man seemed to excite him. 'Not so nice for Michaelov's family, eh? For his wife. For his daughter. For . . . Olga.'

Povin's brain was stirring now. He didn't know the answer, not yet, but at last he saw the line and knew he could follow it.

'This Kulikov knew Olga,' he ventured.

'Got it.'

'Knew her well.'

'*Very* well. Same class, same social scene, both young. She was a good fuck, they say. If you didn't mind the drugs and the tantrums. Kulikov liked to fuck her. Shit. He *loved* her!' The Chechen's face wore a bemused expression, as if there was no accounting for taste. 'She used to like the fucking also.'

'What happened?'

Alexander rose and began to walk up and down the room with a measured tread. He looked as if he too had to think this thing through properly.

'You didn't hear?'

'No.'

The Chechen spent a long time brooding on that. At last he seemed satisfied that it represented the truth, for he said, 'No. That's right. They said they hadn't told you that.'

136

From his position on the couch Povin couldn't see the man's face but suddenly he found the tone of his voice reassuring. The Chechen also wanted to know.

'The boy was connected with the girl. Frolov traced her. You remember *that* name, eh? Frolov, your deputy? He found Olga Michaelov, and she helped him find you. She was in the house the night Kazin told her father all about you. She was upstairs. Screwing.'

'With . . . Kulikov.'

'With *Lev* Kulikov. Lev zero zero zero eight.'

'With . . .?'

'That's right, KGB man.'

'And Olga heard . . .'

'And *he* heard . . . everything.'

There was a long silence. Povin had no doubt that the Chechen was telling him the absolute truth — as it had been told to him.

'So there was some clearing up to do, wasn't there?' Alexander continued to pace up and down the small room, staring at the floor. 'The first one Frolov swept under the carpet was Olga. Then he had to follow through with Lev Kulikov.'

'I understand about Kulikov now,' Povin said slowly. 'This is just the kind of place they'd send him — son of a high-ranking Party official, it all fits. But Olga? Where's she?'

'Underground. Six feet deep, where it's very cold.' The Chechen stopped pacing. 'Frolov had her shot. And the boy knew that. He saw it.'

'*Saw* it?'

'They made him watch. That's what they tell me. It was Frolov's idea. He knew how much the boy liked screwing her.' Again the slightly bemused look. 'How much he loved her.'

It was on the tip of the old man's tongue to ask why they hadn't shot the boy at the same time when suddenly he saw why. He understood everything and wished he didn't.

'They made him watch,' the Chechen repeated. 'Frolov was still tidying up. He'd got your job, he'd become a general, everything was fine. You knew a whole heap of things about him but what the hell — you wouldn't be around much

137

longer. So Frolov sat back comfortably and waited for Kazin to have you shot. But for some reason — ' Alexander lowered himself to a crouch, so that his eyes were level with Povin's — 'for some unimaginable reason . . .'

'He didn't.'

The Chechen smiled, revealing two uneven rows of sharp-looking yellow teeth. 'That is right, KGB man. He didn't. And Frolov got nervous. He began to wonder why. Until after a while it wasn't enough to wonder. He had to do something about it.'

Povin closed his eyes. It all fitted — well, nearly all. Frolov very badly needed to get rid of Povin, but Kazin wanted the old man alive. Frolov got tired of waiting. So he installed Kulikov in the camp without Kazin's knowledge, and told the boy that the traitor who'd brought about Olga's death was working in the bakery.

No, it didn't quite fit.

'Kazin knows he's here,' he said quietly; and Alexander the Chechen smiled again.

'You and me,' he whispered. 'We think the same.' He stood up very slowly, flexing his taut muscles. 'In some ways. That's why I tell you this, Povin. I'm being used. I don't like that. It upsets me. No reason why I should have to know all these things — better I don't know, eh? Safer . . . So then I say to myself: why not ask KGB man? He understands about suchlike.'

'What will happen to Kulikov now?' It was Povin's voice that broke the silence, but Alexander seemed to find the question equally interesting. He wheeled round to face the couch and the old man saw that his eyebrows were raised in amusement.

'You guess.'

Povin thought. For an assault on a prisoner the penalty was usually a month in the isolator followed by strict regime. The boy had used a knife, which made things worse. Three months' solitary? But when he said it aloud the Chechen merely laughed.

'Seventy-two hours in the cooler, then assigned to morgue duty.'

138

Povin rolled off his stomach and sat up. Something was going very badly wrong. 'Frolov . . .?'

'No. You think so?'

Povin was forced to shake his head. Even if Frolov had given birth to the idea originally, now it was Kazin's by adoption. But then, why go to endless trouble arranging for the Chechen to act as his minder? It made no sense.

'There's a lot of coming and going at this place,' said Alexander. 'Average time for a zek here's only a week. Maybe they'll take you too. Who knows? Better pray for it, old man. Better pray they take you *soon*.'

Povin eased himself off the couch, keeping his face averted from the watchful Chechen whose words had sparked off an idea in the old man's mind. Take him away, would they? Perhaps he could save them the trouble . . .

'So now you know what I know, Povin.' Alexander was standing by the door again but this time he was reaching for the handle. 'Think it over, let me know what the hell is happening. You see a lot of me from now on. Better hope I'm fast enough.' His fleshy lips curved in a contemptuous sneer. 'One thing certain. *Zuyev* won't be.'

Povin smiled at him. It suited the old man very well to have his relationship with Zuyev duly noted, although the Chechen couldn't have known that. By all means let Kazin concentrate on his connection with Zuyev and miss the real point . . .

Alexander threw open the door and stood aside to let the old man leave. Then next second Povin was in the corridor and Alexander was . . . the old man looked round . . .

Alexander was nowhere. He had disappeared.

Povin turned this way and that but the passage was empty. His lips parted, one hand leaped to the nape of his neck and again his heart tripped into high gear. Had he dreamed everything? No — the vodka was still sloshing about inside him, exuding its last residue of comforting warmth. Alexander had been real enough. But his story . . .

His story. Was *that* real? Did Alexander belong to Frolov? To Kazin? Whoever had told him that remarkable story must have been very close to the top. Povin wanted time to think about these things, a lot of time. Unfortunately, however, he had less than three days in which to make up his mind about them. Because in another seventy-two hours Lev Kulikov, half-blind in one eye and obsessed with the desire for vengeance, was going to be on the loose.

Assigned — Povin mentally saluted Kazin's macabre sense of humour — to morgue duties.

15

Inna Karsovina slouched in the back seat of the old Moskvich as it bounced its way through the last few miles of darkness which separated her from the prison compound by the side of Lake Not, vainly trying to sleep. It had been a wretched weekend, and then she had been obliged to stop over in Murmansk for a meeting with the Project Committee. With 'them'. She couldn't tell if they thought she was making progress or not; 'they' were invariably noncommittal. 'He knows something,' they repeated, with their usual cynical smiles. 'Yet he doesn't know what it is that he knows. You must help him find out. We've decided to keep him alive; tell him that, if you like.'

Were they playing straight by her? Inna didn't know. 'Why did the zek attack Povin?' she asked them. 'What steps have you taken to ensure his safety? Why aren't you going to shoot him, after all?' But the faces behind the fixed smiles were tightly closed.

She was becoming more and more confused. Twice now she had felt Povin reach out invisible fingers to beckon her; on two occasions she had watched, fascinated, as her mind abandoned the rest of whatever it was that made Inna Karsovina whole and began a weird dance towards that spectral, beckoning hand. Strange how his nascent power over her seemed to march step by step in time with Anfisa's growing ascendancy over Volodiya . . .

Mothers!

At last they reached the camp. Inna lay down on her bed exhausted, but her brain wouldn't let her relax. She tossed and turned this way and that, fretfully dreading the advent of dawn and yearning for sleep to come. Volodiya, Povin, 'them' . . . no respite, no rest, no peace.

It was five o'clock in the morning when the phone rang, rescuing her from some shapeless, incoherent nightmare.

'Karsovina.'

She struggled in vain to still the violent beating of her heart. Kazin had begun to seem more threatening than any nightmare. Dark, atavistic memories rushed to the forefront of her conscious mind: the call in the middle of the night, the dreaded knock at the door . . .

'Karsovina, are you awake?'

'Yes, Comrade Chairman.'

'I have here the short-range weather report for the Murmansk region. It's going to be a fine day. He needs some fresh air and exercise. So do you. Take him out for a walk.'

The line went dead immediately. Inna held the receiver away from her ear and stared at it. She wanted to shake the instrument, strangle it, do anything to make it disgorge more words — but there was nothing.

She sank back on to the bed and stared at the ceiling. After a while she fell into a dream-laden doze which brought no benefit but served only to make her late for the morning session. Povin was already waiting for her when she entered the interrogation room. He rose at once, and although he kept his face downcast she knew that he was silently assessing her dissipated appearance. She flushed with anger at the thought that he might misunderstand and before she could stop herself had flared, 'You needn't look at me like that! I couldn't sleep, that's all.'

His head jerked up in amused surprise and Inna squeezed her fingernails into her palms. But the look on his face was an insult and her next words come out in a flood.

'You know what makes me want to spit? The waste. Christ, what a waste.' (Somewhere deep inside her head a cold voice mildly queried whether she had in fact said 'Christ'.) 'Ninety

141

per cent of what you did for the Motherland was brilliant. Yet you had to throw it all away. Why?'

In the silence that followed Inna Karsovina knew real shame. That outburst had been unforgivable. Worse than unforgivable: unprofessional. It endangered the work. Nothing could justify that.

Except, perhaps, one thing: she meant every word of it. And she cared passionately about his answer.

'Citizen Karsovina, I think you will find that in the top right-hand drawer of your desk there are cigarettes. If you will permit me to enjoy one of those cigarettes, I can more readily give you an answer to your question.'

His eyes held hers with almost malignant intensity. 'You . . . you don't smoke,' Inna said stupidly. Damn this headache . . .

'I didn't. Not when I first came from freedom. That is how we zeks speak of it, did you know that? "From freedom." It means not a physical transition but a state of mind. A newly arrested prisoner is still in freedom, even though his body is confined. It takes time to come from freedom. It requires help. Cigarettes help. In prison they are a bond, a common language, currency, pleasure. And someone in my position is hardly frightened of lung cancer, or concerned by the loss of his tastebuds. That small sacrifice opened many doors. I would like a cigarette. If you please, Citizen Interrogator.'

He was very different this morning: immeasurably stronger and without that false humility which so often drove her wild.

Like a patient under hypnosis Inna watched with dispassionate interest as her right hand crept along the surface of the desk to the drawer and pulled it open. It was as Povin said, there were cigarettes. How did he know that?

He leaned back and inhaled, drawing the smoke deep into his lungs with evident pleasure. Inna realized that he had merely chosen to put the conversation on 'hold', without yet giving her liberty to speak.

'I had a lot of hope, once,' the old man went on reminiscently. 'This bears on your question, by the way — you know, the one about why the waste. When I was young, I hoped for great things from Russia. Much as you do still.' He rested an elbow on the desk and watched the smoke drift through his fingers up to the ceiling. 'Forgive me, Citizen Karsovina, but you remind me very much of Yevtushenko's Sonka. You remember "The First Wave" . . .?'

> *Mother's homemade rolls*
> *were stuffed into my rucksack . . .*
> *Taiga, my new mother,*
> *please accept me in your family!*

'Such idealism, such enthusiasm. I have always thought of that as very beautiful, very moving. And you reminded me of the lines, right from the first day . . .'

'Cut out all the shit, Povin.' But her voice was listless and the old man scarcely paused for long enough to demolish her fitful attempt to re-establish control by enveloping her in a look of contemptuous pity.

'I think, if you don't mind — ' he stopped and delicately picked a strand of tobacco from his tongue before continuing '— that we have reached a point where it is you who should . . . cut out the shit. No!' He raised both hands, palms towards her, commanding silence. (Commanding, or so it later seemed to her, total obedience in all things.) 'You continually ask me questions and then pass on without either considering or even waiting for a reply. This morning, like it or not, you shall have an answer.'

Inna adopted a bored expression and sat back with her hands folded in her lap, like a good child. Povin mentally applauded the brave attempt at irony and continued.

'But like Sonka, there came a moment when I was no longer sure. Well, there were many moments, I don't know why I confine myself to one. But let me tell you of it, anyway. When I was still a young man I commanded a small interrogation cell in Ryazan. There wasn't much to do so we had to make our own amusement. One night we picked up a boy, oh, eighteen or so, and gave him the treatment. You'll find the incident in there — ' he gestured with his half-smoked cigarette at the folders by Inna's side and went on — 'it's very well documented, in fact. He began to pray, so the *gaybists* I was privileged to command killed him. Incidentally, one of them was called Volodiya . . . And you know what I did, citizen? I acquiesced.'

Povin seemed to be winding down. He had begun on a high, commanding pitch, so as to get her whole attention, but now his tone was becoming more conversational.

'I bought it, in other words. I raised no complaints, I criticized no one. Now let me tell you what I should have done.'

Povin's chair grated on the floor as he leaned forward to dislodge a pellet of ash from the cigarette. Their eyes met and he smiled his usual polite smile, as if to say, 'Are you enjoying all this, I hope I'm not boring you?' Inna's face remained unresponsive, but she was not bored. Seeing that, he continued with his story.

'I ought to have gone out into the parade ground and summoned my cell and made them witness the execution of the two bullies who had killed that wholly innocent boy, and then I should have taken my ceremonial sword and drawn a line, so . . .'

Povin moved his forefinger through the air, squinting at it as if anxious to ensure the most perfect accuracy.

'. . . And then I should have said, "Now. Any of you who disagree with what I have done, who think I was wrong and those two corpses are right, to one side of the line I have drawn — there! And I will kill you and have done with it, no matter what the cost . . . " '

His tongue had protruded between his lips, so intent was he on the point of his finger, but now he looked up a fraction and transfixed Inna, so that she was looking straight at him, across the upraised finger.

'. . . No matter what the consequences to me may be; move across the line, and I will strike you . . . dead.'

As he spoke the last word Povin crooked the upraised finger and lowered his hand. 'That's what I ought to have done.'

Inna stirred and muttered, 'You certainly wouldn't be sitting there now, if you had.'

'How funny you should say that. Stolyinovich was the same. "All this yak about conscience," he'd say. "What's the good, when all you'd have achieved is a quick suicide?" He

144

was right, of course. But still — funny you should say that, too.'

He stubbed out the cigarette, making a good job of it, until at last no more smoke rose from the butt.

'There is a God,' he said, with total conviction. 'I need not dwell on that, because you know it as well as I do.'

Inna felt that she should protest, but what was the use? This morning she lacked the resources to make a denial sound convincing.

'Even if there is no God, it is pointless to deny His existence to so many million devout Russians who do believe in Him and raise their children to believe in Him, and their children's children, to the end of eternity. Religious oppression did not stop with Stalin's death. I know that, you know that. Today, every day, people will be arrested, without recourse, for no crime except that they do not fit easily into this society which we have created. And children will be separated from their parents.'

He was starting to grow animated again.

'This will interest you, Citizen Karsovina. I have myself often supervised the separation of infants from their parents. In my youth it needed only a local Party chairman to declare that certain adults were anti-Soviet, and the iron law came into play. Remove the children, before they are corrupted! Isolate them! Quarantine them! To the orphanage! To the special school! To the asylum!'

With unexpected violence he banged his clenched fists on the table, making Inna jump out of her chair.

'*To be shot*!'

His mouth was drawn back in a snarl, the arcane rictus of the death's head, so that for a moment Inna knew real, stark terror; then the old man's face slowly relaxed and she resumed her seat, a little uncertainly, but at least in the knowledge that he had no desire to harm her. And after that there was silence in the room for a very long time.

'I would like to go out,' the woman said at last. 'Will you accompany me?'

It did not sound like a command.

145

'I am very tired,' she went on. 'Also, I have a headache. This room depresses me beyond words. I need to go out. I must go out.'

As she came round the desk he rose unsteadily to his feet, reluctantly but admiringly acknowledging that she knew how to seize the initiative when she chose. Inna suddenly found it very easy to obey Kazin's outrageous instruction. She had to get out in the fresh air, before she suffocated. If the old zek came with her, so be it.

They left the dacha by its imposing front entrance and turned right, past the bakery, their feet scrunching on the coarse grey scalpings of the drive. Povin shambled along half a step behind Inna, every so often stealing sideways glances in her direction. She was wearing a smart coat, he noticed, far too smart for a dump like this. It was pale camelhair with a belt which she tied in a careless knot, as if clothes bored her, yet she was always so well dressed. Povin folded his hands under his armpits, envying the woman her snow mitts.

Instead of following the drive round where it curved towards the main gate Inna struck off across the grass in the direction of the distant perimeter fence. They soon left the cookhouse behind them, but not before the old man had glimpsed the smart black Zhiguli racing past them towards the dacha. Comings and goings, all day every day; Alexander the Chechen was right about that. A flash of gold braid in the window indicated the usual top-ranking Party officials on their way to interrogate some other zek less fortunate than the old man. Later in the day that car would leave, perhaps taking the chosen prisoner with it. Povin shook his head; no good yearning . . .

They walked in silence until at last they reached the fence, a quarter of a mile from the house, and for a long time the two of them stared out at the bleak, empty landscape, filigreed with barbed wire, under a low, grey sky. To the right of them the fence dropped down the slope to the lake, extending into the placid water for a hundred metres or more. There was nothing to see except the lake and the near-flat moorland dotted with clumps of trees which surrounded the camp.

The woman was pale, her forehead sweaty; she looked ill.

She had mentioned a hell of a weekend. Was the child giving her trouble, he wondered? Did she have man problems? Money worries? She was human too. Compared with his miserable existence hers was a bed of roses, but that didn't mean she lacked cares. And was it possible that an awareness of her own untenable position had at last begun to dawn? He smiled. Perhaps — but Kazin didn't often make mistakes. This was like everything else. This was planned. This was danger.

Inna turned to her right and began to walk along the perimeter fence, hands in pockets, keeping her face to the outside world. She could not succeed in dislodging Povin's words from her memory. There was a grain of truth in what he said, more than a grain. His offence lay in speaking out loud what everybody knew. People were arrested for no good cause. The State did separate children from their parents. Was not Kazin even now driving a wedge between her and Volodiya . . .? Inna tossed her head and expelled a sigh. She had lost her bearings. No, that wasn't quite right. Her bearings had always been wrong . . .

To Povin she seemed as much a prisoner as he was, and not for the first time it crossed his mind that this was unsuitable work for a woman, certainly a woman with a young child and no husband. Suddenly she spoke, taking him unawares, so that he had to struggle to capture her line of thought.

'You have quite recovered? From the assault, I mean.'

'Oh yes, thank you. For a while I was like a boy who'd been beaten, but I soon got over it.'

'Do you know why he attacked you?'

'No.'

'I suppose you're lying, as usual.'

Povin smiled again. 'I don't lie. I cooperate, remember?'

Inna laughed sarcastically. 'Tell me, Povin, how does a man of your age keep going, mm? No hope, beatings, interrogation . . . why don't you just fold up?'

The old man shrugged. 'The obvious answer. Faith.'

'Is that all?'

'I think so. What other answer could there be? My faith is real, you know that by now. God listens.'

'Even to someone who's been as wicked as you?'

'Especially to people like me. The saints have all made it home. People like me are still running the course.'

'Why doesn't God help people like *me*, then?' Inna rounded on him. '*I've* never done the things you've done. I've always tried to lead a decent life. Yet you're the one who's calm and confident, not me. Is God always like that — choosing the scum?'

Povin considered it. 'I think so,' he said at last. 'If you want to attract God's attention it helps to be scum. Oh, and it helps to be old, too.'

'Yes,' Inna said dully. 'I think that's true. At least I know now why they chose me. I used to mock your photograph. "Father figure!" I'd scoff. But they were right. Oh my god, how they were right.' She snorted. 'Listen to me! God, indeed . . .'

'Photograph?'

'I keep it on my bedside table. Can you actually *believe* that? My mother says it gives her the willies. I don't blame her.'

'You live with your mother?'

'You didn't know that?' Her face was incredulous. 'You're lying. Or maybe not. I can never be sure now, can I.'

'I didn't know that. About your living with your mother, I mean. For the most part you're a closed book to me.'

'Really.'

'Yes,' he said seriously, ignoring the sarcasm. 'Really and truly.'

Inna continued to walk, kicking forward first one leg then the other, in the same mannered goose step that had caught his attention earlier. 'It's not always easy, living with a mother. But then you know that, of course.'

'You are right about the father figure,' Povin said after a while. 'That would appeal to them. You mustn't underestimate a father's power. Mine was always away; Volodiya's died. It's a recipe for a troubled soul. So when the interrogators supply a father figure it acts like a salve. People think of interrogation as being all kicks and blows. They couldn't be more wrong. Kicks and blows form only a tiny part of a real investigation. For someone like me, they're virtually useless.'

'Oh I know, I know. It doesn't require an IQ of a thousand to see that. With a man like you, it has to be very different. It's necessary to build a relationship, a real bond. There's only one problem.'

'What's that?'

'They haven't told me what they're after. I wish they would. Then we could do a deal.'

Povin presented her with a perplexed look. 'I don't understand.'

'It's not so difficult. You find me a pain in the arse. I can understand that, sympathize even; after all, you have the same effect on me. I want to get out, you want me out. You keep asking me to tell you what I want to know, so you can give me the answers and we can call it quits. But — I don't know the questions!'

In spite of himself, Povin could not help laughing. After a few moments Inna joined in, but half-heartedly, as if she was unable to see the real kernel of the joke.

'You make me feel nostalgic,' said Povin. 'Nothing ever changes. The KGB is incapable of real change, isn't it? "It worked for 'Iron' Felicks Dzerzhinsky, so it'll work for us." Of course, they wouldn't dream of telling you the real questions, because they know I'll use the bonds you forge to ferret the questions out. I used to be in exactly the same position myself.'

'You mean you never told your subordinates what you were really trying to discover?'

'I did, actually. I believed in giving the younger ones their heads — it used to drive Michaelov mad. No, what I meant was that when I was a youngster myself, no one ever trusted me. The high-ups only told me the bare minimum they thought they could get away with. Then, of course, they'd berate me for not getting the results they wanted.' He chuckled. 'Perhaps you haven't got to that part yet.'

Inna shrugged glumly. 'Christ only knows . . .'

'Ah, Christ . . .'

'. . . They just stare blankly down their noses at me and whisper among themselves. I didn't mean to say Christ.'

Povin decided to let it go. 'You're doing all right so far,' he said confidently. 'Look at us now. Just what the committee wants. Top marks.'

'Surely not? They'd have me shot for this. It's only because I'm not feeling well and I'm just a little fool anyway . . .'

'Quite wrong. This counts as distinct progress. Look.' Povin stopped and willed Inna to turn and face him. To his pleasurable surprise, she did so. 'If they'd wanted to hit me with the heavy stuff they'd hardly have chosen you, now would they?' His voice was kind. Inna vaguely noticed that today he seemed much less frail than usual. 'They chose you because you serve other purposes. Don't misunderstand me. There *are* women who can be brutal and bad, stupid women, I've met them. But you're not one of them. No, your job is quite different. Your task is to make friends with me, I know that. If I were Kazin I would send you to interrogate me — you and no one else.'

After a moment of irresolution Inna averted her eyes from his face and walked on. The old man's words rang true; Kazin had openly admitted as much. But then — what was the point of this incredible farce?

'I hate to say it,' she said abruptly, 'but there *are* times when you remind me of my father. You really do, you know.'

'Stop.'

'Why?'

'Because now you're indisputably playing their game for them. Are you sure you want that?'

'Of course.' She glanced at him with irritation. 'That's my job. I thought we were agreed that the sooner we got to the end of the road the better we'd both be pleased.'

'It's easy for you to say. I have to remember what's at the end of that road for me. Nine grammes of lead.'

Inna winced at the familiar Russian euphemism for a bullet. 'They're not going to shoot you.'

'No, of course not. They're going to hand out the Order of Lenin, along with time off for good behaviour.'

'They're not going to shoot you,' she repeated impatiently, as if to a dull child. 'Goodness knows why, but it's all arranged. Kazin briefed the Project Committee last weekend, and they were actually *kind* enough to inform me — for a change.'

It sounded so guileless that Povin stopped dead and stared after her as she walked on along the fence, seemingly lost in her own thoughts. Then, sensing his absence, she also stopped and turned back.

'So tell me,' he said as he came up to her. 'In what ways do I remind you of your father?'

Inna thought. 'He used to meet whatever I said with that same look of polite, bored attention,' she said at last. 'As if he didn't really give a toss, but I was his child and he was going to give me a few minutes of his precious time because that's what children deserved.' She smiled wanly. 'That's the main thing.'

'I see.' Povin considered it at length. 'It's a habit of mine. Nothing personal.'

'No, I gathered that. Perhaps it was the same with Father.'

'Anything else?'

'There are a few other things. The way you reacted to music, for instance.'

Music. *Music*. The old man's step did not falter, but again he felt that remarkable sense of having been brought into the presence of the master inquisitors, his nose suddenly hard up against the real purpose of the investigation. How far did he want to play Kazin's game for him?

'You talk of your father as if in the past,' he said quickly, anxious to steer her away from the danger zone.

'He's dead. Heart. He wasn't very old. He taught English at Moscow University. It was overwork that killed him. That, and the sadness. All he really wanted to do was play the piano: he was a frustrated musician. I don't know if he was any good, but his touch was exquisite. He taught me, when I was young.' She smiled, a little puff of vanity enlivening her face. 'He said I was good, better than he was, in fact.'

'Do you still play?'

Inna shook her head ruefully. 'No. The practising took up too much of my time.'

'Ah yes. Practice is everything. You must do it eight hours a day and more, or you're nothing.'

'That's right. That's what he said. I suppose Pyotr Stoly-inovich practised all the time?'

151

'Every day. It could be a terrible strain. We'd arrange to go somewhere, then he'd decide he hadn't practised enough and scream at me and, oh, it was awful sometimes. Have you noticed that everybody has a few friends who are quite frightful?'

'But not all the time.'

'Ah, you've got it. Just sometimes.'

'It sounds funny to hear you say it, though. I read all the files and I talk to people who used to know you, but I've hardly the least idea of what you were like in the evening, after work. You did relax sometimes, I suppose.'

'Quite a lot, actually. I have all the constitutional Russian laziness. I liked to drink and talk with friends, visit the Bolshoi, go for walks. And there were the records, of course. Thousands of them, by the end.'

He appeared to be paying no attention to her reactions but his sharp eyes missed nothing. The woman wasn't as good at keeping her thoughts to herself as she should be — but then, of course, the Chairman would have allowed for that. At the word 'records' her brow contracted in a frown, but she did not jerk her head towards him as he would have expected her to do if Kazin's briefing had been slanted in that direction. Well, it was only a wild guess on his part; nothing more than a random shot.

Time for a change of subject. 'You were very upset when your father died, I imagine.'

Inna nodded unhappily.

'So like me you had no adult male figure in your childhood.'

'None. There was Mother, and I had lots of aunts. Female teachers. No men, not until I . . .'

'Yes. Go on.'

'It doesn't matter.'

'Until you started going out with boys, is that what you were going to say?'

'*You* said it. You're the expert here. Always I must remind myself of that.' Her voice exuded heavy irony; Povin knew at once that she was parrotting some lesson or other. He pretended to adopt her attempt at humour.

152

'Yes, I'm the expert. Papa knows best. Were there many boys?'

'What do you think?'

He treated the question seriously. 'Not many.'

'Right. One, in fact.'

'That doesn't surprise me. Concentrate the energies, do one job thoroughly. Very laudable.'

'You think so? Mother didn't think so. "Play the field," she'd say. "At your age, that's the best thing." She was right, too. I should've listened to Mamma. You know what happened to Leonid, of course, you said so a moment ago.'

Povin hesitated only a second. 'Of course. Overkill, as usual. Kazin could have had him sent to a camp at the other end of the universe. There was absolutely no need to murder him.'

'Don't talk rubbish, Povin.' The words came out roughly, but somehow they didn't match the sadness in her eyes. The old man was not at all perturbed.

'You'll come to accept it, in time. They've told you they won't shoot me, but they will. On that day, you'll also accept what Kazin did to Leonid.'

'They're not going to shoot you.' Her voice was petulant, the voice of a teacher who cannot make her class learn by rote. 'I've worked it out for myself. It's quite logical, really. They haven't got the guts. You're a . . . a walking encyclopedia. An encyclopedia of Soviet intelligence, going back thirty years. They know damn well that the day after they buried you they'd need you for something and come running, only then it'd be too late, wouldn't it? They can't afford to take that chance. So, it's exile for you, old man. Somewhere frightful, I dare say — they haven't told me where, so don't waste your breath asking.'

Povin walked for several paces without replying. Plainly this was yet another trap; he had long ago abandoned any hope of survival. And yet . . . The girl's words made some kind of tangled sense. Not because he was a walking encyclopedia, but because Kazin should have shot him years ago . . .

'Killing's out of fashion,' said Inna. She had come to a halt by one of the legs of a perimeter watchtower and was resting her back against its splintery wood. 'They let Stolyinovich live, you know.'

There was a second of silence, during which Inna's mind jumped ahead to another topic. What followed was therefore all the more profoundly shocking to her.

'Liar!' snapped Povin. 'Stolyinovich is dead. Many interrogators have told me so, many times. Liar, liar, *liar*!'

Inna reeled under this unexpected onslaught. She could not begin to understand what was happening. During the past hour she had been inhabiting a world in which, despite its falseness, terms like 'interrogator' and 'zek' had lost some of their meaning. Against all the imaginable odds a fragile skein of respect had begun to weave its subtle way between her and this human relic of the past. Now the skein was broken, leaving Inna without any defence against the tidal wave of Povin's anger which reared over her hapless head.

'They were the liars,' she protested weakly. 'Kazin himself told the committee. He's alive, I tell you . . .'

For an instant the wave surged to the very edge of her consciousness and she was aware of nothing except Povin's demented eyes; then he was striding across the boggy grass in the direction of the bakery, leaving Inna to stare after him in amazement, with the shattered remnants of the tender skein lying in the slush by her feet.

But the old man was far from being amazed. Now at last, in spite of rage and grief, the answers to many mysteries were becoming clear to him. Kazin wanted a name. And there was nothing, *nothing* he would not do to get it.

16

On his previous, infrequent visits to England Victor had never strayed outside London. There he felt at home; one big capital city is very like another in its fundamental aspects. Seaside parochialism was a new and not very enlivening experience. He sat on the promenade at Eastbourne, coat collar turned up against the cold, and looked suspiciously about him. Notwithstanding drizzly squalls from the grey-brown sea, the front was crowded. Victor had never seen so many decrepit old people in his life. In the past quarter of an hour he had watched in disbelief as the halt, the lame and the blind paraded before him, their snail-like progress ample proof that all men are mortal. Where were the children, he asked himself in irritation? How could these ancient crones and wizards be expected to manage by themselves, at eighty, ninety — his outraged stare strayed to an arthritic old woman, walking, if that was the right word, with the aid of a frame — a hundred?

Victor snatched an impatient look at his watch. He didn't care for Eastbourne. Apart from the extreme age of most of its inhabitants it was impossible to get a drink in the afternoon, and if there were whores they kept away from the one place where you'd expect to find them — the street.

Bryant was late. Victor angrily shook his watch. Suddenly he became aware of a new presence and he looked up quickly to find himself no longer alone on the hard wooden bench.

'Sorry to have kept you. My Masonic lunch went on rather too long and then I wanted to change.'

'I was getting worried.'

'Sorry.' Bryant sounded genuinely contrite. He was wearing a dark brown suit over a mustard-coloured waistcoat, with a matching handkerchief stuffed carelessly in his top pocket and a trilby half a size too small perched precariously on the crown of his head. Victor gazed at him with grudging professional admiration. Bryant blended into his background like a chameleon. He sat bolt upright, hands on knees, and looked about him with the fierce look of a naval commander on his own bridge.

'I thought this place would be a good deal less conspicuous than in London. Margaret and I own a house up towards Beachy Head. Either your compatriots in Kensington have not yet discovered my seaside retreat or they are sporting enough to leave it alone.'

Victor's eyes flickered sideways. 'You are not under surveillance here?'

'No. Not as far as we are aware. There is a famous saying about this place: a man goes down to Eastbourne to die, and then forgets what he went down for. Perhaps the KGB are of that opinion also; they do not follow me here.' Bryant raised his hands from his knees and examined the backs of the fingers. 'You asked to see me. I'm listening.'

'I need some information before I can make a decision.'

Bryant screwed up his lips and Victor sensed that he was forcing himself to listen, to pay a price long foreseen and often dreaded. 'Go on,' he said eventually.

'I want to know a little more about my employer. At the moment he's making me uneasy. I don't like that. I want you to tell me: why exactly are you doing this?'

Bryant lifted his head and stared out to sea, thus enabling Victor to study him in profile. A strong, determined chin, he noticed; not an altogether easy man to deal with, or so the general had said . . .

'You know of course that Povin and I had . . . have a link. Something in common.'

'The religious thing. Yes, I knew that.'

'There is a parable about the good — '

'The Samaritan, yes, I know my Bible, I had a Russian mother, remember?' Victor did not mean to sound unkind but his words evidently stung, for Bryant said roughly, 'If you're going to ask impertinent questions you might

156

at least have the grace to listen to the answers!'

Victor smiled, but did not apologize. 'All right,' he said. 'Explain to me about the Samaritan.'

'Isn't it obvious? Povin's in the ditch and I don't want to pass by on the other side.'

'Because you're both Catholics?' Victor didn't bother to try to hide his scepticism. 'Is that all?'

'It is not all. But it's bound up with everything else. It's not in my nature to abandon with a shrug someone who has laboured to help me for so long, without thanks, without hope of personal gain. Someone whom I . . . liked.'

'But never met? Or only a couple of times.'

'Someone whom I liked,' Bryant repeated mechanically to the open sea.

Victor let him sit in silence for a while. Then he said, 'Guilt.'

'What?'

'You dropped him in the shit. If it wasn't for you, he'd be back in Moscow right now, wouldn't he? Listening to the pianist play Mozart.'

Bryant might have been turned to stone. He didn't look at Victor. The longer the silence endured, the more curious Victor became as to Bryant's eventual response. 'You know what?' he said at last. 'You just answered my question.'

Bryant turned and subjected the Russian to a haughty, contemptuous stare. 'Did I?' he murmured. 'Yes. Yes, I suppose I did.' He jutted out his lower lip, a man determined to drain the bitter dregs to the very end. 'What else do you want to know?'

'Nothing.'

'I see.' Bryant seemed resigned. 'And that, I suppose, is the end of it, as far as you're concerned.'

'Yes.'

'Then . . . I'm sorry to have troubled you with such a wearisome journey. Naturally I shall reimburse you your expenses.'

'I don't understand what the hell you're talking about, God.'

'I thought you said . . .'

'It's the end of it, yes. I wanted to be sure and now I am. I'll do it. I'll try and get him for you.'

'Why?' Bryant's voice, harsh and cold, rapped out like a parade-ground command. 'Why should my guilt bear on you?'

Victor answered without hesitation. 'Because it makes me very sure of you, that's why. Even though I can't understand what you've got to be guilty about; after all, the General was an adult. But at least I know you're not going to back out on me at crucial moments. Your motives *matter*!' He swung his body round so that he was facing Bryant directly along the bench, his face very close to that of the older man. 'If it was greed, or professional ambition, or anything to do with the General being a KGB man, a spy, then I wouldn't even attempt it. Not for anything you could offer me! If it was religion . . .' Victor flicked his head to one side and casually spat. 'That's what I think of your religion. But it's none of those things. It's guilt. And coming from a man like you, that *means* something, don't you see? Your guilt's worth all the money and all the power and all the threats and terror in the world! Because you feel it. Because you . . .' He raised his clenched fists to the sky and shut his eyes, casting about for the precise, the exact word. 'Because you *suffer*!'

Victor opened his eyes to see a reticent smile wind its way across Bryant's lips. 'And you,' he said gently to the Russian. 'What are your motives, I wonder?'

Victor shrugged again. 'Oh. Loyalty. Boredom. A bit of love, maybe. General Stepan could be a crook and a bastard when he chose, but he was one hell of a master. And I liked it. We Russians do, that's right, eh? We like to be told what to do, and we can put up with the knout when we're slack. I miss all that. So I'm going to try and get him for you. But don't expect too much, that's all.'

Bryant inhaled a very deep breath and blew it out through puffed lips. 'You don't seem very confident.'

'I'm not. I know who I'm dealing with. The chances are virtually nil, you know that, don't you?'

Bryant nodded.

'But some risks are worse than the ones I'll run. Yours, for instance.'

'Mine?'

'Sure. If you go along with this your neck's on the block. I have requirements. Physical requirements which only you can meet — and the most pressing of those is manpower.'

'Manpower?'

'I want Lambe. I want him wholesale, permanent.'

Bryant's face clouded at the memory of Lambe's recent telex. 'I'm afraid I couldn't possibly sanction one of my own men penetrating the Soviet Union in a mission of this kind.'

Victor shook his head impatiently. 'No, no, you don't understand. I need Lambe strictly on the outside. I must have someone in charge of the operation on the ground in Norway, someone I can trust.'

'And you feel you can trust Lambe.'

Victor nodded emphatically. 'Yes.'

Bryant sighed and slowly shook his head. 'It's not as easy as you might think. I *must* contain this project within the smallest possible compass.'

'Of course. But you also have to get me out, along with the General. And you can't do that unless there's a man up there on the ground.'

'But I thought you'd try to get him out alone . . .'

'No. Not possible. We have no information as to the General's physical state. Who knows, maybe he can't even walk. I need a plane, God. A two-seater, low-flying Harrier . . .'

'My gód!' The words were ripped out of Bryant's chest against his will. 'You must be insane!'

'Not insane. You want him out, that's how he comes out. Now perhaps you see why I had to be sure of you, eh? You want him out and I'm willing to try. But you'd better get used to the idea that *I* dictate the arrangements.'

Even as he spoke Bryant's mind went hurtling into the realm of logistics. It was possible, of course it was *possible*, such things had happened in the past; problems only ever occurred when something went wrong. And what if something went wrong now? They would sack him. He would lose his pension. For the first time in his life Bryant coldly faced the prospect of the breadline. His personal fortune was dwindling fast; people like Victor cost money. And there would be others before the payroll was closed, Bryant was sure of that: camp guards, officials, god alone knew how many others.

But it was possible. Always it came back to that. The odds

were terrifying but it could be done. The whole problem boiled down to one simple question: just how badly did he want it done?

Bryant found himself wondering if he had underestimated Victor. It took a clever operator to extract a motive from someone like him and rub his nose in it. But then only a clever operator could hope to pull off such an impossibly audacious coup. Bryant needed Victor. Dear God, he prayed silently, please grant that I have judged the Russian well! Please make him worthy of my trust . . .

'You do realize, don't you,' he said sharply, 'that we shall be quite alone, you and I. There is no help to be had from my government, none at all. If we fail, we shall sink without trace. The General. You. Me. And, if you insist . . Lambe. Do you still want him?'

'I haven't the choice. Don't expect to grab my balls with that kind of crap; I won't "sink" as you piss-put it, I'll die.' Victor grunted. 'You'll just live in this cesspit until the sea ices over.'

Bryant compressed his lips. Now he saw very clearly the point of Victor's earlier observation: it took two to make this decision. He turned his head and stared out across the surface of the mud-coloured sea, seeking inspiration, awaiting the word of God. But God was silent.

'Very well,' Bryant said at last. 'I will give Lambe appropriate instructions, but he will know nothing of the realities underlying your mission. Please bear that in mind.'

'Of course.' Victor sounded relieved. For a mad moment he wondered what Bryant would say if he had the faintest conception of what those 'underlying realities' were in fact: making a British plane complete with pilot and passenger disappear off the face of the earth. 'Now. After Lambe, I need money. Travelling expenses. And once inside, there will be people to buy.'

'I anticipated that. I can arrange to have you put in funds. I take it you want the money in cash?'

'Yes.'

'How much?'

'Ten thousand pounds.'

Bryant was aghast. 'I don't see why . . .'

160

'I can hardly wire home asking Papa for more if I run out in mid-holiday.'

It was a lot of money, more than Bryant could easily afford. As if reading his mind Victor said, 'Whatever is left over comes back to you. I do not charge a fee for this.'

'Thank you.'

'It should not need stating. I will meet you here, tomorrow, at the same time and collect the money then. Unless you wish to propose some other arrangement?'

Bryant hesitated. 'The day after tomorrow. Raising that kind of cash takes time. Will you be staying over?'

'I think not. I prefer to keep on the move. Also, I am afraid.'

'Afraid?'

'Of being watched, followed. Of dying of boredom here.' Victor did not smile. Instead he rose and offered his hand. 'No, don't get up — you'll make us look conspicuous. I will see you here the day after tomorrow. Same seat. Same time.'

He stalked off without waiting for a reply. After he had gone a few yards he glanced over his shoulder. Bryant was sitting in the old position, hands on knees, staring into the wind, out to sea. To Victor he seemed acutely visible, like the focal point of a crowded, 'busy' photograph. But when a few steps later he turned again for a final look, the man whom he laconically designated God was just a part of the crowd, a nice old gentleman in a tweed suit and a hat that was half a size too small for him, sitting on a bench, perhaps waiting — the thought tickled Victor's esoteric sense of humour — for death to come and occupy the vacant space beside him.

17

The old man clung to the wall like an insect, using his hands to haul himself painfully up towards the single, tiny window, while his toes scrabbled for chinks in the mortar which bonded together the breeze blocks of the cell. At last he managed to bring his chin level with the sill. His breathing came in short, laboured gasps. He knew he would not be able to maintain this agonizing position for long, so he made the most of his time. His eyes darted right and left. Thirty metres of cleared grey earth between him and the next blockhouse, two blinding spotlights high up on a pole, underneath them a brace of guards with a dog moving slowly across Povin's line of sight. He felt his hands begin to slip and groaned aloud; then — yes! In the shadows to the right of the blockhouse opposite, a red glow quickly waxed and waned . . .

The old man slid into a heap on the floor and lay there, breathing heavily, for a long time. It wasn't physical exertion that exhausted him tonight. It was fear.

At least Alexander the Chechen had not abandoned him, not yet. The red spark of his cigarette end was all that now stood between the old man and sleepless nights. Not much of a barrier, that glowing tip of ash, but it was his only protection against Lev triple-oh-eight and the old man clung to it like a drowning sailor to a mast.

Saturday night. Tomorrow was a rest day; for once they hadn't cancelled it. But the old man was in no fit state to relax. As soon as he had recovered a little he dragged himself upright and looked to his defences. The stiletto was the main thing; he kept it on him all the time now. The door . . . Povin moved softly across to the entrance to his tiny cell and listened. Out in

162

the corridor all was silent and that was as it should be, for the order 'Lights out!' had been given more than an hour earlier. There was a latrine bucket in the corridor but the occupants of this blockhouse tried not to use it because it stank. These zeks were not *blatnye*, common criminals; they were political prisoners, for the most part civilized men unused to prison conditions.

The old man opened his door a crack and listened. He knew that the steel gate at the end of the passage which led to the outside was sealed for the night, protected by an electronic alarm which sounded in the main guardroom. Kulikov wouldn't find it easy coming in that way. Povin's eyes shifted to the window set high in the wall of the passage. Too risky; the patrol would be bound to see or hear such an approach.

But . . . the old man shook his head wearily. Electronic alarms could be cut. He was too much of a professional *gaybist* to put any faith in modern technology. One man made a lock just so that another could pick it, or bribe his way past it. Kulikov wasn't likely to be deterred for long.

Povin quietly closed the door, and in a sudden gesture of utter despair slammed his clenched fists against the wood. His forehead was running with sweat. Scarlet flashes popped behind eyes that ached with strain and his hearing was concentrated to such a degree that he kept imagining nonexistent sounds. Trapped. He was trapped in a corner.

After a while he lowered his hands and shuffled wearily over to his bunk. He had seen Kulikov that very day. The boy was out and assigned to helping Zuyev, of all people. Was Kazin a wizard? Zuyev's responsibilities included the morgue. Duties were light in the spring, there weren't that many deaths and triple-oh-eight would have plenty of time in which to scheme. Povin shuddered, remembering how that milky-white eye had transfixed him at a distance. Before the disabled zek made his assault he had hated Povin, but guardedly and in silence. The old man didn't mind that. He was used to covert distrust. He knew that in the minds of many he was classed as *nasedka*, a stoolpigeon, but no one had any proof. Now, however, this thing between him and Kulikov was out in the open.

And nobody was doing anything about it.

The old man groped in his jacket pocket for a cigarette and matches. The cigarettes were a great blessing. When he put on his jacket at the end of a shift he invariably found that somebody had put a fresh pack in one of the pockets. Alexander the Chechen was taking his duties seriously. Povin lit up and gasped down the smoke, staring at the ceiling.

Kulikov was after him and nobody cared. He was precious to them, yet still they put him under threat; they gave him a minder when it would have been the simplest thing in the world to transfer Kulikov to another camp. They did every single thing against the grain, did it with the aid of the old man's most insidious enemy — fear.

Fear. At long, long last his nerve was giving out.

He had it all now, or very nearly. A few days ago he came across a newspaper (a month out of date but who cared?) containing an article on a computer science symposium in Leningrad, a very interesting, well-researched article which afforded him a pleasing image. He was the hardware. Kazin had been steadily feeding him a programme. Now at last he had the key to the electronic lock and was ready to compute.

He propped himself up on one elbow and listened. Was that a noise outside? It's nothing, he told himself. Your imagination. Lie down. *Damn you, lie down*!

They were building up the pressure. That's why they had ordered Alexander to tell all he knew. No . . . too crude. They would not have ordered him to do anything, merely dropped a hint and left it at that.

What came next? They wanted the old man to flee but they realized he couldn't manage it alone, so what would they do? Povin knew. Soon they would be sending someone from the West to help the woman free him. Karsovina understood the threat which triple-oh-eight posed to the old man's life, and she was susceptible enough to help him when it came to the crunch. Kid's stuff. He would run all right, but in his own way and at a time of his choosing, not theirs. Run before they gave him up to Kulikov for execution . . . He shivered. The timing was everything. If he got it wrong . . .

He grappled with his fears while he lit a second cigarette

from the butt of the first. Nicotine gave him courage, helped him think.

It must be Chance Medley, *must* be. The old man had patiently worked over the ground again and again, always reaching the same conclusion. Now he was sure. Stolyinovich was alive. That proved everything. 'I have part two of your message,' Kazin was saying to him. 'Give me part one . . .' But the old man wasn't sure he wanted to do that. Or that he didn't want to do it.

Kazin wanted a name. Povin didn't know the name. How far should he do Kazin's work for him, before he fled?

He rolled off the bunk and rested his elbows on his knees. He — he himself — was the last of the Chinese boxes. The logical end of Kazin's programme was to uncover the secret which the old man carried inside his head without knowing what it was. And for that, Kazin had chosen the woman.

Povin took another deep drag on his cigarette and stubbed it out on the floor with a 'tchah' of disgust. What was she doing in the KGB anyway? She didn't belong there. In some ways she was but a child, such a naive child too — yet the hope of all Russia was concentrated in the hands of children like her. God help Russia, then.

He tossed his head roughly, denying the treacherous feelings inside him before they could take proper root. She was there in Kazin's programme and must take her chance with the others. But at least he could pray for her . . . and for the child.

The old man painfully lowered himself on to his knees and raised clasped hands in front of his face. He found it difficult to concentrate tonight. His hands were shaking. With bitterness in his heart he recognized that for all his faith he was still mortally afraid of death.

The familiar words of the prayer refused to come. Where was Kulikov now? Povin shuddered again. He knew that the zek could be in only one place. Wherever Kazin wanted him to be . . .

Somewhere in the darkness outside a cigarette glowed briefly red and was extinguished.

18

It was a long trek out to Dzerzhinsky Recreation Park, situated at the northern end of Mira Prospekt, but Volodiya wanted to go and since his grandmother supported him Inna knew better than to argue. The boy longed to be dazzled by the huge wraparound screen of Circlarama, so that was one expensive outing; then they had to eat, and since the nearby Golden Sheaf restaurant was in such a lovely setting why not have lunch there, suggested Anfisa? And indeed why not, thought Inna furiously; after all, Mother, you aren't paying!

There was a row about what Volodiya ought to wear. The weather was unseasonally warm and Inna saw no reason why he should be wrapped up like a shapeless parcel in layer after layer of woolly clothing. Anfisa, on the other hand, belonged to the old school of Moscow motherhood, which decreed scarves and overcoats on principle until at least the end of April, which was still a few days off. Inna put her foot down, argued the point under the watchful, calculating eyes of her son, and won. The penalty for success, however, was dire: Anfisa refused to talk to her. So Inna sat tight-lipped in the bus, looking resentfully out of the window while Volodiya and his dear *babushka* prattled on the seat opposite about things she had missed in Murmansk.

The film turned out to be a boring propaganda piece on the Baikal-Amur Railway, which made Volodiya fidget and gripe, so Inna was heartily glad to get out. At lunch she provoked Anfisa's disapproval by ordering a litre of sweet white wine, most of which she drank herself. Afterwards she sat with her mother in the watery sun while Volodiya pretended to be an aeroplane, swooping up and down the broad paths and terrorizing the black swans. The wine had made Inna feel better. Normally she would have disciplined the boy, but today his wild behaviour left her cold. Let him get on with it. Anfisa didn't object, so what was the point of making a fuss? Well, perhaps some point.

'You never allowed me to run about like that when I was young.'

'Ah, but you were a girl. Girls don't. Boys have got to let off steam sometimes.'

Anfisa had pulled her knitting from her capacious leather handbag and was busily counting stitches.

'Sexist nonsense.'

'Hoo-ee! What fine Western-style talk! Old Granddad teach you that, did he?'

For some muddled reason which she couldn't fathom Inna wanted to cry, but instead she merely shrugged her shoulders aggressively in an attempt to pull herself together.

She turned her head this way and that, looking for Volodiya, who had disappeared. 'Have you seen the boy?' she asked.

'No. Don't worry, he won't stray far.'

'You never let me out of your sight when I was his age.'

'You were a girl.'

'You talk as if I've turned into a snake.'

Anfisa eyed her daughter darkly over the snip-snap of the needles. 'I don't know what you are any more, and that's a fact.'

'Whose fault is that?' Inna flared. 'I'm a guest in my own house now! Every time I come home on leave I have to ask permission for this and that, find out what you've been doing with the boy and fit myself in somehow . . . I've just about had enough.'

Anfisa said nothing. The clacking of the needles grew faster and louder. Inna turned her head, poised to make another telling point, and to her astonishment saw that her mother was quietly crying.

'What's the matter?'

Anfisa did not reply, but merely wiped away a tear with the back of her hand before redoubling her efforts with the needles.

Inna gnawed her lip. Christ (oh, not *Him* again), how she hated her mother when she did this! It was so unfair. Shed a few tears, start the guilt running freely, put the knife in — the three stages of mother love. Now, of course, Inna was in the wrong. Soon some passer-by would turn to stare disapprovingly at the poor lady seated beside her callous daughter, nasty bit of work, cold, selfish . . . Oh, Inna could have written the script a dozen times over, she'd acted it out often enough. What a performer. What . . . a . . . *star*!

No. She was being unfair. Her mother, too, was a human being with all the needs and weaknesses which that entailed. It couldn't be easy, looking after Volodiya day in and day out. Inna felt the drip, drip, drip of guilt wearing down her granite resolve and silently loathed herself.

'Come on, Mother,' she said at last. 'Don't cry. People will look at you.'

'Let them.'

'I'm sorry.'

'No you're not.'

True, thought Inna. What do I have to be sorry about? 'Really I am.'

Anfisa laid down her knitting and rummaged in her bag for a handkerchief with which she noisily blew her nose. 'Mustn't let the boy see,' she sniffled.

'That's right. It'd only upset him.'

There was an uncomfortable pause. Then Anfisa said, 'I don't know what's come over you lately, I really don't.'

Inna was like water that day: she took the line of least resistance. 'I've been working too hard, that's all. I've not been myself.'

'The monthly business is all right?'

'Yes, of course . . . I mean, yes thank you, Mother.'

'Then what . . .?'

Inna sighed. 'Oh, lots of things. The travelling, I suppose.'

'And Old Granddad?'

'Maybe a bit. You mustn't tell anyone I've told you, you will remember, won't you?'

'Who do you think you're talking to? You think I want to get my own daughter into trouble with the bosses?'

'No, I'm sorry. Of course not.'

'Well, then. But that doesn't stop me worrying. I'm worried sick, I don't mind telling you.'

'What about, for goodness' sake?'

'You. The boy — it's not easy keeping track of a little imp like him when you're my age — I fall into bed at night and wonder if I'll ever see morning. But mainly you. You seem so far away these days. I hardly recognize you when you come home.'

It was on the tip of Inna's tongue to retort, 'I hardly recognize *you* either,' but she shied away from confrontation. Experience taught her that it was much better to let her mother get things out of her system and then the storm would blow over. Until next time.

'I know what you mean,' she said dully. 'I snatch a few hours at home here and there, and all I ever seem to do is try to catch up. Why do men love travelling so, I wonder? It never seems to bother them. They queue up for the mobile jobs these days.'

'That's because they're men. The last thing they want is to sit at home in the nest while the kids run round them and the woman nags for more money. They want to get out, have a bit of fun.'

'And we don't?'

'Some of you do.' Anfisa had dried her tears and seemed keen to mend fences. 'I've seen it. But not the mothers. For them it's too late.

Inna pondered that and came to the conclusion that in her case at least it was sound. 'Let's hope this won't go on for much longer, then.'

'The travelling, you mean?'

'Yes. Old Granddad, as you persist in calling him, though I can't see why. He's not that old, not by today's standards.'

'Too old for you.'

'Hardly a problem, when he's stuck up there for the rest of his life. Besides, he doesn't interest me in *that* way in the slightest.'

Anfisa compressed her lips, seemed to be on the point of saying something, then checked herself. After a little pause she said, 'Aah, let's not talk about him. You have enough of him during the week.'

Inna was only too glad to change the subject. In a moment of weakness she had confided the details of her latest assignment to Anfisa, who disapproved but could do nothing. Inna bitterly regretted her momentary lapse, but the words were out now and she had to live with the consequences. While she cast about for some fresh topic of conversation, Volodiya came flying down the path, zipped past the two women with a burst of imaginary cannon fire and fled into the distance. Inna sighed. The tears had halted just below her eyelids. She really must get a grip on herself.

'You're still all right for money, I suppose?'

'Yes, thank you. We live on what you leave each week. I'm saving my pension for Volodiya's birthday. I'm going to open a savings account for him.'

'You!' Inna was surprised. 'I thought you didn't trust banks.'

Anfisa laid down her knitting and stared across the pond. 'I don't know,' she said at last. 'It's going to be his world, not mine. There'll be banks.'

'I wish I could be as sure of that as you are.'

But Anfisa merely smiled. 'I'm sure.'

There was a long silence. At last Inna scraped up enough courage to take a deep breath and say, 'Is that because you believe in God?'

Anfisa turned round, startled. 'Who said I believed in God?'

'No one. I just know.'

Anfisa looked down at her knitting. 'You don't mind?'

'Why should I mind?'

'You being in the Organs, and all.'

'Mother!' Inna leaned over and put her arm round Anfisa's shoulders, pulling her close.

For a second the old lady resisted; then she gave. 'You're not going to throw me in with Old Granddad?' Her voice, arch and timid at the same time, made Inna smile.

'No. Not you. Not . . . anyone.'

'Me I can understand. I'm your mother, you wouldn't turn me in — although, god alone knows, you can't say that of some! But as for anyone — isn't that your job?'

'It was, once. In a way. But they moved me, remember?'

'Yes. You always said it was boring.'

'I said it was hateful. Not the same thing.'

During their conversation Anfisa's thoughts had evidently been running to catch up, for now she said, 'But you must tell me, how *did* you know I was a believer?'

'You really want to know?'

Anfisa saw the twinkle in her daughter's eyes and cautiously registered that things had taken a turn for the better. 'Yes.'

'I followed you one Easter. When I was about twelve. You went to church.'

Anfisa was silent for a while. 'I took such care,' she said at last. 'I was convinced you never knew. I asked the priest for advice, he agreed I shouldn't come to church too often, it was for the best in a family like ours. But I used to go once a year, each Easter, regular as clockwork.' She shot a defiant look at her daughter. 'I still do.'

'Good for you.'

Inna smiled at the incredulous expression which stole over her mother's face. 'Do you mind if I tell you another secret?'

'Suit yourself.' But she was dying to know.

'You're not to tell anyone.'

'I know what a secret is.'

'I'm not sure, but . . . I think I might believe in God too.'

And then the tears did burst forth in a flood, trickling down her face to dry in broad, salt-white streaks. Anfisa looked as if she feared her daughter had gone mad before suddenly reaching out to take her in her arms, and cradle her like the small child she still conceived Inna to be. For a long time they sat linked together, rocking to and fro, and now the passer-by would have nothing of which to disapprove: a storm-tossed, emotional scene in the grand mainstream of the Russian tradition, played straight from the heart.

At last the worst was over and Inna sat up, using her mother's handkerchief to dab the tears from her face. They huddled together, holding hands in silence, desperately hoping that Volodiya would not choose this precious moment of unity and reconciliation to make his appearance. It was Anfisa who broke the silence.

'But . . . how? Why . . .?'

Inna shook her head wanly. 'I don't know. Honestly I don't

171

know. Even now I'm not certain, it's all so muddled up. It began years ago, I think. In the KGB we have these wonderful libraries. When it was my job to monitor the religious sects, I thought: why not do it properly, get to know the enemy? So I used to stay on, after work, reading. At first it bothered them, I could see that, but I didn't care, and because I was good at my job and it was paying dividends they left me alone after a while. And the more I read, the less I could understand what all the fuss was about. It's not just us, here in the Soviet Union; throughout history people have been persecuting Jews everywhere for no reason, out of sheer jealousy, as far as I could see. Until at last I started to think of repression as being a bad thing — bad in itself, I mean. And from there it was only a step to seeing religion as a *good* thing. There was no harm in it. I had access to the statistics, too — not the rubbish that gets into *Pravda*, but the real figures. Russians are believers. Mother, do you know — this is one of the most genuinely devout societies in the world? Still? After all that's happened . . . Russians are stubborn, aren't they?'

'Yes. Like mules.'

'And then . . .' Inna paused, a faraway look in her eyes. How to say it? She took a cautious first step. 'I began to like what I was reading. In the Old Testament, the beautiful oneness of God and the joys of obedience to His ways; and then later, in the New Testament, all that emphasis on mercy, rather than the law. On forgiveness. Compassion. Turning the other cheek.' The ice did not crack; her confidence grew a little. 'I began to read about the lives of people who had been changed by it. St Augustine. Marcus Aurelius. Changed for the better. And that's when it started to get difficult, because it was setting up tensions between me and the job. But there was nothing I could do about that, so at first I was glad when they changed my assignment and gave me . . . Granddad. Only that muddled me up still more, because he's a Christian too, you see; he started very much as I did and his mother was Orthodox, like you. He's been incredibly wicked in his life, but he always kept a hold on his faith, and it's changed him too . . . and now it's changing me and, oh Mother —' the tears welled up again, — 'I'm so scared and wretched. This isn't *me*. I don't know what I'm going to do!'

Anfisa stroked her daughter's hair and helped her dry the new flood of tears. 'No good crying,' she murmured sympathetically. 'If He decides to take us, He does — and that's the beginning and the end of it. It's like love. You know how they say we women always fall for the least suitable man in sight? It's the same with God. Put a girl down in the Organs and what does she do? She gets religion. Cheer up, Inna. Don't fight what you can't change.'

'I know. You're right. But oh, how I wish you weren't!'

Anfisa struggled to order her thoughts. 'Don't resist,' she said slowly. 'Give it time. You *have* time, you're still young. Things will resolve themselves in ways you can't even begin to imagine.' Oh, how she yearned for it to be true! But her heart was heavy with apprehension.

Anfisa's words were as mundane and well used as her old, dog-eared cookery book, but somehow they brought Inna comfort. For the first time in months she felt a respite, however brief, from tension. She had told her mother everything and the relief that followed was profound.

'Not so young,' she murmured sadly. 'And . . . "No man knoweth the hour", isn't that how it goes?'

'God will give you time,' Anfisa said firmly. 'He will not deal unfairly with one who comes to Him so late and after such trials.'

'Trials. Yes. You're right enough there, Mother. How much longer . . .?' Her voice tailed off.

'Until you're finished with Granddad,' Anfisa said briskly. 'That's what you've got to concentrate on now, my girl. You sort him out as fast as you can and come back to us.'

'You make it sound so easy. He's a long job. I used to wonder why on earth they'd chosen me, so young and inexperienced, but they knew what they were doing, didn't they? *He* started off in just the same way as me. Curiosity, reading. Getting to know the enemy. Going over to the other side. Mother always in the background. Christ yes, they knew what they were about when they dragged me in!'

'Never mind. Maybe he's worth it. Maybe it was his appointed task in life to bring you home, who knows?'

Inna stared at her mother, struck by the thought. 'Do you really think so?' Then she reluctantly shook her head. 'I'm afraid I'm still not far enough along to buy that yet.'

'You don't have to buy anything. But what I can't for the life of me understand . . . No, it doesn't matter.'

'Say it.'

'Well. What beats me is why on earth this old boy in the camp should have got his hooks into you. What is it about him, Inna?'

'God may know, but if He does He isn't letting on. I try to follow the rules but it's so hard. Every time I see him he confuses me just that little bit more until sometimes I wonder who's in control — him or me! And they *knew* it was going to happen, right from the very first day when they selected me for this job! I still don't understand what it is about him . . . No, that's not quite right.' Inna's face wrinkled into a frown while her memory chased back over the past few weeks. 'There is something, though. We've never talked about it, he's not sure if it's in the files I've read, but there was this awful business over his mother. The Organs found out she was a Christian; I think he blames himself for that. Then she recanted, and somehow that's all his fault too. And the man has a conscience: the nearest thing to a genuine Christian conscience I've ever encountered, I think.'

'Yet you say he's so wicked?'

Inna raised her head, lips slightly parted, and stared into space. 'Yes. That's it, you see.'

'I most certainly don't.'

'He's been a part of the system. *My* system. And he's rejected it in the only way he knew how . . .' Her eyes widened. 'My god, my god, I see it, I *see* it! He's been wicked, and he knows he's been wicked. He comprehends the reality of it. And . . . and oh, but he's in such danger, Mother! Of being murdered by one of the others. I don't *want* that! The law's one thing, but when I think of him being dragged out, stabbed maybe . . .'

Her voice faltered. After the initial release of confession, her earlier concern was starting to creep back. 'Mother, you won't tell anyone, will you?' she said anxiously. 'If ever this got out . . .'

Her mother was about to speak again when there was a sudden interruption. The two women simultaneously became aware of an altercation behind the bench on which they were sitting and hastily turned round.

Volodiya, kicking and struggling, was being restrained at arm's length from pummeling another boy into a pulp. The victim, a thin and puny child with a white complexion and blond hair, was obviously one of nature's scapegoats; a cut over his right eye was bleeding freely and he was busily crying himself into a state of hysteria. The person doing the restraining was a middle-aged man with a pained and puzzled expression on his face, who seemed incapable of fully understanding what was going on. One of the park wardens, a fat, short-tempered-looking woman, was trying to comfort the passive recipient of Volodiya's splenetic, childish rage, so far without any evident success.

Inna and her mother jumped up. 'What happened?' shrieked Inna as she ran towards the heaving group.

'It's my grandson,' said the puzzled-looking man. 'This boy, he keeps hitting him. It's my grandson . . .'

'Does this little devil belong with you?' snapped the warden. At the sound of her voice Inna began to shrivel and curl up inside herself, like paper thrust on the fire. She wanted to close her eyes, stop up her ears and walk away from this terrible scene, this debacle, this monument to the sum total of her failures as a parent.

'Yes,' she heard her mother say with a bellicosity equal to that of the warden. 'And what's it to you, eh?'

The warden looked at Anfisa uncertainly, as if recognizing in her a kindred spirit but one who had temporarily gone over to the other side. 'This villain was knocking the bones out of the little one.'

Anfisa reached out and twisted one of her grandson's ears. 'Volodiya. Why were you hitting him?'

'Ow! He hit me first.'

'No I didn't!'

'Yes you —'

Anfisa twisted the boy's ear again and he instantly fell silent. 'Apologize.'

175

'Shan't!'

'A-*pologize!*'

Volodiya stole a glance at Anfisa's face and looked at his feet. Then he stared up at his mother, trying to inject the maximum amount of appeal into his quivering eyelashes. 'Shan't!' he repeated.

For a moment Inna studied him thoughtfully, all the while conscious of three pairs of adult eyes fixed firmly on whatever she was about to do next.

'Volodiya,' she said very quietly. 'Apologize this instant.'

The little boy continued to stare at her for a few seconds more, then rapidly switched his gaze to Anfisa. No help there. He edged towards his mother and laid a hand on her coat. 'No,' he said. 'I *won't!*'

Before he could move Inna had calmly reached out and seized him by his left ear; her eyes lighted on Anfisa's expression of sublime approval, and she smiled a collaborative smile, instantly reciprocated. Then she turned her attention to her son, whose expression of outraged betrayal did Inna's heart, if not good, then at least no harm.

'Volodiya,' she repeated, still very quietly. 'I'm going to tell you one more time . . .'

'I'm sorry, Mummy.'

'Now to him. What's his name?' she said to the man.

'Yuri.'

'Say sorry to Yuri.'

Volodiya's eyes flashed for an instant; then the spark died. 'I'm sorry. Yuri.'

The incident was closed. The warden gave Anfisa another of her uncertain looks and shook her head. 'He's going to catch cold like that. You should wrap him up better. It's not May yet, you know.'

Anfisa shot a quick look at Inna, a look which said as plainly as could be, '*I'll* handle this, if you *don't* mind.' 'And what's that to you, Comrade?' she yelped. 'Since when have you been in charge of child welfare in Moscow? Tell me, Comrade, do they know in the Kremlin yonder how you've taken over?'

The warden flinched. 'All I was trying to do — '

'Thank you, Comrade, thank you very much. But he's my

grandchild, and if I say he's warm enough . . .' Anfisa snatched up Volodiya's hand, linked her arm through Inna's and began to march.

'. . . *He's warm enough!*'

19

Two men stood in the passage facing the double doors, hands folded in front of them, their legs apart. As the elevator hummed to a stop they turned and began to walk without a backward glance. Kazin and Krubykov emerged in the company of two more of the bodyguards assigned to them by the Ninth Directorate and the procession set off briskly down the corridor.

At last the little group arrived at a heavy steel door on which hung a sign: NO ADMITTANCE WITHOUT CHAIRMAN'S PERSONAL ORDER. Krubykov advanced with a large, jangling bunch of keys, and a moment later Kazin stepped across the threshold with his lieutenant.

'Out,' he snapped, and the four bodyguards exited, leaving the Chairman and Krubykov alone together. Kazin extracted a cigarette, fitted it into his little cane holder and waited impatiently for the flash of Krubykov's lighterflame.

'What a mess,' he muttered, looking around him with a grimace.

Oleg Kazin, Chairman of the *Komitet Gosudarstvennoy Bezopasnosti*, was very nearly eighty years old. For a man of his age he enjoyed remarkable physical health. His face invariably glowed, as though he had just stepped from under a hot shower. He walked quickly, his long legs sometimes making assistants run to keep up with him, and although he wore thick spectacles the rest of his senses were keen. Kazin

177

took perverse pleasure in hearing doctors warn him against smoking. He made a point of attending their funerals.

It was hard to say whether this man had ever been sane in a sense which Western psychiatrists would recognize. The issue was clouded by countless myths; very little was known about his personal history. The public facts were these: he had been married in 1929; his wife was killed in a bombing raid in 1941; there had been one child of the union, a daughter.

This girl stood at the very centre of the Kazin mythology. She had died. There were as many rumours about the manner of her death as there were people to relate them, but it was curious how all the stories had two things in common. Her father, it was said, had killed her in one of his awesome paroxysms of rage. And he had used a hammer to do it.

There the resemblances ended and the divergences set in. No two people seemed able to agree on the daughter's name, age, place of death or burial, mental state, physical condition or political affiliation (if any); certainly, no living person ever claimed to have met her. A popular version of the story had it that she sided with the Mensheviks, thus incurring her father's wrath; but the dates were wrong, the last remnants of the Mensheviks having vanished long before she ever came on the scene. Nevertheless, this tale had persisted to the present day.

So there was plenty of material on which to base a judgement that Kazin was never quite 'a hundred kopecks to the rouble', although the other old men, the ones in the Kremlin who had survived alongside him, used the catchphrase with the uneasy circumspection of nervous children who approach the dark corner of the stairs. Whatever the truth about his mental state, there can be little doubt that Kazin for many years displayed the most remarkable command of Soviet affairs, both domestic and foreign. His public fortunes might rise and fall, but the influence which he exerted, whether in power or out of it, never seemed to wane.

It was part of Krubykov's function to keep a close but strictly unofficial eye on his master, watching for signs of instability, although, of course, it was never put quite like that. Occasionally, once a month perhaps, Krubykov went for a lunchtime stroll in the Kremlin gardens, where someone would join him for a while and words would pass; but that was all. There was never any question of asking Kazin to submit to a medical examination. Krubykov had been around long enough to be able to read his master as a fisherman reads the sea or a shepherd his flock. Subtle changes in Kazin's mood communicated themselves to the colonel instantaneously; he would make the appropriate adjustments to the day's schedule, note the incident for his next walk in the Kremlin and keep his thoughts to himself.

One peculiarity which had increasingly begun to force its way on Krubykov's attention of late was Kazin's intense and rapidly growing love of detail. Despite the rumours to the contrary which had reached Inna Karsovina's ears, he paid a good deal more attention to the work of his subordinates than was generally realized. He had taken to descending from on high to lowly departments in obscure directorates and assuming command for perhaps an hour, or it might be a week, until the impetus left him, he became bored and moved on to something else, without ever bothering to ascertain the results of his erratic interventions. Thus it was that Kazin had taken charge of the hunt for the Travel Agency and so far showed no signs of delegating it to others.

Now he was in a basement three floors beneath the KGB's Dzerzhinsky Square headquarters. In fact it was several rooms knocked into one, on Kazin's orders, for the express purpose of creating a secure depository for Povin's belongings. One of Kazin's first acts as Chairman had been to order the ransacking of the general's apartment. All its contents, every movable object, had been taken here to the underground room, which was maintained at a constant temperature and atmospheric pressure, day and night. That was two years ago. Since then, each item in turn had been removed for minute scientific examination by the experts who staffed a committee jointly sponsored by the Eighth Department of the Second Main Directorate (Computers) and the Technical Operations Directorate.

Krubykov viewed the whole exercise as an expensive waste of time and did what he could to contain it within reasonable bounds. When dealing with Kazin, however, that was always difficult. Now that the Chairman had decided to take a personal interest in the Travel Agency Krubykov's hands were virtually tied.

Kazin sat down in one of Povin's best armchairs and stared at the opposite wall, where eight thousand gramophone records, labelled and alphabetically arranged in order of composer's name, stood stacked in rows.

'Unbelievable,' he croaked. 'To spend a fortune on . . . on *that*!'

'There are worse hobbies,' Krubykov ventured mildly.

'Yes — but the repetition! The duplications, the *brak*! Some of those things are completely unplayable, did you know that, eh?'

'Yes. I don't think that was important to them, if you'll forgive me the comment, Comrade Chairman. They wanted to collect everything, irrespective of quality. I'm told there are dealers who would be prepared to pay a high price merely to view the inside of this very room.'

'Tchah! Idiots, then! Eight thousand bits of plastic, gathering dust. But it's there . . .' Kazin jumped to his feet and went across to peer more closely at the record library which Povin and Stolyinovich had assembled between them over nearly twenty years. 'It's in there somewhere, Krubykov.'

'Possibly.'

'No!' The Chairman rounded on his subordinate with a glance of undiluted malevolence. 'I know it's there. I knew as soon as I read the transcript of Stolyinovich's interrogation. Look at that Shakespearean sonnet the English fed him . . . "Music to hear, why hear'st thou music sadly?" Come on, Krubykov! Put yourself in the General's shoes. His friend gives him a pile of records then whispers in his ear, "I have a message for you, 'Music to hear . . .'" Isn't it obvious? Besides, none of this other muck —' he waved an arm so as to embrace the whole room — 'contains anything of the slightest value. I've read the reports, I know. But the records . . .' He swivelled back to them with a greedy look on his pink face and Krubykov uneasily shifted his weight from one foot to the other. 'Oh yes, Krubykov, it's in there, somewhere. The key. The key to Povin's code. The last link he needed in order to make contact

with his courier from the Travel Agency. And when I find it
. . .'

He left the sentence unfinished, but continued to stare avidly at the piles of gramophone records which stretched from floor to ceiling along the length of one whole wall.

'If you find it,' Krubykov muttered to himself, careful not to let Kazin hear. Two years of intensive scientific tests had failed to reveal anything the slightest bit suspicious or out of the ordinary where the records were concerned. Each surface was 'clean', according to the most up-to-date electronic tests. Every note from every piece of music recorded on these discs had been transcribed into Basic and fed into the Eighth Department's computers for analysis; one machine had been working on nothing else for the past six months and, according to Krubykov's latest information, it was not expected to finish the job for another twenty-three thousand years. In Krubykov's book, the chances of discovering anything of the slightest value from these records was remote.

The colonel sat down in one of Povin's other armchairs and stretched his legs out in front of him, content to let Kazin ramble on. He had long ago made his own assessment of the situation. He knew his master's obsession centred on identifying the last batch of discs imported into the USSR by Stolyinovich, so the first thing Krubykov did was examine the customs inventory relating to the pianist's last six trips abroad. Unfortunately, however, the forms merely disclosed 'miscellaneous gramophone records', without giving details of either numbers or titles. A few days after his arrest Stolyinovich's mind gave way under interrogation and he never subsequently recovered, thus ruling out the direct approach. Then Krubykov considered the possibility of dating the records, with a view to identifying those of recent origin, only to realize that, because Stolyinovich might well have imported old pressings, this wasn't necessarily going to lead to the answers he wanted. The colonel lost interest after that.

'Excuse me, Comrade Chairman . . . ' Krubykov addressed himself to Kazin's stooped shoulders, hoping that he wasn't working up to one of his rages. Krubykov tried never to speak to Kazin unless he could see his face.

181

'Well?'

'Is it not at least possible that the time has now come to interrogate Povin directly about these matters?'

'No.' Kazin turned round and Krubykov saw with relief that his face wore only its usual expression of sour severity.

'May I venture to ask you, Chairman . . . why not?'

'Because we could never be sure he was telling the truth, that's why. Use your head, Krubykov, it's not there just to keep your shoulders apart.'

Krubykov smiled sycophantically. 'I realize there would be difficulties of verification . . .'

'Difficulties!' Kazin came to sit beside him, lighting another cigarette from the stub of the old as he did so. 'Impossibilities, you mean.'

'But everything else he's told us has checked out.'

'So?'

'Doesn't that tend to suggest that in this case . . .?'

'No, it doesn't. What do we have to check *this* case out against, eh?'

Krubykov was silent.

'That's just the problem, isn't it? We have no independent sources of information on the Travel Agency. He can say whatever he likes and we'll have no way of knowing if he's telling the truth. Suppose he named you, eh?' Kazin smiled, his white teeth glinting in the fierce neon light. 'I'd have you shot. You want to run that risk?'

Krubykov smiled.

'Well, then. Besides, I've come to the conclusion that Povin couldn't tell us the answer to this one even if he wanted to. The secret's in the records that the pianist brought into the country, but Povin doesn't know that, you see.' His voice had fallen; he was muttering away to himself so quietly that Krubykov had to lean forward to catch the words. 'He was going to be told later, by Stolyinovich. We've got part two of the message, now we need part one. And that's *there*!' His arm shot out in the direction of the stacked records. 'Somewhere. If only I knew how to lay my hands on it!'

'I'm sorry, Comrade Chairman, you are rather a long way ahead of me.'

'Well, it's obvious, isn't it?' Kazin sounded dangerously exasperated and Krubykov shrank back a little farther into his chair, minimizing his visible surfaces in case of attack.

'Theirs was a two-part code. Stolyinovich was the carrier. He comes into Russia with some records, a present for General Povin. The record titles are a communication from the Travel Agency; they mean something when you put them together in the right way. In other words, the titles contain part one of the message. But — Povin doesn't know that! Obviously! The system needs a cutout, so his friends on the outside don't tell him where to look for his message, oh no! Instead they provide him with a part two — Stolyinovich's script. Well, we've got that, haven't we? That's the one thing he *did* tell us before he went under. The trouble is, we still haven't got the faintest idea which records to apply it to! Anyway . . . Stolyinovich reads out his script. Then: click! At that point Povin knows the latest batch of records means something, he sorts through his stock of old codes, and there it is! Clever.' Kazin scorched Krubykov with a scornful look. 'Too clever for you, at any rate. Now all we need do is identify the relevant batch of records.'

'But Chairman, it's all taking so long. Can we really continue to justify the uncovering of the Travel Agency in terms of hours and expense?'

'You've missed your true vocation, Krubykov, you should have been an accountant. Besides . . . ' Kazin sucked his teeth and gave his assistant a sly look. 'We're going after more than the Travel Agency.'

'Chairman?'

'There may be more than one product, Krubykov. Try a little lateral thinking for once.'

The colonel wisely declined the bait. 'You seem so sure, Comrade Chairman. Yet the proofs . . .?'

'Proofs! You're starting to sound like Stanov, d'you know that? Don't get on my nerves, Krubykov, it's not worth it. Flexibility! How many times have I tried to din that into you? Forget the book, try some common sense for once in your life. We'll get the proofs, don't you worry. Karsovina will see to that. Which reminds me — she's got an appointment in five minutes. Let's get going.'

Kazin rose to his feet and made for the door, Krubykov keeping a pace ahead in order to conceal the look of anxiety on his face. Things were rapidly starting to get out of hand. The colonel did not for a moment doubt the importance of the Travel Agency, but it was ridiculous to suppose that such a project could continue to engage the energies of the KGB's Chairman for the foreseeable future. Krubykov found that his thoughts were luring him down enticing but hazardous by-ways and it was something of a relief when Kazin said, 'Tell the committee they're running slow and I'm not happy about it. I want results, and I want them *now*!'

As they came out of the lift on the third floor Kazin began a diatribe against the shortcomings of the KGB's technical support services, which occupied him the length of the generals' corridor and into his secretariat's outer office. A forlorn figure clambered to his feet as the two men entered, and Krubykov recognized Frolov. If Kazin saw his First Deputy Chairman he gave no sign of it, but passed through into Krubykov's sanctum without once breaking either his step or his monologue. Krubykov looked at Frolov and his face darkened. 'Not now,' he hissed. Frolov spread his hands in an imploring gesture of despair, lifting his eyes heavenwards, but Krubykov, un-moved, followed Kazin to the inner office, closing the double doors firmly behind them.

Inna Karsovina was seated next to the colonel's desk. When the Chairman entered she rose, smoothing down her dress, and Kazin paused for long enough to indicate with a circular wave of his hand that she was to follow him. As usual, a single desklamp afforded the immense office its only source of light. Kazin rounded his huge desk, lowered himself into The Chair and studied her for a moment. He registered that she had aged more than the six weeks which separated their two meetings, and was pleasantly surprised.

'Bring your chair round here, sit beside me.'

The woman obeyed after only a second's hesitation. She was completely unnerved by the close atmosphere in the Chairman's room but she would have done anything not to show it. When Kazin pulled his chair a little closer to her own she resisted the impulse to recoil from such hideous bodily proximity. The smell of stale ash was everywhere, the heat in the office seemed suddenly stifling.

After a long pause Kazin said, 'You're doing well. Not perfectly, but better than I expected.'

Inna meekly nodded her head. When Kazin reached out to touch her arm she forced herself to remain absolutely still. At last he sat back very slowly, as if he had not quite decided to let her off the hook. Only when he felt that the educational silence had gone on long enough did he remove his hand and begin, very quietly, to speak.

'What do you think of him, Comrade; now that you have had a chance to get to know him?'

The woman hesitated; the fact that she had been expecting such a question did not mean that she was any better prepared with an answer. 'Disgusting,' she said at last. 'The smell . . . indescribable!'

Her answer appeared to take Kazin by surprise, for his lips pursed in an uncertain smile. 'I suppose we could always arrange for him to have a bath before your sessions . . . '

'Quite unnecessary, thank you, Comrade Chairman. I have become used to it now. I place a vase of fresh flowers on the windowsill at the start of each interrogation and that helps.'

'Ah yes, I heard about the flowers.' He smiled at the look of bafflement which stole over her face and continued, 'But it disturbs you, his physical condition, I mean?'

'After all, it is only to be expected. Two years on the Gulag . . . well.' She left the sentence unfinished, but the shrug with which she accompanied the last words was expressive.

The woman's wide-open eyes bored into his own with what looked like complete detachment. Look at me, she seemed to be saying, do you like what you see? Am I not cool, poised, every inch a professional? Do I please you, Comrade Chairman?

'What is you assessment of progress so far?'

'Slow.' Her hands writhed briefly in her lap and were still. 'I am sorry, Comrade Chairman.'

'And I am not, Comrade Karsovina. No one, I think, has ever tried to give you the impression that this could be hurried.'

Inna became aware that his face had somehow crept even closer to hers. This unsought, enforced intimacy with Kazin had an unnerving effect on her. The Chairman spread his hands.

'What did we ask you to do? To be *friends* with him! Friendship cannot be rushed, can it? Friendship, the true meeting of two minds, has to grow. It cannot be forced in a hothouse, like an orchid.'

When her rigid face did not change the Chairman uttered a loud sigh. 'Karsovina, Karsovina, why are you always so frightened of me? You should not be. I chose you, remember, chose you specially for your peculiar and undoubted qualities, also —' seeing her about to protest he held up his hands — 'also your failings, yes. And I was not wrong. You are succeeding, because you are weak as well as strong, soft as well as hard. Now is the time for confidence . . . Inna.'

The woman quickly raised her head. He had used her first name. By now his face was so close that their noses almost touched and this time she drew back.

'Show him how confident you are. Dazzle him. Take him out of the camp, Inna. Take him to have a drink in the town.'

It struck her as a ridiculous suggestion; but when she tried to put her feelings into words he cut her off with a grim smile. 'Use your head. In such a camp there are many comings and goings, arrivals and departures. What difference will one more make?'

'He is already in great personal danger, Chairman.' Inna's voice was low and urgent. 'He has an enemy there, one of the other zeks. If I take him out of the compound and bring him back again I double the danger. I . . . I single him out.'

Kazin's expression did not alter. 'I agree,' it seemed to be saying. 'How perceptive you are!' But what he actually said was, 'Take him out. One friend with another. *Enjoy* yourselves.'

His face filled her entire consciousness, threatening her with its sickening combination of stained teeth and black gums. 'Do not worry about the General's enemies. I have arranged to neutralize them, do you understand? Povin now has his own personal bodyguard — just like in the old days, when he

186

occupied the office down the corridor. Very like the old days . . . remember what I told you before: that someone is coming to visit the General soon, someone out of the past. Maybe you will meet him too, who knows?'

'Meet? A visitor . . . ?'

'Yes. Someone who plans to help Povin escape.'

'*An agent from the West?*'

'Yes. But not a conventional agent. Someone who plans to spirit the General away from all of us, East *and* West.' His face wore a faraway expression, as if he were prophesying. 'I know the General, know him to the bottom of his soul. And I know the people on the outside who know him.' He nodded his head with heavy emphasis. 'There will be a visitor . . . soon.'

Then she remembered something she had read in Povin's file and knew who it was. Victor.

Suddenly Kazin became animated again. 'The Project Committee tell me that you expressed surprise at the decision to postpone Povin's liquidation indefinitely. Is that true?'

'Yes, Comrade Chairman.' She looked down unhappily at her clasped hands. 'The fate of traitors is to be shot.'

'The fate of traitors . . . is none of your business, Karsovina. Understood?'

Inna turned pale. She didn't know which was more frightening: Kazin intimate or Kazin angry. 'Yes, Chairman. I understand perfectly.' Her calm expression was starting to slip at the edges. Kazin smelled panic and the odour was as pleasing to him as a burnt offering in the nostrils of an Old Testament prophet.

'Good. Remember, you are the General's friend now. My decision to spare him for a while should give you only pleasure.' His voice sharpened. 'Don't get your roles mixed up, will you. Friendship, Karsovina. *Friendship.*'

He rose to his feet, indicating that the meeting was over, and the woman did likewise. Kazin reached out to touch a bell switch located on the side of his desk; a moment later the double doors opened to admit Krubykov.

'Take Karsovina out through the Lubianka exit. I don't want Frolov to see her again.'

Kazin saw the expression of terror on Inna's face and

187

laughed unpleasantly. 'Don't look so scared, girl. I haven't got nine grammes of lead waiting for you in the cellars, if that's what you're thinking. You can tell your friends you went through The Door and survived! It's just a convenient way out when I've got a queue of *churkas* waiting . . .' He remembered who he was talking to and broke off. 'I want to see you again in two weeks' time. In the meanwhile, make sure that you're never far from a phone. Oh, and Karsovina . . . '

Krubykov was holding open the infamous door to the Lubianka Prison for Inna to pass through, a courtly smile on his face. The woman paused, glad of any excuse to put off the evil moment, and turned to face Kazin once more.

' . . . I repeat: you may take it that I am far from displeased with the progress you have made.'

Everything was fine until she got to Pushechnaya Ulicia; then she was sick on the pavement outside Detsky Mir, under the eyes of a party of fascinated schoolchildren who thought they had come to view the biggest toyshop in the world and instead found a pretty young woman throwing up. Somehow she managed to get herself aboard a bus that was heading in the direction of home. She sat right at the back, desperately hoping that no one would turn round, while the memories of her interview with Kazin flayed her alive.

Inna didn't know how she had managed to force herself through the morning's ordeal. Some unconscious part of her brain must have taken over, that was the only explanation; a pilot, programmed for emergencies such as this. In that last instant, as Krubykov was bowing her through the terrible door, she had wanted to say to Kazin, 'I've been fooling you, this isn't me, not any of it — I'm frightened of you, I can't bear being near you, I'd rather be with my old man! He's still got some shreds of human dignity left, compared to you, and when I'm with him I can talk, really *talk* to him, in a way I can't seem to talk to anyone else these days . . .'

But the fuse hadn't blown; the system didn't go up in a puff of smoke. Inna's defence mechanisms had swung smoothly into play: she hesitated, Krubykov swung back the door . . . and then she was safe. For Volodiya's sake, thank god, she was safe.

Her hand was shaking so much she could hardly insert the key into the lock. She let herself into the apartment and with a sigh of relief realized that Anfisa and Volodiya were both out. She went through to the kitchen to make herself some tea. She would have liked to swallow something for the tension headache which had begun to rage behind her eyes but her stomach warned her against it. She carried her tea into the bedroom and lay down on top of the quilt with a sigh.

She really could not go on with this.

Inna sat up again at once. No point thinking along those lines; she had a child to support and raise. Yes, but . . . Inna rubbed her sore eyes helplessly. What sort of world was she going to raise him into? Kazin's world? Povin's?

She had already changed her job once. She could not hope to do so again, at least not without attracting so many black marks on her file that the move would hardly be worth it.

Leave, then.

Leave the KGB . . . How grand it sounded! Wouldn't Povin have loved to hear her say that! But the simplicity of the thought was deceptive. Even in the unlikely event of Kazin agreeing to let her go at such a delicate juncture, leaving the Organs meant forfeited pension rights, demotion to an inferior social grade, loss of access to the cheap, good shops. And what else did it mean? Inna crossed her arms and rubbed her shoulders, suddenly feeling cold. Could one, in fact, leave the KGB? How did one go about it — hand in notice on a Friday night? Inna had never heard of a single person resigning from the Organs. But then, who'd want to? What sane, rational officer would voluntarily surrender a life of privilege in exchange for one of uncertainty and deprivation?

Yet she, Inna Marietta Karsovina, she had to get out. Otherwise she was going to be crushed between the irresistible force of her own free nature and the immovable object that was Kazin.

Inna's eyes lighted on her bedside mirror and involuntarily she shivered. Her face was pale and the skin was drawn tightly over her cheekbones, making her look old. Two pink blotches burned under her eyes, pulsating like plague spots. Her hair was turning brittle, she noticed; the ends had begun to split.

189

She forced the eyeballs to right and left, observing how their whites were overlaid with a filigree of broken veins. The exercise brought her gaze to rest on Povin's photograph.

Inna picked it up and after a second's hesitation rejected the childish idea of flinging it on the floor. Instead, she made a half-affectionate moue at the stern black and white features before carefully replacing the photo on its table and dusting it off with her sleeve. 'Father figure!' she scoffed; but the words sounded wrong when addressed to such a face.

By association of ideas she picked up her handbag and felt inside for the secret pocket. She unzipped it and, after a little rummaging, found what she was looking for: a small picture of her late husband, Leonid. She laid it down next to Povin's photograph. They were so unalike. Povin's face had been moulded by experience; it was a hard weapon used for cutting through the jungle that encroached on Russia from every side, whereas Leonid had scarcely been touched by life when his photograph was taken. His gaze was wide open and eager, a boy's gaze; and his cheeks were still puffy with the after-effects of his mother's cakes and dumplings. A touch of black round each eye — that was the only sign to mark the dissipation awaiting its moment in the wings.

Inna replaced Leonid's photograph in the secret pocket of her handbag and pulled the zip shut. It was necessary to start thinking like a professional again. The interrogation must proceed and in strict accordance with Kazin's orders. Whatever happened, irrespective of her own desires, there was always Volodiya. His future dictated her future, absolutely and without qualification. Even if it meant — Inna faced it resolutely — the sacrifice of her own personality.

The word seemed wrong, somehow. It failed to convey the intensity of her feelings. Her eyes once again fell on Povin's photograph and the right expression presented itself with wounding swiftness.

Her own soul.

20

For Vitali Anissenko the day began just like any other. Although his bedroom faced eastwards the light at this latitude possessed the even, hard quality which artists associate with the north and covet. By 7.30 or thereabouts it had grown strong enough to penetrate the chinks in Vitali's thick winter curtains, striking him full on the face with sufficient power to interrupt his uneasy dreams. Still asleep, he screwed up his face against the insidious grey dawn, ground his teeth a couple of times, sneezed and awoke.

He dragged himself to the side of the bed, swinging his short legs to the floor with a little groan of self-pity, and pulled on a pair of old slippers over his bedsocks. Then he stumbled across to the window, shivering in the damp chill of the unheated bedroom. Activity in the street below tugged anxiously at the corner of his eye. He crouched low so that he could peer through a narrow gap in the curtains without being seen. Old man Yudkin was coming out of the grocer's shop opposite, his stooped frame a sinister shadow in the trough between the buildings which could not yet aspire to the thin daylight. Vitali rubbed his hands together unhappily. His food bill was long overdue now, but there was precious little money in the till downstairs and he had other, more pressing debts to meet. He pulled the curtains to with a jerk and began to drag on his clothes, which this morning seemed to resist his clumsy efforts as if they had somehow developed a corporate mind of their own.

At last he finished dressing and clomped down the wooden stairs to the kitchen, where he brought the stove back to life and made himself a cup of strong, bitter tea. A year after the

191

death of Natasha, his wife, it was hard for him to remember much about marriage. As far as he was concerned, life had always been like this; and from now on things were never going to be any different. His existence had its counterparts everywhere: a widower, fifty, locked into a lifestyle which he hated but which offered no alternative, Vitali knew he was looking at another twenty or so years of quiet desperation which essentially would not differ from those endured by other widowers in big cities and small, one-horse townships across the face of the earth. Nothing in the acrid tealeaves at the bottom of his chipped cup foretold that life was about to change irrevocably for the worse.

He rinsed his cup and saucer under the cold tap, leaving them unwiped on the rough wooden slab which served as a draining board. Then he put on his outdoor clothes, remembering to bank down the stove beforehand, and let himself out of the front door with only a quick look across the muddy street in the direction of old man Yudkin's store. Don't hesitate, he told himself, don't act guilty. But Yudkin was invisibly consuming a hearty breakfast under the calculating eyes of his shrewish wife, every mouthful translated into roubles and kopecks of profit and loss; good luck to him, Vitali thought grumpily, though not without a stab of envy.

As proof against the grocers of this world he began to whistle a mournful tune which accorded well with the damp, cold atmosphere pervading the town that day. By the time he had covered the short distance between his tiny house and the single-storey building next door where he conducted his business operations as the undertaker of Ristikent he had his keys in his hand, and had sorted out the biggest of the bunch, the one that fitted the padlock on the double doors of the garage. He looked up the still-deserted street to where the settlement had reached an uneasy accommodation with the surrounding countryside and tried to gauge the weather, but wet cloud had descended almost to ground level, hiding the sodden peat and the few stripped, bent-over trees from sight. Vitali shrugged and smiled the archetypal smile of his trade. With any luck, that should carry a few of the older ones off before spring set in and ruined the market for the next four months.

Then he took his first proper look at the doors and it dawned on him that all was not quite as it should be. The padlock was open.

Vitali stood back from the doors, keeping his eyes firmly fixed on the padlock, while he digested that. There had been an intruder. No other explanation was possible. But at the same time he was aware that it made no sense. He kept nothing of value in his tiny office and no one in his right mind would want to steal a ten-year-old van used for transporting corpses, which was all that the garage contained. Half-formed, vaguely terrifying images of body snatchers and black magic flitted through his mind, only to be discarded as ridiculous — Ristikent might have a bar and two whores but it was definitely not the sort of place to harbour either penurious medical students or witches.

It was necessary to do something. Old man Yudkin would soon be finishing his breakfast and Vitali wanted to be ensconced in his office before that happened. But still he hesitated. Nothing like this had ever happened before, not since 'Mad' Mikhail Murashev, one of the town's two militiamen, had got furiously drunk and burned down Ristikent's only surviving church as a glorious prelude to his transfer to Murmansk and 'special duties'. Vitali squared his shoulders and tried to think. Shouldn't he perhaps report it before he touched anything; that was what you were supposed to do in case of fingerprints, wasn't it?

Behind him, on the other side of the street, Vitali distinctly heard the sound of a door being unbolted and shoved half open. Yudkin — that door of his was always sticking, but in another second the old man would lean his shoulder against it and be on the street . . . Vitali took a deep breath, stretched out his hand to the padlock and wrenched open the doors.

Inside the garage a light was burning, that was the first thing to strike him. Surely he had switched it off the previous night? His step faltered. But then there came the sound of Yudkin's front door opening with a whine and a crunch; the undertaker of Ristikent dithered no longer, but slipped across his own threshold and eased the double doors shut behind him.

The garage had been designed to hold two vehicles, and indeed until shortly before his wife's death the business had

193

supported both the refrigerated van and a dignified hearse which was much in demand among the older members of the township's community for *na levo* funerals. But when Vitali's financial difficulties began and mounted, he was soon forced to dispose of the hearse as a much regretted but alas unjustifiable luxury — petrol disappeared into the grand old modified Chaika like water down a drain. Now the garage held only the black van. In the light of the single forty-watt bulb suspended from the ceiling by a hank of wire Vitali peered anxiously around, scenting nothing but trouble. Yet it all looked the same: the workbench at the back was undisturbed, several blackened oildrums stood in their usual precarious pile, the old tyre that he had been meaning to fix these many months lay propped up against the wall by the tap as it had done last night and the night before. His eyes strayed to the glass and wood partition which ruled off part of the garage into an office, but that was in darkness. Vitali knew a second of misplaced relief. Like all the other residents of Ristikent, he kept his money in the bedroom, under the floorboards, but there were certain papers in the office which with the benefit of hindsight would have been better off burned. Certain aspects of the way in which Vitali acquired his petrol, for example, and a number of documents relating to claims on the State for paupers' funerals which did not precisely correspond to the entries on the crematorium's weekly bodycount — matters which, of course, were perfectly capable of rational explanation, but which nevertheless caused Vitali to shift his weight uneasily from one foot to the other as they came to mind.

He put his head on one side and listened. Silence. Perhaps the intruder had gone. Vitali took a step forward, then another. The silence remained unbroken. By now his shoulder was level with the van's offside mirror. Seized with a sudden inspiration he lowered himself heavily on to his knees and crawled underneath the vehicle, not really knowing what he expected to find.

What he found was a pair of legs standing outlined in silhouette at the back of the garage. Vitali, terrified, raised his head too quickly and banged it against the bottom of the van. For a second he saw stars and lost control, thus causing his chin to fall forward on to the cracked concrete floor of the garage, and this time he shrieked aloud. Through a rippling blur of sparks and colours he saw the feet turn and begin to walk unhurriedly around the van towards him.

'Get up.'

Vitali hastened to obey. The voice above and behind him was a horrid croak of insolence and power, the kind of voice which every Russian knows and dreads. He backed out from under the van as quickly as his short, fat body would allow and hauled himself upright with the help of the vehicle's offside step. He turned round to find that the owner of the horrid voice was a tall, thick-set, middle-aged man wearing a heavy leather trenchcoat and a cream-coloured silk scarf. To Vitali's relief he realized that the stranger was not immediately interested in him at all — his attention was concentrated on the van. He held a clipboard and every so often he would make a lengthy note, as if crematorium vehicles were a new experience for him and he wanted to be sure of recording everything accurately.

Without looking up from his notes the man said, 'You know what you looked like down there? Eh, Anissenko? You looked like an arsehole, that's what. How long have you had this load of junk, then? Ten years, is it?'

Vitali gulped. 'Yes. Ten.'

The man nodded and went on with his writing. After a while he moved away from the undertaker and resumed his former position at the back of the garage. Vitali gathered up the shreds of his courage and went after him. The more he saw of this intruder the less he liked the look of him. He was tough, a regular thug, as ready to break your bones as pass the time of day, and arrogant with it. That scar on his neck — Vitali saw it and quickly lowered his eyes, as if frightened of being caught in the act. A horrible long scar, running down inside the man's shirt, a knife wound, perhaps?

Vitali was a small man, both physically and mentally, but deep inside him there was a residue of self-respect. 'Who are you?' he said, trying to make his voice match the stranger's for roughness but producing only an indignant squeak. 'What are you doing here?' The man continued to write, as if the undertaker had not spoken. Vitali pitched his voice higher and tried again. 'I'm going for the militia, that's what I'm doing. We'll see how you answer them!'

When the stranger continued to write, Vitali backed away towards the double doors. If he hasn't answered me in half a minute, he promised himself, I'm going for the police. He counted up to thirty, during which time the man tore a sheet of paper off his clipboard, filed it neatly at the back and resumed his note-taking. With growing reluctance Vitali turned away from him and reached out to open the doors. I'll give him another ten seconds, he told himself. One . . . two . . . three . . .

'Anissenko. Arsehole Anissenko.'

In spite of himself, Vitali turned. For a moment he noticed nothing different about the intruder, who continued to scrutinize his clipboard, but then he belatedly noticed that the hand which held the pen now also contained something else: a red something, a pass which bore — Vitali moved closer, drawn like a fish to the proferred bait — a State seal. The seal lured him onwards and he caught sight of the word *Komitet*. Then there was a signature: Konstantin Chernenko's.

'Oh my god.'

The intruder raised an inquiring eyebrow. 'What?'

Vitali was more frightened than he had ever been in his life. 'Nothing,' he whispered. 'Nothing at all. I am sorry, Comrade.'

Sorry, he was saying, for everything: for being here, in your illustrious way, for bothering you, for being alive.

The man in the trenchcoat flicked his hand and the red pass closed with a snap. He tucked it into his inside breast pocket, put the cap on his pen and shut the clipboard. 'Now,' he said, 'we talk. In there.' He nodded towards the office and Vitali fell over his flat feet to lead the way, holding open the door for his visitor — already he had ceased to think of him as an intruder, now he was a visitor — and actually bowing him into the only chair, as if magically transported back through the years to the time when there was competition under the tsars, and politeness mattered.

The man put his feet on to Vitali's desk and sat back with hands folded in his lap, while he subjected the unhappy undertaker to a long, hostile scrutiny. Vitali stood on the other side of the desk and kept his eyes firmly fixed on the floor.

'You have a State contract,' the man said at last, and his voice was thoughtful. 'With Gulag.'

'Yes, Comrade.'

'Not much else, I imagine?'

'Very little, Comrade. This is a pretty deserted part of the world.'

'But not much competition?'

This time Vitali merely shook his head in silence. His short-comings as a black-market businessman needed no high-lighting by the Kremlin Kommandant of the KGB.

'Not much competition ... but still your business is as miserably wretched as it is possible for a business to be and still exist. Am I right?'

Vitali nodded unhappily.

'Tell me, Anissenko, tell me truly. How much do you make on the side out of State-financed funerals, eh? Come on, the truth.' Vitali started to speak, but the man raised one languid hand and said, 'You will realize, of course, that my next stop is the crematorium.'

Vitali swallowed hard. 'A . . . little, perhaps. Since the death of my wife, times have been very hard.' When the stranger said nothing Vitali raised his eyes a fraction and went on timidly, 'I have to do everything myself now. I have asked for assistance, but no one wants to be an undertaker these days.'

The stranger stared at him, as if at a lunatic. 'Why should they?' he said. 'In a place like this . . . hardly what I would call *prospects*, huh? If business is so bad, why do you want an assistant anyway?'

Vitali wondered whether to tell him the truth: in order to attract outside labour to an area like this the State would have to provide at least threequarters of the new man's salary, a subsidy which would be paid directly to the boss. He decided against it. 'I am due to retire in a year or two's time, Comrade. There will be no one to carry on and I shall have to train someone from scratch before I go.'

'Hardly worth it, I'd have thought. Not enough people die, isn't that the truth?'

197

Vitali lowered his head again and stared miserably at the ground. It wasn't just the truth; it was the beginning and end of his whole wretched existence.

'So. You make a little out of the State, do you.' The stranger's voice retained its thoughtful timbre; there was none of the outright hostility which people normally associated with this kind of questioning. 'Well, who doesn't these days? How would you like to set things straight, arsehole Anissenko? A clean sheet.'

Vitali, scenting a trap, said nothing.

'Do you know who I am?'

The undertaker shook his head.

'I'm your new assistant, Igor Ivanov. The Murmansk Area Committee has seen fit to grant your request at last. Don't forget that, if anyone should ask.'

Vitali gawped at him. 'But . . . but, Comrade . . .'

Igor swung his legs off the table and sat up. 'Listen to me, Anissenko. You've been rumbled. We all know the penalties for ripping off the State, you'll end up in one of those camps you service and come out in that.' He jerked his head in the direction of the undertaker's van. 'Ironic, eh? But nailing you would be one great bloody bore. I don't want all the fucking paperwork. So this is how it works. You cooperate, and I'll lose your file. Don't cooperate, and you're screwed. How's that?'

Seeing Anissenko hesitate, Igor moved in for the kill. 'You know what I am, don't you?' His voice was soft and velvety, the voice of a seducer.

'You are . . . with the Organs.'

Igor laughed and shook his head as if he genuinely appreciated Vitali's little joke. 'You saw the pass?'

'Yes.'

'And the signature?'

Vitali was silent.

'How many of those do you suppose are in circulation, eh? How many have you *seen*? Come off it, Anissenko. Don't waste my time and I won't waste yours.' He thumped the desk, sending a tiny cloud of dust spiralling into the air between the two men. 'I can smash you today. All it'll take is one phone call.

Fortunately for you, I've got better things to do. So. What's it to be, eh?'

What Vitali read in the stranger's face destroyed any possibility of argument. All he knew was that from this there was no conceivable escape, and in that knowledge he bowed to the inevitable.

'Anything you need, Comrade. It's yours.'

The stranger sat back in Vitali's chair and recrossed his legs on the desk. This time when he extracted a cigarette he tossed the packet over to the other man and, since Vitali had no match, offered him a light from a smart electronic Ronson. For a while the two of them smoked in silence. Every so often Vitali leaned forward to deposit ash in the old tobacco tin which served as an ashtray; Igor, less fastidious, used the floor.

'I'm going to tell you a few secrets, Anissenko.' Igor's voice was flat and uninterested, as if he were merely proposing to share a Dynamo football result with his reluctant accomplice. 'If you pass them on, even a hint, mind, you know exactly what will happen.'

Vitali nodded. He knew.

'Very well, then. In this region there are fifteen corrective labour and strict regime camps — sixteen if you include the children's detention centre in Kandalaksha. All of them are serviced by the area crematorium at Monchegorsk. One of them is very special: Ristikent MU/12, the other side of the lake. All the camps are sensitive: most of the inmates are engaged on top-secret projects of military construction. Ristikent MU/12 is the most sensitive of all. You know, I know, that the inmates of such camps do not get out.'

Vitali's shirt had turned clammy against his skin. Now he was implicated. Igor was right to say that people knew these things, although technically they were secret, but to talk of them aloud — that was another matter.

Igor dropped a long worm of ash on the grubby floor and continued. 'Yet . . . people do get out. Two in the last year, to be accurate.' He paused to allow this uncomfortable piece of information to sink in and do its work. 'This requires outside assistance. The question I have to answer is: how the hell do they manage it? Where is the break in the security net, eh?

That's what I'm here to find out.' He paused to give his next words their maximum effect. 'And you're going to help me.'

Vitali was at last moved to protest. 'Me, Comrade? But how can I help? These are things beyond my horizon, I know nothing . . .'

'Nothing?' Igor's lips had set in an unpleasantly hard straight line. He was a master of timing: the man's pauses unnerved Vitali more than his words. 'I said earlier, didn't I, that these camps all have one thing in common — they rely on the Monchegorsk crematorium. That brings you squarely into the picture, I'd have thought, eh?'

Vitali cast an imploring look at the stranger. 'But surely, Comrade, you don't imagine that I am in any way involved?' When Igor said nothing the undertaker repeated in a querulous voice, 'Surely?'

'We have studied you, Anissenko,' Igor said at last. 'The provisional conclusion is that you are innocent. But mark: I say provisional. We think that you are being made use of. I hope for your sake that the provisional conclusion becomes the final one also. Your full cooperation will assist in that.'

The blood rushed to Vitali's head and drained away immediately, leaving him giddy. 'Anything,' he heard himself whisper.

'Good.' Another long pause, in which Igor stubbed out his cigarette on the floor and leaned forward across the desk, bringing his face so close to Vitali's that the latter could smell the garlic on the other man's breath. 'This, then, is the situation. Your new assistant has arrived in Ristikent. At long last your pleas for assistance have been answered: Igor's *propiska* is stamped good for work and residence here. Igor stays with you, in your house. Don't worry — ' the stranger held up a deflecting hand — 'Igor keeps himself to himself, your neighbours will scarcely know of his existence.'

I hope not, Vitali thought; my god, I hope not.

'When you go to the camps, I go too — I am your new assistant, after all. What I do there is none of your business, but you may as well know that it is absolutely essential for me to interview certain prisoners without the authorities being aware of it. That may take several visits, we'll just have to see. All that need concern you is that I have to keep my cover at all times. I am Igor, you understand, your assistant, your friend. If anyone asks, no matter who it is, that's what you tell him. Got it?'

Vitali blew out his cheeks. He had no choice; go with the tide. 'Yes, Comrade.'

'Remember . . . *no matter who asks*! Do you understand?'

'Yes, Comrade. I understand perfectly.'

Again that hostile jeer: 'No one, but no one, ever understands perfectly. Not until the bullet enters his skull.' The stranger, seeing the condition Vitali was in, leaned back satisfied. 'There will be compensations. Starting with . . . this.' Igor took out his wallet and extracted some notes which he placed on the desk in front of Vitali. Five hundred roubles. 'I eat,' he explained. 'Also, I drink. That should cover it for a while. If you need more, ask — but be prepared to account for every kopeck of that when you do.'

Vitali's fat hand scuttled across the desktop and closed round the notes before Igor, or whatever his name was, could change his mind.

'Now start earning it. Your routine, I want to be sure I've got it right. You do a weekly round of the camps, is that correct?'

Vitali struggled to pull himself together. 'Yes, Comrade. Not all of them: Olenegorsk Three and Lovozero ITK/1 have their own vans — they only call me in if there's an overload they can't cope with. That doesn't happen very often.'

'So: each week, on Monday, you go to the rest. Including Ristikent MU/12?'

'Yes.'

'Always on a Monday?'

'Always.'

'Does it sometimes happen that there are no bodies?'

'Sometimes. But in winter there is usually at least one.'

'Suppose there are none; do they phone to say that you need not come?'

'No. I only find out what they've got for me when I arrive.'

'Who checks the van in and out?'

'I have to go through the usual security checks on my way in. There is always an officer to supervise the loading of the corpses. Then I —'

'Wait. Who does the loading, the physical handling?'

'Zeks.'

'Not you?'

'No.'

'How many zeks?'

'Two. Nearly always two.'

'Are the corpses wrapped?'

'Not always. It depends on whether the supply of shrouds has run out.'

'Do you personally run any kind of check on the corpses?'

'Check, Comrade?'

'Do you look at them, look inside the shrouds?' Igor became impatient at the dumb look on the undertaker's face. 'To see if they're dead!'

'No, Comrade.' Vitali was shocked.

'So. The zeks load the bodies. The officer looks on. Does he do anything, ask you to sign anything?'

'No.'

'And then?'

'Then I go out.'

'Is there another security check?'

'Sometimes. It depends on the camp.'

Igor drummed his fingers on the desk and said nothing for a while. Then, 'It depends on the camp,' he repeated slowly. 'You mean, some run exit checks and some don't . . . what the devil *do* you mean, Anissenko?'

'What you said, Comrade. Some do and some don't.'

'Well, what about Ristikent MU/12?'

When Vitali did not reply at once the stranger looked up impatiently to find that his face had moulded itself into an expression of painful intensity, as if he were trying to recollect something of importance.

'It is very strange that you should mention that, Comrade. Twelve used to be one of the strictest. Now . . . '

'Yes! Now what?'

'There is no exit check.'

'What, nothing at all?'

'That's right. Before, I had to stop the van at the inner fence and the sentries — there were always three of them — would do a bodycount. Then they'd shout the result across to the sentries on the outer wire. I'd go through; stop; the outer sentries would count again. Then I could go.'

'And do you mean to tell me that now that doesn't happen?'

'That's right, Comrade.'

'What, *none* of it?'

'None of it, Comrade.'

Igor rose abruptly and came round the desk. The two men stood face to face for a long time while Igor studied Vitali's expression for signs of duplicity, and at last the stranger appeared to be satisfied that the undertaker was telling the truth, for he said, 'Good. Today is Monday. What time does your round start?'

Vitali looked at his watch. It had stopped. He must have forgotten to wind it the night before. 'Nine o'clock,' he said mechanically.

'Then you're late.' There was nothing wrong with Igor's Seiko on its elasticated steel strap, which recorded ten past nine. 'Time for work,' the stranger said; and the look on his face was as near jovial as the features would bear. 'I've got to change first — it wouldn't do for me to be seen in these clothes, not in a dump like this. And then we'd better get going, hadn't we, boss?'

It so happened that Ristikent MU/12 was the first port of call on Vitali's roster that day. The road to the camp had suffered badly from the spring rains and the undertaker's driving, never that good, was made worse by the gloomy, lowering presence of Igor in the passenger seat. It was one of the unhappiest journeys that Vitali could remember.

Victor fared little better. His mouth spent the bumpy drive alternating between a cigarette and his fingernails. The setup stank to high heaven. A camp with no exit checks was new in his experience. Were they expecting him? It sounded as if they were; in the course of researching Ristikent and its undertaker he had managed to stir up a lot of mud. Too much could go wrong. He had planned ahead as far as he could, but without official backing from one of the major Western intelligence services there had to be limits. Victor was not looking forward to the coming reconnaissance.

His nerves were thoroughly frayed by the recent session with Anissenko. He knew that he had gone out on a terribly thin limb by showing the undertaker his red pass. The forgery emanated from Shrilenko's legendary document factory in West Berlin and was as authentic as the magicians there could make it, but still the thought of it burning a hole in his breast pocket was enough to bring Victor out in a cold sweat. Fewer than a hundred such passes circulated in the Soviet Union at any one time, the pattern was always changing, and not even Shrilenko could be sure that all his models were current. He had worked from the original which Victor brought out of Russia with him at the end of the AWACS mission: good enough to fool a cursory glance from a frightened puppy like Anissenko, but hardly a guarantee of safety under the searchlights of Ristikent MU/12's guardposts.

Anissenko gave Victor the creeps. He could only hope that some of the undertaker's recent crash course in tradecraft would stick for long enough to do a bit of good.

Then suddenly, there was the camp.

The van breasted a rise and began the descent across the moor to the outer sentry post. The camp was surrounded by a cleared belt extending half a mile in every direction: an unnatural zone of featureless countryside which no zek could hope to cross undetected. Victor leaned forward in the passenger seat and furiously set himself to master details in the few moments which remained. Two lines of wire, each ten metres high; six watchtowers, their machine guns clearly visible, the last tower almost on the lakeshore; carefully raked earth, twenty metres of it, mined, between the wires; one pair of sentries with a dog, slowly patrolling the inner fence — nothing out of the ordinary there. Beyond that lay a dense, broad belt of trees, deliberately planted so as to screen off the house from those who had no business beyond the wire.

The van was drawing very close to the outer perimeter, and Victor focused his attention on the single-storey clapboard blockhouses which stood at either side of the first gate — a proper gate, he noticed grimly, with thick reinforced metal bars and six guards, now all facing in the direction of the approaching van. Notices, red lettering on white boards. '*Ispravitel' no-trudovaya Koloniya MU/12.*' And the hollow admonition, 'Honest Labour: the Road Home!'

Through sheer nervousness Vitali forgot to let out the clutch and the van humped its way to a stall. Victor casually rested his arm on the windowledge, looking straight ahead through the windscreen.

'You want to take a driving test, eh?' The two sentries on the driver's side were familiar with Anissenko; their round, Mongolian faces demonstrated only good humour. Victor guessed that the van's arrival marked one of the few moments of human contact that these men enjoyed and was therefore pleasurably anticipated. 'Who's this, then?'

Three more sentries materialized by Victor's elbow. The expressions on their faces were unfriendly. One of them immediately stood back a couple of paces and raised his sub-machine-gun. Victor noted from their shoulder-boards that these men were from Guards Directorate (Gulag), not the KGB. Nevertheless, he felt the muscles of his stomach tense and for a second had difficulty breathing.

'He's my new assistant, Igor,' Vitali said, with a fair stab at conviction. 'Hey, whaddyou think, I got a helper at last, huh?' But the sentries' faces did not change.

'Your identification. Quick!'

Victor reached into his pocket. Inside his coat were two plastic folders, one containing an internal passport made out in the name of the real Igor and the other his red pass. There was a small nick in the edge of the passport folder. Victor identified it without hesitation and put the *propiska* in the gloved hand which forcefully thrust its way under his chin. The sentry stared at it for a long time, then went into a huddle with his colleagues. Although Victor could hear them muttering together he wasn't able to distinguish the words. He longed to take out a cigarette, but knew it would be tantamount to an admission of something to hide.

'Wait.'

One of the sentries paused for long enough to issue the terse instruction before returning to the guardhouse. Out of the corner of his eye Victor traced the telephone wire which stretched between the two fences, and his stomach muscles screwed an extra turn.

'Smoke?'

Victor's head jerked sharply. The undertaker had produced a pack of cigarettes and was offering them to the sentries on his side of the van. His movements were calm and unhurried. When the sentries' cigarettes were lit he held out the pack to Victor without looking at him. 'Pass them round your side, will you, Igor?'

After a second's hesitation, Victor took the packet. Anissenko's composure shook him. It was flawless. Could natural fear alone explain such unexpected talent in a supposed amateur? Victor pushed the disturbing thought from his mind and offered the packet out of the window. With scarcely a pause the sentry holding the sub-machine-gun lowered it and moved forward to join his two colleagues, who were already sparring with their frozen fingers to be the first to accept. Victor fumbled in his pocket for a light, remembering to leave his Ronson alone. Undertakers' mates didn't carry fashionable electronic lighters, although KGB high-ups might. 'Matches,' he hissed, and Vitali, once he had got over his momentary panic, fumbled for a box of Vestas.

A sergeant was walking down the corridor between the outer and the inner fence. He stopped short of the van while one of the sentries went up to him with Victor's papers. There was a muttered colloquy, after which the sergeant approached the passenger window. He held Victor's photograph in his cupped hands, evidently comparing it with the original subject, while Victor stared past him with studied unconcern. The sergeant was young, he noticed, and had the face of a child on his first day at a new school, ingratiating his way towards friendship. The NCO evidently mistook the expression in Victor's eyes for hostility, for his own face fell and he said, 'Your mate's been moaning on about how they won't give him an assistant . . . I'm glad to see he's got one at last.'

'Ah . . . oh, yes, yes indeed, thank you, Captain.'

The sergeant perked up at that, and Victor remembered just in time to offer him the by now much depleted cigarette packet before the gates swung open. Vitali started the engine and they were through. The sergeant evidently commanded the farther line of wire as well, for there were no more difficulties: the second set of gates parted to admit the van and a moment later Victor found himself inside the strict regime corrective labour camp known as Ristikent MU/12.

Anissenko drove slowly, as he had been instructed, while he treated Victor to a running commentary. 'Over there, on the right, the hospital wing . . . that's the kitchen . . . that low extension, see, next to the bakehouse, that's the cold room. That's where they keep the corpses, along with the meat . . .'

Victor leaned forward excitedly, craning for a better view. 'Stop as close as you can to the kitchen by stalling the engine, like you did at the gate. Leave the rest to me.'

The crude gravel track curved round the front of the dacha, leading down a short slope to the kitchen block. Vitali hesitated. 'Are you sure . . .?'

'I'm sure,' Victor snarled and with his left heel kicked down hard on Anissenko's instep. The driver yelped, took his foot off the clutch and stalled the van just as it reached the side door of the bakery.

Victor jumped out and ran round to the bonnet, which he yanked open with the expertise of a born mechanic. No one saw him slip his hand down between the battery casing and the side of the engine block to pull loose a wire which he had carefully designated in the course of his morning's inspection. As Vitali alighted from the cab and went to join him Victor began to curse.

'Electrical. Alternator's bust. *Shit*!'

Vitali put his head under the bonnet and whimpered, 'We've been spotted.'

Victor raised his head a fraction and looked out from under the bonnet. About fifty metres away from where they had stalled was the door of the extension to the kitchen building: the cold store. Outside it stood an officer and two zeks, all looking in their direction. As Victor's eyes focused, the officer began to walk towards the stationary van. 'Move it up,' he snapped. 'You expect them to carry bodies over that distance?'

Vitali stood upright and spread his hands in a despairing gesture. From under his eyelids Victor saw that the undertaker was sweating, his puffy face the very picture of guilt and apprehension.

'Who's this?' The officer eyed Victor coldly. 'I haven't seen you before.'

'I'm his assistant, Colonel. Here's my papers.' Victor didn't wait to be asked; he held out his *propiska* to the officer with a bold gesture which betokened a confidence he was very far from feeling. But the officer waved it away after a single contemptuous glance, 'They checked your papers at the gate, didn't they? Well, then! And don't you civilian scum know anything? This —' he pointed brusquely at his left shoulder-board — 'means I'm a captain, not a fucking colonel. Now move on, damn you, or I'll put you in the cold store myself.'

'Can't.'

The captain was not accustomed to being disobeyed, particularly not by strange civilians with direct, fishy stares. 'Can't!' he exploded. 'Why the fucking hell not?'

'Breakdown. Alternator's gone.'

The two zeks had come up to stand behind the furious officer, their eyes darting hither and thither in search of something to filch. Victor bypassed the captain and addressed himself to them. 'Either of you know anything about engines?' They shook their heads.

'No talking to them!'

'Sorry.'

There was a long silence while the officer's eyes shifted indecisively back and forth between Vitali and his new assistant, a silence broken by Victor asking, 'Have you got a maintenance section here, Captain?'

The officer hesitated. 'That's a State secret.'

Victor allowed a look of resignation to seep across his face. He leaned his back against the side of the van and folded his arms; then he said, 'Sorry I spoke,' and one of the zeks sniggered.

'Shut up, you!' The zek subsided. When after another moment of silence the officer spoke again, his tone had become fractionally more reasonable. 'Who normally maintains your van?'

'That garage out near Monchegorsk,' said Vitali. 'Glukhovsky's place.'

'Somebody'll have to get in touch with them, then.' The officer looked around him, stuck for choice. He couldn't very well send the zeks off to telephone, but he was damned if he was letting a couple of civilians use the camp facilities. Why the devil weren't there any guards around?

'Can't we use your phone, please, Captain?' Victor's voice bordered on the insolent; it was as if he were laughing at the officer somewhere behind his fishy eyes.

'No.'

'Haven't you got one of them either?' Victor asked innocently; and the other zek sniggered like the first one. The officer wheeled round, but now both prisoners stood with their eyes fixed on the ground, their faces expressionless.

Victor silently drew a long breath and willed the officer to do the thing he had to do, he must do, the one inescapable, inevitable, incontestable act which was staring him in the face, obliterating all other options. Do it, he grated to himself, do it, do it, *do it!*

'Wait here. I'll telephone myself. Glukhovsky, you say?'

Vitali hastened to reply. 'Yes, Captain. And thank you, thank you very much indeed, I'm so sorry this should have happened . . .'

'Never mind all that shit, what's the number, moron?'

Vitali rifled through his pockets until he came up with a tattered black notebook, which he proceeded to consult. He found the number and haltingly repeated it to the enraged officer, who snatched the book from the undertaker's hands and walked off with it. After he had gone a few metres he was struck by a thought and wheeled round. 'You two,' he yelled at the zeks. 'Wait over by the cold store until I get back.' 'Yes, Captain,' they chorused, but did not move.

On this, his first visit to the camp, Victor had no particular plan. He expected to accomplish very little. His intention was to conduct a lightning recce and then get out as fast as possible. Five minutes. That utterly arbitrary time-limit was the best he could do. Three hundred seconds from now, the officer would return. Everything had to be slotted into that scintilla of time, and it meant working at breakneck speed. He counted off five seconds from his precious allocation, allowing the captain to pass out of earshot, and drew a deep breath.

'You two. I'm looking for someone. Old, beaten up a lot, piercing blue eyes, tall, pointy ears. Kitchen worker. Mean anything?'

He showed his hands, each of which contained two packs of cigarettes. They were a cheap Russian brand: poor stuff as bribes go, but less risky if he were caught than American smokes. The zeks looked questioningly at each other, but did not move.

'I thought you didn't look like a bodies man,' one of them said at last. Victor focused all his attention on him. The zek who had spoken looked young but he was obviously blind in one eye — it had turned milky white. There was something malevolent about his gaze, as if behind the ruined eye there lurked a baleful intelligence. 'Too much like someone who belongs this side of the wire, if you ask me,' the zek went on, and his companion nodded. Victor grinned wolfishly and said, 'You're not so wrong at that, friend.' Then he beckoned to the trembling figure of Anissenko. 'Keep an eye open, Vitali. As soon as he comes back, start whistling.'

'What shall I whistle?'

Victor stared at his troubled, stupid face and knew rage. 'You bloody fool, anything you fucking well like!' Vitali backed away until he had placed the protective barrier of the van comfortably between him and the explosive stranger who in a few short hours had turned his life upside down. Victor followed his progress with smouldering eyes before feverishly rounding once more on the zeks.

'Are you another *gaybist*?' the half-blind zek asked suddenly; and Victor's expression hardened. 'Never you mind who I am,' he said savagely. 'Do you want the smokes or not?'

The zeks exchanged glances; they seemed to be engaged in some kind of telepathic debate. All the while Victor was counting, at least one minute gone, sixty-five, sixty-six, why the hell didn't they decide . . .?

210

'In there.' The evil-looking zek nodded towards the kitchen, an unpleasant smile on his face. He seemed to be calculating. 'There's one in there sounds like him.'

'Then,' Victor said, forcing himself to sound rational, 'go and get him for me. Will you. Please.'

Another moment of indecision, again the furtive glances crossed and entwined, a mutual shrug. Seventy-nine, eighty, eighty-one . . .

Then the half-blind zek was slouching towards the kitchen, while his companion expertly lifted the packets from Victor's hands.

The young zek reached the kitchen door, hesitated and laid his hand against the wood as if testing the resistance. The door opened suddenly and a burly figure filled the frame, blocking any possibility of entry. Victor's eyes narrowed. A Chechen . . . What was a Chechen doing in a camp like this? The boy stopped at once; his shoulders drooped and after a second he actually withdrew a couple of steps. So the Chechen frightened him, did he? Victor grunted. The boy was no fool, then.

The Chechen looked at Victor and pursed his lips. Then he said something to the boy who retreated, keeping his face towards the man in the doorway, until he was almost back where he started by Victor's side.

'Get lost, you.' The zek directed a murderous glance at Victor, who returned it in good measure, before spitting at his feet and slouching off towards the coldroom. A moment later Povin emerged at the door, wiping his hands on his denim jacket and blinking owlishly in the watery morning sun.

His gaze lighted on Victor, but for a moment he betrayed no reaction. He cocked his head, as if listening, his eyes flickered this way and that, seeking out potential watchers, the hands continued their restless movement . . . then he sank down on to his haunches like a robot whose master has switched off the power, his face as white as the flour he'd left behind on the table, and softly groaned.

The other zek had come to stand behind Victor, listening curiously for what was about to happen. 'You fuck off too.' On hearing Victor's command he pouted, but the overwhelming smell of KGB was too much for him. He disappeared behind the van with a half-smothered laugh, taking Vitali's one remaining box of matches with him, and Victor was free at last to concentrate on what Kazin had done to his former boss.

The sight filled him with such anger that for a giddy second he wasn't sure whether to weep or find the two zeks again and work off his fury by beating them to a bloody pulp. The fit passed as quickly as it had come. Later. That could all come later. Right now there were more important things to deal with.

'Stepan,' he whispered. His voice came out as a dry sob and Povin matched it with his own.

'You . . . *fool*.' He sounded as if he were in the grip of mortal despair; then, as quickly as Victor had recovered, he contrived to get a hold on himself. With trembling fingers Victor somehow managed to light a cigarette. He rested his shoulder against the wall of the kitchen blockhouse and casually looked around him. There was nobody about. Anyone watching would see only an idle zek taking an unauthorized break and an undertaker's assistant standing a few metres away from him, cigarette in hand, while he waited for the mechanic to come. Just two minutes left now. One hundred and twenty seconds. The scenario wasn't perfect, but it would do. One hundred and nineteen, one hundred and eighteen . . .

'Keep your voice low.'

Povin nodded.

'I think I can get you out. They don't do a bodycount at the gate. Find a way of getting inside one of the shrouds, leave the rest to me, I'm part of the body disposal unit now — '

'You . . . stupid . . . bloody . . . *fool!*' Povin shook his head very slowly, as if astounded that anyone could be so dumb. 'Get out fast, Victor. They're expecting you. Can't you *smell* it? Where are the guards? Where are the sentries? Where has the officer gone? *They know you're here*! Turn round and get the hell out, now!'

Eight-seven, eighty-six . . .

'I know . . . but I'll think of a way round that. I'll be back, and I won't leave you here . . .'

Povin raised his voice and spoke steadily across Victor's rising protests, spoke in a tone that Victor knew of old and obeyed as instinctively as his eyes turned towards the light.

'I am coming out, Victor, but in my own way and in my own time. If I'm spared, which I won't be if you send that bloody boy anywhere near me again. Yet you can help me, you come like a gift from God, there is one thing you can do for me, one thing *only*, and you must listen now, and not talk again, because we have a few seconds left and they will not give us another chance, please believe that, Victor, you have to contact the Travel Agency, do you hear me, Victor, do it now, today, through Bryant, however you can, and you must tell them to arrange a one-way passage, now, immediately, a single ticket out . . .'

Notwithstanding the old man's injunction Victor could not resist interrupting, 'From the camp?'

'From Moscow.'

'*Moscow*!'

'From Moscow, yes, please, *please* listen, dear Victor . . .'

'A one-way passage. For you . . .'

'For a child . . .'

As the officer approached the broken-down van he could see that someone was sitting on the kitchen step and he quickened his pace. 'Hey! You there! You get back to work, or I'll have you thrown in the isolator!' Then he recognized the old man and his expression altered.

'I can assure you, Captain Zuyev —' it was the old man who spoke — 'I was merely taking a few moments' break. Nothing more.' Povin staggered painfully to his feet, willing Victor away with a single flash of his steel-blue eyes, and disappeared inside the kitchen. Victor tore his gaze back to the flustered captain's face and studied it with curiosity.

'The mechanic's coming. Kandalaksha's already been on the line, demanding to know where the hell you've got to. You two'll be working late tonight, don't think otherwise.'

'Thank you, Captain. While we're waiting, perhaps I'll just take another look inside the hood. Maybe if I poke around a bit . . .'

'You do that! And your bloody boss here can start help carrying the bodies to the van before they turn into soup!'

It was a peculiar thing, but a few minutes of fiddling under the bonnet served to bring the engine back to life, which caused all Zuyev's circuits to blow at once. He exacted two roubles from the hapless Anissenko as the price of his phone call to the mechanic, and the two men could hear his curses ringing in their ears long after they had left the kitchen block. The sentries let them out with half-hearted waves of commiseration (for word travels fast in a camp), while the sergeant was even moved to offer Victor and Anissenko a cigarette apiece for consolation. He watched the van from the outer guardpost; only when it had disappeared over the moors did this fresh-faced, eager young man, who was neither a sergeant nor assigned to the Guards Directorate (Gulag), go back to the unit commander's office and place a phone call to Moscow, status most immediate, for the personal attention of General Boris Frolov.

21

Inna sat at the desk in the big interrogation room overlooking the lake and considered her position. There was nothing enviable about it; she was still marginally better off than her old man, but that was about all. How long would her immunity last, she wondered? Especially now that the Project Committee had decided on Povin's fate . . .

She put her head in her hands and tried to work out what her latest instructions actually meant. The words were plain enough. What mattered was the truth which lay behind them.

This afternoon she was to tell Povin of 'their' decision: something so outrageous that even now the woman had difficulty taking it in. The problem was that she no longer believed

214

in 'them', or what they told her. And the old man would know it. Inna raised her eyes to the door and slowly nodded. Yes. He would know.

'Today,' Inna Karsovina said briskly, 'we are going out for a nice drive in the countryside. Wouldn't you like that?'

The old man smiled at what he took to be a pleasantry. After their last encounter he hadn't been sure whether she would opt for ferocious, overweening brutality or submissive weakness at their next meeting. Her midway choice of nursery discipline, firm but caring as he mentally described it, struck him as wholly admirable; and once again he gave her credit for doing the unexpected. The image of a nanny not only pleased him, it stirred up a memory.

'You remember how I told you you had a child?'

'Ah yes, I'd been meaning to ask you about that again, Povin. Come on, now. How the devil did you manage to guess? For you were guessing, that first time, weren't you.'

Povin modestly lowered his eyes. 'I was about to tell you. Something you said just now, the way you said it, I mean — it reminded me of those early days when we were both still . . . guessing.'

'I don't understand you.'

'It is your manner of speech, Citizen Karsovina. You spoke to me just then as you would to a difficult, perhaps even exasperating child — as you would to Volodiya, in fact. "A nice drive in the country . . . " It was an early clue.'

'So very clever.'

Povin, hearing the sarcasm in her voice, was abashed. 'Might I ask one thing?'

'Well?'

'I remember you said you would not report my little trick about Volodiya to the authorities. Why was that?'

Inna answered without hesitation. 'It would have been too much of a waste of time. That sort of thing can wait for later. Don't think I've forgotten it.'

'I see. So time is important on this interrogation?'

'Apparently. Now. Are you coming for that drive or not?'

Povin smiled good-naturedly. He couldn't perceive the point

of this folly, not yet, but he was happy to go along with it in the faith that something would emerge. 'So you've decided to get rid of me at last,' he ventured.

'What?'

'The old trick. The prisoners go out on a work detail. A guard says: You! Go pick up that log of wood, over there. The chosen one goes, and crosses the line dividing the work area from the rest of the forest. So . . . ' He shrugged.

'So what?'

'So they shoot him, of course. For attempting to escape.'

'You're not serious.' The words were dragged out of Inna against her will. He was doing it again. He was distracting her, beguiling her . . .

'But I am. The reward to the guard is a day's leave.'

'*Reward*!'

'Certainly.' It was obvious that the woman had never heard of this practice, yet how could she live in Kazin's world and not know? 'It is a well-recognized method of dealing with trouble-makers.'

He could see from her eyes that she believed what he told her while at the same time resenting his insistence on telling the truth, and remorselessly he followed the point through. 'That is why I say, my time has come. You will take me for a drive and shoot me.' Povin raised his hands a few inches from his knees and lowered them again. 'Well, so be it.'

Inna appeared to detect in his words a meaning of which Povin himself was unaware. It occurred to the old man that she had an unwelcome secret to impart, but was determined to choose the right moment. His words had presented her with an opportunity to speak but she was going to pass it up, gambling that there would be a more favourable opening later on. The thought disturbed him.

'You must have seen a lot, I suppose.' The woman's voice was slow, reflective.

'Many things. Terrible things.'

'What was the worst thing?' He could tell that she didn't really want to pursue this, but some devil inside her was overriding the day's appointed programme and he reflected (not for the first time) that she did not know what she was

216

really looking for, or why. 'The very worst thing you can remember?'

Povin treated her question seriously. It was a difficult one to answer, so he spent several minutes dredging about in his memory. He had no desire to spare her, but he recognized that the choice of incident was important.

'I remember a zek eating himself,' he said at last. He tried to keep his voice flat and unemotional, like a newscaster reporting an atrocity, but the woman was very shocked.

'I don't believe you,' she said after a second's hesitation; but he could tell that she did so only to test her own reaction, so he ignored her and continued.

'We were all starving. I was being interrogated round the clock, I didn't go out, but the others were required to work, of course. Conditions were appalling, beyond your imagination. The camp was in northern Siberia, near Norilsk. Winter. Forty below at night. Many prisoners froze to death. Those that survived worked until they dropped, at the uranium mines near there.' Povin shuddered. 'It was a death camp. Then one night I saw this thing I will never forget. One of the zeks had a knife. He used it to carve off a tiny slice of his own calf, here . . .' Povin bent down to indicate the precise spot on his own leg and Inna leaned forward, as if mesmerized. 'Then . . .'

'Yes? Then?'

Povin slowly shook his head, bringing the mental kaleidoscope into focus. 'There were some old books in the camp, piles and piles of them, all rotting. No one ever read them, or even knew where they came from They ended up in the latrines, usually. But that night, this old zek tore off some of the sheets lying around and used them to make a small fire. On which he . . . cooked . . . his own flesh . . .'

'Stop it!'

'. . . But they found him, the guards came in and found what he was doing, you see, and they shot him.'

Inna wiped her forehead. The room was stuffy, she found it hard to breathe.

'They shot him . . . but, this is the interesting part —' the old man grew suddenly animated — 'do you know why they shot him, Citizen Karsovina?'

217

The woman looked up to see Povin's eyes fixed beseechingly on her own, as if he needed her help in order to get through the story to the end, and mutely shook her head.

'They shot him . . . because those old books, those mouldy piles of paper that nobody wanted . . . when the guards picked them up and read them, it turned out they were the collected works of Lenin. And he had taken some of the pages to make a fire, so that he could . . . '

'Stop it, stop it, *stop it*!'

There was a long silence. The tense relationship had unexpectedly launched itself into a void which neither of them had sought or desired, a desolation where there was no communication between the old man and his interrogator, no contact of any kind.

After a while Povin was struck by an inconsequential thought and he said, 'It is a lie, to say that no man is an island. Men *are* islands. But they are also *like* islands, in this way . . . they are connected. Beneath the surface. They are linked.'

'I think,' Inna said, 'that we should go out now.' It was hard for the old man to know what her thoughts were. She pulled her chair towards the desk and picked up the phone.

'Bring his clothes in.'

As she replaced the receiver her eyes came level with his own and she managed a wan smile. 'I have been instructed to provide you with some proper clothing. You cannot go into town wearing zek's rags, can you?'

'You are serious — about going out? I don't understand this. Do you?'

Before she could answer there was a knock at the door and a young KGB lieutenant entered the room. He carried a large parcel wrapped up in brown paper which he proceeded to place on a chair over by the wall. Inna waved a hand in acknowledgement and said, 'The car is here?'

'At the front door, Comrade. Whenever you're ready.'

She nodded and the officer withdrew. Povin waited until the door had closed behind him before he said, 'What's in the parcel?'

'Clothes. Your own clothes, brought specially from Moscow.'

218

'Everything of mine was destroyed,' the old man said bitterly. 'They told me so, often.'

'Yes, they did — and they meant to destroy everything. But you know the KGB ... ' Her voice was scornful. 'I'm told they've made some alterations, on account of your new measurements. Let's see ...'

She rose and walked over to collect the parcel from the chair, placing it on the desk in front of Povin. The string holding it together was tied in a loose bow which came undone at the first tug. She unfolded the paper ... and for a long moment the two of them sat staring helplessly at what Kazin had done.

Povin recognized the garments. An officer's peaked cap, the greatcoat with its sky-blue shoulder-boards, tunic, trousers, cotton shirt and tie. The uniform of a full general in the KGB. His uniform.

'This is a joke. This is ... *monstrous*!' Her hand was already on the telephone when he reached out to restrain her, a tired smile hovering round his lips.

'No joke, Citizen Karsovina.'

She stared at him blankly. 'But ... you realize what he's done? You realize what will happen if you are seen wearing these?'

'Of course.'

'Then how ...?'

'Because it represents the next move. Do not be so stupid as to deceive yourself that you are in charge of my life, my fate, for you are not. No, Citizen ...' He shook his head wearily. 'This is planned. Of course, when we go out to the car they will see me and they will think — just another big-hat involved in a high-level interrogation, a plant, a stoolpigeon. We both know that. But my days are numbered anyway.'

'They're not!' She seemed to be on the point of disclosing her mysterious secret but again she resisted the temptation; instead, she roughly shook off his restraining hand and grabbed the telephone.

Nine-eight, six-four, double-four: Krubykov would have been proud of her. She let it ring thirty-five times before allowing herself to face the fact that Kazin wasn't going to answer.

219

'It's not your fault,' he said kindly. 'You imagine you're in charge here — well, you did, anyway. But you're not in charge. Inside this room, Kazin is king.' He rose to his feet. 'I'd better put these on.'

But Inna was dialling again. 'Send up my driver!'

Povin sighed good-naturedly and sat down. Several minutes passed. At last there came another knock on the door and the lieutenant put his head round it.

'There has been a mistake,' the woman said coldly. 'Take these clothes away and bring proper ones.'

'I am sorry, Comrade, but that is not possible.'

'Why not?'

'We have nothing else in the correct size. And the instructions — written instructions, Comrade — were very precise.'

'I see. We shall not be going out today, after all.'

'*Very* precise, Comrade.' The officer's boyish face had suddenly grown hard.

'Wait downstairs.'

After the lieutenant had left the room Povin took up the cap and thoughtfully turned it round and round, as if he had never seen one like it. Then his fingers ran over the tunic, feeling its rough texture, before passing to the shirt, the trousers, the tie . . . 'Yes, they're mine,' he said at last.

'But . . . *why?*'

'Oh, plenty of reasons. Perhaps because you're going to shoot me and for some reason you want the holes in my uniform and my blood on the cloth.' His smile radiated jollity. 'Come on, Citizen, use your imagination!'

She sat in silence, her rounded shoulders eloquent testimony to what she was feeling. 'You're determined to go through with this . . . this farce?'

'What choice do either of us have?' he asked gently. 'You heard what the Lieutenant said . . .'

A resigned smile flickered across the woman's lips and was gone. 'Then you'd better have your instructions.'

'Ah, that's more like it! Marching orders.'

'Only one.' She hauled her body into a more upright position and wriggled her shoulders as if to ease the tension. 'For as long as we are outside you are to call me . . . ' She hesitated, shook her head, tried again. 'By my first name. Inna. And I will call you Stepan.'

The old man's eyes closed in a long, slow blink but he displayed no other sign of surprise.

'While we are off camp limits, you are to call me by my given name because to do otherwise would be to attract suspicion. That is the . . . the *theory* of it.' She made no attempt to conceal her scepticism.

'You are growing a little tired of other people's theories, I think?'

She made no reply, but turned away from him and faced the window. For several more minutes Povin looked down at the clothes, then up at his interrogator, then down to the clothes again. Suddenly he seemed to reach a decision. His hands went to the neck of his denim jacket and he started to undress.

She hurried him out to the car as if making a midnight arrest, using her own body in a vain attempt to conceal him from curious eyes. There was hardly anyone about, yet everybody knew. Even when Inna Karsovina snapped at the driver to get a move on they both realized that it was nothing but a forlorn gesture; Alexander the Chechen was coming out of the bakehouse and, although he never raised his eyes to the car, it was clear that he saw. As they accelerated away from the dacha Povin could not resist sneaking a quick glance through the rear window. The Chechen stood looking after them with a thoughtful expression on his face which said: 'A peaked cap and gold braid, a chauffeur too. Well, well . . .'

The woman sat in the back seat next to Povin, looking out of the window at the drenched moors, as if expecting the dreary Kola countryside to provide her with consolation.

'It surprised me when the snow began to melt,' she said absently. 'I thought it was always white up here. In fact, spring should be quite pleasant. Soon there will be wild flowers. I am looking forward to that.'

Povin cautiously eyed the back of the driver's neck. It was the same young KGB lieutenant, and the old man mentally congratulated Kazin on the standard of the production. Set design and props were perfect.

'Suppose I wanted to get out,' he said, suddenly keen to take her mind off things. 'Go for a walk and pick you some of those flowers.'

'Certainly. In a week or two's time, when they start to bloom.'

Povin raised an ironic eyebrow and the woman laughed. 'Am I frightened you'll try to escape, do you mean? Oh, it's all right, you don't have to speak in riddles — ' a gesture at the driver's back — 'he's one of us, he is. No, I'm not in the least worried, Povin. Sorry, I forgot . . . Stepan Ilyich. An old man like you couldn't hope to survive out there. Besides, which way would you go? Camps in every direction, camps and military installations.'

'I might risk it, don't you think?' he said lightly. 'After all, what have I got to lose? There are farms out there, and peasants who would help me perhaps.'

She was starting to pick up his mood. 'Hardly. Do you know what the KGB offers for help in recapturing an escaped prisoner? Sixteen kilogrammes of flour and a sheep. That's more than you're worth.'

Povin chuckled. 'Perhaps I could outbid the KGB. Even if I couldn't, I might just risk it for other reasons.' He assumed a mock official tone. 'It would hardly look well on your dossier, would it, Inna? They might even think, heaven forbid, that you were guilty of assisting me in some way.'

The woman laughed, actually managing to sound gay — she for one was glad to be out, the old man noticed — and tapped the driver on the back. 'Show him.'

Without taking his eyes off the road the man reached down to the seat beside him and lifted a Kalashnikov machine pistol into Povin's range of vision.

'Convinced?'

Her eyes sparkled. Povin shrugged, but did not reply. For several minutes they travelled in silence.

'How did such a person as yourself come to be in the Organs?' he said.

'Oh, *that*.' As the car put more miles between them and the dacha Inna felt her heart perceptibly begin to lighten.

'I was in my last year at Lomonosov. They wanted statis-

222

ticians in the Fifth Direction and my maths degree looked all right to them, I suppose.'

'How did they recruit you, though?'

'On the forehead.'

Povin smiled at this idiomatic Russian description of the direct approach. 'How sensible. Just the kind of invitation which would be calculated to appeal.'

'You think so?'

'I know it. Why did you agree?'

'It looked like an excellent job. Money, prospects. Something useful to do.'

'Does it still seem that way?'

Inna allowed her eyes to linger on the driver's mirror for a fraction longer than was necessary before replying, 'Of course. The service of the State is always worthy. I was lucky to be picked.'

Povin wondered if the chauffeur's ears were as finely attuned to nuances as his own. Inna was going to be in trouble if they were.

'Did your husband mind?'

'Of course not. He was very pleased.'

'Did you ever think of remarrying?'

'No.'

'May I ask why not?'

Inna tossed her head. After a while he prompted her gently. 'There are those lines of Yevtushenko's, in "Irene", how do they go . . .?

> How could it be
> > that now you have
> someone to sleep with
> > but no one to wake up with?

Inna jerked her head round and he saw that he had gone too far. 'How dare you!' she snapped. Her eyes flickered towards the driver's unresponsive back, but only for a moment; it was as if she sensed the all-male conspiracy in the car, for when next she spoke her voice was milder. 'That was impertinent, Povin.'

'I am sorry.' He sounded genuinely contrite. 'But I'm

curious, and you must admit that, however tactlessly it may have been expressed, I do have a point. You are a most attractive woman, Inna. There must have been suitors, since Leonid's death?'

Inna turned back to the window. 'Some.' Her voice had lost all its former gaiety. 'You're presumptuous, Povin.'

He pressed on regardless. 'But never "The Man".'

'Never The Father Man.'

'Ah! Volodiya.'

'Of course.'

'To love me, you must love my son.'

'Exactly. Would you like to change the subject, please.'

'I am sorry, it's just that in this liberated world of ours . . .'

'*Liberated*!' This time even the driver sniggered. Inna shot him a furious glance before rounding on Povin. 'Did you know that as recently as the end of the last war the Turkmenians were burying unfaithful wives up to their noses in sand, as a punishment? Is that liberated? Have things changed so much?'

'Let us change the subject at least, then.'

'You men. All the same! Liberated, yes, for you maybe. Do you know what it's like for a woman who wants a career, any career? Well, *do* you? Of course, you haven't got the faintest conception . . .'

He wondered what she was seeing through those vacant eyes, what memories held her down, until at last her gaze fell and she sat back in her seat. 'It's hardly surprising,' she said. 'What should I expect, after all? From someone like you . . .'

'I am not myself today. All this . . .' He lifted his hands in an apologetic gesture and let them fall again.

They were approaching a township; the poorly made gravel track gave way to rough tarmac and houses began to appear in ones and twos, each surrounded by its meagre plot of garden.

'May I ask . . . where is this, please?'

The driver turned his head sideways and answered with a pleasant smile. 'This is Ristikent, General.' If Povin noticed his reinstatement to the ranks of power he did nothing to show it. 'Not much of a place, I am afraid, but I hope you will enjoy your visit. There is a bar.' He slowed down, made a U-turn in the narrow high street and stopped. 'Please to get out here,

224

General. Comrade Karsovina will be your guide. I shall wait for your return in . . .' His eyes switched inquiringly to Inna's face. 'Half an hour,' she said, and the driver nodded. He enjoyed this role much more than that of sergeant on the gate detail.

Povin got slowly out of the car and looked around him. Ristikent, or what he could see of it, was all the pathetic little settlements of outback Russia rolled into one: a pitted street, houses much in need of repair and maintenance, high-tension cables strung between posts like an endlessly blank musical score. Then he spied a knot of soldiers slouching down the street towards them and instinctively he looked for somewhere to hide. Too late: the soldiers had seen them! The oncoming group had quickened their pace; they were staring at Inna and Povin as if there was something odd about them, now they were straightening out of their former shambling walk, next second they would break into a run. 'Hey you,' they would shout, 'stop, or we shoot!'

As the soldiers — there were four of them — came level with Povin they threw back their shoulders, straightened their backs and with one accord saluted him. For a moment he couldn't respond, then his hand automatically raised itself in a half-remembered gesture until it was brushing the rim of his cap, and the soldiers were gone.

Povin's face had turned chalk white; his hands were shaking. 'Are you all right?' Inna murmured, and then saw that he was very far from being all right, so with rough firmness she grabbed his arm and used her free hand to push open the door of the Friendship Bar. She led him to a table beside the stove and continued to hold his arm while he lowered himself into a chair with a mumble of thanks.

Inna looked around her, oblivious to the quick, penetrating glance which the old man darted at her from under his eyelids. At this time of day the place was deserted and for a moment she wasn't sure that it was even open, although she knew that in the far north shopkeepers hardly recognized the distinction between 'open' and 'closed'. Here, and in all the other places like it, business was business, a sale was a sale.

It was a poor enough place: little more than a narrow front room with five or six tables scattered around the bare concrete floor and a collection of wooden, cushionless chairs to sit on. Several panes of window glass were cracked, and once beyond the pitifully restricted range of the stove draughts criss-crossed every square inch of the bar. Inna wandered towards the far end of the room, taking off her gloves and throwing back the fur hood of her coat, so that her hair tumbled free of constriction. The woman inside her could not help turning back to see if Povin had noticed, but he was sitting hunched in the same position, hands clasped and writhing in his lap, apparently indifferent to their surroundings. She pursed her lips and directed her attention to the bar itself. It was a pine plank laid across trestles, behind which a bank of dusty shelves held no more than a dozen bottles at most.

'Is there anyone here?'

She heard a noise and diverted her attention to a low door by the side of the trestles, through which it was possible to see the soiled tiles and grimy sink of a kitchen. A woman emerged, wiping her hands on a patched apron, and stared at Inna as if customers represented some kind of unwelcome intrusion.

'We want something to drink. Do you have any vodka fit for human consumption?'

The other woman looked towards the stove, where Povin still sat motionless, and Inna could see the fear gather from the corners of her mind. The woman was old and fat and blowzy, the product of too much alcohol and not enough tension in her life to keep away the cobwebs. Inna rapped on the pine plank to bring her attention back to the business in hand.

'Yes, we have vodka.' The barmaid's voice was strangely light and high-pitched for such a fat, bloated body.

'Two glasses, then. Ah!' Inna had been surveying the shelves behind the plank. 'What's that one there? It looks as though it hasn't been opened.'

The barmaid followed her gaze and piped, 'That's Petrovka, that is, Miss. It's awful old.'

Inna gave the plank a delighted slap. 'We'll have that. How much for the bottle?'

The barmaid's eyes travelled round in unhurried circles while she attempted to do the calculation. After a few seconds Inna grew impatient, plonked ten roubles down on to the bar and made a long arm for the bottle on its shelf. 'Now I want two glasses, and then you can keep the change.'

The astonished barmaid could hardly believe her luck. She produced the glasses, took one last, troubled look at the outlandish strangers who had descended into her cosy world without warning, and waddled back into the kitchen.

Inna placed the bottle and glasses on the table in front of Povin, but his apathetic face remained as immobile as the rest of his body. She sat down and waited for the mood to work its way through his system while she uncorked the bottle and filled their glasses. She had a message for him, the time had come when she must deliver it, but — how to broach matters? How to explain what she herself did not fully understand?

The glasses were filled to the brim. When Povin finally raised his eyes from his lap she saw that they were empty of life.

'What is this?'

'Drink. Here.'

He lifted one of his hands, very slowly, like an invalid whose strength has deserted him, and picked up the glass.

'*Zah vahsheh zdahrov'yeh,*' Inna said with artificial heartiness, and the two of them drank. Povin held his upturned glass suspended in the air above his head, a look of disbelief on his face. Then he said, 'This . . . is Petrovka.'

'Right. The woman said it was old, but it tastes all right to me. More?'

Povin lowered his glass to the surface of the rickety table and shook his head. 'I gave it up.'

'What?' His voice was so low that Inna had to strain to make out the words. The old man shivered and came back to life.

'I gave it up. It was my penance for Kyril. No more Petrovka. Ever.'

'Oh. Did you really? I didn't know that.' Then, as the effect of his words sank in, 'Should I get us something else?'

He hesitated for a moment, as if considering it seriously, then shook his head. 'No. It doesn't matter, after all. Who cares?' He laughed and repeated it. 'Who cares?'

He reached out for the bottle and poured each of them another tot. This time he was the one to call a toast. 'To Bucharensky. Kyril!'

They drained their shotglasses and wiped their mouths. Inna was beginning to realize that Kazin's order to take her Young Pioneer into town, although dangerous, did not lack logic. At first she had convinced herself that it was merely a trap but now she saw the sense of the idea. Povin was visibly loosening up before her eyes. His lips had become a pale mauve colour and he was smiling into the distance as if at some pleasant memory of his youth — very much an old man's look, Inna thought. What could he see? Was it Kyril? She knew that was the casename of Stanov's agent, the one who had come closest to uncovering Povin's secret double life. The old man had managed to turn the thing on its head by pointing the finger of suspicion at General Michaelov, inheriting his job in the process. Funny how history repeated itself: Povin in his turn had been usurped by his own deputy, Frolov. How cruel life was . . . Inna felt the by now familiar internal softening process begin its subtle shifts and roughly seized the bottle.

'I told myself that I would take one last glass of Petrovka, as a treat, on my deathbed.' He looked down into the shotglass, as if he half expected to find the grim reaper at the bottom. 'What the hell. Pour.'

Inna obeyed. Then she recorked the bottle and unostentatiously placed it just out of Povin's reach. She could not put off her message any longer. 'This is a celebration,' she said quietly, folding her arms on the table in front of her.

'Mm? What are we celebrating, Inna?'

'You and I are to part.'

'Ah.' He picked up his glass and drummed it on the table. 'I was right to drink the Petrovka, then. The timing's perfect.'

'No, it's not. Here, Stepan, are you sober?'

He smiled sheepishly, half closing his eyelids and thereby causing Inna to miss the undimmed intensity of his gaze. 'What do you think? You take a ravenous zek out of his camp, dress him up as a general, march him into the nearest bar and fill him up with vodka. 'Course I'm sober. Happens every day.'

For all Povin's rigid self-control, not even he could altogether stem the tide of memory. He wondered if the bar had been bugged by Kazin's men, decided not to worry. He'd last drunk Petrovka vodka with Victor. And before that, when?

How many years ago had he first tasted it . . .?

'Did I ever tell you about my mother?' he said suddenly. 'Eh? Did I?'

'Stepan.' Inna leaned farther across the table. 'There is something I have to say . . .'

'Sright. Go 'head. My *mother* —' he pushed his glass aside and beamed at the woman — '*loved* this stuff, she did. Loved it! Drank it all the time. Stepan, she'd say, when she'd had a few of these . . . Stepan, my dear, don't you ever pull the plug on anybody.' Povin rested his elbow on the table and waved one forearm like a windscreen wiper in front of Inna's bemused face. 'Not those words, you understand. 'Swat she meant, though. Don't . . . tell . . . tales.'

'Stepan, please.' It dawned on Inna that the eyes in front of her now were sharp and piercing, according ill with the old man's drunken manner, which had overwhelmed him with remarkable swiftness; was he perhaps trying to tell her something which he could not handle in any other way . . .?

'Aach . . .' Povin's hand fell back to the tabletop. 'Know how I met Michaelov? Telling tales. Ryazan Officers' Training School. There was a cadet, Illyin his name was. Called Lenin a bleating nanny goat, and I told the commandant. Sneaks to the front! Party card for you, my boy, you're just the kind of officer material we need. Meet Michaelov, he'll look after you, he's a sneak as well. Mother . . . never forgave me . . . for what I did, you know. She always thought I . . . '

He stared into her eyes for a long moment, willing her to understand, before his gaze slid away. Inna rubbed her forehead and sighed. How was she going to tell him . . .?

'I'm sorry,' he said suddenly.

'It doesn't matter. I'm sorry too . . . about your mother, Stepan.'

She sensed that he was striving to atone for a treason far greater than anything the KGB recognized, treachery of a kind which she herself had had to live with and which little Volodiya might some day come to know.

'You had a message for me?'

'Yes. I have been ordered to tell you something. It concerns your future, Stepan.' Seeing him draw breath to speak, she held

229

up her hand and went on rapidly. 'No, please just listen. They say they've reached a decision and I've been authorized to tell you what it is. They seem to think that this interrogation has been useful — goodness knows why, but they do. And they want it to go on indefinitely. Not from one day to the next, as before, but at odd intervals, when they have a major problem over internal security. And they're also honest enough to admit that they need you, need your memory, I mean. So they're proposing a deal. It's not much of a deal, but it's a hell of a sight better than what you've got now.'

The smile on his face was lopsided, as though his attention was less than perfect. 'I'm listening.'

'I hope you are, because you have to agree to all the terms or it's off. Is that understood?'

'Yes.'

But she wasn't sure if he really was listening. Should she go on or stop? Go on, what choice did she have . . . ?

'They are going to instal you in a dacha. Nothing grand, just two bedrooms, somewhere near Moscow. You'll be under house arrest for the rest of your life, I'm afraid, but that'll hardly come as a surprise. If you behave yourself, there'll be trips like this one now and then, but nobody's promising anything. You have to cooperate, all the time. Any refusals, any lies, and that's the end — they'll shoot you and bury you in the garden of the house. As long as you cooperate, you can lead a reasonable life — no visitors, but books and music and food and drink.'

When she stopped he looked up at her inquiringly, and she saw that she had his complete attention after all — saw that she had had it from the start, that there was never a time when he did not listen to her every word as if his life depended on it.

'There's more,' he said with unaccustomed asperity. 'I know there's more. Tell me.' When she hesitated he leaned across until his face was very close to her own, close enough for her to smell the vodka on his breath, and repeated with emphasis, 'Tell me.'

'If you will promise not to become angry.'

'I promise. Now *tell me!*'

'It's . . . Stolyinovich. He *is* alive, Stepan, I wasn't joking.

They're going to make you responsible for him.' Seeing his lips start to move soundlessly, she hurried on, stumbling over the words. 'You must be prepared for some terrible changes. Physically and mentally, he's a broken man, although the doctors say they can see some hope for his mind. He'll be entirely dependent on you for every little thing: an exhausting burden. But that's the deal. You can take all of it. Or you can leave all of it. There is nothing in between.'

For a long time he merely looked at her and his eyes gave nothing away. 'He is alive,' he said at last, and somehow it was neither a statement nor a question, but a curious kind of indeterminate hypothetical proposition.

'Yes. Stepan, there is one thing more. So as to give you a proper chance of assessing the deal which they have offered, they propose to bring him up here, on a visit. In two days' time. I repeat — you must start to prepare yourself for changes.'

There was another long silence. Then Povin said, 'What if I refuse this . . . offer?'

'I do not know. They have not told me. I have thought about it, of course. They could shoot you, and draw a line underneath everything. But I don't think they'll do that. I believe they will keep you in a camp, this one or another, harsher one, until you die. You see, it is your cooperation they want. They are prepared to pay for that — in their terms, they are prepared to pay quite a lot. For some of them, keeping a traitor alive is the worst kind of heresy. You are very lucky to be given the choice at all. And it has been made very clear to me that it will not be offered again.'

'They are offering me . . . life?'

'Life. And a measure, however small, of rehabilitation.'

Povin smiled at that. 'Do you know the old joke? "Under the constitution, every Russian is entitled to three *arshins* of earth and a posthumous rehabilitation"?'

'I know it.'

'I never thought that last bit would apply to me.'

'It doesn't apply to you. You'll have your three *arshins* for a grave when you die, which may be years off yet. Don't you realize, that's what I've been telling you?'

He was silent for so long that eventually Inna could bear the

231

6570.

suspense no longer. 'Stepan,' she murmured. Then, when he was still silent, she tried again. 'Stepan, won't you please talk to me? Won't you tell me what you're thinking?'

He shrugged. 'I was thinking . . . I don't believe a word of it. And neither do you.'

She hesitated only a second before replying, 'No. At least . . . no, not in the essentials.'

'There will be no dacha, no trips into town.'

'No rehabilitation, no books, no music.'

'No hope.'

She shook her head in wordless assent and he knew that she was on the verge of tears. The knowledge brought him no comfort but it was not his way to ignore another's pain. He stretched out a hand and the woman took it, entwining their fingers, and when the old man laid his other hand on top of hers she made no attempt to withdraw.

'It's not your fault,' he said absently. 'None of this is your fault, Inna. They used you, that's all. They . . . exposed you.'

'I *want* to believe it! The dacha and . . . and everything else. Because it means you'd be out of that terrible camp, out of danger. But . . .'

He patted her hand. 'Never mind.'

And then at last she did withdraw, but in a way which he did not expect. She folded her arms on the table, lowered her forehead until it was resting on the cradle they made, and began to weep. At first her tears fell silently, with only the heaving of her shoulders to mark her distress, but as time went by the soft hiss of her breath grew into sobs which racked her frame, wrenching themselves free while her heart at last abandoned the futile attempt to control its grief.

Povin slowly reached out to stroke her hair, soothing her into a semblance of calm, and when she had recovered a little he asked her wonderingly, 'Why do you waste your tears?'

She raised her stricken face and managed a feeble smile. 'Oh, I don't know. Because of all the Russian bars like this one, perhaps. Because of all the sad faces like yours, Stepan.'

She wasn't sure if he understood; indeed, she wasn't sure if she herself understood, but it didn't seem to matter. With one accord they helped each other up, putting on their coats and

232

gloves, helping with a sleeve here, a wayward button there, until at last they were ready to go. The smiling lieutenant helped them into the car and draped a rug over their knees. As he pulled out from the kerb he glanced in the mirror to see his two charges staring out of their respective windows; but, because his view was restricted, he was not to know that they had placed their hands on the seat with the little fingers just touching, so as to make a fragile bridge across the gulf which lay between them.

22

Valyalin knew that things had reached rock bottom when Frolov actually came down to see him off. The major, seeing his chief in natural daylight, was even more appalled by his changed appearance. Frolov had lost over ten kilos in weight during the past month alone. Dark circles round his eyes stood out in sharp contrast to the puffy white flesh of his face. The general kept his hands in his pockets, out of sight, but Valyalin knew that the nails were bitten to the quick; and the twill of Frolov's trousers did nothing to conceal the nervous fidgeting of his fingers.

'You've got the flowers?'

'Yes, I've got the flowers.'

'Know what to say? Eh?'

'I'll think of something.'

'You've had enough time to come up with a few ideas! It's been weeks . . . Valyalin!'

The major leaned out of the car window with an inquiring look on his face, but Frolov had run out of steam. The imploring expression in his eyes filled the major with contempt.

'Valyalin . . don't fuck this one up, that's all.'

As the car drove away from the forecourt the major could

see Frolov still standing under the canopy, his shrunken figure dwarfed by the façade of the First Main Directorate's prestigious headquarters building, a flagship which in theory he commanded but which in practice was all adrift.

Now the rain slashed horizontally along Arbat Street, whipping umbrellas from the hands of drenched, frustrated pedestrians and slowing traffic to a crawl.

Valyalin, slumped in the back seat of Frolov's official Chaika, could not remember a time when he had felt so depressed. Between his legs lay a huge, cellophane-wrapped bouquet of flowers, tossed in casually by the driver at the last moment, their heads crushed from resting on the carpet. Valyalin had neither the energy nor the inclination to pick them up. This afternoon it was his job to deliver the flowers to Inna Karsovina. He was dreading the prospect.

The major's principal problem at the moment was lack of support from above. There was no longer any doubt about it: Frolov's mind wasn't on the job. What made it worse was his failure to confide in his staff. The general had taken to closeting himself in his private room and making endless long-distance calls to Murmansk. No one knew why Murmansk, or who was up there, or anything about the matter at all. It was just a mystery, one of far too many.

For a long while Frolov seemed mercifully to have forgotten his plan of sending Valyalin to pimp for the Directorate, but a few days ago he had hauled in his assistant and demanded with a frown to know what progress had been made. When Valyalin said, 'None,' Frolov exploded with rage, and the major had been required to spend the better part of the last forty-eight hours tracking down the blonde who was rumoured to haunt the offices of Chairman Kazin. At first it looked as though this required more clout than the First Main Directorate, at what was surely the nadir of its existence, possessed. Slowly, however, the ice began to crack: Valyalin phoned round his contacts, ending up with one of Krubykov's personal typists, and at long last a name had emerged.

The driver drew into the kerb opposite the Vakhtangov Theatre and Valyalin put on his cap. The flowers were better protected against the weather than he was; at least they came wrapped up. He told the driver to wait and dived for the narrow archway that he had been told to look out for. He carried the flowers with one hand; in the other was a note-book with directions helpfully written down by Krubykov's *sekretutka*. A courtyard, there ought to be a courtyard . . . yes. Valyalin came out into the open again and a squall of rain hit him full in the face. Then, to the right of the fountain, another passageway . . .

Valyalin made a run for it, scarcely noticing the hardy individual who sat patiently on the low wall which surrounded the ornamental fountain. They asked Valyalin about this man later, much later, when the memories (such as they were) had faded, and he was able to tell them little if anything. The man — Valyalin was sure of the sex, at least — was wearing a long, shiny leather raincoat, with a scarf wound round the lower part of his face and a hat pulled well down over his eyes, so that not much of him was visible to messenger boys in a hurry, like the major. His approach to nature was stoical enough: he sat with his hands in his pockets, while rain dripped off the brim of the hat, falling in a near continuous stream before his partially concealed face. Such a description hardly helped the interrogators and it did Valyalin no good at all.

At last he found the entrance to the old apartment house and hauled himself slowly up to the second floor. As he progressed his pace became more and more snail-like, until by the time he arrived at his destination he was scarcely moving. What on earth was he supposed to say, dammit? That he had 'noticed' her and instantly been smitten? (This was Frolov's idea. Valyalin discarded it with a withering sneer.) A mutual friend had suggested . . . (Who?) He lived on the floor below and had come to get acquainted? (He didn't, and she would know he didn't.)

Valyalin rested his shoulder against the wall of Inna's apart-ment and blew out his cheeks. Actually, the choice facing him was quite simple. He could go through with it, or he could tell his boss that when it came to the crunch he'd chickened out. Some choice. Valyalin rang the bell.

At the moment, the very precise moment when his finger found the button, the door flew open, causing Valyalin to step back in alarm. An old woman rushed out of the flat and seized him violently by the shoulders. Valyalin found it unnerving to be assaulted with such force by someone so much shorter and less able-bodied than he was. While the old bat babbled on at a rate of knots his mind steadied for long enough to remember Krubykov's secretary saying something about a mother. A mother and ...

'Have you seen a boy, a little boy with sandy hair and a sweet face, my lord, my lord, I'm in such a muddle I can't think ...' The woman was quite obviously on the brink of hysteria. 'He's only six years old and he'll be wanting his mummy, yes he will ... have you *seen* him?'

The major coughed in embarrassment and struggled to free his shoulders from the old woman's manic grasp. 'A boy ... no. Who ...?'

'It's my daughter's son, Volodiya.'

'Inna's son?'

'Yes! You know her, then? Oh sir, what a terrible thing ...' Two tears had forced themselves out of Anfisa's eyes and were trickling down her cheeks; for some reason the sight put Valyalin in mind of rain dripping off a hat, a detail he was to remember much later, but before he could make the conscious connection the old woman had launched back into her rambling tirade. 'The hospital called, there's been a horrible accident, the car skidded in the rain, they said, it wasn't the driver's fault, he's in shock, but Inna, they wouldn't tell me how bad it was, they said I was to go at once ...'

Valyalin, still reeling under this verbal assault, struggled to assert himself. 'Inna? She's been hurt, you say?'

'Knocked down by a car outside the Peking Hotel, I can't think what she was doing there at this time of day, now she's in hospital unconscious, intensive care, that's what they said, oh sir, can you help me please?'

Valyalin tut-tutted soothingly and guided her back inside the apartment, where he lowered her into the nearest chair. The old woman gave way to another quick bout of crying, which dried up almost as soon as it began, and knitted her hands together in a tight ball of desperation.

'You want to go to the hospital?' he said doubtfully.

236

'Yes! They say I must go as soon as possible.'

'So . . . what's the problem?'

'The boy. He'll be home from school any minute, I don't want just to leave him a message, what would the poor mite think?'

'A neighbour, perhaps?' Valyalin struggled manfully to overcome an unworthy feeling of relief at the knowledge that he wasn't going to have to face Inna after all. 'Somebody could look out for him?'

'All the people he knows are away, I've tried, and I wouldn't trust the rest, oh why did he have to choose today to be late . . . ?'

Valyalin put the bunch of flowers down on a nearby table and tried to organize a plan of action. 'Would you like me to stay for a bit?' he asked reluctantly.

'Oh, would you, sir? I can see you're one of her colleagues, you understand these things, I'd feel safe knowing you were here, Volodiya knows the uniform, he'll trust you.'

Valyalin blew out his cheeks again and considered the matter. It was warm and dry inside the apartment, and he did not relish the prospect of telling Frolov that his last hope was hanging by a thread in a hospital ward. Besides, if he waited for the boy he would have more time in which to concoct a plausible story, soften the edges a bit perhaps.

'What shall I tell . . . Volodiya, is it?'

'Volodiya, yes sir, tell him that I've had to go out for a bit, I was called away, don't say anything about his mother.'

'All right. He won't be long, will he?'

The old woman was in such a confused state that she couldn't think what to do for the best, and certainly she had no spare energies for concentrating on Valyalin's question. 'He knows how to make his own tea,' she muttered, 'and he's got his key with him, and say I'll telephone, but sir, if you please wouldn't leave him, at least until I call, he's only six.'

The major escorted Anfisa to the door and saw her down the stairs, waiting until the sound of her anxious lament no longer echoed up the well before he retreated into the flat and closed the door. Not a bad little place, he reflected as he looked around; not bad at all. If the boy didn't come home within the next few minutes he would have to go out and make some arrangement or other with his driver, but the rain was still pouring down and so the driver could wait awhile. For the present Valyalin could afford to sit down and take the weight off his feet.

He chose the most comfortable-looking chair and lowered himself gratefully into it with a glance at his watch. Nearly 4.30. He'd give it until the half hour, then go down. Pity about the girl, it sounded serious. Nice apartment she had, warm too. What the devil was he going to tell the boy, though . . . ?

Valyalin closed his eyes. Murmansk. That was domestic, and First weren't supposed to stick their noses into domestic. Risky . . . but who did he know up there? Who could he ask? There must be *someone* . . .

Valyalin slept.

He awoke to the sound of the front door opening and then closing again. After a second of panic he remembered where he was and looked hastily at his watch. Half past six.

Half past six! Valyalin sprang to his feet. What on earth had the boy been up to, coming home so late? He cocked his head, listening, while he planned his next move. It was vital not to frighten the boy. 'Volodiya,' he called, trying to make his voice sound soft and gentle. There was no reply. The major tried again, but still the hallway was silent. He moved slowly across to the door of the living room, his head full of uneasy premonitions. What if the boy started to cry, became hysterical? No, don't think about that, just go out to him, be nice, be kind . . .

Valyalin peered round the door. There was no little boy in the hall. Instead, he saw the old woman, Inna's mother. Her face was paper-white. At first she did not appear to notice him. Her eyes were fixed on the carpet and when his cautious approach made a floorboard creak she gave no sign of having heard. Then she looked up and began to walk unsteadily towards him. For a moment Valyalin felt relief. If the mother had come home, presumably Inna was out of danger.

He cleared his throat. 'Ah . . . how is she, then?' No reply. Nervously he tried again. 'Your daughter? Inna?'

Anfisa stopped when she was only a few inches away from the KGB officer, never taking her eyes from his face. Valyalin swallowed. His earlier feeling of relief was rapidly yielding to a conviction that something was wrong.

'Not there.' Her voice came out in a hoarse croak.

'*What?*'

'No record of such an accident involving a person of that name . . .'

Then the woman raised her hands to take hold of his lapels and, small though she was, began to shake him from side to side as if he weighed no more than a sack of flour; her eyes narrowed to slits, the muscles stood out rigidly from her neck and her mouth opened wide enough (or so it seemed to the petrified major) to swallow him whole.

'Monster!' she howled. '*What have you done with my grandchild?*'

23

Povin sat huddled up on the middle of the bunk, listening to his tremulous heartbeats. It was past midnight; all the other denizens of the camp were asleep, or should have been. But the old man did not sleep. He was lecturing himself.

He would have to keep awake more, take fewer catnaps. Impossible. *No!* If it meant staying alive, anything was possible. Only a few more days now. *Believe it*! One day you'll walk into the interrogation room and she'll be there: you'll take a look at her face, just one, and then you'll know, old man, *this is the day*!

The day that God will set you free.

Povin lay down very slowly, giving his exhausted body space in which to unwind its taut sinews. Each time it was harder to muster the energy necessary to repel the expected attack; each day it took longer to untense. No man, however fit, could maintain such a regime indefinitely. For someone in Povin's position, a zek old and undernourished, the future shrank a little every time he commanded his tired, emaciated body to defend itself.

The lecture continued on its well-worn course. Maybe the day won't come. Victor would be caught. The Travel Agency would fail. Not would . . . will. Povin licked his dry lips. Part of him wanted that failure. It was not right that Inna should suffer.

Her or you.

How many more nights like this one can you endure? How much longer can you stay awake? How many dawns have you left? How many hours?

How many seconds?

What will happen when you die, old man? Where will you go? Heaven or hell?

When will you die? How will it happen?

When . . .?

Povin had been in enough cells to know the ways of rats. You could fob them off for a while with a blazing torch, if you were fortunate enough to have one, or a determined rush, but they would retreat only a short distance, just far enough to allow the darkness to swallow them while they regrouped; and whenever you backed off they would advance, each time coming a little nearer, each time retreating a little less, until at last they had you surrounded, and at last their courage sufficed . . .

The camp was infested with rats.

He slithered off the bunk and for the third time that night made the effort to haul himself up to the narrow window. Everything looked the same. Blockhouse, grey earth, spotlights . . . He craned his neck round as far as it would stretch, first to the right, then to the left. Yes, there it was, the solitary red glow as tiny and yet as powerful as a lamp burning in the sanctuary. The old man slipped back to the floor with a groan. One night he would look out of the window to see no comforting glow, and then . . .

He would pray. He had prayed before Alexander arrived and somehow God had kept him going; when Alexander left the old man would pray again. Nothing else, not even the strong arm of Alexander the Chechen, could match the power of those prayers. Alexander did not believe in God. Povin was alone, always alone.

The old man crept back to his bunk and lay down. He would not sleep tonight, he decided. He would stay awake and think. Fatigue gnawed at his defences, whittling away his resistance almost without him knowing. *Think*! Think of the future, *make* it happen! Frolov, Boris Frolov. He was responsible for all this. One day, Frolov. The old man's eyes closed. One day . . .

The transition from sleep to wakefulness was smooth and immediate. As Povin's eyes opened he stirred very slightly, shuffling the wooden stiletto into the palm of his right hand with a flick of the wrist. The tiny sound which had caused him to wake was not repeated.

He never slept without the stiletto in his hand, not since the day when Alexander had revealed himself. He knew he was not infallible. He could not stay tuned into danger for ever. There had to be times when the guard dropped and the fortress was undefended; this was one such time.

The blockhouse was in total darkness. Povin could not see an inch in front of his face, let alone the end of the bed. But someone was out there in the corridor. He knew someone was there. Not who, or what his purpose was, all that could come later. For now what mattered was his nebulous presence, unseen and unheard, but *felt*.

Whoever it was had no concerted plan, or he would have rushed in to finish the job. A maverick. Kulikov.

Povin had been holding his breath. Now he let it escape in a long, soft sigh. He still had a chance.

Where was Alexander? What had gone wrong? The old man propped himself up on one elbow, not caring if he made a noise, and was rewarded by the sound of a floorboard creaking in the corridor. Whoever was out there was afraid — but not so afraid that he would scuttle away at once at the slightest disturbance, like a bird hearing a human footfall. A vulture, perhaps. A vulture who waited for the all-clear before it swooped . . .

'Alexander?' Povin's voice came out clearly, but soft and

241

low-pitched — the last thing he wanted was to wake up anyone else. Please God, let it just be Alexander . . .

No response.

He closed his eyes and concentrated on listening for the giveaway sounds. When the attack came he would have only an instant's warning — a single step, perhaps, or the rush of air as Kulikov flung himself along the bunk. The old man's heart was throbbing painfully fast, making his chest heave and his lungs hurt with the effort of supplying his body and brain with the oxygen they so desperately needed to stay alive. A second, less than a second, and in that time he must defend himself with perfect, reflex thoroughness against an assailant whom he could not even see.

Povin began to count, very slowly, in a controlled attempt to relax. The hard edges of the stiletto were grinding into his palm, making the muscles of his hand ache and the skin chafe, but he dared not loosen his grip. Somewhere on the other side of the impenetrable black curtain before his eyes a man shifted his weight, and Povin heard. Was he still outside in the passage? Or had he already entered the cell? No. He made too much noise. If he had so much as touched the inner door Povin would have known.

He squeezed his wooden dagger a couple of times for reassurance and held it out blindly in front of his face. Any second now Kulikov would come for him, brushing aside the veil of darkness which presently separated the two adversaries, pinning his arms to the bunk, and then he was done for. He must go on to the attack. There was no other choice. It was that or die.

'Dear God,' he breathed. 'Please help me.' Such a simple prayer. Why could he not always be so honest in his dealings with the Almighty? And the prayer was answered at once: remember, said a voice inside the old man's brain, if you cannot see him, no more can he see you . . .

Povin slipped from the bunk and tiptoed silently across to the wall which contained the window. This time he did not even try to climb; he jumped, putting all his last feeble reserves of strength into the spring. The split second during which his eyes were level with the sill enabled him to see everything doused in the glow from the spotlights: cleared earth, block-house wall opposite . . .

No red glow.

Povin fell back in a crouch. He was breathing heavily, the man in the passage could not but hear. Alexander had moved, that's all. Perhaps he had heard, even now he was coming to rescue Povin . . .

The old man took a deep breath and held it. In the pause that followed he heard two things: the frantic beating of his own heart and the sound of the door handle being slowly turned.

'Alexander?' he croaked.

But it wasn't Alexander. The Chechen would have answered the old man, would have offered him reassurance. Whereas the person standing just the other side of darkness said nothing at all.

Far away to the south another old man was beset by troubles, although these were largely of his own making. His surroundings contrasted strongly with Povin's. The Palace Etelaranta is one of Helsinki's finest hotels, with a fabulous view of the southern harbour and the cathedral on the opposite shore. Bryant's triple-glazed quarters were warm and comfortable. His was a single room, but still there was ample space for him and Lambe to face each other across a low table on which stood a half-empty bottle of *akvavit*.

The human atmosphere inside Bryant's room, however, was a good deal less agreeable than its physical counterpart. He was not feeling well. His flight from Heathrow had landed late, he was exhausted, the hotel's food, though wonderful, was over-rich for his jaded taste. He was all on his own now, flying on a wing and a prayer, one hand holding up the elastic and the other frantically trying to replace the pins as they came un-stuck. It occurred to him, and not for the first time, that this was an almost spectacularly vile way to end a career.

He screwed up his eyes against the light and tried to concen-trate on what Lambe was telling him. He had been dreading this interview ever since the major requested it. Demanded was a better word, perhaps.

'What you're saying, then, is that you don't trust this man? Is that it?'

It came out with a good deal more hostility than he'd intended and the pained expression on Lambe's face made him wince. For an embarrassed moment Bryant couldn't recall the officer's first name, although he'd been using it on and off all evening. Something outlandish, un-English. Dominic.

'I'm sorry, Dominic, I'm not trying to needle you. I just want to know where you stand, that's all. I have to know that.'

As he looked at the hard expression on C's face it seemed to Lambe that the boot was on the other foot. He was being lured deeper and deeper into an enchanted forest, a dense, deceptive thicket of thorns and vines strong enough to throttle a man who didn't look out for himself. None of the usual procedures had been followed. There was no casefile, no project committee, no logistics team, no strategic planners' meeting, no nothing. And Lambe, who now found himself faced with the unpalatable task of ferrying his chief up to the very edge of the Soviet Union, was starting to become very chary of it all.

His face assumed a thoughtful, slightly pained expression. 'I can't lay my hand on my heart and say that anything's wrong. It's just part of having a nose for the job. After a while you like to think you can smell a wrong 'un.'

'I see.' Bryant looked into his glass. 'The man you met . . . Victor, has been known to me for quite some time now.'

'Excuse me for asking, but might I just inquire . . . in the field, sir?'

For the umpteenth time Bryant fought back his headache to the edge of consciousness and strove to discern the question's implications. 'Not in what you would call the field, no.'

'That's the trouble. That's exactly the point. I sense that he's a field operator — please don't think that I'm asking questions, because I'm not — and that he's awfully sharp, yet he's been out of action for a long time.'

'That is . . . It's possible.'

Lambe bit his lip. He was a senior officer and entitled to expect better treatment, yet Bryant wanted to deal with him as if he were a Grade 6 records clerk. Lambe liked his chief and respected him enormously. No one who was familiar with the man's private record could fail to respect him. The major's personal code of ethics suggested that he ought to tell the Head of the Service what was actually going through his mind at that point: to bypass him altogether and telephone London for confirmatory instructions.

'I'm sorry —' Bryant's brain temporarily veered off course again — 'Dominic. As you know, I have never been a believer in secrecy for its own sake. But on this one, the less you know the better.' There was an increasingly sharp edge to his voice. 'That goes for everybody connected with the operation.'

'Does it have a name?'

'Does what have a name?'

'The operation. The mission. The whatever you want to label it.' Lambe smiled thinly. 'You see, sir, I don't even know what this thing is called. The usual procedures just don't appear to figure in this at all. And I'm puzzled, I don't mind admitting.'

If he had been hoping to lure Bryant out on to more open ground he was disappointed. 'What you're saying,' he concluded lamely, 'is that I'm to do what I'm told and keep my mouth shut. Is that correct, sir, or is there something I've missed?'

After one whole minute by Lambe's watch it was clear to him that he had his answer. For an officer of his seniority and experience it was hardly acceptable. He sat back in his chair and placed his hands on his knees, trying to keep a neutral expression on his face. But it wasn't easy.

'I have to tell you, Sir Richard,' he said quietly, 'that I don't regard this as a very sound or even satisfactory way of mounting what is obviously an important operation.'

To his surprise Bryant said at once, 'I respect that.'

'You do?'

'Yes. I don't agree with it. But I can't ignore that it's your view.'

If it was intended as a peace offering it didn't go nearly far enough, but still Lambe hesitated. 'Then may I be permitted at least to make one or two suggestions . . . ?'

Bryant shook his head like a huffy bird. 'No.'

'I see.' Lambe drew a deep breath and straightened his back. He had reached a point which he had foreseen weeks ago, at the end of his dinner with Victor, and he had been praying ever since that the hour should not strike. 'I'm afraid that what I'm about to say will sound almost desperately offensive to you, Sir Richard. I've never done this before and I hope I shall never have to do it again, but it's my right and I'm going to exercise it. I want your signature on a document.'

Bryant looked at him wearily. Lambe was not to know it, but he too had long ago anticipated this moment and prepared for it.

'Certainly.'

Lambe's eyes flickered in surprise. It was the last response he'd expected to hear. The major had come to the meeting prepared to face hostility, arguments, all the manifestations of the tactless exercise of autocratic power, and instead he found sweet reasonableness . . . of a kind which served only to lure him deeper and deeper into the enchanted thicket. He searched Bryant's face for signs of weakness. There were none.

'You do understand what that'll mean, sir.'

'Of course.' Bryant's tone was impatient. They had an early start in the morning, he was anxious to get to bed. 'Victor's message was quite explicit. He's coming out in forty-eight hours, he said, and that means tomorrow night.'

Lambe struggled to suppress his rising anger. 'And on the strength of that one message you're prepared to risk a pilot and a two-seater training Harrier over the Kola Peninsula, knowing that it will be used in an attempt to bring out not one passenger but two, an operation for which it was never designed and which when put to the test may not be physically possible?' His voice was incredulous. 'You're prepared to go and oversee all that *yourself*?'

Lambe would never know what was passing through the chief's mind in the minutes of silence that followed, but later on, after the operation was over and the secret armies had gone home, it seemed to him that it was here, at this point, that the old man finally faced up to the realities of the decision in front of him and for the first time was appalled. It was as though — Lambe had trouble finding the right image — a theoretical chessplayer had been flushed out on to a real board, with a real opponent, real stakes to be played for and a whole lifetime of achievement to lose.

Bryant stood up and went over to the dressing table, on which lay an elegant, thick leather folder. He removed a sheet of the hotel's stationery and brought it over to where Lambe was sitting. He placed the piece of paper squarely on the surface of the low table, poured himself another glass of *akvavit* and unscrewed the cap of his fountain pen. 'Now,' he said quietly. 'Tell me what to write.'

24

The door to the cell was wide open now. Povin couldn't see anyone but he pricked up his ears and listened. Breathing. Quite close to him a man was breathing. The breaths came in short, nervous gasps, signs of intense strain. A desperate man, then.

Povin rose to his feet, trying to make the moves silently, but his body let him down with a creak of worn-out joints. He too was breathing fast; a band of pain stretched across his chest as he fought for oxygen. He knew his assailant must be in the room.

Povin edged along the wall, straining to see what was happening in front of him. His eyes might have been swathed in black velvet for all the good it did. The breathing was nearer now. He shifted the stiletto a little more snugly into his palm and held it out.

Lunge . . .

His arms swept the darkness, right, left, right, but the breathing was by his side and edging closer. He swung round to face it but as he did so the source of the quick breaths dodged backwards, avoiding the blade.

Blind. Kulikov was nearly blind. He was used to the darkness. He'd had more practice.

Povin retreated until his calves touched the edge of the bunk.

Christ, no! He raised his right foot, desperately feeling backwards for the hard wooden surface, and levered himself up with an effort. High ground, seize the high ground . . .

By this time neither of them was making any attempt to preserve the silence. Povin could hear Kulikov's footfalls as he padded towards the bed. But noises wouldn't bring help; no one else wanted to get involved in something like this.

Was Kulikov armed? Did he have a knife? A gun? How could he have a gun? Povin ground his teeth. In this camp almost anything was possible, but not that.

Silence. The breathing had stopped.

For a moment the old man couldn't believe it. Where was Kulikov? He held out the stiletto once more, probing the darkness with its tip, but he encountered only empty air. A sound to his right, he stabbed forward . . . Nothing. Povin recovered his balance and strove to control his panting. The pain in his chest tightened. Keep control, he silently screamed to himself. Don't lose consciousness, don't fall, your heart can take it, *concentrate*!

Something touched the edge of his bunk, he felt the tremor. Kulikov was here. He heard a rustle; the zek was climbing on to the bunk, level with the old man. Before he could help himself Povin had taken a step backwards . . . and as the corner of his cell enfolded him he knew he had suicidally reduced his chances to nil.

He leaped forward, cutting and slashing with his blade, but Kulikov was ready for him. He grabbed the old man's arm and wrenched, allowing himself to fall backwards with Povin on top. As the old man shrieked a hand came out of the darkness to stop his mouth, and Povin remembered that although the zek was half-blind he was very strong. The boy threw his weight to the right but it was only a feint; next second he had rolled in the opposite direction and was lying on Povin's chest, his knees already bending forward to pin the old man down.

His hand came away from Povin's mouth but before the old man could shriek again Kulikov was strangling him. The boy's fingers forced their way round his victim's scrawny neck almost without meeting resistance. Povin's chest pain was like a saw cutting him in half. He could no longer breathe. Bright

248

red flashes exploded in front of his eyes. With a supreme final effort he tried to drive his stiletto into the body which crouched over him, but Kulikov anticipated the blow with a sudden downwards lurch, pinning the old man's forearms to the bed with his elbow. Agony flickered up and down Povin's right side like an electric current and he dropped the stiletto. Kulikov's fingers seemed to meet through the folds of his scraggy neck, squeezing his windpipe, stemming the flow of blood. The red flashes grew ever more brilliant, his heartbeat was slowing, his exhausted body had nothing more to give. Only seconds left now ...

He tried to pray but couldn't. His last thought was not of God. It was of Frolov.

'All out, all out, *out, out, out*!'

A burst of machine-gun fire, whistles, dogs barking — at first the old man was aware only of half-made impressions, vague and indistinct; then his mind cleared and he realized that Kulikov was no longer kneeling on his chest. His eyes focused on the window. Torch beams, voices. Panic.

He gulped down air in great heaving gasps. Alive, he was alive. The cell was empty. Kulikov had gone.

'Out, out, *out*! Hands behind your backs. Roll call, now! Out or we send in the dogs.'

It wasn't yet morning, the sky was still dark. What was happening? Povin rolled off his bunk on to the concrete floor, clasping his throat. He choked up a little phlegm and struggled to rise. It was no use expecting help from the guards, they'd be in any minute with the dogs. He couldn't get up, no matter how hard he tried; his neck was burning ... *Pull yourself together*! *Breathe*!

He scrabbled on the floor for his wooden knife. He must find it, he *must*! Ah, there it was, behind the bunk ...

His heart was steadying now; he still couldn't swallow but he'd live.

'You! Come on, outside.'

He was in the act of buttoning his jacket when the guard put his head round the door, and the man appeared to notice nothing suspicious. Povin was the last to stagger from the block-house. The scene which met his eyes was sheer pandemonium.

All the camp guards had been mustered. Machine guns were set up at one end of the strip of earth between the old man's blockhouse and the next in the line, giving the gunners a clear field of fire into the zeks as they assembled for roll call. They were sleepy and disorientated but none of them protested. Tension filled the air like static, sharpening fear. All the spotlights were on; the dogs strained at their leashes baying for blood; the compound commander, Trofimov himself, stood next to the machine guns with his officers grouped around him as if to form a protective shield.

A senior NCO took the roll in double time. The zeks, responsive to the danger in the charged atmosphere, were quick to answer. No one wanted to give the gunners an excuse to open fire, or the dog-handlers some reason for slipping the Dobermans off their chains. At last the roll call of numbers was completed and every zek was accounted for, even Kulikov.

All the zeks . . . except one.

The protective cordon of officers surrounding their commander suddenly parted and he barked an order. A searchlight beam lazily traversed the ranks of prisoners before coming to rest on something which lay at the commander's feet. A body. The beam flickered across it several times before homing in on the face.

The old man stood at the very end of his line. He could see without even having to turn his head. Not that he had to see, not really. Some part of him already knew who it was.

Alexander the Chechen.

A bullet had entered his forehead above the right eye. Povin was less than ten metres away, he could see everything down to the minutest detail. The corpse's head lay in a dark red pool and he knew that the exit wound would be a damn sight less tidy than the neat hole at the front. A silencer, of course, that went without saying.

Povin raised his eyes a fraction and found himself staring at Zuyev, who returned his gaze without expression. A small-calibre bullet, the old man was thinking, fired at close range from a silenced pistol. By someone familiar to the victim, someone whose approach would not cause Alexander to cry out.

His eyes strayed to the holster at Zuyev's side. How many bullets did a pistol magazine hold? Answer — his lips crinkled in a humourless smile — one more than Zuyev's did now.

Kazin had ordered Alexander to keep a watch over Povin. Povin had leaned on Zuyev, leaned a little too hard, it seemed; so Zuyev released Kulikov, countered the electronic alarms, killed the Chechen. It was a reasonable deduction: none of the zeks had access to a gun and only Zuyev could have such an overwhelming motive for getting rid of Povin's minder. Neat, too — there would have been nothing to implicate Zuyev if Kulikov had succeeded. But . . . why now? On whose orders? Someone grown desperate, tired of waiting . . . Someone terrified of what the old man might say. Logic dictated only one answer. It had to be Frolov.

Dawn was coming. The commander conferred briefly with his officers. He wanted the area cleared and, besides, it wasn't worth allowing the prisoners to go back to bed.

'Right turn! No talking! Hands behind your backs!'

Povin summoned up reserves of energy he didn't know he possessed and drew a deep breath. He was defenceless now. Already he could sense a change in the atmosphere. Many eyes were upon his back, speculating, hostile . . . As they began to march he pretended to count the steps, one, two, three, four; but it was the last seconds of his own life that he heard ticking away.

25

Bryant and Lambe flew into Banak soon after midday. The airport was thick with troops when they landed; at first Bryant couldn't understand why, but Lambe pointed wordlessly through the window of the terminal and he saw the Harrier swoop down low over the nearby mountains on the last leg of its flight from Lossiemouth.

'On time. Good.'

'I hope so,' Lambe said curtly. 'The Norwegians have left us in no doubt that they want it out of their way as soon as possible. This is Lakselv, a big NATO military area. It attracts enough attention from the Russians as it is, without having Harriers based here.'

'Don't worry, Dominic. She came on time, she'll leave on time. By dawn tomorrow that plane will be back in its hangar with scarcely anyone the wiser.'

But he knew that Lambe was unconvinced.

The drive to Kirkenes, on the northern tip of Finnmark, was long and uncomfortable. Bryant had never visited this part of Scandinavia before. In places it reminded him of Scotland; he would have liked to spend a few days fishing in the torrential rivers they passed on their way north, but that belonged to a part of his life which no longer figured in any of the permutations before him.

Lambe drove. 'I'm sorry we can't make better speed,' he said at one point, after a particularly difficult passage. 'They call this the Blood Road round here. It was built by slave labour under the Nazi occupation. Water- and oil-bound gravel, mainly. Back-breaking work. Germans during the day and wolves at night, Christ, can you imagine it!' Bryant's lips curved in a sour smile. He used to have a reputation for coming down hard on blasphemy but that, it seemed, was now like so much else — a thing of the past. And after all, what did it matter? Christ, he thought with sudden bitterness, can look after himself.

After a while the drive began to bore Bryant. Everywhere it was the same: a few scattered birch trees, waterlogged moor, moss and lichen; in the distance mountains, their tops lost in thick cloud, with vast boulders embedded in scree at their feet. Occasionally they would pass through a small village, and once Bryant commented on the brightly painted houses, red, yellow and white, all standing out vividly against the sombre background of the moors.

'It's their way of protesting,' said Lambe. 'Against the past, the dark, the *mørkesyke*.'

'I'm sorry?'

'A kind of depression brought on by the winter darkness. They say you can't imagine it until you've lived through it. I hope I never have to. I've seen what it does to people.'

The landscape had grown steadily more desolate. Now the mountains were black and less shy of approaching the road. The car was crossing an ill-drained plateau when great sheets of rain unfolded themselves down from the peaks, engulfing the car in a flash flood. Lambe switched the wipers to double speed and slowed almost to a crawl.

'I see what you mean. About the depression.'

'Let's just hope we're not here long enough to catch the real thing.'

The rain stopped as suddenly as it had begun, to be replaced by watery sunshine. Lambe took one hand off the wheel and pointed across Bryant. 'This is another military area — see that sign?'

Bryant looked. No Photographs: No Camping: It is Dangerous to Move off the Road. 'What's that stone?' he asked. 'It looks like some kind of monument.'

'It is. A lot of Russians were killed there in the war. It's a mass grave.'

'Russians?'

'Yes. Some of the population of East Finnmark are Russian.

253

Things tend to blur in a place like this, sir. Frontiers, well, they're just lines drawn on maps by civil servants in centrally heated offices miles and miles away from where it counts. That's one reason why our mutual friend chose this place. There's a boundary, of sorts, although after a winter like the one we've just had the maintenance teams are going to be kept busy for a couple of months at least, I'd say. But the line's very arbitrary. People have relatives on both sides of it. There's more irregular traffic than the authorities admit to.'

'But is there no supervision?'

'Not much. The odd flight, once a day, depending on conditions. Foot patrols are out of the question whatever the time of year. And it doesn't matter who you are, you can't control the Lapps. They don't recognize any authority except their own. They're the biggest offenders. The Russians just ignore them. It wouldn't surprise me to learn that's how Victor got in — with a Lapp caravan. You see that road, there?'

Bryant craned his head to see the turning they had just passed. 'Yes.'

'That's the road to Høybuktmoen. There's an airfield there, quite a good one. SAS use it — the airline, not our chaps. We're based there for tonight's op. I've booked us into a hotel in Kirkenes. Not quite what you're used to, I'm afraid.'

'It's of no consequence. Can I ask a favour of you?'

Lambe's 'Of course' was mechanical and late. Bryant knew perfectly well that he had already demanded too much of this man, but the condemned cell is a privileged place.

'Is it possible to go up into the hills and look down on to the frontier with the USSR? Or is that too dangerous? I would like to see where . . . things happen.'

Lambe laughed. 'I'll take you right up to the border, if you like.'

'Would that not be a little foolhardy?'

But Lambe only smiled. 'Watch out for the sign to Grense-Jakobselv. Route 886.'

Route 886 turned out to be little more than a gravel track connecting a long succession of potholes. In places it was so narrow that Lambe had to inch the car forward, using Bryant to check their clearance on the nearside. For the most part the road lay through thick pine forest, with only the barest occasional glimpse of farmland, or a lake. Then they turned off and after another ten minutes' drive suddenly emerged from under the trees into a cleared strip. The road ran straight ahead for about a hundred metres to what looked like an ordinary gate. Lambe disengaged gear and they coasted gently up to the barrier. Bryant could see that it was indeed a five-bar gate of a kind which would have been familiar to any English farmer. The wood was not in very good condition but the large pad-lock looked new. On either side of the gate was a simple three-strand barbed-wire fence, stretched between rusty L-shaped metal stakes.

'I suppose we can't go any farther,' Bryant said. He sounded disappointed. 'Private property.'

'Sort of.' Lambe took out a cigarette and pointed towards the gate. 'That's Russia.'

Bryant spun round to glare at Lambe, but the major's face was serious. Then he caught sight of something which had hitherto escaped his attention: a notice, weatherbeaten and obviously very old, enjoining people in four languages not to fire shots or shout abuse across the border. He stared at it uncomprehendingly, still not quite willing to trust the evidence of his own eyes.

'Fancy a stroll?' Lambe opened the driver's door and got out. After a moment's hesitation Bryant followed him. Lambe rested his arms on the gate and smoked for a while in silence.

'See those trees over there?' He nudged Bryant and pointed across the border. 'There's a lookout post behind them, you can only just see it. Sometimes it's manned, sometimes it isn't. Let me take a look . . .' He went back to the car and returned a moment later with a pair of binoculars which he focused on the clump of trees about a quarter of a mile away. 'Empty. Ever been to Russia, sir?'

Bryant shook his head.

'Come on, then.' And with that Lambe vaulted over the five-bar gate into the Soviet Union. Bryant watched him with a wistful expression on his face, but did not move.

Lambe's face softened. 'You never know, it may be your last chance,' he coaxed. For a few moments longer Bryant dithered; then, very slowly and awkwardly, he clambered over the gate.

Nothing happened. No shots rang out, no armoured car roared up to them, no sentry's challenge disturbed the stillness. As an experience it lacked spice. The landscape on this side of the wire was exactly the same as in Norway. Bryant blinked and looked around him. So this was the 'other side'. Enemy territory. Russia.

He pointed at the gate and said hesitantly, 'That . . . is the Iron Curtain?'

'That.'

'I see. This side doesn't seem to be much different, does it?'

'Not much.'

'Yet all my life I've tried to believe that there was a difference. I have made myself believe that. Tell me, Dominic, do *I* look different on this side of the wire?'

Lambe considered him seriously. 'No,' he said at last.

'Is that . . . why you brought me here?'

'Not . . . consciously, no.'

'So then . . . what is the difference between them and us?'

Lambe smiled and shook his head. He was a serving officer who did his duty, not a philosopher and still less any kind of politician. The question had very little meaning for him. 'Thoughts,' he said eventually. 'Attitudes. They wouldn't see it in your terms, Sir Richard. They couldn't stand here and say, "It's all the same land, the same people." It wouldn't occur to them to say that.' Lambe frowned. 'I'm talking about the Kremlin, you understand. Here, in the next field, I could perhaps find a farmer who thinks like you.'

'But who'd never admit it . . . ' Bryant stood for a long time with his hands thrust deep in the pockets of his overcoat, head bowed as if in remembrance. 'Perhaps that's the difference. The only one that matters. It is a question of what a man would admit to . . . ' He looked up. 'No one in the Politburo would do what I'm doing now. Introspection's not for them.'

There was a long silence, punctuated only by the sough of the wind through the nearby strands of wire. Eventually Bryant shook himself and seemed to come back to the present, for he smiled and said, 'Thank you, Dominic. When I asked you for a favour I didn't realize just how thoroughly you were going to oblige me. Indulge me, I should say.'

'My pleasure.' The major's smile was polite rather than warm. 'But perhaps we ought to be getting on to Kirkenes now.' He looked at his watch. 'There's not much light left, and I'd rather be back on the main road before dusk, if you don't mind.'

'Of course.'

They climbed back over the gate and got into the car. As Lambe reversed into a three-point turn Bryant treated himself to one final, lingering look at the Dark Tower of his nightmares, in some vague and troubled fashion feeling the need to reconcile a lifetime's dedicated work with the bleak but peaceful scene beyond the humble gate. When the car finally moved off slowly down the pitted track, along that segment of it which was supposed to lead to peace and democracy and freedom, he was almost overwhelmed by the temptation to turn round for a last assessment, but with a formidable act of will he checked himself. In the course of his life he had lived by many rules, breaking some and bending others, but there was one immutable rule which he always obeyed.

Never look back.

26

As the Yak-40 roared up into the gathering dusk Oleg Kazin lifted a slim attaché case on to his knees and opened it to extract a couple of glossy black and white photographs. He studied the first for a moment, then slipped it behind the elasticated net of the seat in front of him. Krubykov recognized the second photograph at a glance and as the Chairman reached across him to mount it on the back of the seat he murmured, 'Povin.'

'Povin. A much younger and healthier Povin. News?'

'Nothing. All the border directorates have reported in now and there's no trace of the child. He's disappeared into thin air. The militia are combing Moscow; I gather it looks like 1937 all over again, suspects piled three deep on each other's shoulders, the Butyrki crammed to bursting point. Nothing.'

'What would *you* remember of 1937, Krubykov?' The Chairman's voice was disdainfully grim.

'Very little. I am sor —'

'You were only a boy then. Those of us who remember it do so because we are fortunate enough to be alive. We are hardly likely to forget it. Watch your language, Krubykov. You never know where it may lead you.'

The plane forged on towards the north and the two men sat in silence while many miles slipped away behind them. Krubykov knew better than to try to reopen the subject; Kazin was lost in a deep study of the photographs in front of him. 'Clever,' he said at last, and Krubykov jerked himself fully awake.

'Forgive me, Chairman, I'm afraid . . .'

Kazin nodded his head in the direction of Povin's photograph. 'A clever *churka*, that one. To spirit the boy away like that. I knew he might try, but it's still ingenious. He had help, of course, that goes without saying, but the inspiration's his.'

Krubykov wasn't sure if he was supposed to take this observation seriously. 'From the camp?' he said hesitantly.

'Oh yes, certainly. Camps are not islands, Krubykov. There are roads in and out. A resourceful zek can always find a way.' Another nod in the direction of Povin. 'He's resourceful. So is Victor.'

Krubykov decided to go along, at least for the moment. That was always the easiest line to take with Kazin. 'Have you told Karsovina that he was responsible?'

'No. She doesn't even know yet that the boy is missing.'

'What!'

Kazin shook his head and frowned. 'Certainly not.'

'But as the boy's mother . . .'

'I do not employ her to be a mother.'

'Surely she must know?'

'How? She has only two lines of inquiry. One. She can telephone her home. Her mother has been removed to our safe house, so the phone will ring and ring, but no one will answer it. Two. She can telephone me. And I . . . am unavailable.'

'She'll be out of her mind with worry.'

'Possibly.' Kazin squinted at the plane's ceiling, testing the proposition like a vintage that was new to him. 'But you're presupposing she's made some attempt to contact anyone. She may not have done so.'

Krubykov kept his face impassive. Once, long ago, there might have been a tiny corner of his brain that protested against Kazin. Now familiarity had dulled it to the point where it was no longer extant.

Kazin leaned forward and tapped the first photograph. 'You recognize him?'

'Bryant. C.'

Kazin nodded. 'Head of the British Secret Intelligence Service, DI6.' He sighed. 'A pity. We are about to lose him. And it's a waste. He's a better man than . . . ' He jabbed his thumb at Povin's photograph, denting its glossy finish with the nail. 'Both men of principles, but Bryant's always stay the course that little bit longer.'

'It was his choice to become involved.'

'Not really.' Kazin shook his head again. 'I don't think he had a choice, a real choice. Povin didn't think so. Men like Bryant don't "choose" to do the decent thing — you know that's what they say in England, Krubykov, "the decent thing"? He had to come to get Povin out. His peculiar code of conduct required that, because it was the only way, just as our military code requires troops to bury an enemy machine gun under the weight of their bodies, if *that's* the only way. But it's a pity.'

'Might I suggest that it's also a triumph? Not every Chairman of the KGB can claim to have brought down the head of a foreign intelligence service.'

'It's not a triumph. It's a waste of energy. The man at the top is never dangerous, Krubykov. The organization continues without so much as a hiccup when he goes, at least, that's if the organization's even half good. No, he's a figurehead, a man for dealing with the politicians. If I stop him, I don't stop DI6. And it's DI6 that I'm committed to destroy.'

'But in that case does it matter one way or the other?'

Kazin shrugged. 'Marginally. There are two candidates for the position of C when Bryant goes. Each of them is slightly less desirable than he is, from our point of view. I would prefer to face Bryant.'

'Then why bother to destroy him?'

Kazin did not answer immediately. After a while Krubykov turned his head and to his surprise saw that the Chairman's face was transfigured. The blood had drained from his normally pink cheeks, leaving only blotchy islets of broken veins in the surrounding pallor. His eyes were half-closed and vacant. Kazin's thoughts appeared to be concentrated far, far away on a scene which the colonel could not begin to imagine. Krubykov's lips parted, his breathing slowed to the lightest whisper, he was paralysed. Even after years of dealing with this crazed old man, responding to his slightest whim or change of mood, the colonel could not remember ever having seen him look so strange. It gave him an eerie feeling. At first he couldn't identify the vital factor that was new; then he realized what it was and for a moment his breathing stopped altogether. The quivering watchspring of inner malice which motivated Kazin's every waking moment had temporarily shut down.

'Do you know anything about cooking, Krubykov?'

The colonel jumped. 'I think I can boil an egg, Comrade Chairman.'

Kazin's lips stretched in a tolerant smile. 'That's a good start, then. Eggs . . . There was a time when I did a lot of cooking. I even studied it for a while. Sauces. Pastries. Soups, I was famous for my soups.' He turned his head towards the colonel, who once again held his breath, but still the old man's eyes were sightless and empty. Krubykov realized that his master was existing in another time, another place. But it was more than that. Wherever he was, whatever he saw, it provoked within Kazin a feeling akin to tenderness of which Krubykov would not have believed him capable.

260

'I had a good teacher, you see. An excellent teacher . . .' Kazin paused. For a moment everything hung in suspense; then his face clouded and the disquieting spell seemed to be broken. 'A long time ago.' His voice was growing brisker, but had not yet quite regained its normal stridency. 'A time when things were different. Do you know how to make meringues, Krubykov?'

The colonel wordlessly shook his head.

'You have to separate the white of the egg from the yolk. You have no choice: no separation, no meringue. Do you follow me?'

'Yes.'

'You don't want the yolk at all. You can throw it away, but that's wasteful. Or sometimes, if you've got the right ingredients, and the time, and the patience, you can make custard with that unwanted yolk, or mayonnaise, but often, you know, you don't want custard or mayonnaise. Not really. So you make yourself swallow it anyway. Or perhaps you just throw out the yolk, and shrug.'

He looked at Krubykov, and the colonel saw that Kazin wanted to find out if he'd understood the parable. Slowly, and very reluctantly, Krubykov shook his head. Kazin stretched out his hand towards the two photographs. 'Meringue,' he said, tapping Povin's face. Then his finger hovered over Bryant. 'Yolk . . . and perhaps on this occasion mayonnaise as well, who knows?'

A curious feeling of weakness pervaded Krubykov's body, making him limp. He looked down at his hands and saw that they were trembling, ever so slightly. Experienced though he was in treading his daily, deadly tightrope, the last five minutes had unmanned him. Kazin had gone from brutal disregard for Inna Karsovina to sympathy for the head of an enemy intelligence service via some mysterious memory of the unimaginable past. Krubykov had never seen anything like it. And if there was one thing he had learned to dread above all others in his dealings with Kazin, it was the unprecedented.

Kazin reached up and pressed the call button. When the steward came running he said, 'Give me a report on Stolyinovich.'

The steward hurried towards the rear of the aircraft, where he disappeared behind a curtain. On his return a few moments later he said, 'The prisoner is quiet, Comrade Chairman. The doctor says he is fully conscious and receptive.' He hesitated, aware that he was about to venture into dangerous territory. 'The doctor respectfully suggests, however, that it might be as well if you did not — '

'Get out.'

The steward retired, grateful for the opportunity. The crew of the Chairman's private plane were highly paid and not overworked. But they earned their money.

'He's got over it, then.' Kazin laughed his usual coarse laugh and Krubykov fractionally relaxed. 'My, my, what a temper!'

'You'd hardly think he'd remember.'

'Oh, he remembered me all right. Just as well you were so close, Krubykov. He might have killed me, for all those fucking guards cared.'

Krubykov did not correct the Chairman, although this was an unjust slur on the guards who had brought Stolyinovich to the third floor at Dzerzhinsky Square. The former pianist had shown all the legendary speed and strength of a madman. His curled fingers went straight for Kazin's face. If the colonel had not been standing mere inches away, the attack might have been fatal.

'A good sign, nevertheless,' Kazin went on. 'It means he'll recognize Povin also. He's getting better, Krubykov, just at the very moment when we want him to. Everything is falling into place.' He rubbed his hands with satisfaction. 'Povin, Stolyinovich, Victor and Karsovina in Ristikent — such a stimulating combination! Bryant in Kirkenes. And the Travel Agency — ' he brought his palms together in a gentle clap — 'nowhere.'

The fasten-seat-belts sign came on as the plane began to sink down towards the Kola Peninsula. Ten minutes later it was taxiing towards the military terminal. The two men descended the steps into a wall of driving sleet to be met by an officer with much gold braid on his epaulettes. At a gesture from Kazin Krubykov ran into the terminal, glad of its fuggy warmth, and watched through the thick windows while Stolyinovich was led down the steps to a waiting car. Kazin and the officer stood under an arclight. The Chairman's hands were thrust deep into the pockets of his coat; and from the way he held his head Krubykov knew that he was intent on the other man's words. At last the officer saluted and withdrew into the surrounding darkness.

Kazin began to stalk towards the terminal. As he approached he removed his hands from his pockets and pounded a fist into his other palm. 'Alexander is dead. Murdered. Come on, Krubykov, we've got to get up there fast before that little psychopath of Frolov's sticks a knife in Povin's ribs.'

As they settled into the waiting car Kazin touched Krubykov's arm. 'One other piece of news. They have monitored the arrival of a British Harrier at Banak.' He smiled, and for a second the colonel detected a pale shadow of the Chairman's former mood. 'We've smashed the egg, Krubykov. And the next thing we've got to do is separate it!'

27

Povin sat patiently waiting for the interrogation to begin but he could see that the woman's mind was elsewhere. He had entered the room to find the tape recorder playing Rachmaninov's Piano Concerto No. 1 in F-sharp minor. The old man found that an interesting choice.

It was part of Russian musical folklore that Stolyinovich had a blind spot about Rachmaninov, but his one-off interpretation of this particular work left the hearer feeling breathless and awed. Long ago, when he was still in his twenties, he had played it to win the Leeds Piano Competition; Decca recorded it, and somehow a tiny flicker of the original magic always managed to re-create itself across the years. But the pianist had never repeated that one early triumph. Out of a sense of national pride he had cut several commercial recordings of Rachmaninov's works; they were not a success and somewhere in the middle years of his meteoric career they were tactfully allowed to die. For that reason Povin treasured the first victory all the more; only a few of the pressings from the Leeds concert survived.

He was convinced that the woman knew the recording's history, what it meant; hence this was a gesture that gave him hope.

No sign of tension showed through Povin's calm exterior. He knew that everything now depended on the precise order of events. The events themselves were predestined. All that mattered was the timing.

He cleared his throat. 'Please forgive me, but you seem a little distant today. No questions?'

She had been sitting with her elbows on the desk, chin supported in cupped hands, looking at the tape recorder. Now she stood up and began to walk nervily about the room, pausing every so often to straighten a file or move the vase of flowers from one end of the sill to the other. Povin watched her carefully. When at last she turned to face him her eyes failed to meet his by just a fraction.

'It's nothing, really.'

'Nothing . . . "really". That suggests there is something, doesn't it?'

Inna shrugged. 'I was drafting my resignation, if you really want to know.'

The old man shook his head very slowly, as if to indicate astonishment. He was in truth a little surprised. She thought she had failed, when in fact she had succeeded beyond Kazin's grandest expectations.

'And . . . I can't seem to get through on the phone to my flat.'

'Ah.' Povin hesitated. So events had begun their course. 'The lines are often bad. Soviet technology, dare I say it — or will you put a note in the file if I do?'

She flashed him a quick shadow of a smile and resumed her aimless pacing without bothering to reply.

'It's hard being a mother,' Povin mused aloud. 'I wish . . .'

264

Inna halted and folded her arms. 'Wish . . . what?'

'Oh, nothing important.'

'Come on, tell me.' She hitched herself on to the edge of the desk, tucking one leg behind the other, and for the first time that day gave him her complete attention.

'Well, then . . . Oh I don't know why I'm telling you all this. I wish I'd had more time with my own mother. To understand her. To . . . get to grips with her, if you like.'

When Inna smiled this time, there was warmth in her face. 'I've never seen anyone so eaten up by guilt at his failure to relate to his parents.'

'Mother only. There was no problem with Father; I didn't bother to try and relate to him at all. No, it was Mother I messed it up with.'

'Because you think you could have saved her, is that it? Then you're a fool. You're being a Young Pioneer again. No one could have saved your mother from a beating. You're lucky they didn't finish her off, right then and there.' She hesitated, struck by a thought. 'Is that one reason why you became a Christian, d'you think? To assuage your guilt? Guilt transference?'

Povin made no reply. Inna dropped off the edge of the desk and went back to her perambulation of the room. 'I don't mean to sound harsh,' she said eventually.

'I know.'

'Life is harsh.'

'I know.'

'My mother . . . '

'Yes?'

'My own mother . . . There've been problems. Sometimes. Over Volodiya, mainly. You can't change what's done.'

'You can learn from it, though. So you don't make the same mistakes when it's your turn.'

Inna flopped back down into her chair. She had come to recognize the times when Povin put more into his words than their face value would suggest, and this was one such time. 'What do you mean?'

'You have a son of your own. Learn from the mistakes your mother made. Learn from your own mistakes. I want to ask you something.' He leaned forward to rest his forearms on his knees and clasp his hands in front of him. 'It concerns guilt. It's also important.'

She wanted to look away but his steady gaze held her fast; they had reached a point in their relationship where he no longer had to convince her that something was important.

'Suppose you were forced to make a choice . . . a choice between Volodiya and your own mother . . . the kind of choice which would mean never seeing one of them again, ever . . . what would you do?'

He sat back very slowly, keeping his eyes fixed on her face, and it seemed to Inna Karsovina that the roles were reversed; that she, the prisoner, must answer Povin, the interrogator. Then the illusion passed, and with it the desire to snap some angry putdown.

'I . . . I don't know. Listen, I want to tell you something, Stepan. I want to say that I'm sorry.' Genuine grief flooded across her face. 'At the beginning perhaps, then I was with them, truly with them . . . but it's been a long time since the beginning, hasn't it?'

'Yes. So help me to escape.'

It took her a few moments to assimilate that. 'Help you . . .?'

'Our conversations are, of course, recorded; I have to hope that they are not also monitored simultaneously. In a moment I propose to walk out that door. I want you to come with me.'

'But you'll never make it.' Inna's voice was tired and flat, as if she no longer cared what happened.

'Yes, I will. I will make it, Inna, with your help.' The old man looked into her eyes and what he saw there contradicted her voice: concern and pity. A flicker of real affection, maybe. The ice was creaking beneath their feet but time was short, events were happening in the right order and from now on there must be no dawdling . . .

'I can't help you.'

'Yes, you can.'

'But how?'

'Don't interrupt. We have minutes, seconds maybe — you really can't conceive how little time we have. You will walk with me. You will be my safe conduct, no one will question you or try to prevent us from leaving. You and I, we come and go, everyone knows that; sometimes in uniform, sometimes not, today not. You will help me, Inna. And then you will accompany me to freedom . . . '

Inna gaped at him, not understanding, her eyes wide with fear. 'Don't be ridiculous. I . . . I can't!'

She was about to speak again, but Povin used every ounce of energy he possessed to will her absolute obedience. '*Do it!*'

'Why should I?' she wailed; and Povin, hearing the anguished conflict within, finally told her. 'Because Volodiya, your child, is now in the West waiting for you, Inna, for *you*, nobody else, and only I can send you to him. *Only I!*'

Inna was suffocating. She could not breathe. She swayed groggily on her feet like a punchdrunk fighter, sensing without fully comprehending the imminence of tragedy. Across a vast distance, the other side of an abyss, she heard Povin say, 'Help us, Inna. Because of Volodiya. Because of your soul, and his future. Because . . . *you want to*!'

It was true about Volodiya. It was a lie that she wanted to help Povin. It was true . . . *It was all true!*

She grabbed up the phone and frantically dialled the number which Kazin had given her so many weeks ago, in some previous incarnation. No reply. She tried her flat. No reply.

It was all true.

As if from outside herself Inna saw a woman pounding her fists against the old man's chest, head thrown back, keening for her little boy. Povin made no attempt to defend himself. He let the storm whirl itself out, until at last Inna collapsed at his feet in a fit of sobbing. She cringed before him, almost doubled up, and then in a low voice she said, quite rationally, 'Give me back my child.'

'All these weeks, and you still don't understand me.' His voice was weary, weary . . . 'Haven't you listened to anything I've said, Inna Marietta? Haven't you known me? Have you learned *nothing* about me? The boy is unharmed! If I have misjudged you, if I have failed . . . he will be brought back to you. My god, woman, can you doubt that? Can you? *But* . . . if you want to . . . if you are ready, as I believe with all my heart and soul and strength that you are ready . . . come with me.'

His arm shot out towards the window. 'Out there. But in the name of God, for the sake of your child, for all our sakes, Inna — do it *now*!'

She gazed up at him through terrified eyes, incapable of knowing what to do. Before she could decide there came an interruption. The door was wrenched open, Lev Kulikov surged into the room . . . and Povin instantly saw that the odds had changed. The zek was holding a knife. Not a sliver of wood like the old man's, but the real thing. Triple-oh-eight held his arms out in front of him, tossing the knife from one hand to the other. Povin backed off very slowly, never once taking his eyes from the zek's face. So somebody *was* monitoring their sessions, then. Frolov's man . . . the moment he'd heard Povin begin to talk of escape he'd have alerted Kulikov . . .

'No guards,' Povin said bitterly. ' "They put me off my stroke," you remember saying that? They won't give you *time* to resign, Inna Karsovina. They'll put you up against a wall and . . . '

He broke off, distracted by remote sounds. Suddenly they could all hear it: a concatenation of many voices and the crash of boots on the stairs.

Kulikov hesitated only a second. He knew that he would be overpowered before he could stab Povin with the dagger, but he had been awaiting his opportunity for too long to be thwarted now. He flicked the point of the blade between the first two fingers and thumb of his right hand and flung back his arm. Povin's eyes widened as the zek bared his teeth in a grimace of triumph. The knife had reached the very back of its arc; Povin saw the boy's teeth grind and he ducked, knowing it was already too late . . .

Krubykov was the first to come through the door. With scarcely a pause he hurled himself at triple-oh-eight, already off balance as he prepared to throw the knife, bringing him crashing down. Inna shrieked; then, conscious of yet another presence in the room, raised both hands to her mouth. Povin slowly stood upright, unable or unwilling to believe what he saw.

Oleg Kazin, Chairman of the KGB, stepped casually over the zek's prostrate body and walked quickly round the desk until he stood only a few inches away from Inna Karsovina. Again his face was blotchy and pale; again his eyes were far away in another dimension. His gaze was directed at Inna, but it was not her that he saw cowering in front of him. Instead, he saw another woman, of similar age, with a pretty face and the same kind of smile that had betrayed him once before . . .

Kazin flung out his arm to its fullest extent, clenched his fist and threw all his weight behind a blow to Inna Karsovina's jaw.

The force of it spun her round through ninety degrees, propelling her body against the windowledge so that the flowers were knocked over and water from the vase began to run down the wall in broad streaks of grey against the white-wash. It was the water that held Povin's attention. For some indefinable reason he could not look at anything except the ugly, wet runnels, which mirrored those on his cheeks.

Then the young lieutenant who had driven them to Ristikent brought Stolyinovich into the room, and at the same moment, with precision timing, the Rachmaninov concerto attained its glorious, triumphant climax. The hiss of the empty tape seemed to go on for a very long time, while the two men stared at each other with no words to speak. Kazin fitted a cigarette into his cane holder and waited for Krubykov's sycophantic match. 'Remove *that*.' The lieutenant stepped forward to pick Inna up from the floor and drag her, whimpering, from the room. Her eyes were closed and her face was veiny-white, like marble.

Kazin sat down in the interrogator's chair. The KGB lieu-tenant quickly came back to stand behind his left shoulder while Krubykov flanked him on the right, and for a moment Kazin surveyed the battlefield in silence.

'Pick up that one,' he said at last, pointing towards Kulikov. 'Give me the knife.'

The lieutenant obeyed. Kazin took the weapon by the blade, weighing it thoughtfully. 'Bring him here.'

Krubykov helped the lieutenant to drag triple-oh-eight round the desk and made him kneel in front of Kazin. The boy was snivelling. At a sign from the Chairman Krubykov pulled back his head by the hair.

'You either see not enough,' Kazin hissed, 'or you see . . . too *much*!'

He drove the knife forward. Povin was aware of confused impressions: a spurt of rich, red blood, something globular halfway down Kulikov's cheek, screams that went on for a very long time as guards came in to haul the blinded zek away. At last the room was quiet again and Kazin turned towards Povin with a pleasant smile.

'Stepan Ilyich,' he murmured. 'It's been a long time.'

Povin said nothing.

'Sit, sit.'

Povin pulled upright the chair which had been knocked over by Stolyinovich's forced entry and after a second's hesitation lowered himself into it, his face an expressionless mask.

'I nearly misjudged the situation there,' Kazin said with mock humility. 'Dear General Boris . . . such a boor when it comes to things like that. What a shocking thing. Almost as shocking as you arranging to kidnap Karsovina's child . . . Kazin brought the tips of his fingers together in front of his face and shook his head judicially. 'Make a note . . .' He turned his head and addressed the lieutenant. 'I shall want to see the *oper* of this camp before I leave. The security here is simply terrible. Atrocious! If it wasn't for Kulikov, why, they'd almost have got away with it!' The young man's lips twitched in a smile but he did not otherwise move. The Chairman seemed to be in an excellent, albeit malign humour.

'Well, well. Quite a gathering, isn't it. Old faces, old friends.' Kazin enlarged his sphere of observation. 'Pyotr . . . Stepan Ilyich. We've even got Victor waiting downstairs; you can see him later. A close thing — he nearly gave us the slip, we found him less than a kilometre from the border. I really don't understand him at all.' The Chairman took a long drag on his cigarette, addressing the smoke to Povin. 'Did it never occur to him that it was just a little bit too easy? You here, right on the border with the West, over the frontier he came without so much as a patrol to worry about, in and out of the camp . . . did he never *once* stop to think, "Victor, my lad, this smells"?'

There was no answer, but the Chairman did not seriously expect one. 'Well now, I'll tell you something, Stepan Ilyich,' he said, leaning forward. 'I said that's how he'd behave. Nobody else agreed with me, but *I* knew. No one else thought he'd be stupid enough . . . he'll cry off, they told me, he'll read the signs.' Kazin slowly shook his head. 'But — he didn't. He thought it worth the risk, and after all, perhaps he was right: he was — is — the best. Otherwise you would not have chosen him in the first place. Although I doubt very much whether Bryant would have got value for money at the end of the day. Where did he plan to take you, eh? South America, perhaps?'

Stolyinovich had dragged himself upright and was staring at Povin. Now he stretched out a trembling hand towards the general as if he feared the dream might shimmer and collapse on touch. Although Povin had rigidly kept his gaze averted from Stolyinovich, he knew the hand was there. Like a man on the hypnotist's couch he felt his own arm jerk against his will and move towards the point in space where he sensed Pyotr's hand to be. Kazin saw it and shook his head with a loud tut-tut.

'I'm afraid he hasn't been a very cooperative guest, Stepan Ilyich. I doubt if you'd approve. At one point it was even necessary to put him in a special psychiatric hospital.' He rolled the words around his mouth — *spetspsikhbol'nitsa tyur'ma* — and as Povin heard the satisfaction reverberating in the Chairman's voice his hand completed the transition across time and space to close round Pyotr's. 'That was at Alma-Ata. He didn't get on with them there at all, I'm sorry to say. Why, do you know at one time he even accused them of administering neuroleptic drugs?'

Povin's hand tightened its grip. He knew all about the drugs. If given in sufficient quantities over a long enough period they would turn a man into a living corpse, a zombie without hope of resurrection.

Kazin pursed his lips, evidently engaged in some calculation or other. 'Perhaps he'll behave better for you, who knows. I suppose the girl told you the deal I'm proposing, before she went off the rails?'

Povin cleared his throat. It was an effort to speak to Kazin as though the Chairman was a human being but somehow he managed it. He even made himself sound pleasant. 'The dacha, and all that, Comrade Chairman?'

'The dacha.'

'She told me.'

'It still holds. There's one variation, though.'

'I thought there might be. The girl . . . '

'Of course, yes, the girl.' Kazin stubbed out his cigarette and looked at the ceiling, where he seemed to be finding a lot of his inspiration. 'I suppose there's no chance of persuading you to return the child?'

Povin's silence was answer enough for the Chairman.

'No.' Kazin's eyes returned to the ceiling, he was still thinking aloud. 'And now Volodiya's gone, he's gone. We'll never find him, or if we do, a snatch will be more trouble than it's worth. Very neatly thought out, as usual. I must confess I hadn't foreseen about the child. The one thing I didn't manage to foresee. Ingenious. Quite in keeping with past form, I would say, wouldn't you, Krubykov?'

'Indeed, Chairman.'

'It's an ill wind, however. So. What are we to do, then?' The ceiling seemed to have yielded all its secrets, for now Kazin fixed his eyes on Povin's face. 'Where do we go from here?'

He drummed his fingers on the table while waiting in vain for Povin to speak. 'We could always have her shot,' Kazin said at last. He spoke slowly, as if the idea held little attraction for him. 'The mother too, of course. That would at least have the merit of tidiness.'

Povin somehow managed to repress the words that boiled up inside him. Kazin witnessed the struggle and raised an eyebrow. 'Yes?'

Povin shook his head, but very slowly, as if he had trouble moving it.

'You wouldn't care for that, would you, Stepan Ilyich. One more burden of guilt to hang round your scrawny neck, eh? And perhaps — ' the Chairman's face clouded — 'enough to deprive us of your cooperation. You've got quite enough ideals for two.'

He continued to drum his fingers on the desk, keeping Povin in suspense for a few moment longer. 'Of course,' he said softly, as if the idea were wholly new to him, 'we could always send her to the West, to join the boy.'

'You won't do that, Chairman.' Povin's voice was bored and contemptuous.

'I might. Did they tell you what your friend Victor had arranged? No? Then you'd better come and see. Obviously you won't take it from me.' Kazin turned round to the lieutenant. 'Get him his clothes. Besides, it's high time we went and saw this Harrier for ourselves.'

So at Kazin's insistence they dressed Povin up as a general of the KGB for the last time and took him out to the waiting car where he sat in the back like a very important person, with the Chairman on one side of him and Krubykov on the other. They drove through the darkness over progressively worsening roads, until eventually the tarmac ran out altogether and they had to walk through the rain to a waiting army Jeep. Then they bumped and bored along a stony track which led into the taiga, where the Jeep was forced to crawl at ten kilometres an hour, with branches and brambles scratching its canvas roof. At last they came to a clearing and by the light of the headlamps Povin saw the dark shape of an aircraft with soldiers all around it.

They got out. It was very cold. The never-ending rain came down like a curtain between the three men as they trudged and slithered through the mud. The plane was a training Harrier and to Povin it looked undamaged.

'Fetch the pilot.' At Kazin's command one of the soldiers hurried away into the darkness. A door slammed and seconds later an escort was coming into the light, bringing with them a man clad in flying gear. Kazin turned to Povin. 'You can talk to him.'

'In front of you?' His ironical tone did not escape the Chairman.

'Since the object of the exercise is to satisfy you that the man is genuine, that would tend to be self-defeating, wouldn't it,' he said. 'No. Alone.'

As Povin approached the pilot the escort released his arms and pushed him forward. The two men met in the criss-cross of light beams from the army vehicles which surrounded the clearing. Povin had only the vaguest impression of the pilot's face. He looked over his shoulder. The nearest soldier was ten metres away.

'We don't have a lot of time,' he murmured in English.

'I will give you my name, rank and number. That is all, sir.' The airman's voice was stiff with tension and fatigue. Povin sighed and lifted a hand to the man's shoulder. The pilot stared down in surprise but made no move to dislodge it.

'We don't have a lot of time,' Povin repeated. 'Save all that nonsense for the others, they'll enjoy it as much as you will. You had orders to come and collect a man called Victor. You were to recognize him by means of a photograph, I suppose.' Suddenly he realised why Kazin had wanted him dressed in his uniform: to minimize problems of recognition. 'Perhaps they showed you my photograph too?' The sudden twitching on the airman's face was confirmation enough for Povin, who nodded and went on, 'They were expecting you, but they meant to let you go, along with the Harrier, at least from here, from this clearing. But there will be a different passenger. A woman. Whatever happens, don't fly the shortest way home. Don't fly west. They'll be waiting for you there with half the guns and planes of the Kola Peninsula. Fly south, with everything you've got. That will give you the necessary start. Then it's up to you.'

Povin turned away, putting his hands into his pockets, and then stopped as if struck by an afterthought. 'Tell Bryant I'm sorry,' he said over his shoulder. 'Tell him . . . we shall meet in another place. Have you got that? In another place. He'll understand.'

He waited until they were out of the taiga and back in the car before he spoke again.

'And now the price, Chairman.' His words were brisk and to the point, the words of a man who wants to conclude a deal and be about his other business.

'Price?' Kazin's voice, in contrast, was smooth and sweet as molten chocolate.

'Yes. The plane's there, the pilot's English, I've seen enough. You can't hold it for ever, time's short, I realize all that. You're going to send the woman across the wire if I do . . . what?'

'The woman, the pianist and Victor. I've got no quarrel with them.'

'All right, dammit!' Povin's body was quaking with anger. 'Whoever! Just tell me what I have to do.'

Kazin smiled. 'It's really very simple, Stepan Ilyich. I want you to cast your mind back a couple of years and tell me who you were due to meet at the other end, when you got to Tbilisi. The name of your courier in the Travel Agency. That's all.'

'That's *all*?'

'Yes.'

Kazin wanted a name.

There was a long silence. The old man realized that he must now make a decision. It was not really much of a choice that faced him; he had always known what the price of failure would be.

Make it look real.

Povin began to laugh. He laughed and he laughed, until the tears were rolling down his cheeks, his throat hurt and the muscles of his stomach ached with the unfamiliar exercise; and only when he could laugh no more did he wipe his eyes and say, 'I don't know.'

'And is that your answer?'

'Oh yes. That's my answer all right.' Povin chuckled one last bitter time. 'There is an irony of fate here, Comrade Chairman, and it will delight you. The Travel Agency, that legendary model of silent efficiency . . . in my case it made a mess of things. I was told to expect the name of a courier. It never reached me.'

'No, it never reached you.'

Povin realized without surprise that Kazin believed him, and breathed a prayer of gratitude. He strained to penetrate the darkness inside the car, but the Chairman's face was shrouded in shadow.

'It never reached you . . . and yet you know the name.'

'No.'

Kazin reached out to tap Povin on the knee. '*Yes*, General. It'll come to you. Think it over, why don't you. Until the morning . . . '

28

As Colonel Krubykov surveyed the narrow confines of Ristikent MU/12's largest penalty isolator cell it came home to him with forceful clarity that here he was faced with a situation which could not be allowed to develop unchecked for much longer.

'I'm sorry, Chairman,' he murmured, 'but is it really your intention to spend the . . . *whole* night in this place?'

Kazin did not even bother to reply. He pushed past Krubykov and sat down at the table in silence. The lieutenant entered, carrying a paraffin stove; he was followed by two camp guards struggling under the weight of a substantial-looking tape recorder.

'You have checked the machine, I take it?' Kazin's voice hissed through the icy atmosphere inside the cell as if projected from a sinister whispering gallery.

'Yes, sir.' It was the lieutenant who answered. He looked down at Kazin, wrapped up in an old overcoat which reached almost to the floor and wearing only thin kid gloves. 'The stove, Chairman. Will one suffice?'

'Yes.'

'The paraffin will cause an unpleasant stench by dawn. The confined space . . .'

'Never mind.'

The lieutenant and the colonel exchanged uneasy glances behind Kazin's back. During the night the temperature inside the bare, brick-built hut might fall as much as twenty degrees below freezing. The Chairman was known to be tough, yes, but at his age, dressed like that, with only an oil stove to heat what was intended as a punishment cell . . .

Kazin donned the tape recorder's headphones and Krubykov hastened forward to switch on the machine. The Chairman raised his hand to the phones, frowned and blinked.

'It is working now. But what happens if it should fail during the night?'

'There is a second machine in the cell next door, Comrade Chairman.' For one dreadful moment the lieutenant thought that Kazin was going to order him to monitor it, but the old man merely grunted. Then he asked, 'What is the position with regard to Stolyinovich?'

'The doctors are confident, Chairman,' said Krubykov. 'They have spent the last few hours dinning the second part of the code into him and say it is inconceivable that he can last out the night without repeating it to Povin.'

'Confident.'

'Chairman, they guarantee it. And sooner rather than later.'

'They'd better be right, Krubykov.' Kazin grunted again, and subsided once more into grim-faced silence. The temperature was falling rapidly, notwithstanding the portable stove. The lieutenant gnawed his lip and tried to catch Krubykov's eye. No help there. He resolved to make one last attempt.

'Comrade Chairman, it would be a very simple matter for us to install these recorders in the house, where it is warm . . .'

To Krubykov's surprise and mild irritation Kazin did not lose his temper. Instead, he rammed a cigarette into the little cane holder with enough force to tear the paper and said, 'You would be observed laying the wires, Lieutenant. It is impossible to keep such things secret in a camp. Besides . . .' He paused, as if reluctant to trust his underlings with some personal, perhaps slightly embarrassing secret. 'I want to know. I want to know what it is like.' His eyes dissolved into the faraway look which had become so familiar to Krubykov over the past few hours and his voice faltered. Then, just as quickly, he recovered.

'No. This is how it has to be. Here I am . . . ' He lit the cigarette and sucked a lungful of smoke down hard. 'Here I stay. Now get out.'

This time the colonel allowed his eyes to meet those of the lieutenant in a sympathetic, conspiratorial glance, narrowing them slightly as a sign of warning, and the young man shrugged. He snapped his fingers at the guards, who left the cold, damp cell, followed by Krubykov; the lieutenant hesitated in the doorway, checking that all was as it should be and permitting himself one last look at the seated figure of the old man hunched over the table beside the tape recorder, motionless and ominously silent, a cigarette smouldering between his kid-clad fingers . . . then the lieutenant was closing the door quietly behind him with ostentatious care and the vigil had begun.

Penalty isolator. *ShIzo*. Each camp had its own little idiosyncratic variations. 'Solitary' might be a small cell with just enough room for one man to lie down, the kind of thing which one would expect anywhere in the world, although in a Soviet strict-regime camp that would be derided as poor, unimaginative stuff. There the isolator might consist of a hole in the ground, a disused septic tank, an underground cellar half full of water; in some places it had a rounded bar running its length, astride which the solitary occupant would be forced to maintain his balance for hour after hour; in the warm south the cell was frequently nothing more than a crude oven fabricated from corrugated-iron sheets left out in the sun, a human incinerator.

At Ristikent MU/12 the isolator was known as 'the box'. The box consisted of a row of six cells, each just large enough to hold a man standing with his shoulders hunched but not quite long enough to enable that man to lie down. These cells had no windows and were without light or heat of any kind. Now, in spring, the natural warmth of the sun sufficed to melt a little of the top layer of permafrost, thus enabling water to flood up through the rotten floorboards of the isolator block. This water was icy cold.

While a man was in solitary he was entitled to receive fifteen ounces of bread and one cup of gruel a day. He was given no fresh water, but Gulag regulations were humane in not forbidding the prisoner to drink the frozen mush which rose about his ankles. The camp authorities reckoned by a working rule of thumb that, in spring, ten days of the box were enough to kill the average zek, while five days would deprive him of his reason.

On Kazin's orders, two of these cells had been knocked together into one. When Povin was brought to this half-underground room, Victor had already been left alone there for several hours; he did not know exactly how long, because in the box time soon lost its values.

The guards unwittingly pushed Povin straight into Victor's arms.

'Stepan . . . Not good. Sorry.'

Povin hugged him tightly to his chest, patting his broad shoulders. 'It doesn't matter,' he whispered. 'You did all I could ever have asked. You got the message through to Bryant, about the child.'

'Yes.' Victor sighed, and Povin heard how the cold introduced a shiver into his voice. 'I did that. They caught me just short of the wire, you know? Another half hour and . . .'

'Don't think about it, Victor. No use.'

'No use. Here, Stepan, are we going to get out of this place, eh?'

Yes, Povin thought. If my hunches are right, I can get us out of here any time. Kazin wants a name. *If* . . . But not now, not yet. Make it look real . . . 'Of course.'

'Cocky bastard!'

Povin laughed. 'Fuck you!'

The two men hugged each other close again. They knew better than to dwell on their circumstances while they were still strong enough to distract themselves. Povin eased himself into a more comfortable position and asked the question which had been troubling him for days. 'What in hell's name possessed you, Victor? To come here like that . . . surely you knew it was a trap?'

'Yes. Bryant knew.'

'Yet the two of you risked everything — for what?'

'You want an answer? Eh? Stupid bastard . . .'

'Not worth it. You played right into their hands, you and Bryant. Crazy. In the old days I'd have had you shot for that.'

'Shit on the old days.' Victor laughed; but again Povin heard that ominous shiver. 'In the old days I had to count my pay each week to see you hadn't filched half of it. You did once, remember?'

'Well, I'd lost money at cards. A debt of honour, I ask you . . .'

Both men were laughing now.

'. . . Honour! Your honour, my money . . .'

'You could afford it. The way you robbed me blind . . . *I* even used to count the chess pieces after we'd finished the game, to make sure you hadn't pocketed them as well as half my salary.'

'You remember when we last played chess?'

'Two years ago.'

'Almost to the very day.'

'I hate anniversaries.'

'And how I hate them.'

They talked easily, but they were listening for unspoken truths, each man striving to assess the other's capacity for survival. The initial experience meant little to Victor. He was cold, but he was also a hard man. During his years of service under Povin he had seen and endured so many horrors that this latest one had no immediate noticeable effect on him. He knew himself well enough to understand that the real testing time lay in the future, when darkness and cold would merge into a blur of numbing, timeless disorientation. For the present, he could bear it. Just. So he wedged himself into a corner, near his master, and resolved to keep talking about the past until he was ordered to stop.

The box had a different effect on Povin. It produced in him a strange combination of profound despair and intense mental effort. Throughout his time in Gulag he had gone to any lengths, broken every rule, in order to stay out of *ShIzo*. He knew that at his age and in his condition he could not survive solitary confinement in a place such as this for more than a night at most. After waging so long and successful a battle, for him the box represented endgame: that last series of hopeless moves which heralds checkmate.

But at the same time, and by way of curious paradox, *ShIzo* also spelled hope. Ever since the day when he first entered the dacha to find Inna Karsovina waiting, Povin had realized that Kazin wanted something from him; he also knew that, once he perceived the Chairman's desire, he would be able to manipulate it. What followed had been a farce: there was no 'interrogation' and Kazin never intended that there should be. If the woman asked him no direct questions, it was only because the Chairman wanted to save his ammunition for a last assault, at the end. When he was exhausted, and forgetful, and muddled in his mind. When in Kazin's eyes the old man was finished, ready for his 'nine grammes of lead', followed by the 'three *arshins* of earth' which he had mentioned to Inna.

Now that time had come. So Povin stood with bowed head, the ceiling of the box hard against his neck, and he thought, and conserved his energies, and like Victor was strong.

They brought Inna Karsovina in much later, when the temperature had dropped below freezing, and for her this was but another scene in a long, unfolding vista of Hell.

She had suffered much since Povin last saw her: suffered in body and also in mind. The guards had dragged her from the interrogation room and thrown her into a cell occupied by a deranged prisoner who had not been in close proximity with a female for more than a year; and there the guards left her, coming back after two hours to remove a woman who superficially looked the same, but was not.

As the door of the box swung open Povin saw who it was by the beam of the guard's torch and instinctively reached out to grab her as she fell inside. She was shivering and feverish; in the darkness Povin was aware only of moisture wherever he touched her — blood or sweat, he wasn't sure. She was desperate to talk but her words came out as incoherent ramblings punctuated by an occasional scream or whimper, and it was all Povin could do to soothe her into silence and the semblance of repose. At last he managed it; she sank down to the cold, wet floor and reluctantly he resigned himself to leaving her there until she could muster enough strength to stand. But the score to be levelled was growing, growing all the time.

Then at last they brought Pyotr Stolyinovich to make the reunion complete, and after the guards had gone away there was silence in the box for many minutes.

It is difficult for two people to embrace in a confined space not much bigger than a broom cupboard, but Stepan and Pyotr managed it somehow — awkwardly yet unselfconsciously, smiling a little at the awkwardness, although they could not see each other's faces. Povin had not held anyone close to him with tenderness for more than two years. His body quivered and ached but his mind spun wild with unlooked-for joy, whirling out of the camp, out of Russia, free; it was as if Stolyinovich unlocked the cell and released him for a time to wander at will. But then the journey through space ended; the water sapped blood from his feet, his back creaked with pain and Povin remembered where he was.

Now he had work to do. This reunion had been arranged with a purpose in mind. Kazin wanted a name. Victor's presence alone wasn't enough to produce it, so they brought Inna, and Pyotr as well for good measure. He had to make a decision.

'It's been a long time,' he murmured. Pyotr withdrew until his face was opposite the old man's and just a few inches away, so that the general could smell the fetid stink which two years' imprisonment leaves on a man's breath, in his throat, his guts . . . but he didn't care. All that mattered was that they should be together again now, where it counted, at the end.

'A long time, Stepan, yes.'

The old man started. He had prepared himself for great changes, heeding Inna's advice and finding it sound, but the voice which spoke to him out of the darkness was the one he remembered from long ago. Not when they parted: on that day Pyotr was in pain, afraid, and his voice broke pitifully; but the voice of before, of the time when they had first met and love was something new for both of them. It gave the old man an eerie feeling to know that Kazin could abrogate time thus.

'How are you, Pyotr?' Stupid question, Povin thought to himself and wished it recalled — but to his surprise Stolyinovich answered rationally, 'Not bad now. In the beginning it was bad, very bad, Stepan.' His voice dropped and the old man heard him swallow a couple of times before resuming. 'I wasn't very good. In fact I was very naughty. Now I behave myself, it's all right. They don't try to give me . . . things any more.'

Things. Drugs, that's what he meant. Pyotr was there in the

cell and yet a part of him was absent. They had put him through the mill and now he had come out the other side looking and sounding much the same, but the product wasn't quite perfect. It was slightly flawed, irremediably so, but in a way which the old man couldn't hope to fathom. He felt Pyotr's trembling hand stroke his cheek, ever so gently, and made himself believe that the flaws didn't matter. Nothing mattered. Here, at the end, second best was enough.

'And you, Stepan? How are you?'

'All right. I survived. I'm better for seeing you, for holding you like this . . .'

So much to say. All the things I promised myself if ever . . . They're gone now. There's nothing left, Stepan. Nothing.' Pyotr spoke with the extreme simplicity and precision of a serious-minded child.

'It doesn't matter. Nothing matters any more. Except . . . one thing I must say. Useless though it is, Pyotr . . . I want to tell you I am sorry for getting you into this. I am sorry.'

Pyotr chuckled and the sound, so unexpected and so heart-rendingly reminiscent of good times past, made the old man's ears tingle. 'Just words, Stepan. Saying sorry for all . . . this, it doesn't mean a thing. You cannot say, "Sorry for all this," can you? And when I say, "It doesn't matter," that doesn't mean anything either.'

Povin choked back tears and said, 'You're right.'

'We are together. And they're not going to separate us again, are they, Stepan?'

Suddenly it was like hearing that same solemn child plead for his mummy, and Povin had to wait seconds before he trusted himself to speak what was, after all, the literal truth. 'No, Pyotr. We're never going to be apart again.'

The pianist relaxed his grip and eased himself backwards as far as the restricted space would allow. At once he came into contact with another body and cried out, 'Who's there?' Povin could hear the sudden terror at the back of his throat, lying in wait for his words.

'Victor . . .'

'Victor!'

'Yes. It's a long story, Pyotr.' Povin felt his friend's hand

283

brush his chest and realized that he was reaching out to touch the other man.

'Here, Pyotr.'

'Victor!' Their hands met and clenched hard; Povin could feel them both trembling.

'Also, a woman. Inna Karsovina. My interrogator. She is quiet now, but before you came she was rambling — they've worked her over good. Try not to fall over her, Pyotr. She's hurt.'

'You want me to look out for your interrogator?'

His voice was puzzled, as if here was a great and wonderful mystery. Povin sighed, momentarily unsettled by the thought of the tortuous road he had been made to tread. 'Another long story. She became a friend. I used Victor to get a message to the Travel Agency and they kidnapped her child. I meant to hold him as hostage, but that's all history now.'

'Hostage! Why? I don't . . .'

'She was allowed to take me out of the camp, Pyotr. She could have helped me across the border. She would have done, if the conditions were right. Please . . . don't ask any more.'

Stolyinovich was silent for a moment. Then he said slowly, 'The Travel Agency.'

Povin did not reply, but he heard.

'You know, Stepan, there is so much I want to tell you.'

'Yes, Pyotr.' The old man murmured his response gently, anxious to preserve his friend's feeble concentration. Very close now . . . But the pianist's voice had become childlike again and Povin knew he was once more lost in the maze of the mind.

'Yet it's . . . it's *gone*, Stepan. All that I wanted to tell you. All gone.'

This time Povin only smiled and stroked Pyotr's hand.

'All gone, all gone. "Music to hear, why hear'st thou music sadly . . . " But, Stepan . . . all the rest has gone.'

Pyotr had spoken in English.

'Music, Pyotr?'

' "Music to hear, why hear'st thou music sadly, sweets with sweets . . . " Something. I can't remember any more. But something.'

Deep inside Povin there had formed a pool of intense and gathering stillness. More than close, now . . . on the threshold. He must not blow the seed away before it rooted.

'Let me try to help you, Pyotr. "Music to hear, why hear'st thou music sadly?" And then perhaps . . . "Sweets with sweets war not, joy delights in joy . . ."?'

' "Why lovest thou that which thou receivest not gladly . . ." ' Pyotr sounded full of wonder. Povin began to recite the next line, but before he could complete it the pianist's voice blended with his own. ' "Or else receivest with pleasure thine annoy?" '

'That is very pretty, Stepan. So pretty. What is it?'

What was it? Confirmation of a conclusion reached painfully, after long effort. Chance Medley: a code once common, now fallen into disuse — a musical code. Records. The verses represented all these things, and more. But . . .

'It is a sonnet, Pyotr.' The old man spoke slowly and quietly, choosing each word only after deliberation. 'Shakespeare.'

'Shakespeare . . .' The pianist's voice had become dreamy and slack; Povin knew he was wandering across the border which separated mind's day from mind's night and the knowledge chilled him. He *had* to choose now. Choose whether to give Kazin what he wanted. A name.

'Help me. Help me . . .'

The whimper came from the floor. It was a while before Povin heard it. For a moment he tried to pierce the veil of darkness which separated him from Inna, cutting them off from support and hope.

'Wait. Don't try to move until I reach you.' The old man felt forwards with his hands until he located the woman on the floor. 'You must try to stand, at least for a little while. The water . . . it freezes to the bone. Frostbite.' He became aware of Victor on the other side of Inna, trying to help her up. 'Easy, easy now. Rest your back against the wall, there's nowhere to sit . . .'

'What is this place?' Her voice rippled with hysteria and pain. Povin answered forcefully, knowing that in her condition only plain words could help. 'It is the penalty isolator of Ristikent MU/12. It is very small — a box. There is no heat.

285

There is no light. There is no bed, no chair. It is freezing. There is nothing any of us can do about this. *Nothing*! Do you understand?'

Her teeth were chattering; the old man realized that she did not even have a coat. Unless something happened she would be dead long before morning. Unless . . .

He struggled out of his greatcoat and awkwardly managed to drape it round her shaking shoulders. What the hell did it matter . . .? 'Tell me what has happened to you, Inna. Tell me now.'

She could not control her shivering. Several times she tried to speak, but failed. Povin clasped her to him tightly and began to massage her back. At first she resisted his touch, placing her hands against his chest to push him away; then she seemed to lose all her strength and she succumbed, but unwillingly, as if to necessary evil.

'Did they beat you? Did they?'

She shivered less now, but when she spoke her voice was a scarcely audible whisper. 'Yes. And they . . .'

'What? Inna! *What*?'

'N-nothing. You w-w-won't l-leave me?'

'I cannot leave you, Inna, even if I wanted to. I do not want to. You are in prison now. We are all in prison. Do you understand what I am saying, Inna?'

Silence.

'Do you understand, Inna?'

'P-prison. Here.'

'Yes. Here.'

'Why . . . me?' There was a long pause between the two words, as if after the first she lost the thread and had to struggle to regain it.

'Because you betrayed him. You betrayed Kazin. That is why he chose you, Inna. You and no one else. The *real* reason. So that you might betray him. And he might punish you through your own child, at the end. He knew I would take the boy, if I could.'

She had stopped shivering, although the tiny cell was deathly cold. Now she laid her head on his shoulder and as the tears began to flow he stroked her hair, very gently, like a father soothing his daughter to sleep. The image struck him with great and peculiar force.

'You are so like his own daughter, Inna.' Povin raised his voice. 'Did he tell you that?'

'No.'

'In looks. In manner. In age. All the same. All . . . different.'

She lifted her head. 'You knew his daughter.' He could hear the wonder in her voice. When he did not reply she said again, 'You knew his daughter.' There was a long pause. Then, 'You know what happened to her. Don't you?'

Silence.

'Don't you?'

Silence.

'Stepan. Answer me, Stepan. *Please, Stepan*!'

But he continued to stroke her hair, until at last she lowered her head in defeat. 'Is that what will happen to me?' she murmured into his shoulder. 'Is that what will happen to Volodiya?' As she spoke the child's name tears sprang into her eyes again and she began to weep, but still Povin said nothing.

They had been in the cell a long time now. The old man guessed that it was still before midnight, but only just. He could no longer feel any sensation in his feet. The numbness was climbing slowly but steadily up his legs, towards the knees. There was very little room to move and no space at all for exercise. Victor would make it, probably, but Pyotr and the girl were marked out for extinction. He didn't know about himself. Over the past two years he had often been surprised by his own resilience. It was possible he might see another dawn, but on the whole he thought it unlikely.

Should he speak, or say nothing?

He could die in silence, and they would all die. The defeat of Kazin was a triumph for which their deaths represented only a trifling price . . . No, he didn't believe that, it wasn't true. That was the negation of all he had fought for. What about the boy, Volodiya? What kind of hell awaited the soul of a man who wrought such destruction? 'Better that a millstone should be hung round his neck . . .'

Povin longed to speak. He wanted his revenge. But if he spoke, Kazin won.

The maze inside his head was not static. Every time he focused on a path it would shift and weave until he could no longer follow where it led.

'Inna.'

She told him that she had heard by a sudden tensing of her body, but that was all.

'Did they talk to you about the records? At the end . . . ?'

She raised her head and vainly tried to penetrate the implacable darkness, searching for his face in wonderment. 'Records?'

Silence.

'Did they mention . . . the Chance Medley code?'

'Yes.'

'Yes . . . they would have to let you know that much. Pyotr told them.'

The pianist stirred his cramped limbs, bumping against both Povin and Inna. 'What did I do, Stepan?'

'Nothing.' Povin lowered his voice to a whisper. 'There was a code, Inna. The Chance Medley, they told you that. It comes in two parts. I had one. Pyotr was given the other. He told Kazin, he had no choice. Now he's told me, just a few moments ago. And for the first time I know what my part of the message was. Records. Gramophone records. The ones Pyotr brought me as a gift from his last trip abroad. That's what you were supposed to find out, Inna. And now you know.'

She shook her head and cried a little. 'I don't know anything, Stepan.'

The maze dissolved, re-formed itself, steadied. Povin was thinking again. His conclusions had been sound, then. Chance Medley, the only musical code London ever used. Although it was old, Povin never forgot a cipher. He'd long ago sent his brain in search of this one and found it intact. But that was only part of the exercise. The records. He had to be able to remember the names of the records.

Kazin was right to say the old man knew the answer. The answer was there, locked into the interstices of his brain, if only he had the wit to recover it. And Povin had done the necessary calculations many weeks ago now. The question which could no longer be deferred was a simple one: did he want to use them?

He had to remember the records. *Some* records. Six of them. Six letters . . .

He was suddenly infected by claustrophobia, a mounting panic which longed to find release in physical violence. The sense of oppression in the tiny cell was overwhelming, terrifying. He had to stop it. *Soon.*

The old man chose.

'Pyotr.'

The pianist had drifted off into the mysterious world for which Kazin's torturers had shaped him. He came back to reality with a start. 'Stepan. I'm cold, Stepan. And hungry. Please let us out. Please, Stepan. Let us out . . . '

'Pyotr, listen to me . . . '

'Please, Stepan.'

'*Listen*! The records you brought me, as a present . . .'

'Records? I'm hungry, Stepan . . .'

'There was . . . Grieg's Piano Concerto. A minor, Opus 16. A 16. Then . . . Prokofiev. The seventh piano sonata. B-flat major, that's B 7 — it's coming, my god, it's *there*!'

The maze shimmered for the last time and was perfectly still. Now he merely had to follow the appointed path to the end.

'Stepan, I . . . I have to get out.'

The woman's words distracted him and he had to fight down the sarcastic rejoinder which came to his lips. 'You cannot leave, Inna,' he said evenly. 'They will not let you.'

'But I need to . . . Stepan. I need to use the . . . the lavatory.'

She was coming between him and his calculations, but again he struggled for self-control. 'You can call, if you like.'

She raised her voice and cried out, but nobody came. After five minutes she realized that nobody would ever come.

'Then what am I to do?' she wailed; and now he could no longer restrain himself, nor resist his small, mean moment of revenge. 'This is a Soviet prison, Inna. Socialism made real. The triumph of ideology over humanity. *Do it on the floor!*'

At first she could not believe he was serious. Her mind refused to believe it. Then, slowly, her body overcame conscious thought and she began to sob: long, drawn-out gulps of misery which tore at the old man's heart but brought Inna no relief; for the more she cried the more the pressure on her bladder tightened until at last she could bear it no longer and let loose the flood which flowed down her legs to the floor in great gouts to match her racking sobs of utter humiliation and despair.

But now Povin was in the grip of a rising emotion which threatened to drive him crazy, for the emotion was rage and it had no outlet.

'Socialism made real, Inna Marietta,' he grated. 'The real thing, the best that man can do. I'll tell you something funny, if you like. This'll bring a smile to your lips. This'll make you laugh, it was Frolov, stinking, crawling Boris fucking Frolov, Colonel that was, my *god*!'

He raised both hands to his forehead then smashed clenched fists against the ceiling with all his strength.

'*God damn you, Frolov! God rot you! God rot your fucking, fucking, fucking soul for ever and ever and a day!*'

He launched himself forward. He was crying. Victor grabbed him, missed, tried again and this time succeeded in getting a hold. They fought, locked together in the restricted confines of the box, scarcely able to move but struggling with all their strength. Inna shrieked and shrieked again; Stolyinovich cowered away, holding his hands over his head, and slid to the floor; suddenly Victor managed to jerk Povin's head against the brick wall of the cell and the old man, stunned, released his grip.

He sank down to the floor with a groan and began to retch. Icy water flooded into his clothes, soaking him to the skin within seconds. 'Frolov,' he cried at last. 'F-fucking F-Frolov. All the while pretending to bring me down, chasing me, hating me, wanting my job. And he was the Moscow Travel Agent. What . . . a . . . *joke*! I w-wonder what he'd have done if I'd m-made it . . .'

Outside the penalty isolator there was a sudden clatter of many footsteps followed immediately by the clash of a key in the lock and the command: 'Open!'

Light flooded into the box. By the torch beams Povin caught a hateful glimpse of its other occupants. Inna and Pyotr lay hunched up together on the icy wet floor. The woman cried quietly to herself while they picked her up and carried her out. Victor had dark spots on his face; at first the old man thought they were shadows, tricks of the light, but when someone shone a torch full on him he saw the blood which his fingernails had drawn, and shuddered.

'And now, General . . . ' A shadow stood on the threshold sideways to the old man, who thus saw it in profile: a shadow wearing a long overcoat, tightly belted at the waist, with a cigarette holder from which the smoke twisted upwards like curls of incense in a Russian Orthodox Church . . .

'The records. All of them. If you please.'

Povin looked up at him stonily. 'You heard . . .'

'Everything.'

The old man buried his head in his hands and fought to stem the tears. 'Will you at least let the others go?'

'A deal's a deal,' Kazin said equably. 'You can all go. Yes, General, even you. Tomorrow morning. When it's light.'

As Povin keeled over sideways Kazin turned to the young KGB lieutenant and said, 'Get him out of there.'

29

It was a wonderful dawn: the best the old man had ever seen.

They'd carried him out of the isolator with the others and escorted them to the administration block, where hot coffee and food were waiting, followed by dry beds with soft down pillows and heavy blankets. The four prisoners slept as if drugged. Povin, whose habits had become deeply ingrained over the past two years, was the first to be awoken by the light in the eastern sky. He dragged himself across the room to the window and peered through the curtains (real curtains!), resting his arms on a radiator (hot!) for support.

'What a day! Blue sky wherever you look; no clouds anywhere.' Pyotr had risen silently and come to stand behind him. Povin, still half lost in his reverie, scarcely heard. Far away on the other side of the watchtowers and the fences a dazzling yellow hem joined the dark earth to the sky. The old man's eyes caressed it lovingly. Black Russian earth melding with the light of the rising sun, and above that the last, faint stars. Soon it would be fully light. Soon it would be day: the first day of an Arctic spring. A wave of maudlin melancholy swept over the old man, making his eyes bright with unsheddable tears. 'Sad,' he murmured softly. 'Sadness as Russian as that rich earth on the horizon and the watchtowers in the foreground.' He wiped his forehead with the sleeve of his jacket, inwardly cursing himself for his stupid weakness, and turned to present Pyotr with a cheerful face. Think of the realities facing you, he told himself brusquely. There is bread to eat. There is water to drink. There is air to breathe. Beyond that . . . nothing.

But yes, there was something. This morning they were accompanied by a white-coated steward instead of armed guards with dogs, and not to the bakery either, but to the officers' mess, where a table had been set aside for their breakfast. Kazin, Krubykov and the lieutenant were already seated there when Povin shambled in behind the rest.

'Good morning, Stepan Ilyich. You're just in time for breakfast. Come. Eat!' And Kazin thrust back the chair next to him with his own hand, that Povin might sit down. The old man smiled, slipping into his place as if he had been invited to join the communal table at the Armed Forces Officers' Club in Moscow.

There were eggs fried in butter, rolls, jam, more of that delicious hot coffee, and some fruit. Povin hadn't tasted an apple for over two years. He looked at it curiously before sinking his teeth into its soft flesh, relishing its very existence.

The other three captives sat in silence, but Povin, who knew he shortly faced the prospect of interminable silence, was in a mood to talk. 'You have a good appetite, Chairman,' he said jovially.

'Certainly. People think the old don't like to eat, Stepan Ilyich. We know better, eh?'

'What did the young ever know?' Povin grunted. 'Kulikov was young.'

Kazin puckered up his face in a contrite frown. 'Yes, I'm sorry about him. I knew Frolov would try to finish you off, but I had to take the risk of leaving Kulikov up here.'

'How little faith you have in my ability to take care of myself.'

Kazin grinned. 'I don't think so, Stepan Ilyich. And there was always Alexander.' He lowered his voice to a conspiratorial whisper. 'Anyway, the girl needed a bit of encouragement. Kulikov made her feel sorry for you. She really likes you, you know. Ever thought of getting married, eh?'

Povin laughed and reached across Kazin for the bread basket. He was enjoying his breakfast. And why not? It was his last.

'How was the trip up? You still flying that old Yak?'

'Yes. It'll need replacing soon. Tell me, what do you think I ought to have next, eh?'

'I'm out of touch, Chairman. What are Tupolev up to these days?'

'Wrecking. As usual.'

The two old men laughed, slapping their legs and causing the coffee to spill from their cups.

'Stop it!'

They paused in mid-guffaw, astonished to be thus interrupted. Inna Karsovina had risen to her feet. Her face was white as snow, even to the lips. Povin thought that he had never seen anyone look so ill.

'How can you do this? How can you?' She was not hysterical. All her remaining few drops of strength were channelled into anger. But it was hard for her to sustain the performance — she reminded the old man of a car with a flat battery, its headlights fighting for life. There was no volume to her words, no spark to inflame her righteous indignation.

Her dull eyes moved away from Povin's face, travelling the length of the table and back again. All she could see was male stares fixed upon her with varying degrees of puzzlement and displeasure. Only Povin looked amused. Inna sat down very slowly and rested her head in her hands. She longed to weep and could not.

'Eat your breakfast.' Kazin spoke as if to a child who must shortly go to school. Inna had used the words herself to Volodiya, many times, but never quite achieving that perfect tone of easygoing firmness. 'I've got good news for you, Inna Marietta. Last night we monitored a cable from Berlin. The British say they took the boy through the Wall yesterday. He's safe and sound. Now eat.'

But Inna cried a little and pushed away the plate with its two fried eggs set in a sea of congealed fat. Povin at once reached out for it.

'You want one of these?' Kazin shook his head. 'Come on. Split it with me.' Povin picked up the plate and used his fork to shunt one of the eggs on to Kazin's.

'Oh, all right. It's cold enough to freeze the feathers off a duck's arse up here.'

His words must have struck a responsive chord in Povin, for suddenly the old man shivered. No! *Don't think*! 'Tell me about Moscow, Chairman. What's going on?'

As the two men chatted Povin's concentration never once slipped. From under his eyelids he could keep sly watch on the rest of the table without difficulty. He saw that no one else understood the game he and Kazin were playing, not even Krubykov, who was puzzled almost beyond endurance. Povin knew that the colonel felt betrayed and the thought gave him much pleasure.

If this were to be my Last Supper, the old man mused, and if they asked me, 'Is it I, Lord?' . . . to which of these would I give the piece of bread, the token of Iscariot?

His past was so rich in betrayals. Pyotr had betrayed him over and over again in petty ways, but never maliciously. Victor? Perhaps. Then again, no. His rescue attempt hadn't made matters any worse than they were already. A well-intentioned mistake, that's all. No wilful treason there. Inna . . . ?

'Why are you looking at me like that?'

But he only grinned and turned back to face Kazin, rejecting all thought of a nonexistent future. It wasn't anybody's fault that this had to be a last supper. 'So what happened in the GRU then, after Kronkin was shot . . .?'

Kazin answered him seriously. He played the same game as Povin and for the same reason: it was necessary to distract the others, on both sides. There must be no thinking about the future, not today. For the present the sole art lay in concealment: of motives, emotions, thoughts. Awkward questions about the things that did not quite fit must be left for later. Afterwards. When it was over.

'Give Stepan Ilyich a cigarette, Krubykov. He's got some new habits since we saw him last.'

Povin smoked. It was a long time since he had enjoyed a cigarette as much. But all too soon the day was fully light and it was time to go. As they pushed back their chairs he remembered inconsequentially that Soviet fighter planes were no good at night . . .

'Now,' said Kazin as they walked to the waiting convoy. 'To business. There's the pilot.' He pointed, and the old man saw the British airman being led to a Moskvich. 'He can take one of you in the Harrier. The rest will go in a helicopter. We're negotiating a passage through Norwegian airspace but that shouldn't hold us up long. I'll see you later, Stepan Ilyich; we can save our goodbyes until then.'

Kazin watched Povin clamber into the back of a ten-tonner and lean down to help Inna up. 'You know,' he called, 'it's a relief to get out of the office for a while.'

'Of course. It was the same with me.' The old man tried to keep his tone light, but it was harder for him now. 'Listen, Chairman . . . '

Inna Karsovina slithered out of Povin's grasp and crawled to the front of the lorry, where she lay down as far away from him as possible. The engine started, making the whole lorry quake. Kazin approached, a look of curiosity on his face.

'You can use it?'

'Use what?' Kazin's face was puzzled.

'The evidence. It is in a form that you can use?'

The Chairman took a long, deliberate drag on his cigarette while he regarded Povin through narrowed eyes, until at last the old man became impatient. 'Against Frolov.'

Kazin smiled. 'Oh yes,' he murmured. 'Thank you very much, Stepan Ilyich. The record of the interrogation is perfect in every respect.' He spread his arms wide in a theatrical gesture of amusement. 'You can imagine my horror when I learned the truth!'

'Truth!' They laughed easily together, like old friends. 'But it should be all right,' Povin mused. 'They'd never believe a straight accusation, coming from you, but this should hold up.' He raised his eyes to Kazin's face. 'It had better.'

The hardness in the Chairman's expression matched his own. 'It will. I — I personally, Stepan Ilyich — *guarantee* it!'

They were almost ready to leave. Victor scrambled quickly up, followed more clumsily by Stolyinovich. Povin rested his back against the tail-board and waved cheerily to Kazin. The Chairman raised his right hand to his forehead in an ironical salute, the lieutenant banged on the side of the lorry, and they were off.

Povin slipped his arm through Victor's. 'Enough to eat?'

'Yes. Stepan . . . ?'

'Let's not talk.'

It was good to be out in the fresh air, instead of stuck in the kitchen hard at work. Besides, Povin was determined to enjoy himself today. There was nothing to distract him from the scent of the peat bogs, steaming in the newly warm sun, which stretched away from the road to where the taiga signalled the horizon.

Rodina. Motherland. Again the insidious, maudlin sentimentality plucked at Povin's eyes and he shook his head roughly. No time for that, not now. Later, maybe. Soon. But now he must be strong.

The same journey, to the same spot in the forest, only this time it was light and he could savour the scenery. There was a helicopter waiting for them in the clearing, alongside the Harrier; as Povin jumped from the back of his lorry he saw the pilot climb up to the cockpit and strap himself in. They wheeled up an air-compressor and moments later the engines fired, their mournful whine rising slowly on the fresh morning air to screaming pitch before once more sinking down to idle. For a second the pilot looked straight at Povin, and as the general read doubt in the man's eyes he threw all his will into his own gaze, staring at the pilot with rigid attention until he thought he saw him nod once; then he knew that he could do no more and he turned away, towards the present, towards choice.

'Well, well. This, then, is the end.' Kazin's face wore a cheerful expression which scarcely accorded with his sad words. He rubbed gloved hands together and puffed hard on a cigarette. 'Goodbye, Stepan Ilyich. Give them hell in the West, won't you. Make them feed you, tell them nothing: that's my advice, but you'll do what you want, of course. If you come back, I'll shoot you myself.' Suddenly he spread his arms wide and after only a second's hesitation Povin walked into them. Conceal, beguile, distract: do the job for which you've lived your whole life . . . He could feel Kazin's body tremble against his own and — Not long, he was thinking, not much time left for you, and what's more you know it . . . Then he stood back, holding Kazin at arm's length for a last, almost affectionate look, before the Chairman once more inserted the little cane holder in his mouth and said, 'Who will go in the Harrier?'

It sounded like a genuine question, rather than a veiled order. Povin looked at him expressionlessly for a long moment before diverting his gaze to the candidates. Victor stood a little to one side, watching his master's face. Povin smiled at him reassuringly but shook his head. Now he wished he had talked to Victor after all, asked him how he'd planned to force the pilot to fly them away from Bryant and the waiting Western world, but it was too late for that. And it was a trifle; what did it matter? There was a plan. Victor would have managed it somehow, just as he always had done in the old days.

Pyotr was still humming the same tune. He must have felt cold, for his hands were clasped under his armpits and every so often he would shuffle his feet in a desultory attempt to inject a little blood into them. The old man wanted so much to see into his eyes, but the pianist resolutely stared at the ground, as if seeking there the answer to some insoluble problem. After a moment Povin turned his back on Pyotr, lest his hesitation should give the game away to Kazin, who was observing him keenly. Not even to say goodbye to Pyotr . . . Povin swallowed hard and for a moment clenched his teeth. The price was high.

Inna.

In stark contrast with Stolyinovich she looked about her boldly, defying her fate to the end. Had she betrayed him? The image of the Last Supper came back into his mind and he smiled; she had greater claim to the mantle of Judas than all the rest, but still, it was a question without meaning. The old man studied her long and hard but could see no answer on this side of the frontier which separated Russia from Norway, life from death; and anyway, the past was dead now, there was only the future, and that was Volodiya, which in turn meant . . .

Kazin knew the odds as well as Povin; better, in fact. He understood perfectly that the Harrier represented a chance, the only chance, of life. He was offering one of them — just one — that chance. Povin directed a level gaze at Kazin, who met it unflinchingly, and he said, 'Not much of a choice, Chairman. Not what I would call a real choice at all.'

'I don't understand you.'

'You lied about the child.' Povin's voice was flat, it brooked no denials. 'You pretended you didn't foresee what I would do, but you did. It's your way: to give and take back at the same time. A chance, that's what you're offering. But don't pretend it's a choice.'

Kazin curved his lips into a rueful smile. 'Perhaps I exaggerated a little,' he said at last. 'I'm a modest man. And you must remember, Stepan Ilyich, that for almost anyone else . . . this would be a choice.' He shook his head. 'Don't fix me with all your weaknesses, Povin.'

This, their last conversation, was conducted in low voices so that the others should not hear it. Now Povin looked at the ground, shrugged and stepped back.

'Inna Karsovina,' he said, raising his voice. 'Let her go in the Harrier, Chairman. She's in a bad way, it'll be over quicker.'

Did Kazin smile once more as he heard those last words? Povin thought he did; at least, his own expression exactly matched that on the Chairman's face and certainly he was smiling. Over quicker, oh yes . . .

'Very well.' Kazin snapped his fingers at the lieutenant. 'Put her in the plane.'

But before the officer could step forward Povin held up his hand and said, 'Wait.' While the others looked on inquiringly he approached Inna and made as if to take her in his arms. Krubykov, startled, jumped forward.

'Stand back!'

'Don't be ridiculous, Krubykov.' Kazin's face assumed an expression of pure disdain. 'You sound like a sergeant in charge of some piffling camp convoy.'

Povin exchanged one last ironic smile with the Chairman of the KGB before enfolding Inna in his arms and stroking her fine golden hair. She did not protest, neither did she resist, but instead laid her head on his chest and held him tightly, as if at last she knew. She was crying quietly — for him? For Volodiya?

'Goodbye, Inna,' he murmured, 'For a little while.'

At that she raised her head and searched his eyes; and this time it seemed to her that there was a message, but one that she could not decipher in time; a message that she must remember for the rest of her life, because it was important, so she strove to fix his expression in her memory whence she could recall it later, in peace and freedom.

'Kiss Volodiya for me. You promise, mm?' She nodded. ' "We shall all be changed." You know that don't you?' His voice cracked and she heard him swallow. 'Go quickly now. Don't look back. Whatever happens, don't look back. Goodbye.' Then he was disengaging her suddenly desperate grasp and handing her over to Krubykov, who half dragged, half carried her to the waiting Harrier, while she cried, 'Stepan! I don't want to go, not without you. Stepan! *Stepan*!'

Povin's heart was beating very fast. All his senses were at full stretch and the fear which had been nibbling at his consciousness since dawn was gone. The pain in his leg, the cold air on his skin were as intense as his awareness of the pattern of frost on the nearest leaves, or the song of the birds in the trees. Everything he focused on was magnified beyond reality, every blade of grass, each twig, each ray of sun scything through the tall boles of the surrounding forest. He was alive!

Kazin would honour the bargain, his revenge on Frolov was complete — and he had preserved the secret of the Travel Agency's courier. Nothing else mattered. He had achieved it all. He knew he ought to pray, but now, at the end, the one time when it really mattered, he could not find the words.

The Harrier was sealed and ready to fly. The pilot ran the turbo-fan up to its limit, holding it there until the whole forest seemed to reverberate with its urgent shriek; then his gaze sought Povin once more, that same look of uncertainty in his eyes, as if pleading for a final confirmation, and the old man shot a quick glance around him. Everyone's attention was on the Harrier. He drew in a deep breath, raised both arms to full stretch and screamed, 'Now!'

As the others looked round in astonishment, Povin began to stumble towards the treeline.

He heard the sudden roar of the Harrier's engine deflecting towards the earth and knew that it was rising. Behind him there came a sudden commotion: Krubykov shouting orders and cries from the troops as they ran about in disarray. Then the Harrier was directly above his head, still hovering, still uncertain. Povin lowered his arms and set himself to run as never before, ignoring the agony in his chest, his legs, but fighting for the treeline as if for life itself. He wasted no energy in looking up, but suddenly the note of the plane's engine changed and he knew that the pilot had made his decision.

South. He was flying south, not west: away from where the Soviet fighters waited in ambush. Scattered, disorientated thoughts dashed through the old man's head. It would take time to radio from this godforsaken spot; there would be endless delays in verifying the message, the fighters would have to divert . . .

He was nearly at the trees now. Behind him he thought he could hear Kazin say, 'Wait! Let him go'; above his head the Harrier roared away into the distance, its engine developing maximum thrust against the crisp atmosphere, the sun was up and rising . . . Povin lifted his arms again in farewell and laughed. Another fifty metres and he would be in the forest. The click of rifle bolts, a shot, another . . .

His heart was pounding at his ribcage as if demanding to be let out, he was breathless, he felt his legs begin to slow. The pain in the left one was excruciating, but it didn't matter, nothing mattered, the plane had gone south and his spirit was light with the knowledge that for once, just this once, he had chosen the correct path and was following it all the way home . . .

The sten gun's clatter ripped through his thoughts; he saw as branches to the left, high up, shivered and splintered, but he only laughed again and began to zigzag, distracting their attention from the one thing that still mattered, the Harrier's flight-path. Now the steady stream of bullets was stripping the bark from the trees immediately ahead of him . . .

'Young Pioneer,' he heard a voice say, a woman's voice of indeterminate age, a mother's voice — Povin threw back his head one last time and laughed out loud for sheer joy.

Then a bullet found his heart and laid him down to his rest.

WILLIAM DIEHL

IS BACK WITH AN EXPLOSIVE NEW THRILLER

HOOLIGANS

Jake Kilmer wasn't in Dunetown for the sightseeing –
nor to play the slot machines. He was there on racket
squad business, checking out a nice bunch of *cosa
nostra* boys called the Cincinnati Triad who were
taking the town for every cent they could get. Now, it
seemed, someone was taking the law into their own
hands to try and clear Dunetown of the mobsters –
someone who, like Kilmer, was trained to kill in
Vietnam . . .

ADVENTURE THRILLER   0 7221 30074   £2.75

NORMAN MAILER

TOUGH GUYS DON'T DANCE

**The brilliant new novel from America's
greatest living writer –
author of the classic bestsellers
An American Dream,
The Naked And The Dead
and the Pulitzer Prizewinners
Armies Of The Night and
*The Executioner's Song***

Tim Madden is an unsuccessful writer addicted to bourbon,
cigarettes and blondes with money. On the twenty-fifth
morning after the departure of his wife, Patty Lareine, he wakes
with a hangover and considerable sexual excitement.

He remembers nothing of the night before – but there's a fresh
red tattoo on his arm bearing a name from the painful past, and
the front passenger seat of his Porsche is drenched with blood . . .

So begins Madden's disquieting journey into the dark recesses
of America's psyche.

'Hypnotic . . . thrilling, blood-spilling.' *Mail On Sunday*

General Fiction   0 7221 5768 1   £2.50

A selection of bestsellers from SPHERE

FICTION

HOOLIGANS	William Diehl	£2.75 ☐
UNTO THIS HOUR	Tom Wicker	£2.95 ☐
ORIENTAL HOTEL	Janet Tanner	£2.50 ☐
CATACLYSM	William Clark	£2.50 ☐
THE GOLDEN EXPRESS	Derek Lambert	£2.25 ☐

FILM AND TV TIE-INS

SANTA CLAUS THE NOVEL	£1.75 ☐
SANTA CLAUS STORYBOOK	£2.50 ☐
SANTA CLAUS JUMBO COLOURING BOOK	£1.25 ☐
SANTA CLAUS: THE BOY WHO DIDN'T BELIEVE IN CHRISTMAS	£1.50 ☐
SANTA CLAUS: SIMPLE PICTURES TO COLOUR	95p ☐

NON-FICTION

HORROCKS	Philip Warner	£2.95 ☐
1939 THE WORLD WE LEFT BEHIND	Robert Kee	£4.95 ☐
BUMF	Alan Coren	£1.75 ☐
I HATE SEX		£0.99 ☐
BYE BYE CRUEL WORLD	Tony Husband	£1.25 ☐

All Sphere books are available at your local bookshop or newsagent, or can be ordered direct from the publisher. Just tick the titles you want and fill in the form below.

Name _____

Address _____

_____

Write to Sphere Books, Cash Sales Department, P.O. Box 11, Falmouth, Cornwall TR10 9EN

Please enclose a cheque or postal order to the value of the cover price plus:

UK: 45p for the first book, 20p for the second book and 14p for each additional book ordered to a maximum charge of £1.63.

OVERSEAS: 75p for the first book plus 21p per copy for each additional book.

BFPO & EIRE: 45p for the first book, 20p for the second book plus 14p per copy for the next 7 books, thereafter 8p per book.

Sphere Books reserve the right to show new retail prices on covers which may differ from those previously advertised in the text or elsewhere, and to increase postal rates in accordance with the PO.